Tales from the
Italian and Spanish

Three complete novels, one Italian and two Spanish

Manzoni's "Betrothed Lovers"
Cervantes' "Don Quixote" and
Valdés' "Marta y Maria"

Four other famous stories:

Valera's "Pepita Jiménez"
Aleman's "Guzman of Alfarache"
Mendoza's "Lazarillo of Tormes"
and Quevedo's "Paul of Segovia"

159 Short Stories
118 Italian
41 Spanish Tales of To-day
49 Translated for the first time for this set
26 Stories of Love and Revenge
34 Stories of Heroism and Romance
58 Stories of Humor and Adventure

Originals of famous literary works: "Patient Grisel-da," "Romeo and Juliet," and "Merry Wives of Windsor" (Shakespeare), the stories of "Gil Blas," and some of the comedies of Moliére, and of the grand opera, "Cavalleria Rusticana."

32 Illustrations, chiefly from famous paintings

Full explanatory introductions to each volume, with descriptive historical notes to many of the stories.

Stories of Humor   Stories of Revenge
Stories of Adventure   Stories of Romance
Stories of Love   Stories of Local Color

Authors Represented

Italian

Manzoni, Boccaccio, Machiavelli, Masuccio, Fogazzaro, D'Annunzio, Verga, Deledda, De Roberto, Da Porto, De Marchi, Firenzuola, Capuana, Bandello, Neera, Manni, Fiorentino, Boito, Giacosa, Sabbadino, Ojetti, Pirandello, Rovetta, Palmarini, Gozzi, Da Ceno, Bottari, Doni, Sacchetti, Sanvitale, Parabosco, Cinthio, Soave, Sozzini, Lando, Grazzini, Colombo, Fucini, Malespini, Serao, Brevio, Straparola, Da Lodi, De Amicis, Erizzo, Granucci, Fortini, Martini, Sansovino, Castelnuovo, Bisaccioni, Illicini.

Spanish

Cervantes Velera, Valdés, Galdos, Calderon, Aleman, Mendoza, Quevedo, Ibañez, Picón, De Truba, Pardo-Bazan, Caballero, De Alarçón, Selgas, Nieto, Antor, Blasco, Solano, De Anellano, Calson, Ruiz, Becquer, Hartzenbusch.

Mexico:
López-Portillo y Rojas
De Zayas

Chile:
Gana y Gana
Varas

Cuba:
Castellanos

Venezuela:
Blanco-Fombona

Costa Rica:
Guardia

Peru:
Palma

Colombia:
Isaacs

Argentine:
Ugarte

Philippines:
Rizal

"WHEN I MAKE THEE A COUNT THEN THOU ART AT ONCE A GENTLEMAN"

(From the painting "The Banquet of Sancho Panza, Governor," by the Spanish artist, José Moreno Carbonero, reproduced here by permission of the artist)

TALES
FROM THE
ITALIAN
AND
SPANISH

A NEW SORT OF FICTION

REALISM AND ROMANCE,
ADVENTURE AND HUMOR,
REVEALING THE SOUL
OF THE LATIN LANDS

IN EIGHT VOLUMES
ILLUSTRATED

WILDSIDE PRESS

TALES FROM THE SPANISH

———————

DON QUIXOTE OF LA MANCHA

BY

MIGUEL de CERVANTES

With Four Illustrations

Contents

CERVANTES' "DON QUIXOTE"

iii

CERVANTES' "DON QUIXOTE"

CERVANTES' "DON QUIXOTE"

Illustrations

DON QUIXOTE

INTRODUCTION

"**I**T is certainly the best novel in the world beyond all comparison," said Macaulay in mature years on re-reading *Don Quixote*. He is not alone in the belief. When it appeared, in the first month of 1605, in the city of Madrid, the publisher was astonished at its popularity. Within a month he had to bring out a new edition to protect his copyright in Portugal and the remaining provinces of Spain. Five editions appeared within a year, not richly bound for the critical and the wealthy, but carelessly printed on cheap paper for that great mass of bookbuyers who read what they enjoy and only because they enjoy it. Before long its fame spread to foreign lands, and has continued to spread for three centuries until today no book except the Bible has ever been so widely translated as *Don Quixote*. Even *Robinson Crusoe* is far from showing so prodigious a number of translations and editions.

Yet this world-famous novel is thoroughly and intensely Spanish, and the national qualities are preserved with remarkable simplicity. As one of the characters says, "There's nothing in it to puzzle over." That is why Cervantes himself could affirm: "It is thumbed and read and got by heart by people of all sorts; the children turn its leaves, the young people read it, the grown men understand it, the old folks praise it."

One of the chief reasons for this universal popularity is the humor of Cervantes. It was a quality that never deserted him. His whole life was made up of reverses. His young manhood was spent in a series of adventures more crushing than ever confronted a Monte Cristo. His middle years were consumed in unceasing struggle against poverty, in repeated disappointment and frequent injustice. This very book, which has carried his name to the ends of the earth, was begun in a prison in Seville, where he was confined for debt. Thus was conceived the richest specimen of Spanish humor. The natural gravity of the Spaniards appears in the most ridiculous remarks. Cervantes seems unconscious of the absurdity of even his most preposterous scenes.

Behind this serious air lies a great variety of comic incident and dialogue. Everywhere we perceive a contrast or incongruity that sets us smiling—the unwitting mockery by the droll and stupid Sancho of his master's fantastic hopes and romantic ideals. The very scene of the story is a travesty on the world of romance. Of all the provinces of Spain, La Mancha is the most unpicturesque, mean, and monotonous. The inn that Don Quixote took for a castle is one of the shabbiest roadside inns on the entire peninsula. Of a truth, everyone on turning the last page must declare this one of the most humorous books he has read in his life.

But it is something more. The characters win our interest and affection, so that we call them to mind time and again to linger over their burlesque adventures and comical conversations. Even the minor ones, such as the girlish Clara and the singing muleteer, occupy a charming niche in the memory as winning and graceful figures in a delightfully natural love story. But the characters that have been familiar as household words for nearly three centuries are the pauper gentleman riding on crazy quests of knight-errantry in a world from which chivalry had vanished, and his inseparable attendant, who can never see anything but the humdrum surroundings of a dull and prosaic universe. Don Quixote receives his chief characteristics from a mad delusion that he is a knight devoted by a grotesque idolatry to proclaim in many an encounter the charms of a country wench whom he never sees and who knows nothing of his worship.

Sancho has been called the most humorous creation in fiction. His stolidity is unsurpassable. He might talk forever and commit a thousand impertinences without having an inkling of the slightest impropriety. He is so devoid of imagination that he can understand only the familiar and the commonplace, yet he carries off the palm as a liar by sticking to plain, homely reality, as in his answers to Don Quixote's questions in Chapter xxiii. In short, master and man represent an antagonism that meets us everywhere in life—the eternal antagonism between the dreamer and the business man, between idealism and phlegmatic common sense.

The present edition omits certain episodes that have never been much read because they interrupt the flow of the narrative. Cervantes was making so utterly new a venture in writing *Don Quixote* that he was very doubtful whether anyone would read it. He therefore inserted tales of the tiresome kind the Spanish public of that day was accustomed to peruse. One of these, the story of the captive, has been retained because of its soldierly air and more because it follows even in its most improbable incidents the course of Cervantes' own life. Therefrom may be gained some faint notion of what kind of man was he whose name Spain is now most proud to remember.

Cervantes' "Don Quixote"

CHAPTER I

WHICH TREATS OF THE CHARACTER AND PURSUITS OF THE FAMOUS GENTLEMAN DON QUIXOTE OF LA MANCHA

IN a village of La Mancha, the name of which I have no desire to call to mind, there lived not long since one of those gentlemen that keep a lance in the lance-rack, an old buckler, a lean hack, and a greyhound for coursing. An *olla* of rather more beef than mutton, a salad on most nights, scraps on Saturdays, lentils on Fridays, and a pigeon or so extra on Sundays, made away with three-quarters of his income. The rest of it went in a doublet of fine cloth and velvet breeches and shoes to match for holidays, while on week-days he made a brave figure in his best homespun. He had in his house a housekeeper past forty, a niece under twenty, and a lad for the field and market-place, who used to saddle the hack as well as handle the bill-book. The age of this gentleman of ours was bordering on fifty; he was of a hardy habit, spare, gaunt-featured, a very early riser and a great sportsman. They will have it his surname was Quixada or Quesada (for here there is some difference of opinion among the authors who write on the subject), although from reasonable conjectures it seems plain that he was called Quixana. This, however, is of but little importance to our tale; it will be enough not to stray a hair's breadth from the truth in the telling of it.

You must know, then, that the above-named gentleman whenever he was at leisure (which was mostly all the year round) gave himself up to reading books of chivalry with such ardor and avidity that he almost entirely neglected the pursuit of his field-sports, and even the management of his property; and to such a pitch did his eagerness and infatuation go that he sold many an acre of tillage-land to buy books of chivalry to read, and brought home as many of them as he could get. But of all there were none he liked so well as those of the famous Feliciano de Silva's composition, for their lucidity of style and complicated conceits were as pearls in his sight, particularly when in his reading he came upon courtships and cartels, where he often found the passages like *"the reason of the unreason with which my reason is afflicted so weakens my reason that with reason I murmur at your beauty,"* or again, *"the high heavens, that of your divinity divinely fortify you with the stars, render you deserving of the desert your greatness deserves."* Over conceits of this sort the poor gentleman lost his wits, and used to lie awake striving to understand them and worm the meaning out of them; what Aristotle himself could not have made out or extracted had he come to life again for that special purpose. He was not at all easy about the wounds which Don Belianis gave and took, because it seemed to him that, great as were the surgeons who had cured him, he must have had his face and body covered all over with seams and scars. He commended, however, the author's way of ending his book with the promise of that interminable adventure, and many a time was he tempted to take up his pen and finish it properly as is there proposed, which no doubt he would have done, and made a successful piece of work of it too, had not greater and more absorbing thoughts prevented him.

Many an argument did he have with the curate of his village (a learned man, and a graduate of Siguenza) as to which had been the better knight, Palmerin of England or Amadis of Gaul. Master Nicholas, the village barber, however, used to say that neither of them came up to the Knight of Phœbus, and that if there was any that could compare with *him* it was Don Galaor, the brother of Amadis of Gaul, because he had a spirit that was equal to every occasion, and was no finikin knight, nor lachrymose like his brother, while in the matter of valor he was not a whit behind him. In short, he became so absorbed in his books that he spent his nights from sunset to sunrise, and his days from dawn to dark, poring over them; and what with little sleep and much reading his brains got so dry that he lost his wits. His fancy grew full of what he used to read about in his books, enchantments, quarrels, battles, challenges, wounds, wooings, loves, agonies, and all sorts of impossible nonsense; and it so possessed his mind that the whole fabric of invention and fancy he read of was true, that to him no history in the world had more reality in it. He used to say that Cid Ruy Diaz was a very good knight, but that he was not to be compared with the Knight of the Burning Sword who with one back-stroke cut in half two fierce and monstrous giants. He thought more of Bernardo del Carpio because at Roncesvalles he slew Roland in spite of enchantments, availing himself of the artifice of Hercules when he strangled Antæus the son of Terra in his arms. He approved highly of the giant Morgante, because, although of the giant breed which is always arrogant and ill-conditioned, he alone was affable and well-bred. But above all he admired Reinaldos of Montalban, especially when he saw him sallying forth from his castle and robbing every one he met, and when beyond the seas he stole that image of Mahomet which, as his history says, was entirely of gold. And to have a bout of kicking at that traitor of a Ganelon he would have given his housekeeper, and his niece into the bargain.

In short, his wits being quite gone, he hit upon the strangest notion that ever madman in this world hit upon, and that was that he fancied it was right and requisite, as well for the support of his own honor as for the service of his country, that he should make a knight-errant of himself, roaming the world over in full armor and on horseback in quest of adventures, and putting in practice himself all that he had read of as being the usual practices of knights-errant; righting every kind of wrong, and exposing himself to peril and danger from which, in the issue, he was to reap eternal renown and fame. Already the poor man saw himself crowned by the might of his arm Emperor of Trebizond at least; and so, led away by the intense enjoyment he found in these pleasant fancies, he set himself forthwith to put his scheme into execution.

The first thing he did was to clean up some armor that had belonged to his great-grandfather, and had been for ages lying forgotten in a corner eaten with rust and covered with mildew. He scoured and polished it as best he could, but he perceived one great defect in it, that it had no closed helmet, nothing but a simple morion. This deficiency, however, his ingenuity supplied, for he contrived a kind of half-helmet of pasteboard which, fitted on to the morion, looked like a whole one. It is true that, in order to see if it was strong and fit to stand a cut, he drew his sword and gave it a couple of slashes, the first of which undid in an instant what had taken him a week to do. The ease with which he had knocked it to pieces disconcerted him somewhat, and to guard against that danger he set to work again, fixing bars of iron on the inside until he was satisfied with its strength; and then, not caring to try any more experiments with it, he passed it and adopted it as a helmet of the most perfect construction.

He next proceeded to inspect his hack, which, with more *quartos* than a *real* and more blemishes than the steed of Gonela, that *"tantum pellis et ossa fuit,"* surpassed in his eyes the Bucephalus of Alexander or the Babieca of the Cid. Four days were spent in thinking what name to give him, because (as he said to himself) it was not right that a horse belonging to a knight so famous, and one with such merits of his own, should be without some distinctive name, and he strove to adapt it so as to indicate what he had been before belonging to a knight-errant, and what he then was; for it was only reasonable that, his master taking a new character, he should take a new name, and that it

4

"A COUPLE OF SLASHES, THE FIRST OF WHICH UNDID IN AN INSTANT
WHAT HAD TAKEN HIM A WEEK"

(From the tercentenary edition of "Don Quixote," published in Madrid
in 1905)

should be a distinguished and full-sounding one, befitting the new order and calling he was about to follow. And so, after he had composed, struck out, rejected, added to, unmade and remade a multitude of names out of his memory and fancy, he decided upon calling him Rocinante, a name, to his thinking, lofty, sonorous, and significant of his condition as a hack before he became what he now was, the first and foremost of all the hacks in the world.

Having got a name for his horse so much to his taste, he was anxious to get one for himself, and he was eight days more pondering over this point, till at last he made up his mind to call himself Don Quixote, whence, as has been already said, the authors of this veracious history have inferred that his name must have been beyond a doubt Quixada, and not Quesada as others would have it. Recollecting, however, that the valiant Amadis was not content to call himself curtly Amadis and nothing more, but added the name of his kingdom and country to make it famous, and called himself Amadis of Gaul, he, like a good knight, resolved to add on the name of his, and to style himself Don Quixote of La Mancha, whereby, he considered, he described accurately his origin and country, and did honor to it in taking his surname from it.

So then, his armor being furbished, his morion turned into a helmet, his hack christened, and he himself confirmed, he came to the conclusion that nothing more was needed now but to look out for a lady to be in love with; for a knight-errant without love was like a tree without leaves or fruit, or a body without a soul. As he said to himself, "If, for my sins, or by my good fortune, I come across some giant hereabouts, a common occurrence with knights-errant, and overthrow him in one onslaught, or cleave him asunder to the waist, or, in short, vanquish and subdue him, will it not be well to have some one I may send him to as a present, that he may come in and fall on his knees before my sweet lady, and in a humble, submissive voice say, 'I am the giant Caraculiambro, lord of the island of Malindrania, vanquished in single combat by the never sufficiently extolled knight Don Quixote of La Mancha, who has commanded me to present myself before your Grace, that your Highness dispose of me at your pleasure?'" Oh, how our good gentleman enjoyed the delivery of this speech, especially when he had thought of some one to call his lady! There was, so the story goes, in a village near his own a very good-looking farm-girl with whom he had been at one time in love, though, so far as is known, she never knew it nor gave a thought to the matter. Her name was Aldonza Lorenzo, and upon her he thought fit to confer the title of Lady of his Thoughts; and after some search for a name which should not be out of harmony with her own, and should suggest and indicate that of a princess and great lady, he decided upon calling her Dulcinea del Toboso—she being of El Toboso—a name, to his mind, musical, uncommon, and significant, like all those he had already bestowed upon himself and the things belonging to him.

CHAPTER II

THESE preliminaries settled, he did not care to put off
any longer the execution of his design, urged on to
it by the thought of all the world was losing by his delay,
seeing what wrongs he intended to right, grievances to redress, injustices to repair, abuses to remove, and duties
to discharge. So, without giving notice of his intention to
any one, and without anybody seeing him, one morning
before the dawning of the day (which was one of the
hottest of the month of July) he donned his suit of armor,
mounted Rocinante with his patched-up helmet on, braced
his buckler, took his lance, and by the back door of the
yard sallied forth upon the plain in the highest contentment and satisfaction at seeing with what ease he had made
a beginning with his grand purpose.

But scarcely did he find himself upon the open plain,
when a terrible thought struck him, one all but enough to
make him abandon the enterprise at the very outset. It
occurred to him that he had not been dubbed a knight, and
that according to the law of chivalry he neither could
nor ought to bear arms against any knight; and that even
if he had been, still he ought, as a novice knight, to wear
white armor, without a device upon the shield until by his
prowess he had earned one. These reflections made him
waver in his purpose, but his craze being stronger than
any reasoning he made up his mind to have himself dubbed

7

a knight by the first one he came across, following the example of others in the same case, as he had read in the books that brought him to this pass. As for white armor, he resolved, on the first opportunity, to scour his until it was whiter than an ermine; and so comforting himself he pursued his way, taking that which his horse chose, for in this he believed lay the essence of adventures.

Thus setting out, our new-fledged adventurer paced along, talking to himself and saying, "Who knows but that in time to come, when the veracious history of my famous deeds is made known, the sage who writes it, when he has set forth my first sally in the early morning, will do it after this fashion? 'Scarce had the rubicund Apollo spread o'er the face of the broad spacious earth the golden threads of his bright hair, scarce had the little birds of painted plumage attuned their notes to hail with dulcet and mellifluous harmony the coming of the rosy Dawn, that, deserting the soft couch of her jealous spouse, was appearing to mortals at the gates and balconies of the Manchegan horizon, when the renowned knight Don Quixote of La Mancha, quitting the lazy down, mounted his celebrated steed Rocinante and began to traverse the ancient and famous Campo de Montiel;'" which in fact he was actually traversing. "Happy the age, happy the time," he continued, "in which shall be made known my deeds of fame, worthy to be moulded in brass, carved in marble, limned in pictures, for a memorial forever. And thou, O sage magician, whoever thou art, to whom it shall fall to be the chronicler of this wondrous history, forget not, I entreat thee, my good Rocinante, the constant companion of my ways and wanderings."

Presently he broke out again, as if he were love-stricken in earnest, "O Princess Dulcinea, lady of this captive heart, a grievous wrong hast thou done me to drive me forth with scorn, and with inexorable obduracy banish me from the presence of thy beauty. O lady, deign to hold in remembrance this heart, thy vassal, that thus in anguish pines for love of thee."

8

CERVANTES' "DON QUIXOTE"

So he went on stringing together these and other absurdities, all in the style of those his books had taught him, imitating their language as well as he could; and all the while he rode so slowly and the sun mounted so rapidly and with such fervor that it was enough to melt his brains if he had had any. Nearly all day he traveled without anything remarkable happening to him, at which he was in despair, for he was anxious to encounter some one at once upon whom to try the might of his strong arm.

Writers there are who say the first adventure he met with was that of Puerto Lapice; others say it was that of the windmills; but what I have ascertained on this point, and what I have found written in the annals of La Mancha, is that he was on the road all day, and towards nightfall his hack and he found themselves dead tired and hungry, when, looking all around to see if he could discover any castle or shepherd's shanty where he might refresh himself and relieve his sore wants, he perceived not far out of his road an inn, which was as welcome as a star guiding him to the portals, if not the palaces, of his redemption; and quickening his pace he reached it just as night was setting in. At the door were standing two young women, girls of the district as they call them, on their way to Seville with some carriers who had chanced to halt that night at the inn; and as, happen what might to our adventurer, every thing he saw or imagined seemed to him to be and to happen after the fashion of what he had read of, the moment he saw the inn he pictured it to himself as a castle with its four turrets and pinnacles of shining silver, not forgetting the drawbridge and moat and all the belongings usually ascribed to castles of the sort. To this inn, which to him seemed a castle, he advanced, and at a short distance from it he checked Rocinante, hoping that some dwarf would show himself upon the battlements, and by sound of trumpet give notice that a knight was approaching the castle. But seeing that they were slow about it, and that Rocinante was in a hurry to reach the stable, he made for the inn door, and perceived the two

gay damsels who were standing there, and who seemed
to him to be two fair maidens or lovely ladies taking their
ease at the castle gate.

At this moment it so happened that a swineherd who
was going through the stubbles collecting a drove of pigs
(for, without any apology, that is what they are called)
gave a blast of his horn to bring them together, and forthwith it seemed to Don Quixote to be what he was expecting, the signal of some dwarf announcing his arrival; and
so with prodigious satisfaction he rode up to the inn and
to the ladies, who, seeing a man of this sort approaching
in full armor and with lance and buckler, were turning in
dismay into the inn, when Don Quixote, guessing their
fear by their flight, raising his pasteboard visor, disclosed
his dry, dusty visage, and with courteous bearing and gentle
voice addressed them:

"Your ladyships need not fly or fear any rudeness, for
that it belongs not to the order of knighthood which I profess to offer such to any one, much less to high-born maidens
as your appearance proclaims you to be." The girls were
looking at him and straining their eyes to make out the
features which the clumsy visor obscured, but when they
heard themselves called maidens, a thing so much out of
their line, they could not restrain their laughter, which
made Don Quixote wax indignant, and say:

"Modesty becomes the fair, and moreover laughter that
has little cause is great silliness; this, however, I say not to
pain or anger you, for my desire is none other than to
serve you."

The incomprehensible language and the unpromising
looks of our cavalier only increased the ladies' laughter,
and that increased his irritation, and matters might have
gone farther if at that moment the landlord had not come
out, who, being a very fat man, was a very peaceful one.
He, seeing his grotesque figure clad in armor that did not
match any more than his saddle, bridle, lance, buckler,
or corselet, was not at all indisposed to join the damsels
in their manifestations of amusement; but, in truth, stand-

"THEY COULD NOT RESTRAIN THEIR LAUGHTER, WHICH MADE DON QUIXOTE WAX INDIGNANT"

(From the tercentenary edition of "Don Quixote," published in Madrid in 1905)

ing in awe of such a complicated armament, he thought
it best to speak him fairly, so he said:

"Señor Caballero, if your worship wants lodging, bat-
ing the bed (for there is not one in the inn) there is
plenty of everything else here." Don Quixote, observing
the respectful bearing of the *alcaide* of the fortress (for
so innkeeper and inn seemed in his eyes), made answer:

"Sir Castellan, for me anything will suffice, for

> "My armor is my only wear,
> My only rest the fray."

The host fancied he called him *castellan* because he took
him for a "worthy of Castile," though he was in fact an
Andalusian, and one from the Strand of San Lucar, as
crafty a thief as Cacus and as full of tricks as a student
or a page. "In that case," said he,

> "Your bed is on the flinty rock,
> Your sleep to watch alway;

and if so, you may dismount and safely reckon upon any
quantity of sleeplessness under this roof for a twelvemonth, not to say for a single night."

So saying, he advanced to hold the stirrup for Don
Quixote, who got down with great difficulty and exertion (for he had not broken his fast all day), and then
charged the host to take great care of his horse, as he
was the best bit of flesh that ever ate bread in this world.
The landlord eyed him over, but did not find him as good
as Don Quixote said, nor even half as good; and putting
him up in the stable, he returned to see what might be
wanted by his guest, whom the damsels, who had by this
time made their peace with him, were now relieving of his
armor. They had taken off his breastplate and backpiece,
but they neither knew nor saw how to open his gorget
or remove his make-shift helmet, for he had fastened it
with green ribbons, which, as there was no untying the
knots, required to be cut. This, however, he would not
by any means consent to, so he remained all the evening

with his helmet on, the drollest and oddest figure that can be imagined; and while they were removing his armor, taking the baggages who were about it for ladies of high degree belonging to the castle, he said to them with great sprightliness:

> "Oh, never, surely, was there knight
> So served by hand of dame,
> As served was he, Don Quixote hight,
> When from his town he came;
> With maidens waiting on himself,
> Princesses on his hack——

—or Rocinante, for that, ladies mine, is my horse's name, and Don Quixote of La Mancha is my own; for though I had no intention of declaring myself until my achievements in your service and honor had made me known, the necessity of adapting that old ballad of Lancelot to the present occasion has given you the knowledge of my name altogether prematurely. A time, however, will come for your ladyships to command and me to obey, and then the might of my arm will show my desire to serve you."

The girls, who were not used to hearing rhetoric of this sort, had nothing to say in reply: they only asked him if he wanted anything to eat. "I would gladly eat a bit of something," said Don Quixote, "for I feel it would come very seasonably." The day happened to be a Friday, and in the whole inn there was nothing but some pieces of the fish they call in Castile *abadejo,* in Andalusia "*bacallo,*" and in some places *curadillo,* and in others troutlet; so they asked him if he thought he could eat troutlet, for there was no other fish to give him. "If there be troutlets enough," said Don Quixote, "they will be the same thing as a trout; for it is all one to me whether I am given eight *reals* in small change or a piece of eight; moreover, it may be that these troutlets are like veal, which is better than beef, or kid, which is better than goat. But whatever it be let it come quickly, for the burden and pressure of arms cannot be borne without support to the inside."

CERVANTES' "DON QUIXOTE"

They laid a table for him at the door of the inn for the sake of the air, and the host brought him a portion of ill-soaked and worse cooked stockfish, and a piece of bread as black and mouldy as his own armor; but a laughable sight it was to see him eating, for having his helmet on and the beaver up, he could not with his own hands put anything into his mouth unless some one else placed it there, and this service one of the ladies rendered him. But to give him anything to drink was impossible, or would have been so had not the landlord bored a reed, and putting one end in his mouth poured the wine into him through the other; all which he bore with patience rather than sever the ribbons of his helmet.

While this was going on there came up to the inn a sow-gelder, who, as he approached, sounded his reed pipe four or five times, and thereby completely convinced Don Quixote that he was in some famous castle, and that they were regaling him with music, and that the stockfish was trout, the bread the whitest, the wenches ladies, and the landlord the *castellan* of the castle; and consequently he held that his enterprise and sally had been to some purpose. But still it distressed him to think he had not been dubbed a knight, for it was plain to him he could not lawfully engage in any adventure without receiving the order of knighthood.

CHAPTER III

WHEREIN IS RELATED THE DROLL WAY IN WHICH DON
QUIXOTE HAD HIMSELF DUBBED A KNIGHT

HARASSED by this reflection, he made haste with his
scanty pothouse supper, and having finished it called
the landlord, and shutting himself into the stable with him,
fell on his knees before him, saying:

"From this spot I rise not, valiant knight, until your
courtesy grants me the boon I seek, one that will redound
to your praise and the benefit of the human race." The
landlord, seeing his guest at his feet and hearing a speech
of this kind, stood staring at him in bewilderment, not
knowing what to do or say, and entreating him to rise, but
all to no purpose until he had agreed to grant the boon
demanded of him.

"I looked for no less, my lord, from your High Mag-
nificence," replied Don Quixote, "and I have to tell you
that the boon I have asked and your liberality has granted
is that you shall dub me knight tomorrow morning, and
that tonight I shall watch my arms in the chapel of your
castle: thus tomorrow, as I have said, will be accomplished
what I so much desire, enabling me lawfully to roam
through all the four quarters of the world seeking adventures on behalf of those in distress, as is the duty of
chivalry and of knights-errant like myself, whose ambition
is directed to such deeds."

The landlord, who, as has been mentioned, was something of a wag, and had already some suspicion of his
guest's want of wits, was quite convinced of it on hearing
talk of this kind from him, and to make sport for the night
he determined to fall in with his humor. So he told him
he was quite right in pursuing the object he had in view,
and that such a motive was natural and becoming in cava-

14

liers as distinguished as he seemed and his gallant bearing showed him to be; and that he himself in his younger days had followed the same honorable calling, roaming in quest of adventures in various parts of the world, among others the Curing-grounds of Malaga, the Isles of Riaran, the Precinct of Seville, the Little Market of Segovia, the Olivera of Valencia, the Rondilla of Granada, the Strand of San Lucar, the Colt of Cordova, the Taverns of Toledo, and divers other quarters, where he had proved the nimbleness of his feet and the lightness of his fingers, doing many wrongs, cheating many widows, ruining maids and swindling minors, and, in short bring himself under the notice of almost every tribunal and court of justice in Spain; until at last he had retired to this castle of his, where he was living upon his property and upon that of others; and where he received all knights-errant, of whatever rank or condition they might be, all for the great love he bore them and that they might share their substance with him in return for his benevolence. He told him, moreover, that in this castle of his there was no chapel in which he could watch his armor, as it had been pulled down in order to be rebuilt, but that in a case of necessity it might, he knew, be watched anywhere, and he might watch it that night in a courtyard of the castle, and in the morning, God willing, the requisite ceremonies might be performed so as to have him dubbed a knight, and so thoroughly dubbed that nobody could be more so.

He asked if he had any money with him, to which Don Quixote replied that he had not a farthing, as in the histories of knights-errant he had never read of any of them carrying any. On this point the landlord told him he was mistaken; for, though not recorded in the histories, because in the author's opinion there was no need to mention anything so obvious and necessary as money and clean shirts, it was not to be supposed therefore that they did not carry them, and he might regard it as certain and established that all knights-errant (about whom there were so many full and unimpeachable books) carried well-furnished purses in case of emergency, and likewise carried shirts and a little box of ointment to cure wounds they received.

For in those plains and deserts where they engaged in combat and came out wounded, it was not always that there was someone to cure them, unless indeed they had for a friend some sage magician to succor them at once by fetching through the air upon a cloud some damsel or dwarf with a vial of water of such virtue that by tasting one drop of it they were cured of their hurts and wounds in an instant and left as sound as if they had not received any damage whatever. But in case this should not occur, the knights of old took care to see that their squires were provided with money and other requisites, such as lint and ointments for healing purposes; and when it happened that knights had no squires (which was rarely and seldom the case), they themselves carried everything in cunning saddle-bags that were hardly seen on the horse's croup, as if it were something else of more importance, because, unless for some such reason, carrying saddle-bags was not very favorably regarded among knights-errant. He therefore advised him (and, as his godson so soon to be, he might even command him) never from that time forth to travel without money and the usual requirements, and he would find the advantage of them when he least expected it.

Don Quixote promised to follow his advice scrupulously, and it was arranged forthwith that he should watch his armor in a large yard at one side of the inn; so, collecting it all together, Don Quixote placed it on a trough that stood by the side of a well, and bracing his buckler on his arm he grasped his lance and began with a stately air to march up and down in front of the trough, and as he began his march night began to fall.

The landlord told all the people who were in the inn about the craze of his guest, the watching of the armor, and the dubbing ceremony he contemplated. Full of wonder at so strange a form of madness, they flocked to see it from a distance, and observed with what composure he sometimes paced up and down, or sometimes, leaning on his lance, gazed on his armor without taking his eyes off it for ever so long; and as the night closed in with a light from the moon so brilliant that it might vie with his that lent it, everything the novice knight did was plainly seen by all.

Meanwhile one of the carriers who were in the inn thought fit to water his team, and it was necessary to remove Don Quixote's armor as it lay on the trough; but he, seeing the other approach, hailed him in a loud voice:

"O thou, who ever thou art, rash knight that comest to lay hands on the armor of the most valorous errant that ever girt on sword, have a care what thou dost; touch it not unless thou wouldst lay down thy life as the penalty of thy rashness."

The carrier gave no heed to these words (and he would have done better to heed them if he had been heedful of his health), but seizing it by the straps flung the armor some distance from him. Seeing this, Don Quixote raised his eyes to heaven, and fixing his thoughts, apparently, upon his Lady Dulcinea, exclaimed, "Aid me, lady mine, in this the first encounter that presents itself to this breast which thou holdest in subjection; let not thy favor and protection fail me in this first jeopardy;" and, with these words and others to the same purpose, dropping his buckler, he lifted his lance with both hands and with it smote such a blow on the carrier's head that he stretched him on the ground so stunned that had he followed it up with a second there would have been no need of a surgeon to cure him. This done, he picked up his armor and returned to his beat with the same serenity as before.

Shortly after this, another, not knowing what had happened (for the carrier still lay senseless), came with the same object of giving water to his mules, and was proceeding to remove the armor in order to clear the trough, when Don Quixote, without uttering a word or imploring aid from any one, once more dropped his buckler and once more lifted his lance, and without actually breaking the second carrier's head into pieces made more than three of it, for he laid it open in four. At the noise all the people of the inn ran to the spot, and among them the landlord. Seeing this, Don Quixote braced his buckler on his arm, and with his hand on his sword exclaimed:

"O Lady of Beauty, strength and support of my faint heart, it is time for thee to turn the eyes of thy greatness on this thy captive knight on the brink of so mighty an adventure." By this he felt himself so inspirited that he would not have flinched if all the carriers in the world had assailed him.

The comrades of the wounded perceiving the plight they were in began from a distance to shower stones on Don Quixote, who screened himself as best he could with his buckler, not daring to quit the trough and leave his armor unprotected. The landlord shouted to them to leave him alone, for he had already told them that he was mad, and as a madman he would not be accountable even if he killed them all. Still louder shouted Don Quixote, calling them knaves and traitors, and the lord of the castle, who allowed knights-errant to be treated in this fashion, a villain and a low-born knight whom, had he received the order of knighthood, he would call to account for his treachery.

"But of you," he cried, "base and vile rabble I make no account; fling, strike, come on, do all ye can against me, ye shall see what the reward of your folly and insolence will be." This he uttered with so much spirit and boldness that he filled his assailants with a terrible fear, and as much for this reason as at the persuasion of the landlord they left off stoning him, and he allowed them to carry off the wounded, and with the same calmness and composure as before resumed the watch over his armor.

But these freaks of his guest were not much to the liking of the landlord, so he determined to cut matters short and confer upon him at once the unlucky order of knighthood before any further misadventure could occur; so, going up to him, he apologized for the rudeness which, without his knowledge, had been offered to him by these low people, who, however, had been well punished for their audacity. As he had already told him, he said, there was no chapel in the castle, nor was it needed for what remained to be done, for, as he understood the ceremonial of the order, the whole point of being dubbed a knight, lay in the accolade and in the slap on the shoulder, and that could be administered in the middle of a field; and that he had now done all that was needful as to watching the armor, for all requirements were satisfied by a watch of two hours only, while he had been more than four about it. Don Quixote believed it all, and told him he stood there ready to obey him, and to make an end of it with as much dispatch as possible; for, if he were again attacked, and felt himself to be a dubbed knight, he would not, he thought, leave a soul alive in the castle, except such as out of respect he might spare at his bidding.

Thus warned and menaced, the *castellan* forthwith brought out a book in which he used to enter the straw and barley he served out to the carriers, and, with a lad carrying a candle-end, and the two damsels already mentioned, he returned to where Don Quixote stood, and bade him kneel down. Then, reading from his account-book as if he were repeating some devout prayer, in the middle of his delivery he raised his hand and gave him a sturdy blow on the neck, and then, with his own sword, a smart slap on the shoulder, all the while muttering between his teeth as if he were saying his prayers.

Having done this, he directed one of the ladies to gird on his sword, which she did with great self-possession and gravity, and not a little was required to prevent a burst of laughter at each stage of the ceremony; but what they had already seen of the novice knight's prowess kept their laughter within bounds. On girding him with the sword the worthy lady said to him, " May God make your worship a very fortunate knight, and grant you success in battle." Don Quixote asked her name in order that he might from that time forward know to whom he was beholden for the favor he had received, as he meant to confer upon her some portion of the honor he acquired

19

by the might of his arm. She answered with great humility that she was called La Tolosa, and that she was the daughter of a cobbler of Toledo who lived in the stalls of Sanchobienaya, and that wherever she might be she would serve and esteem him as her lord. Don Quixote said in reply that she would do him a favor if thenceforward she assumed the " Don " and called herself Doña Tolosa. She promised she would, and then the other buckled on his spur, and with her followed almost the same conversation as with the lady of the sword. He asked her name, and she said it was La Molinera, and that she was the daughter of a respectable miller of Antequera; and of her likewise Don Quixote requested that she would adopt the " Don " and call herself Doña Molinera, making offers to her of further services and favors.

Having thus, with hot haste and speed, brought to a conclusion these never-till-now-seen ceremonies, Don Quixote was on thorns until he saw himself on horseback sallying forth in quest of adventures; and saddling Rocinante at once he mounted, and embracing his host, as he returned thanks for his kindness in knighting him, he addressed him in language so extraordinary that it is impossible to convey an idea of it or report it. The landlord, to get him out of the inn, replied with no less rhetoric though with shorter words, and without calling upon him to pay the reckoning let him go with a Godspeed.

CHAPTER IV

OF WHAT HAPPENED TO OUR KNIGHT WHEN HE LEFT THE INN

DAY was dawning when Don Quixote quitted the inn, so happy, so gay, so exhilarated at finding himself dubbed a knight, that his joy was like to burst his horse-girths. However, recalling the advice of his host as to the requisites he ought to carry with him, especially that referring to money and shirts, he determined to go home and provide himself with all, and also with a squire, for he reckoned upon securing a farm-laborer, a neighbor of his, a poor man with a family, but very well qualified for the office of squire to a knight. With this object he turned his horse's head towards his village, and Rocinante, thus reminded of his old quarters, stepped out so briskly that he hardly seemed to tread the earth.

He had not gone far, when out of a thicket on his right there seemed to come feeble cries as of someone in distress, and the instant he heard them he exclaimed, "Thanks be to heaven for the favor it accords me, that it so soon offers me an opportunity of fulfilling the obligation I have undertaken, and gathering the fruit of my ambition. These cries, no doubt, come from some man or woman in want of help, and needing my aid and protection;" and wheeling, he turned Rocinante in the direction whence the cries seemed to proceed. He had gone but a few paces into the wood, when he saw a mare tied to an oak, and tied to another, and stripped from the waist upwards, a youth of about fifteen years of age, from whom the cries came. Nor were they without cause, for a lusty farmer was flogging him with a belt and following up every blow with scoldings and commands, repeating, " Your mouth shut and your eyes open! " while the youth made answer, " I won't do it again, master mine; by God's passion I won't do it again, and I'll take more care of the flock another time."

Seeing what was going on, Don Quixote said in an angry voice, " Discourteous knight, it ill becomes you to assail one who cannot defend himself; mount your steed and take your lance " (for there was a lance leaning against the oak to which the mare was tied), " and I will make you know that you are behaving as a coward." The farmer, seeing before him this figure in full armor brandishing a lance over his head, gave himself up for dead, and made answer meekly:

" Sir Knight, this youth that I am chastising is my servant, employed by me to watch a flock of sheep that I have hard by, and he is so careless that I lose one every day, and when I punish him for his carelessness and knavery he says I do it out of niggardliness, to escape paying him the wages I owe him, and before God, and on my soul, he lies."

" Lies before me, base clown! " said Don Quixote. " By the sun that shines on us, I have a mind to run you through with this lance. Pay him at once without another word; if not, by the God that rules us I will make an end of you, and annihilate you on the spot; release him instantly."

The farmer hung his head, and without a word untied his servant, of whom Don Quixote asked how much his master owed him.

He replied, nine months at seven *reals* a month. Don Quixote added it up, found that it came to sixty-three *reals,* and told the farmer to pay it down immediately, if he did not want to die for it.

The trembling clown replied that as he lived and by the oath he had sworn (though he had not sworn any) it was not so much; for there were to be taken into account and deducted three pairs of shoes he had given him, and a *real* for two blood-lettings when he was sick.

"All that is very well," said Don Quixote; "but let the shoes and the blood-lettings stand as a set-off against the blows you have given him without any cause; for if he spoiled the leather of the shoes you paid for, you have damaged that of his body, and if the barber took blood from him when he was sick, you have drawn it when he was sound; so on that score he owes you nothing."

"The difficulty is, Sir Knight, that I have no money here; let Andres come home with me, and I will pay him all, *real* by *real*."

"I go with him!" said the youth. "Nay, God forbid; no, señor, not for the world; for once alone with me, he would flay me like a Saint Bartholomew."

"He will do nothing of the kind," said Don Quixote; "I have only to command, and he will obey me; and as he has sworn to me by the order of knighthood which he has received, I leave him free, and I guarantee the payment."

"Consider what you are saying, señor," said the youth; "this master of mine is not a knight, nor has he received any order of knighthood; for he is Juan Haldudo the Rich, of Quintanar."

"That matters little," replied Don Quixote; "there may be Haldudos knights; moreover, every one is the son of his works."

"That is true," said Andres; "but this master of mine— of what works is he the son, when he refuses me the wages of my sweat and labor?"

"I do not refuse, brother Andres," said the farmer; "be good enough to come along with me, and I swear by all the orders of knighthood there are in the world to pay you as I have agreed, *real* by *real*, and perfumed."

"For the perfumery, I excuse you," said Don Quixote; "give it to him in *reals*, and I shall be satisfied; and see that you do as you have sworn; if not, by the same oath I swear to come back and hunt you out and punish you;

and I shall find you though you should lie closer than a lizard. And if you desire to know who it is lays this command upon you, that you may be more firmly bound to obey it, know that I am the valorous Don Quixote of La Mancha, the undoer of wrongs and injustices; and so, God be with you, and keep in mind what you have promised and sworn under those penalties that have been already declared to you."

So saying, he gave Rocinante the spur and was soon out of reach. The farmer followed him with his eyes, and when he saw that he had cleared the wood and was no longer in sight, he turned to his boy Andres, and said, "Come here, my son, I want to pay you what I owe you, as that undoer of wrongs has commanded me."

"My oath on it," said Andres, "your worship will be well advised to obey the command of that good knight—may he live a thousand years—for, as he is a valiant and just judge, by Roque, if you do not pay me, he will come back and do as he said."

"My oath on it, too," said the farmer; "but as I have a strong affection for you, I want to add to the debt in order to add to the payment;" and seizing him by the arm, he tied him up to the oak again, where he gave him such a flogging that he left him for dead.

"Now, Master Andres," said the farmer, "call on the undoer of wrongs; you will find he won't undo that, though I am not sure that I have quite done with you, for I have a good mind to flay you alive as you feared." But at last he untied him, and gave him leave to go look for his judge in order to put the sentence pronounced into execution.

Andres went on rather down in the mouth, swearing he would go to look for the valiant Don Quixote of La Mancha and tell him exactly what had happened, and that all would have to be repaid him sevenfold; but for all that, he went off weeping, while his master stood laughing.

Thus did the valiant Don Quixote right that wrong, and, thoroughly satisfied with what had taken place, as

he considered he had made a very happy and noble beginning with his knighthood, he took the road towards his
village in perfect self-content, saying in a low voice, " Well
mayest thou this day call thyself fortunate above all on
earth, O Dulcinea del Toboso, fairest of the fair! since it
has fallen to thy lot to hold subject and submissive to thy
full will and pleasure a knight so renowned as is and will
be Don Quixote of La Mancha, who, as all the world
knows, yesterday received the order of knighthood, and
hath today righted the greatest wrong and grievance that
ever injustice conceived and cruelty perpetrated: who hath
today plucked the rod from the hand of yonder ruthless
oppressor so wantonly lashing that tender child."

He now came to a road branching in four directions;
immediately he was reminded of those crossroads where
knights-errant used to stop to consider which road they
should take. In imitation of them he halted for a while,
and after having deeply considered it, he gave Rocinante
his head, submitting his own will to that of his hack, who
followed out his first intention, which was to make straight
for his own stable. After he had gone about two miles
Don Quixote perceived a large party of people, who, as
afterwards appeared, were some Toledo traders, on their
way to buy silk at Murcia. There were six of them coming along under their sunshades, with four servants
mounted, and three muleteers on foot. Scarcely had Don
Quixote descried them when the fancy possessed him that
this must be some new adventure; and to help him to imitate as far as he could those passages he had read of in
his books, here seemed to come one made on purpose, which
he resolved to attempt. So with a lofty bearing and determination he fixed himself firmly in his stirrups, got his
lance ready, brought his buckler before his breast, and
planting himself in the middle of the road, stood waiting
the approach of these knights-errant, for such he now considered and held them to be; and when they had come
near enough to see and hear, he exclaimed with a haughty
gesture:

TALES FROM THE SPANISH

"All the world stand, unless all the world confess that in all the world there is no maiden fairer than the Empress of La Mancha, the peerless Dulcinea del Toboso."

The traders halted at the sound of this language and the sight of the strange figure that uttered it, and from both figure and language at once guessed the craze of their owner; they wished, however, to learn quietly what was the object of this confession that was demanded of them, and one of them, who was rather fond of a joke and was very sharp-witted, said to him:

"Sir Knight, we do not know who this good lady is that you speak of; show her to us, for, if she be of such beauty as you suggest, with all our hearts and without any pressure we will confess the truth that is on your part required of us."

"If I were to show her to you," replied Don Quixote, "what merit would you have in confessing a truth so manifest? The essential point is that without seeing her you must believe, confess, affirm, swear, and defend it; else ye have to do with me in battle, ill-conditioned, arrogant rabble that ye are; and come ye on, one by one as the order of knighthood requires, or all together as is the custom and vile usage of your breed, here do I bide and await you, relying on the justice of the cause I maintain."

"Sir Knight," replied the trader, "I entreat your worship in the name of the present company of princes, that, to save us from charging our consciences with the confession of a thing we have never seen or heard of, and one moreover so much to the prejudice of the Empresses and Queens of the Alcarria and Estremadura, your worship will be pleased to show us some portrait of this lady, though it be no bigger than a grain of wheat; for by the thread one gets at the ball, and in this way we shall be satisfied and easy, and you will be content and pleased; nay, I believe we are already so far agreed with you that even though her portrait should show her blind of one eye, and distilling vermilion and sulphur from the other, we would nevertheless, to gratify your worship, say all in her favor that you desire."

"She distills nothing of the kind, vile rabble," said Don Quixote, burning with rage, "nothing of the kind, I say, only ambergris and civet in cotton; nor is she one-eyed or humpbacked, but straighter than a Guadarrama spindle; but ye must pay for the blasphemy ye have uttered against beauty like that of my lady."

And so saying, he charged with leveled lance against the one who had spoken, with such fury and fierceness that, if luck had not contrived that Rocinante should stumble midway and come down, it would have gone hard with the rash trader. Down went Rocinante, and over went his master, rolling along the ground for some distance; and when he tried to rise he was unable, so encumbered was he with lance, buckler, spurs, helmet, and the weight of his old armor; and all the while he was struggling to get up, he kept saying, "Fly not, cowards and caitiffs! Stay, for not by my fault, but my horse's, am I stretched here."

One of the muleteers in attendance, who could not have had much good nature in him, hearing the poor prostrate man blustering in this style, was unable to refrain from giving him an answer on his ribs; and coming up to him he seized his lance, and having broken it in pieces, with one of them he began so to belabor our Don Quixote that, notwithstanding and in spite of his armor, he milled him like a measure of wheat. His masters called out not to lay on so hard and to leave him alone, but the muleteer's blood was up, and he did not care to drop the game until he had vented the rest of his wrath, and gathering up the remaining fragments of the lance he finished with a discharge upon the unhappy victim, who all through the storm of sticks that rained on him never ceased threatening heaven, and earth, and the brigands, for such they seemed to him. At last the muleteer was tired, and the traders continued their journey, taking with them matter for talk about the poor fellow who had been cudgeled. He, when he found himself alone, made another effort to rise; but if he was unable when whole and sound, how was he to rise after having been thrashed and well-nigh knocked to pieces? And yet he esteemed himself fortunate, as it seemed to him that this was a regular knight-errant's mishap, and entirely, he considered, the fault of his horse. However, battered in body as he was, to rise was beyond his power.

CHAPTER V

F INDING, then, that in fact he could not move, he
bethought himself of having recourse to his usual
remedy, which was to think of some passage in his books,
and his craze brought to his mind that about Baldwin and
the Marquis of Mantua, when Carloto left him wounded
on the mountain side, a story known by heart by the children, not forgotten by the young men, and lauded and even
believed by the old folk; and for all that not a whit truer
than the miracles of Mahomet. This seemed to him to
fit exactly the case in which he found himself, so, making
a show of severe suffering, he began to roll on the ground
and with feeble breath repeat the very words which the
wounded knight of the woods is said to have uttered:

> Where art thou, lady mine, that thou
> My sorrow dost not rue?
> Thou canst not know it, lady mine,
> Or else thou art untrue.

And so he went on with the ballad as far as the lines:

> O noble Marquis of Mantua,
> My uncle and liege lord!

As chance would have it, when he had got to this line
there happened to come by a peasant from his own village,
a neighbor of his, who had been with a load of wheat
to the mill, and he, seeing the man stretched there, came up

to him and asked him who he was and what was the matter with him that he complained so dolefully.

Don Quixote was firmly persuaded that this was the Marquis of Mantua, his uncle, so the only answer he made was to go on with his ballad, in which he told the tale of his misfortune, and of the loves of the Emperor's son and his wife, all exactly as the ballad sings it.

The peasant stood amazed at hearing such nonsense, and relieving him of the visor, already battered to pieces by blows, he wiped his face, which was covered with dust, and as soon as he had done so he recognized him and said, " Señor Don Quixada " (for so he appears to have been called when he was in his senses and had not yet changed from a quiet country gentleman into a knight-errant), " who has brought your worship to this pass? " But to all questions the other only went on with his ballad.

Seeing this, the good man removed as well as he could his breastplate and backpiece to see if he had any wound, but he could perceive no blood nor any mark whatsoever. He then contrived to raise him from the ground, and with no little difficulty hoisted him upon his ass, which seemed to him to be the easiest mount for him; and collecting the arms, even to the splinters of the lance, he tied them on Rocinante, and leading him by the bridle and the ass by the halter he took the road for the village, very sad to hear what absurd stuff Don Quixote was talking. Nor was Don Quixote less so, for what with blows and bruises he could not sit upright on the ass, and from time to time he sent up sighs to heaven, so that once more he drove the peasant to ask what ailed him. And it could have been only the devil himself that put into his head tales to match his own adventures, for now, forgetting Baldwin, he bethought himself of the Moor Abindarraez, when the Alcaide of Antequera, Rodrigo de Narvaez, took him prisoner and carried him away to his castle; so that when the peasant again asked him how he was and what ailed him, he gave him for reply the same words and phrases that the captive Abencerrage gave to Rodrigo de Narvaez, just as he had read in the story in the *Diana* of Jorge de Montemayor, where it is written, applying it to his own case so aptly that the peasant went along cursing his fate that he had to listen to such a lot of nonsense; from which, however, he came to the conclusion that his neighbor was mad, and so made all haste to reach the village to escape the wearisomeness of this harangue of Don Quixote's; who, at the end of it, said:

"Señor Don Rodrigo de Narvaez, your worship must know that this fair Xarifa I have mentioned is now the lovely Dulcinea del Toboso, for whom I have done, am doing, and will do the most famous deeds of chivalry that in this world have been seen, are to be seen, or ever shall be seen."

To this the peasant answered: "Señor—sinner that I am!—cannot your worship see that I am not Don Rodrigo de Narvaez nor the Marquis of Mantua, but Pedro Alonso, your neighbor, and that your worship is neither Baldwin nor Abindarraez, but the worthy gentleman Señor Quixada?"

"I know who I am," replied Don Quixote, "and I know that I may be not only those I have named, but all the Twelve Peers of France and even all the Nine Worthies, since my achievements surpass all that they have done all together and each of them on his own account."

With this talk and more of the same kind, they reached the village just as night was beginning to fall, but the peasant waited until it was a little later that the belabored gentleman might not be seen riding in such a miserable trim. When it was what seemed to him the proper time he entered the village and went to Don Quixote's house, which he found all in confusion, and there were the curate and the village barber, who were great friends of Don Quixote, and his housekeeper was saying to them in a loud voice:

"What does your worship think can have befallen my master señor licentiate Pero Perez?" (for so the curate was called). "It is six days now since anything has been seen of him, or the hack, or the buckler, lance, or armor.

Miserable me! I am certain of it, and it is as true as that I was born to die, that these accursed books of chivalry he has, and has got into the way of reading so constantly, have upset his reason; for now I remember having often heard him saying to himself that he would turn knight-errant and go all over the world in quest of adventures. To the devil and Barabbas with such books, that have brought to ruin in this way the finest understanding there was in all La Mancha!"

The niece said the same, and, indeed, more: "You must know, Master Nicholas"—for that was the name of the barber—"it was often my uncle's way to stay two days and nights together poring over these unholy books of misventures, after which he would fling the book away and snatch up his sword and fall to slashing the walls; and when he was tired out he would say he had killed four giants like four towers; and the sweat that flowed from him when he was weary he said was the blood of the wounds he had received in battle; and then he would drink a great jug of cold water and become calm and quiet, saying that this water was a most precious potion which the sage Esquife, a great magician and friend of his, had brought him. But I take all the blame upon myself for never having told your worships of my uncle's vagaries, that you might put a stop to them before things had come to this pass, and burn all these accursed books—for he has a great number—that richly deserve to be burned like heretics."

"So say I, too," said the curate, "and by my faith, tomorrow shall not pass without public judgment upon them, and may they be condemned to the flames lest they lead those that read them to behave as my good friend seems to have behaved."

All this the peasant heard, and from it he understood at last what was the matter with his neighbor, so he began calling aloud, "Open, your worships, to Señor Baldwin and to Señor the Marquis of Mantua, who comes badly wounded, and to Señor Abindarraez, the Moor, whom the valiant Rodrigo de Narvaez, the Alcaide of Antequera, brings captive."

At these words they all hurried out, and when they recognized their friend, master, and uncle, who had not yet dismounted from the ass because he could not, they ran to embrace him.

"Hold!" said he, "for I am badly wounded through my horse's fault; carry me to bed, and if possible send for the wise Urganda to cure and see to my wounds."

"See there! plague on it!" cried the housekeeper at this. "Did not my heart tell the truth as to which foot my master went lame of? To bed with your worship at once, and we will contrive to cure you here without fetching that Hurgada. A curse I say once more, and a hundred times more, on those books of chivalry that have brought your worship to such a pass."

They carried him to bed at once, and after searching for his wounds, could find none, but he said they were all bruises from having had a severe fall with his horse Rocinante when in combat with ten giants, the biggest and the boldest to be found on earth.

"So, so!" said the curate, "are there giants in the dance? By the sign of the cross, I will burn them tomorrow before the day is over."

They put a host of questions to Don Quixote, but his only answer to all was—give him something to eat, and leave him to sleep, for that was what he needed most. They did so, and the curate questioned the peasant at great length as to how he had found Don Quixote. He told him all, and the nonsense he had talked when found and on the way home, all which made the licentiate the more eager to do what he did the next day, which was to summon his friend the barber, Master Nicholas, and go with him to Don Quixote's house. . . .

CHAPTER VI

OF THE SECOND SALLY OF OUR WORTHY KNIGHT DON QUIXOTE OF LA MANCHA

H E was still sleeping, but at length began shouting out, " Here, here, valiant knights! here is need for you to put forth the might of your strong arms, for they of the court are gaining the mastery in the tourney! "

When they reached Don Quixote he was already out of bed, and was still shouting and raving, and slashing and cutting all round, as wide awake as if he had never slept.

They closed with him and by force got him back to bed, and when he had become a little calm, addressing the curate, he said to him, " Of a truth, Señor Archbishop Turpin, it is a great disgrace for us who call ourselves the Twelve Peers, so carelessly to allow the knights of the court to gain the victory in this tourney, we the adventurers having carried off the honor on the three former days."

" Hush, gossip," said the curate; " please God, the luck may turn, and what is lost today may be won tomorrow; for the present let your worship have a care of your health, for it seems to me that you are over-fatigued, if not badly wounded."

" Wounded, no," said Don Quixote, " but bruised and battered no doubt, for that bastard Don Roland has cudgeled me with the trunk of an oak tree, and all for envy, because he sees that I alone rival him in his achievements. But I should not call myself Reinaldos of Montalvan did he not pay me for it in spite of all his enchantments as

34

soon as I rise from this bed. For the present, let them
bring me something to eat, for that, I feel, is what will
be more to my purpose, and leave it to me to avenge myself."

They did as he wished; they gave him something to eat,
and once more he fell asleep, leaving them marveling at
his madness.

One of the remedies which the curate and the barber
immediately applied to their friend's disorder was to wall
up and plaster the room where the books were, so that
when he got up he should not find them (possibly the cause
being removed, the effect might cease), and they might say
that a magician had carried them off, room and all; and
this was done with all dispatch. Two days later Don
Quixote got up, and the first thing he did was to go and
look at his books, and not finding the room where he had
left it, he wandered from side to side, looking for it. He
came to the place where the door used to be, and tried it
with his hands, and turned and twisted his eyes in every
direction without saying a word; but after a good while
he asked his housekeeper whereabouts was the room that
held his books.

The housekeeper, who had been already well instructed
in what she was to answer, said, "What room or what
nothing is it that your worship is looking for? There are
neither room nor books in this house now, for the devil
himself has carried all away."

" It was not the devil," said the niece, "but a magician
who came on a cloud one night after the day your worship
left this, and dismounting from a serpent that he rode, he
entered the room, and what he did there I know not, but
after a little while he made off, flying through the roof,
and left the house full of smoke; and when we went to
see what he had done we saw neither book or room; but
we remember very well, the housekeeper and I, that on
leaving, the old villain said in a loud voice that, for a
private grudge he owed the owner of the books and the
room, he had done mischief in that house that would be

35

discovered by-and-by: he said, too, that his name was the Sage Muñaton."

"He must have said Friston," said Don Quixote.

"I don't know whether he called himself Friston or Friton," said the housekeeper, "I only know that his name ended with 'ton.'"

"So it does," said Don Quixote, "and he is a sage magician, a great enemy of mine, who has a spite against me because he knows by his arts and lore that in process of time I am to engage in single combat with a knight whom he befriends and that I am to conquer, and he will be unable to prevent it; and for this reason he endeavors to do me all the ill turns that he can; but I promise him it will be hard for him to oppose or avoid what is decreed by Heaven."

"Who doubts that?" said the niece; "but, uncle, who mixes you up in these quarrels? Would it not be better to remain at peace in your own house instead of roaming the world looking for better bread than ever came of wheat, never reflecting that many go for wool and come back shorn?"

"Oh, niece of mine," replied Don Quixote, "how much astray art thou in thy reckoning: ere they shear me I shall have plucked away and stripped off the beards of all who would dare to touch only the tip of a hair of mine."

The two were unwilling to make any further answer, as they saw that his anger was kindling.

In short, then, he remained at home fifteen days very quietly without showing any signs of a desire to take up his former delusions, and during this time he held lively discussions with his two gossips, the curate and the barber, on the point he maintained, that knights-errant were what the world stood most in need of, and that in him was to be accomplished the revival of knight-errantry. The curate sometimes contradicted him, sometimes agreed with him, for if he had not observed this precaution he would have been unable to bring him to reason.

Meanwhile Don Quixote worked upon a farm laborer,

a neighbor of his, an honest man (if indeed that title can
be given to him who is poor), but with very little wit in
his pate. In a word, he so talked him over, and with such
persuasions and promises, that the poor clown made up
his mind to sally forth with him and serve him as esquire.
Don Quixote, among other things, told him he ought to be
ready to go with him gladly, because any moment an adventure might occur that might win an island in the twin-
kling of an eye and leave him governor of it. On these
and the like promises Sancho Panza (for so the laborer
was called) left wife and children, and engaged himself as
esquire to his neighbor. Don Quixote next set about getting some money; and selling one thing and pawning another, and making a bad bargain in every case, he got
together a fair sum. He provided himself with a buckler,
which he begged as a loan from a friend, and, restoring
his battered helmet as best he could, he warned his squire
Sancho of the day and hour he meant to set out, that he
might provide himself with what he thought most needful.
Above all, he charged him to take a double wallet with
him. The other said he would, and that he meant to take
also a very good ass he had, as he was not much given to
going on foot. About the ass, Don Quixote hesitated a
little, trying whether he could call to mind any knight-
errant taking with him an esquire mounted on ass-back,
but no instance occurred to his memory. For all that,
however, he determined to take him, intending to furnish
him with a more honorable mount when a chance of it
presented itself, by appropriating the horse of the first
discourteous knight he encountered. Himself he provided
with shirts and such other things as he could, according
to the advice the host had given him; all which being
settled and done, without taking leave, Sancho Panza of
his wife and children, or Don Quixote of his housekeeper
and niece, they sallied forth unseen by anybody from the
village one night, and made such good way in the course
of it that by daylight they held themselves safe from discovery, even should search be made for them.

Sancho rode on his ass like a patriarch with his wallet and wine-bag, and longing to see himself soon governor of the island his master had promised him. Don Quixote decided upon taking the same route and road he had taken on his first journey, that over the Campo de Montiel, which he traveled with less discomfort than on the last occasion, for, as it was early morning and the rays of the sun fell on them obliquely, the heat did not distress them.

And now said Sancho Panza to his master, " Your worship will take care, Señor Knight-errant, not to forget about the island you have promised me, for be it ever so big I'll be equal to governing it."

To which Don Quixote replied, " Thou must know, friend Sancho Panza, that it was a practice very much in vogue with the knights-errant of old to make their squires governors of the islands or kingdoms they won, and I am determined that there shall be no failure on my part in so liberal a custom; on the contrary, I mean to improve upon it, for they sometimes, and perhaps most frequently, waited until their squires were old, and then when they had had enough of service and hard days and worse nights, they gave them some title or other, of count, or at the most marquis, of some valley or province more or less; but if thou livest and I live, it may well be that before six days are over, I may have won some kingdom that has others dependent upon it, which will be just the thing to enable thee to be crowned king of one of them. Nor needst thou count this wonderful, for things and chances fall to the lot of such knights in ways so unexampled and unexpected that I might easily give thee even more than I promise thee."

" In that case," said Sancho Panza, " if I should become a king by one of those miracles your worship speaks of, even Juana Gutierrez, my old woman, would come to be queen and my children *infantes*."

" Well, who doubts it?" said Don Quixote.

" I doubt it," replied Sancho Panza, " because for my part I am persuaded that though God should shower down

kingdoms upon earth, not one of them would fit the head of Mari Gutierrez. Let me tell you, señor, she is not worth two *maravedis* for a queen; countess will fit her better, and that only with God's help."

"Leave it to God, Sancho," returned Don Quixote, "for he will give her what suits her best; but do not undervalue thyself so much as to come to be content with anything less than being governor of a province."

"I will not, señor," answered Sancho, "especially as I have a man of such quality for a master in your worship, who will be able to give me all that will be suitable for me and that I can bear."

CHAPTER VII

A T this point they came in sight of thirty or forty
windmills that there are on that plain and as soon
as Don Quixote saw them he said to his squire, " Fortune
is arranging matters for us better than we could have
shaped our desire ourselves, for look there, friend Sancho
Panza, where thirty or more monstrous giants present
themselves, all of whom I mean to engage in battle and
slay, and with whose spoils we shall begin to make our
fortunes; for this is righteous warfare, and it is God's
good service to sweep so evil a breed from off the face
of the earth."

" What giants? " said Sancho Panza.

" Those thou seest there," answered his master, " with
the long arms, and some have them nearly two leagues
long."

" Look, your worship," said Sancho; " what we see there
are not giants, but windmills, and what seem to be their
arms are the sails that turned by the wind make the millstone go."

" It is easy to see," replied Don Quixote, " that thou art
not used to this business of adventures; those are giants;
and if thou art afraid, away with thee out of this and
betake thyself to prayer while I engage them in fierce and
unequal combat "

CERVANTES' "DON QUIXOTE"

So saying, he gave the spur to his steed Rocinante, heedless of the cries his squire Sancho sent after him, warning him that most certainly they were windmills and not giants he was going to attack. He, however, was so positive they were giants that he neither heard the cries of Sancho, nor perceived, near as he was, what they were, but made at them, shouting, "Fly not, cowards and vile beings, for it is a single knight that attacks you."

A slight breeze at this moment sprang up and the great sails began to move, seeing which Don Quixote exclaimed, "Though ye flourish more arms than the giant Briareus, ye have to reckon with me."

So saying, and commending himself with all his heart to his lady Dulcinea, imploring her to support him in such a peril, with lance in rest and covered by his buckler, he charged at Rocinante's fullest gallop and fell upon the first mill that stood in front of him; but as he drove his lance-point into the sail the wind whirled it round with such force that it shivered the lance to pieces, sweeping with it horse and rider, who went rolling over the plain, in a sorry condition. Sancho hastened to his assistance as fast as his ass could go, and when he came up found him unable to move, with such a shock had Rocinante fallen with him.

"God bless me!" said Sancho, "did I not tell your worship to mind what you were about, for they were only windmills? and no one could have made any mistake about it but one who had something of the same kind in his head."

"Hush, friend Sancho," replied Don Quixote, "the fortunes of war more than any other are liable to frequent fluctuations; and moreover, I think, and it is the truth, that that same sage Friston who carried off my study and books, has turned these giants into mills in order to rob me of the glory of vanquishing them, such is the enmity he bears me; but in the end his wicked arts will avail but little against my good sword."

"God order it as he may," said Sancho Panza, and helping him to rise got him up again on Rocinante, whose shoulder was half out; and then, discussing the late adventure, they followed the road to Puerto Lapice, for there, said Don Quixote, they could not fail to find adventures in abundance and variety, as it was a great thoroughfare. For all that, he was much grieved at the loss of his lance, and saying so to his squire, he added:

"I remember having read how a Spanish knight, Diego Perez de Vargas by 'name, having broken his sword in battle, tore from an oak a ponderous bough or branch, and with it did such things that day, and pounded so many Moors, that he got the surname of Machuca, and he and his descendants from that day forth were called Vargas y Machuca. I mention this because from the first oak I see I mean to rend such another branch, large and stout like that, with which I am determined and resolved to do such deeds that thou mayest deem thyself very fortunate in being found worthy to come and see them, and be an eye-witness of things that will with difficulty be believed."

"Be that as God will," said Sancho, "I believe it all as your worship says it; but straighten yourself a little, for you seem all on one side, maybe from the shaking of the fall."

"That is the truth," said Don Quixote, "and if I make no complaint of the pain it is because knights-errant are not permitted to complain of any wound, even though their bowels be coming out through it."

"If so," said Sancho, "I have nothing to say; but God knows I would rather your worship complained when anything ailed you. For my part, I confess I must complain, however small the ache may be; unless indeed this rule about not complaining extends to the squires of knights-errant also."

Don Quixote could not help laughing at his squire's simplicity, and he assured him he might complain whenever and however he chose, just as he liked, for, so far, he had never read of anything to the contrary in the order of knighthood.

Sancho bade him remember it was dinner-time, to which

his master answered that he wanted nothing himself just
then, but that *he* might eat when he had a mind. With
this permission Sancho settled himself as comfortably as
he could on his beast, and taking out of the wallets what
he had stowed away in them, he jogged along behind his
master, munching deliberately, and from time to time
taking a pull at the wine-skin with a relish that the thirst-
iest tapster in Malaga might have envied; and while he
went on in this way, gulping down draught after draught,
he never gave a thought to any of the promises his master
had made him, nor did he rate it as hardship but rather
as recreation going in quest of adventures, however dangerous they might be. Finally they passed the night among
some trees, from one of which Don Quixote plucked a dry
branch to serve him after a fashion as a lance, and fixed
on it the head he had removed from the broken one. All
that night Don Quixote lay awake thinking of his lady
Dulcinea, in order to conform to what he had read in his
books, how many a night in the forests and deserts knights
used to lie sleepless, supported by the memory of their mistresses. Not so did Sancho Panza spend it, for having his
stomach full of something stronger than chicory water
he made but one sleep of it, and, if his master had not
called him, neither the rays of the sun beating on his face
nor all the cheery notes of the birds welcoming the approach of day would have had power to waken him. On
getting up he tried the wine-skin and found it somewhat
less full than the night before, which grieved his heart, because they did not seem to be on the way to remedy the
deficiency readily. Don Quixote did not care to break his
fast, for, as has been already said, he confined himself to
savory recollections for nourishment.

They returned to the road they had set out with, leading
to Puerto Lapice, and at three in the afternoon they came
in sight of it. "Here, brother Sancho Panza," said Don
Quixote when he saw it, "we may plunge our hands up
to the elbows in what they call adventures; but observe,
even shouldst thou see me in the greatest danger in the

world, thou must not put a hand to thy sword in my defense, unless indeed thou perceivest that those who assail me are rabble or base folk; for in that case thou mayest very properly aid me; but if they be knights, it is on no account permitted or allowed thee by the laws of knighthood to help me until thou hast been dubbed a knight."

"Most certainly, señor," replied Sancho, "your worship shall be fully obeyed in this matter; all the more as of myself I am peaceful and no friend to mixing in strife and quarrels: it is true that as regards the defense of my own person I shall not give much heed to those laws, for laws human and divine allow each one to defend himself against any assailant whatever."

"That I grant," said Don Quixote, "but in this matter of aiding me against knights thou must put a restraint upon thy natural impetuosity."

"I will do so, I promise you," answered Sancho, "and I will keep this precept as carefully as Sunday."

While they were thus talking there appeared on the road two friars of the order of St. Benedict, mounted on two dromedaries, for not less tall were the two mules they rode on. They wore traveling spectacles and carried sunshades; and behind them came a coach attended by four or five persons on horseback and two muleteers on foot. In the coach there was, as afterwards appeared, a Biscay lady on her way to Seville, where her husband was about to take passage for the Indies with an appointment of high honor. The friars, though going the same road, were not in her company; but the moment Don Quixote perceived them he said to his squire, "Either I am mistaken, or this is going to be the most famous adventure that has ever been seen, for those black bodies we see there must be, and doubtless are, magicians who are carrying off some stolen princess in that coach, and with all my might I must undo this wrong."

"This will be worse than the windmills," said Sancho. "Look, señor; those are friars of St. Benedict, and the coach plainly belongs to some travelers: mind, I tell you

44

to mind well what you are about and don't let the devil mislead you."

"I have told thee already, Sancho," replied Don Quixote, "that on the subject of adventures thou knowest little. What I say is the truth, as thou shalt see presently."

So saying, he advanced and posted himself in the middle of the road along which the friars were coming, and as soon as he thought they had come near enough to hear what he said, he cried aloud, "Devilish and unnatural beings, release instantly the high-born princesses whom you are carrying off by force in this coach, else prepare to meet a speedy death as the just punishment of your evil deeds."

The friars drew rein and stood wondering at the appearance of Don Quixote as well as at his words, to which they replied, "Señor Caballero, we are not devilish or unnatural, but two brothers of St. Benedict following our road, nor do we know whether or not there are any captive princesses coming in this coach."

"No soft words with me, for I know you, lying rabble," said Don Quixote, and without waiting for a reply he spurred Rocinante and with leveled lance charged the first friar with such fury and determination that, if the friar had not flung himself off the mule, he would have brought him to the ground against his will, and sore wounded, if not killed outright. The second brother, seeing how his comrade was treated, drove his heels into his castle of a mule and made off across the country faster than the wind.

Sancho Panza, when he saw the friar on the ground, dismounting briskly from his ass, rushed towards him and began to strip off his gown. At that instant the friar's muleteers came up and asked what he was stripping him for. Sancho answered them that this fell to him lawfully as spoil of the battle which his lord Don Quixote had won. The muleteers, who had no idea of a joke and did not understand all this about battles and spoils, seeing that Don Quixote was some distance off talking to the travelers in the coach, fell upon Sancho, knocked him down, and leaving hardly a hair in his beard, belabored him with kicks and left him stretched breathless and senseless on the ground; and without any more delay helped the friar to mount, who, trembling, terrified, and pale, as soon as he found himself in the saddle,, spurred after his companion, who was standing at a distance looking on, watching the result of the onslaught; then, not caring to wait for the end of the affair just begun, they pursued their journey, making more crosses than if they had the devil after them.

Don Quixote was, as has been said, speaking to the lady in the coach: "Your beauty, lady mine," said he, "may now dispose of your person as may be most in accordance with your pleasure, for the pride of your ravishers lies prostrate on the ground through this strong arm of mine; and lest you should be pining to know the name of your deliverer, know that I am called Don Quixote of La Mancha, knight-errant and adventurer, and captive to the peerless and beautiful lady Dulcinea del Toboso; and in return for the service you have received from me I ask no more than that you should return to El Toboso, and on my behalf present yourself before that lady and tell her what I have done to set you free."

One of the squires in atteudance upon the coach, a Biscayan, was listening to all Don Quixote was saying, and, perceiving that he would not allow the coach to go on, but was saying it must return at once to El Toboso, he made at him, and seizing his lance addressed him in bad Castilian and worse Biscayan after this fashion:

"Begone, *caballero,* and ill go with thee; by the God that made me, unless thou quittest coach, slayest thee as art here a Biscayan."

Don Quixote understood him quite well, and answered him very quietly:

"If thou wert a knight, as thou art none, I should have already chastised thy folly and rashness, miserable creature." To which the Biscayan returned:

"I no gentleman!—I swear to God thou liest as I am Christian: if thou droppest lance and drawest sword, soon shalt thou see thou art carrying water to the cat: Biscayan,

46

on land, *hidalgo* at sea, *hidalgo* at the devil, and look, if thou sayest otherwise thou liest."

" 'You will see presently,' said Agrajes," replied Don Quixote; and throwing his lance on the ground he drew his sword, braced his buckler on his arm, and attacked the Biscayan, bent upon taking his life.

The Biscayan, when he saw him coming on, though he wished to dismount from his mule, in which, being one of those sorry ones let out for hire, he had no confidence, had no choice but to draw his sword; it was lucky for him, however, that he was near the coach, from which he was able to snatch a cushion that served him for a shield; and then they went at one another as if they had been two mortal enemies. The others strove to make peace between them, but could not, for the Biscayan declared in his disjointed phrase that if they did not let him finish his battle he would kill his mistress and every one that strove to prevent him. The lady in the coach, amazed and terrified at what she saw, ordered the coachman to draw aside a little, and set herself to watch this severe struggle, in the course of which the Biscayan smote Don Quixote a mighty stroke on the shoulder over the top of his buckler, which, given to one without armor, would have cleft him to the waist. Don Quixote, feeling the weight of this prodigious blow, cried aloud, saying, "O lady of my soul, Dulcinea, flower of beauty, come to the aid of this your knight, who, in fulfilling his obligations to your beauty, finds himself in this extreme peril." To say this, to lift his sword, to shelter himself behind his buckler, and to assail the Biscayan was the work of an instant, determined as he was to venture all upon a single blow. The Biscayan, seeing him come on in this way, was convinced of his courage by his spirited bearing, and resolved to follow his example, so he waited for him, keeping well under cover of his cushion, being unable to execute any sort of manœuvre with his mule, which, dead tired and never meant for this kind of game, could not stir a step.

On, then, as aforesaid, came Don Quixote against the

wary Biscayan, with uplifted sword and a firm intention of splitting him in half, while on his side the Biscayan waited for him sword in hand, and under the protection of his cushion; and all present stood trembling, waiting in suspense the result of blows such as threatened to fall, and the lady in the coach and the rest of her following were making a thousand vows and offerings to all the images and shrines of Spain, that God might deliver her squire and all of them from this great peril in which they found themselves. But it spoils all, that at this point and crisis the author of the history leaves this battle impending, giving as excuse that he could find nothing more written about these achievements of Don Quixote than what has been already set forth. It is true the second author of this work was unwilling to believe that a history so curious could have been allowed to fall under the sentence of oblivion, or that the wits of La Mancha could have been so undiscerning as not to preserve in their archives or registries some documents referring to this famous knight; and this being his persuasion, he did not despair of finding the conclusion of this pleasant history, which, heaven favoring him, he did find in a way that shall be related later.

CHAPTER VIII

IN WHICH IS CONCLUDED AND FINISHED THE TERRIFIC
BATTLE BETWEEN THE GALLANT BISCAYAN AND THE VA-
LIANT MANCHEGAN

I N the First Part of this history we left the valiant Biscayan and the renowned Don Quixote with drawn
swords uplifted, ready to deliver two such furious slashing
blows that if they had fallen full and fair they would at
least have split and cleft them asunder from top to toe
and laid them open like a pomegranate; and at this so critical point the delightful history came to a stop and stood
cut short without any intimation from the author where
what was missing was to be found.

This distressed me greatly, because the pleasure derived
from having read such a small portion turned to vexation
at the thought of the poor chance that presented itself
of finding the large part that, so it seemed to me, was
missing of such an interesting tale. It appeared to me
to be a thing impossible and contrary to all precedent that
so good a knight should have been without some sage to
undertake the task of writing his marvelous achievements;
a thing that was never wanting to any of those knights-
errant who, they say, went after adventures; for every
one of them had one or two sages as if made on purpose,
who not only recorded their deeds, but described their most
trifling thoughts and follies, however secret they might be;
and such a good knight could not have been so unfortunate
as not to have what Platir and others like him had in

abundance. And so I could not bring myself to believe that such a gallant tale had been left maimed and mutilated, and I laid the blame on Time, the devourer and destroyer of all things, that had either concealed or consumed it. . . .

One day, as I was in the Alcana of Toledo, a boy came up to sell some pamphlets and old papers to a silk mercer, and, as I am fond of reading even the very scraps of paper in the streets, led by this natural bent of mine I took up one of the pamphlets the boy had for sale. . . .

It proved to be the *History of Don Quixote of La Mancha, written by Cid Hamet Benengeli, antiral historian.* I thereupon bought all the papers and pamphlets from the boy for half a *real.*

In the first pamphlet the battle between Don Quixote and the Biscayan was drawn to the very life, they planted in the same attitude as the history describes, their swords raised, and the one protected by his buckler, the other by his cushion, and the Biscayan's mule so true to nature that it could be seen to be a hired one a bowshot off. The Biscayan had an inscription under his feet which said, *Don Sancho de Azpeitia,* which no doubt must have been his name; and at the feet of Rocinante was another that said, *Don Quixote.* Rocinante was marvelously portrayed, so long and thin, so lank and lean, with so much backbone and so far gone in consumption, that he showed plainly with what judgment and propriety the name of Rocinante had been bestowed upon him. Near him was Sancho Panza holding the halter of his ass, at whose feet was another label that said, *Sancho Zancas,* and according to the picture, he must have had a big belly, a short body, and long shanks, for which reason, no doubt, the names of Panza and Zancas were given him, for by these two surnames the history several times calls him. Some other trifling particulars might be mentioned, but they are all of slight importance and have nothing to do with the true relation of the history; and no history can be had so long as it is not true. . . .

Its Second Part began in this way: With trenchant swords upraised and poised on high, it seemed as though the two valiant and wrathful combatants stood threatening heaven, and earth, and hell, with such resolution and determination did they bear themselves. The fiery Biscayan was the first to strike a blow, which was delivered with such force and fury that had not the sword turned in its course, that single stroke would have sufficed to put an end to the bitter struggle and to all the adventures of our knight; but that good fortune which reserved him for greater things turned aside the sword of his adversary, so that, although it smote him upon the left shoulder, it did him no more harm than to strip all that side of its armor, carrying away a great part of his helmet with half of his ear, all which with fearful ruin fell to the ground, leaving him in a sorry plight.

Good God! Who is there that could properly describe the rage that filled the heart of our Manchegan when he saw himself dealt with in this fashion? All that can be said is, it was such that he again raised himself in his stirrups, and, grasping his sword more firmly with both hands, he came down on the Biscayan with such fury, smiting him full over the cushion and over the head, that—even so good a shield proving useless—as if a mountain had fallen on him, he began to bleed from nose, mouth, and ears, reeling as if about to fall backwards from his mule, as no doubt he would have done had he not flung his arms about its neck; at the same time, however, he slipped his feet out of the stirrups and then unclasped his arms, and the mule, taking fright at the terrible blow, made off across the plain, and with a few plunges flung its master to the ground.

Don Quixote stood looking on very calmly, and, when he saw him fall, leaped from his horse and with great briskness ran to him, and, presenting the point of his sword to his eyes, bade him surrender, or he would cut his head off. The Biscayan was so bewildered that he was unable to answer a word, and it would have gone hard with him, so blind was Don Quixote, had not the ladies in the coach, who had hitherto been watching the combat in great terror, hastened to where he stood and implored him with earnest entreaties to grant them the great grace and favor of sparing their squire's life; to which Don Quixote replied with much gravity and dignity, " In truth, fair ladies, I am well content to do what ye ask of me; but it must be on one condition and understanding, which is that this knight promise me to go to the village of El Toboso, and on my part present himself before the peerless lady Dulcinea, that she deal with him as shall be most pleasing to her."

The terrified and disconsolate ladies, without discussing Don Quixote's demand or asking who Dulcinea might be, promised that their squire should do all that had been commanded on his part.

" Then, on the faith of that promise," said Don Quixote, " I shall do him no further harm, though he well deserves it of me."

CHAPTER IX

NOW by this time Sancho had risen, rather the worse for the handling of the friar's muleteers, and stood watching the battle of his master, Don Quixote, and praying to God in his heart that it might be his will to grant him the victory, and that he might thereby win some island to make him governor of, as he had promised. Seeing, therefore, that the struggle was now over, and that his master was returning to mount Rocinante, he approached to hold the stirrup for him, and, before he could mount, he went on his knees before him, and taking his hand, kissed it saying:

"May it please your worship, Señor Don Quixote, to give me the government of that island which has been won in this hard fight, for be it ever so big I feel myself in sufficient force to be able to govern it as much and as well as any one in the world who has ever governed islands."

To which Don Quixote replied:

"Thou must take notice, brother Sancho, that this adventure and those like it are not adventures of islands, but of cross-roads, in which nothing is got except a broken head or an ear the less: have patience, for adventures will present themselves from which I may make you, not only a governor, but something more."

Sancho gave him many thanks, and again kissing his hand and the skirt of his hauberk, helped him to mount Rocinante, and mounting his ass himself, proceeded to follow his master, who at a brisk pace, without taking leave, or saying anything further to the ladies belonging to the coach, turned into a wood that was hard by. Sancho followed him at his ass's best trot, but Rocinante stepped out so that, seeing himself left behind, he was forced to call to his master to wait for him. Don Quixote did so, reining in Rocinante until his weary squire came up, who on reaching him said:

"It seems to me, señor, it would be prudent in us to go and take refuge in some church, for, seeing how mauled he with whom you fought has been left, it will be no wonder if they give information of the affair to the Holy Brotherhood and arrest us, and, faith, if they do, before we come out of gaol we shall have to sweat for it."

"Peace," said Don Quixote; "where hast thou ever seen or heard that a knight-errant has been arraigned before a court of justice, however many homicides he may have committed?"

"I know nothing about omecils," answered Sancho, "nor in my life have had anything to do with one; I only know that the Holy Brotherhood looks after those who fight in the fields, and in that other matter I do not meddle."

"Then thou needest have no uneasiness, my friend," said Don Quixote, "for I will deliver thee out of the hands of the Chaldeans, much more out of those of the Brotherhood. But tell me, as thou livest, hast thou seen a more valiant knight than I in all the known world; hast thou read in history of any who has or had higher mettle in attack, more spirit in maintaining it, more dexterity in wounding or skill in overthrowing?"

"The truth is," answered Sancho, "that I have never read any history, for I can neither read nor write, but what I will venture to bet is that a more daring master than your worship I have never served in all the days of my life, and God grant that this daring be not paid for where I have said; what I beg of your worship is to dress your wound, for a great deal of blood flows from that ear,

54

and I have here some lint and a little white ointment in
the wallets."

"All that might be well dispensed with," said Don
Quixote, "if I had remembered to make a vial of the balsam of Fierabras, for time and medicine are saved by one
single drop."

"What vial and what balsam is that?" said Sancho
Panza.

"It is a balsam," answered Don Quixote, "the recipe
of which I have in my memory, with which one need have
no fear of death, or dread dying of any wound; and so
when I make it and give it to thee thou hast nothing to do
when in some battle thou seest they have cut me in half
through the middle of the body—as is wont to happen frequently—but neatly and with great nicety, ere the blood
congeal, to place that portion of the body which shall have
fallen to the ground upon the other half which remains
in the saddle, taking care to fit it on evenly and exactly.
Then thou shalt give me to drink but two drops of the
balsam I have mentioned, and thou shalt see me become
sounder than an apple."

"If that be so," said Panza, "I renounce henceforth
the government of the promised island, and desire nothing
more in payment of my many and faithful services than
that your worship give me the recipe of this supreme
liquor, for I am persuaded it will be worth more than two
reals an ounce anywhere, and I want no more to pass the
rest of my life in ease and honor; but it remains to be
told if it costs much to make it."

"With less than three *reals* six quarts of it may be
made," said Don Quixote.

"Sinner that I am!" said Sancho, "then why does your
worship put off making it and teaching it to me?"

"Peace, friend," answered Don Quixote; "greater
secrets I mean to teach thee and greater favors to bestow
upon thee; and for the present let us see to the dressing,
for my ear pains me more than I could wish."

Sancho took out some lint and ointment from the wallets;

but when Don Quixote came to see his helmet shattered, he was like to lose his senses, and clapping his hand upon his sword and raising his eyes to heaven, he said:

"I swear by the Creator of all things and the four Gospels in their fullest extent, to do as the great Marquis of Mantua did when he swore to avenge the death of his nephew Baldwin (and that was not to eat bread from a table-cloth, nor embrace his wife, and other points which, though I cannot now call them to mind, I here grant as expressed), until I take complete vengeance upon him who has committed such an offense against me." Hearing this, Sancho said to him:

"Your worship should bear in mind, Señor Don Quixote, that if the knight has done what was commanded him in going to present himself before my lady Dulcinea del Toboso, he will have done all that he was bound to do, and does not deserve further punishment unless he commits some new offense."

"Thou hast said well and hit the point," answered Don Quixote; "and so I recall the oath in so far as relates to taking fresh vengeance on him, but I make and confirm it anew to lead the life I have said until such time as I take by force from some knight another helmet such as this and as good; and think not, Sancho, that I am raising smoke with straw in doing so, for I have one to imitate in the matter, since the very same thing to a hair happened in the case of Mambrino's helmet, which cost Sacripante so dear."

"Enough," said Sancho; "so be it then, and God grant us success, and that the time for winning that island which is costing me so dear may soon come, and then let me die."

"I have already told thee, Sancho," said Don Quixote, "not to give thyself any uneasiness on that score; for if an island should fail, there is the kingdom of Denmark, or of Sobradisa, which will fit thee as a ring fits the finger, and all the more that being on *terra firma* thou wilt all the better enjoy thyself. But let us leave that to its own time; see if thou hast anything for us to eat in those wallets, because we must presently go in quest of some castle where we may lodge tonight and make the balsam I told thee of, for I swear to thee by God, this ear is giving me great pain."

"I have here an onion and a little cheese and a few scraps of bread," said Sancho, "but they are not victuals fit for a valiant knight like your worship."

"How little thou knowest about it," answered Don Quixote; "I would have thee to know, Sancho, that it is the glory of knights-errant to go without eating for a month, and even when they do eat, that it should be of what comes first to hand; and this would have been clear to thee hadst thou read as many histories as I have, for, though they are very many, among them all I have found no mention made of knights-errant eating, unless by accident or at some sumptuous banquet prepared for them, and the rest of the time they passed in dalliance. And though it is plain they could not do without eating and performing all the other natural functions, because, in fact, they were men like ourselves, it is plain too that, wandering as they did the most part of their lives through woods and wilds and without a cook, their most usual fare would be rustic viands such as those thou dost now offer me; so that, friend Sancho, let not that distress thee which pleases me, and do not seek to make a new world or pervert knight-errantry."

"Pardon me, your worship," said Sancho, "for, as I cannot read or write, as I said just now, I neither know nor comprehend the rules of the profession of chivalry: henceforward I will stock the wallets with every kind of dry fruit for your worship, as you are a knight; and for myself, as I am not one, I will furnish them with poultry and other things more substantial."

"I do not say, Sancho," replied Don Quixote, "that it is imperative on knights-errant not to eat anything else but the fruits thou speakest of; only that their more usual diet must be those, and certain herbs they found in the fields which they knew and I know too."

"A good thing it is," answered Sancho, "to know those herbs, for to my thinking it will be needful some day to put that knowledge into practice."

And here taking out what he said he had brought, the pair made their repast peaceably and sociably. But anxious to find quarters for the night, they with all despatch made an end of their poor dry fare, mounted at once, and made haste to reach some habitation before night set in; but daylight and the hope of succeeding in their object failed them close by the huts of some goatherds, so they determined to pass the night there, and it was as much to Sancho's discontent not to have reached a house, as it was to his master's satisfaction to sleep under the open heaven, for he fancied that each time this happened to him he performed an act of ownership that helped to prove his chivalry.

CHAPTER X

HE was cordially welcomed by the goatherds, and Sancho, having as best he could put up Rocinante and the ass, drew towards the fragrance that came from some pieces of salted goat simmering in a pot on the fire; and though he would have liked at once to try if they were ready to be transferred from the pot to the stomach, he refrained from doing so as the goatherds removed them from the fire, and laying sheepskins on the ground, quickly spread their rude table, and with signs of hearty goodwill invited them both to share what they had. Round the skins six of the men belonging to the fold seated themselves, having first with rough politeness pressed Don Quixote to take a seat upon a trough which they placed for him upside down. Don Quixote seated himself, and Sancho remained standing to serve the cup, which was made of horn. Seeing him standing, his master said to him:

"That thou mayest see, Sancho, the good that knight-errantry contains in itself, and how those who fill any office in it are on the high road to be speedily honored and esteemed by the world, I desire that thou seat thyself here at my side and in the company of these worthy people, and that thou be one with me who am thy master and natural lord, and that thou eat from my plate and drink from whatever I drink from; for the same may be said of knight-errantry as of love, that it levels all."

"Great thanks," said Sancho, "but I may tell your wor-

ship that provided I have enough to eat, I can eat it as well,
or better, standing, and by myself, than seated alongside
of an emperor. And, indeed, if the truth is to be told,
what I eat in my corner without form or fuss has much
more relish for me, even though it be bread and onions,
than the turkeys of those other tables where I am forced
to chew slowly, drink little, wipe my mouth every minute,
and cannot sneeze or cough if I want or do other things
that are the privileges of liberty and solitude. So, señor,
as for these honors which your worship would put upon
me as a servant and follower of knight-errantry (which
I am, being your worship's squire), exchange them for
other things which may be of more use and advantage to
me; for these, though I fully acknowledge them as received, I renounce from this moment to the end of the
world."

"For all that," said Don Quixote, "thou must seat thyself, because him who humbleth himself God exalted;" and
seizing him by the arm he forced him to sit down beside
himself.

The goatherds did not understand this jargon about
squires and knights-errant, and all they did was to eat in
silence and stare at their guests, who with great elegance
and appetite were stowing away pieces as big as one's fist.
The course of meat finished, they spread upon the sheepskins a great heap of parched acorns, and with them they
put down a half cheese harder than if it had been made
of mortar. All this while the horn was not idle, for it
went round so constantly, now full, now empty, like the
bucket of a water-wheel, that it soon drained one of the
two wine-skins that were in sight. When Don Quixote
had quite appeased his appetite he took up a handful of
the acorns, and contemplating them attentively delivered
himself somewhat in this fashion:

"Happy the age, happy the time, to which the ancients
gave the name of golden, not because in that fortunate age
the gold so coveted in this our iron one was gained without
toil, but because they that lived in it knew not the two

words '*mine*' and '*thine*'! In that blessed age all things were in common; to win the daily food no labor was required of any save to stretch forth his hand and gather it from the sturdy oaks that stood generously inviting him with their sweet ripe fruit. The clear streams and running brooks yielded their savory limpid waters in noble abundance. The busy and sagacious bees fixed their republic in the clefts of the rocks and hollows of the trees, offering without usance the plenteous produce of their fragrant toil to every hand. The mighty cork trees, unenforced save of their own courtesy, shed the broad light bark that served at first to roof the houses supported by rude stakes, a protection against the inclemency of heaven alone. Then all was peace, all friendship, all concord; as yet the dull share of the crooked plough had not dared to rend and pierce the tender bowels of our first mother that without compulsion yielded from every portion of her broad fertile bosom all that could satisfy, sustain, and delight the children that then possessed her. Then was it that the innocent and fair young shepherdesses roamed from vale to vale and hill to hill, with flowing locks, and no more garments than were needful modestly to cover what modesty seeks and ever sought to hide. Nor were their ornaments like those in use today, set off by Tyrian purple, and silk tortured in endless fashions, but the wreathed leaves of the green dock and ivy, wherewith they went as bravely and becomingly decked as our court dames with all the rare and far-fetched artifices that idle curiosity has taught them. Then the love thoughts of the heart clothed themselves simply and naturally as the heart conceived them, nor sought to commend themselves by forced and rambling verbiage. Fraud, deceit, or malice had then not yet mingled with truth and sincerity. Justice held her ground, undisturbed and unassailed by the efforts of favor and of interest, that now so much impair, pervert, and beset her. Arbitrary law had not yet established itself in the mind of the judge, for then there was no cause to judge and no one to be judged. Maidens and modesty, as I have said, wandered at will alone and unattended, without fear of insult from lawlessness or libertine assault, and if they were undone it was of their own will and pleasure.

"But now in this hateful age of ours not one is safe, not though some new labyrinth like that of Crete conceal and surround her; even there the pestilence of gallantry will make its way to them through chinks or on the air by the zeal of its accursed importunity, and, despite of all seclusion, lead them to ruin. In defence of these, as time advanced and wickedness increased, the order of knights-errant was instituted, to defend maidens, to protect widows, and to succor the orphans and the needy. To this order I belong, brother goatherds, to whom I return thanks for the hospitality and kindly welcome ye offer me and my squire; for though by natural law all living are bound to show favor to knights-errant, yet, seeing that without knowing this obligation ye have welcomed and featested me, it is right that with all the good-will in my power I should thank you for yours."

All this long harangue (which might very well have been spared) our knight delivered because the acorns they gave him reminded him of the golden age; and the whim seized him to address all this unnecessary argument to the goatherds, who listened to him gaping in amazement without saying a word in reply. Sancho likewise held his peace and ate acorns, and paid repeated visits to the second wine-skin, which they had hung up on a cork tree to keep cool.

Don Quixote was longer in talking than in finishing his supper, at the end of which one of the goatherds said, "That your worship, señor knight-errant, may say with more truth that we show you hospitality with ready good-will, we will give you amusement and pleasure by making one of our comrades sing: he will be here before long, and he is a very intelligent youth and deep in love, and what is more he can read and write and play on the rebeck to perfection."

The goathered had harly done speaking, when the notes

of the rebeck reached their ears; and shortly after, the player came up, a very good-looking young man of about two-and-twenty. His comrades asked him if he had supped, and on his replying that he had, he who had already made the offer said to him, "In that case, Antonio, thou mayest as well do us the pleasure of singing a little, that the gentleman, our guest here, may see that even in the mountains and woods there are musicians: we have told him of thy accomplishments, and we want thee to show them and prove that we say true; so, as thou livest, pray sit down and sing that ballad about thy love that thy uncle the prebendary made thee, and that was so much liked in the town."

"With all my heart," said the young man, and without waiting for any more pressing he seated himself on the trunk of a felled oak, and tuning his rebeck, presently began with right good grace to sing to these words:

ANTONIO'S BALLAD

Thou dost love me well, Olalla;
  Well I know it, even though
Love's mute tongues, thine eyes, have never
  By their glances told me so.

For I know my love thou knowest,
  Therefore thine to claim I dare:
Once it ceases to be secret,
  Love need never feel despair.

True it is, Olalla, sometimes
  Thou hast all too plainly shown
That thy heart is brass in hardness,
  And thy snowy bosom stone.

Yet for all that, in thy coyness,
  And thy fickle fits between,
Hope is there—at least the border
  Of her garment may be seen.

Lures to faith are they, those glimpses,
  And to faith in thee I hold;
Kindness cannot make it stronger,
  Coldness cannot make it cold.

TALES FROM THE SPANISH

If it be that love is gentle,
  In thy gentleness I see
Something holding out assurance
  To the hope of winning thee.

If it be that in devotion
  Lies a power hearts to move,
That which every day I show thee,
  Helpful to my suit should prove.

Many a time thou must have noticed—
  If to notice thou dost care—
How I go about on Monday
  Dressed in all my Sunday wear.

Love's eyes love to look on brightness;
  Love loves what is gayly drest;
Sunday, Monday, all I care is
  Thou shouldst see me in my best.

No account I make of dances,
  Or of strains that pleased thee so,
Keeping thee awake from midnight
  Till the cocks began to crow;

Or of how I roundly swore it
  That there's none so fair as thou;
True it is, but as I said it,
  By the girls I'm hated now.

For Teresa of the hillside
  At my praise of thee was sore;
Said, " You think you love an angel;
  It's a monkey you adore;

" Caught by all her glittering trinkets,
  And her borrowed braids of hair,
And a host of made-up beauties
  That would Love himself ensnare."

'Twas a lie, and so I told her,
  And her cousin at the word
Gave me his defiance for it;
  And what followed thou hast heard.

Mine is no high-flown affection,
  Mine no passion *par amours*—
As they call it—what I offer
  Is an honest love, and pure.

64

CERVANTES' "DON QUIXOTE"

Cunning cords the holy Church has,
  Cords of softest silk they be;
Put thy neck beneath the yoke, dear;
  Mine will follow, thou wilt see.

Else—and once for all I swear it
  By the saint of most renown—
If I ever quit the mountains,
  'Twill be in a friar's gown.

Here the goatherd brought his song to an end, and though
Don Quixote entreated him to sing more, Sancho had no
mind that way, being more inclined for sleep than for listening to songs; so said he to his master, " Your worship
will do well to settle at once where you mean to pass the
night, for the labor these good men are at all day does
not allow them to spend the night in singing."

"I understand thee, Sancho," replied Don Quixote; " I
perceive clearly that those visits to the wine-skin demand
compensation in sleep rather than in music."

"It's sweet to us all, blessed be God," said Sancho.

"I do not deny it," replied Don Quixote; " but settle
thyself where thou wilt; those of my calling are more becomingly employed in watching than in sleeping; still it
would be as well if thou wert to dress this ear for me again,
for it is giving me more pain than it need."

Sancho did as he bade him, but one of the goatherds seeing the wound told him not to be uneasy, as he would ap-
ply a remedy with which it would be soon healed; and
gathering some leaves of rosemary, of which there was a
great quantity there, he chewed them and mixed them with
a little salt, and applying them to the ear he secured them
firmly with a bandage, assuring him that no other treatment
would be required, and so it proved. . . .

CHAPTER XI

IN WHICH IS RELATED THE UNFORTUNATE ADVENTURE THAT
DON QUIXOTE FELL IN WITH WHEN HE FELL OUT WITH
CERTAIN HEARTLESS YANGUESANS

THE sage Cid Hamet Benengeli relates that as soon as
Don Quixote took leave of his hosts he and his squire
passed into a wood and after having wandered for more
than two hours in all directions, they came to a halt in a
glade covered with tender grass, beside which ran a pleasant cool stream that invited and compelled them to pass
there the hours of the noontide heat, which by this time
was beginning to come on oppressively. Don Quixote and
Sancho dismounted, and turning Rocinante and the ass
loose to feed on the grass that was there in abundance,
they ransacked the wallets and without any ceremony very
peacefully and sociably, master and man, made their repast
on what they found in them. Sancho had not thought
it worth while to hobble Rocinante, feeling sure, from what
he knew of his staidness and freedom from incontinence,
that all the mares in the Cordova pastures would not lead
him into an impropriety. Chance, however, and the devil,
who is not always asleep, so ordained it that feeding in
this valley there was a drove of Galician ponies belonging
to certain Yanguesan carriers, whose way it is to take
their midday rest with their teams in places and spots
where grass and water abound; and that where Don Quixote chanced to be suited the Yanguesans' purpose very
well. It so happened, then, that Rocinante took a fancy
to disport himself with their ladyships the ponies, and

66

abandoning his usual gait and demeanor as he scented them, he, without asking leave of his master, got up a briskish little trot and hastened to make known his wishes to them; they, however, it seemed, preferred their pasture to him, and received him with their heels and teeth to such effect that they soon broke his girths and left him naked without a saddle to cover him; but what must have been worse to him was that the carriers, seeing the violence he was offering to their mares, came running up armed with stakes, and so belabored him that they brought him sorely battered to the ground.

By this time Don Quixote and Sancho, who had witnessed the drubbing of Rocinante, came up panting, and said Don Quixote to Sancho, "So far as I can see, friend Sancho, these are not knights but base folk of low birth: I mention it because thou canst lawfully aid me in taking due vengeance for the insult offered to Rocinante before our eyes."

"What the devil vengeance can we take," answered Sancho, "if they are more than twenty, and we no more than two, or, indeed, perhaps not more than one and a half?"

"I count for a hundred," replied Don Quixote, and without more words he drew his sword and attacked the Yanguesans, and incited and impelled by the example of his master, Sancho did the same; and to begin with, Don Quixote delivered a slash at one of them that laid open the leather jerkin he wore, together with a great portion of his shoulder. The Yanguesans, seeing themselves assaulted by only two men while they were so many, betook themselves to their stakes, and driving the two into the middle they began to lay on with great zeal and energy; in fact, at the second blow they brought Sancho to the ground, and Don Quixote fared the same way, all his skill and high mettle availing him nothing, and fate willed it that he should fall at the feet of Rocinante, who had not yet risen; whereby it may be seen how furiously stakes can pound in angry boorish hands. Then, seeing the mischief they had done, the

Yanguesans with all the haste they could loaded their team and pursued their journey, leaving the two adventurers a sorry sight and in sorrier mood.

Sancho was the first to come to, and finding himself close to his master he called to him in a weak and doleful voice, " Señor Don Quixote, ah, Señor Don Quixote ! "

" What wouldst thou, brother Sancho ? " answered Don Quixote in the same feeble tone as Sancho.

" I would like, if it were possible," answered Sancho Panza, " your worship to give me a couple of sups of that potion of the fiery Blas, if it be that you have any to hand there; perhaps it will serve for broken bones as well as for wounds."

" If I only had it here, wretch that I am, what more should we want ? " said Don Quixote; " but I swear to thee, Sancho Panza, on the faith of a knight-errant, ere two days are over, unless fortune orders otherwise, I mean to have it in my possession, or my hand will have lost its cunning."

" But in how many does your worship think we shall have the use of our feet ? " answered Sancho Panza.

" For myself I must say I cannot guess how many," said the battered knight Don Quixote; " but I take all the blame upon myself, for I had no business to put hand to sword against men who were not dubbed knights like myself, and so I believe that in punishment for having transgressed the laws of chivalry the God of battles has permitted this chastisement to be administered to me; for which reason, brother Sancho, it is well thou shouldst receive a hint on the matter which I am now about to mention to thee, for it is of much importance to the welfare of both of us. It is that when thou shalt see rabble of this sort offering us insult thou art not to wait until I draw sword against them, for I shall not do so at all; but do thou draw sword and chastise them to thy heart's content, and if any knights come to their aid and defense I will take care to defend thee and assail them with all my might; and thou hast

already seen a thousand signs and proofs what the might of
this strong arm of mine is equal to "—so uplifted had the
poor gentleman become through the victory over the stout
Biscayan.

But Sancho did not so fully approve his master's ad-
monition as to let it pass without saying in reply, " Señor,
I am a man of peace, meek and quiet, and I can put up
with any affront because I have a wife and children to
support and bring up; so let it be likewise a hint to your
worship, as it cannot be a mandate, that on no account
will I draw sword either against clown or against knight,
and that here before God I forgive all the insults that
have been offered me or may be offered me, whether they
have been, are, or shall be offered me by high or low,
rich or poor, noble or commoner, not excepting any rank
or condition whatsoever."

To all which his master said in reply, " I wish I had
breath enough to speak somewhat easily, and that the pain I
feel on this side would abate so as to let me explain to
thee, Panza, the mistake thou makest. Come now, sinner,
suppose the wind of fortune, hitherto so adverse, should
turn in our favor, filling the sails of our desires so that
safely and without impediment we put into port in some
one of those islands I have promised thee, how would it
be with thee if on winning it I made thee lord of it? Why,
thou wilt make it well-nigh impossible through not being
a knight nor having any desire to be one, nor possessing
the courage nor the will to avenge insults or defend thy
lordship; for thou must know that in newly conquered
kingdoms and provinces the minds of the inhabitants are
never so quiet nor so well disposed to the new lord that
there is no fear of their making some move to change
matters once more, and try, as they say, what chance
may do for them; so it is essential that the new possessor
should have good sense to enable him to govern, and
valor to attack and defend himself, whatever may befall
him."

" In what has now befallen us," answered Sancho, " I'd

have been well pleased to have that good sense and that valor your worship speaks of, but I swear on the faith of a poor man I am more fit for plasters than for arguments. See if your worship can get up, and let us help Rocinante, though he does not deserve it, for he was the main cause of all this thrashing. I never thought it of Rocinante, for I took him to be a virtuous person and as quiet as myself. After all, they say right that it takes a long time to come to know people, and that there is nothing sure in this life. Who would have said that, after such mighty slashes as your worship gave that unlucky knight-errant, there was coming traveling post and at the very heels of them, such a great storm of sticks as has fallen upon our shoulders?"

"And yet thine, Sancho," replied Don Quixote, "ought to be used to such squalls; but mine, reared in soft cloth and fine linen, it is plain they must feel more keenly the pain of this mishap, and if it were not that I imagine— why do I say imagine?—know of a certainty that all these annoyances are very necessary accompaniments of the calling of arms, I would lay me down here to die of pure vexation."

To this the squire replied, "Señor, as these mishaps are what one reaps of chivalry, tell me if they happen very often, or if they have their own fixed times for coming to pass; because it seems to me that after two harvests we shall be no good for the third, unless God in his infinite mercy helps us."

"Know, friend Sancho," answered Don Quixote, "that the life of knights-errant is subject to a thousand dangers and reverses, and neither more nor less is it within immediate possibility for knights-errant to become kings and emperors, as experience has shown in the case of many different knights with whose histories I am thoroughly acquainted; and I could tell thee now, if the pain would let me, of some who simply by might of arm have risen to the high stations I have mentioned; and those same, both before and after, experienced divers misfortunes and miseries; for the valiant Amadis of Gaul found himself in the power of his mortal enemy Araclaus the magician, who, it is positively asserted, holding him captive, gave him more than two hundred lashes with the reins of his horse while tied to one of the pillars of a court; and moreover there is a certain recondite author of no small authority who says that the Knight of Phœbus, being caught in a certain pit-fall which opened under his feet in a certain castle, on falling found himself bound hand and foot in a deep pit underground, where they administered to him one of those things they call clysters, of sand and snow-water, that well-nigh finished him; and if he had not been succored in that sore extremity by a sage, a great friend of his, it would have gone very hard with the poor knight; so I may well suffer in company with such worthy folk, for greater were the indignities which they had to suffer than those which we suffer. For I would have thee know, Sancho, that wounds caused by any instrument which happen by chance to be in hand inflict no indignity, and this is laid down in the law of the duel in express words: if, for instance, the cobbler strikes another with the last which he has in his hand, though it be in fact a piece of wood, it cannot be said for that reason that he whom he struck with it has been cudgelled. I say this lest thou shouldst imagine that because we have been drubbed in this affray we have therefore suffered any indignity; for the arms those men carried, with which they pounded us, were nothing more than their stakes, and not one of them, so far as I remember, carried rapier, sword, or dagger."

"They gave me no time to see that much," answered Sancho, "for hardly had I laid hand on my brand when they signed the cross on my shoulders with their sticks in such style that they took the sight out of my eyes and the strength out of my feet, stretching me where I now lie, and where thinking of whether all those stake-strokes were an indignity or not gives me no uneasiness, which the pain of the blows does, for they will remain as deeply impressed on my memory as on my shoulders."

"For all that let me tell thee, brother Panza," said Don Quixote, "that there is no recollection which time does not put an end to, and no pain which death does not remove."

"And what greater misfortune can there be," replied Panza, "than the one that waits for time to put an end to it and death to remove it? If our mishap were one of those that are turned with a couple of plasters, it would not be so bad; but I am beginning to think that all the plasters in a hospital almost won't be enough to put us right."

"No more of that: pluck strength out of weakness, Sancho, as I mean to do," returned Don Quixote, "and let us see how Rocinante is, for it seems to me that not the least share of this mishap has fallen to the lot of the poor beast."

"There is nothing wonderful in that," replied Sancho, "since he is a knight-errant too; what I wonder at is that my beast should have come off scot-free where we come out scotched."

"Fortune always leaves a door open in adversity in order to bring relief to it," said Don Quixote; "I say so because this little beast may now supply the want of Rocinante, carrying me hence to some castle where I may be cured of my wounds. And moreover I shall not hold it any dishonor to be so mounted, for I remember having read how the good old Silenus, the tutor and instructor of the gay god of laughter, when he entered the city of the hundred gates, went very contentedly mounted on a handsome ass."

"It may be true that he went mounted as your worship says," answered Sancho, "but there is a great difference between going mounted and going slung like a sack of manure."

To which Don Quixote replied, "Wounds received in battle confer honor instead of taking it away; and so, friend Panza, say no more, but, as I told thee before, get up as well as thou canst and put me on top of thy beast in whatever fashion pleases thee best, and let us go hence ere night come on and surprise us in these wilds."

"And yet I have heard your worship say," observed Panza, "that it is very meet for knights-errant to sleep in wastes and deserts the best part of the year, and that they esteem it very good fortune."

"That is," said Don Quixote, "when they cannot help it, or when they are in love; and so true is this that there have been knights who have remained two years on rocks, in sunshine and shade and all the inclemencies of heaven, without their ladies knowing anything of it; and one of these was Amadis when, under the name of Beltenebros, he took up his abode on the Peña Pobre for—I know not if it was eight years or eight months, for I am not very sure of the reckoning; at any rate he staid there doing penance for I know not what pique the Princess Oriana had against him; but no more of this now, Sancho, and make haste before some other mishap like Rocinante's befalls the ass."

"The very devil would be in it in that case," said Sancho; and letting off thirty "ohs," and sixty sighs, and a hundred and twenty maledictions and execrations on whomsoever it was that had brought him there, he raised himself, stooping half-way bent like a Turkish bow without power to bring himself upright, but with all his pains he saddled his ass, who too had gone astray somewhat; yielding to the excessive license of the day; he next raised up Rocinante, and as for him, had he possessed a tongue to complain with, most assuredly neither Sancho nor his master would have been behind him. To be brief, Sancho fixed Don Quixote on the ass and secured Rocinante with a leading rein, and taking the ass by the halter, he proceeded more or less in the direction in which it seemed to him the high road might be; and, as chance was conducting their affairs for them from good to better, he had not gone a short league when the road came in sight, and on it he perceived an inn, which to his annoyance and to the delight of Don Quixote must needs be a castle. Sancho insisted that it was an inn, and his master that it was not one, but a castle, and the dispute lasted so long that before the point was settled they had time to reach it, and into it Sancho entered with all his team, without any further controversy.

CHAPTER XII

OF WHAT HAPPENED TO THE INGENIOUS GENTLEMAN IN THE
INN WHICH HE TOOK TO BE A CASTLE

THE innkeeper, seeing Don Quixote slung across the ass,
asked Sancho what was amiss with him. Sancho
answered that it was nothing, only that he had fallen down
from a rock and had his ribs a little bruised. The innkeeper had a wife whose disposition was not such as those
of her calling commonly have, for she was by nature kind-
hearted and felt for the sufferings of her neighbors, so
she at once set about tending Don Quixote, and made her
young daughter, a very comely girl, help her in taking care
of her guest. There was besides in the inn, as servant, an
Asturian lass with a broad face, flat poll, and snub nose,
blind in one eye and not very sound in the other. The elegance of her shape, to be sure, made up for all her defects;
she did not measure seven palms from head to foot, and her
shoulders, which over-weighted her somewhat, made her
contemplate the ground more than she liked. This graceful lass, then, helped the young girl, and the two made up
a very bad bed for Don Quixote in a garret that showed
evident signs of having formerly served for many years
as a straw-loft, in which there was also quartered a carrier whose bed was placed a little beyond our Don Quixote's,
and, though only made of the pack-saddles and cloths of
his mules, had much the advantage of it, as Don Quixote's
consisted simply of four rough boards on two not very
even trestles, a mattress, that for thinness might have passed

75

for a quilt, full of pellets which, were they not seen through the rents to be wool, would to the touch have seemed pebbles in hardness, two sheets made of buckler leather, and a coverlet the threads of which any one that chose might have counted without missing one in the reckoning.

On this accursed bed Don Quixote stretched himself, and the hostess and her daughter soon covered him with plasters from top to toe, while Maritornes—for that was the name of the Asturian—held the light for them, and while plastering him, the hostess, observing how full of wheals Don Quixote was in some places, remarked that this had more the look of blows than of a fall.

It was not blows, Sancho said, but that the rock had many points and projections, and that each of them had left its mark. "Pray, señora," he added, "manage to save some tow, as there will be no want of some one to use it, for my loins too are rather sore."

"Then you must have fallen too," said the hostess.

"I did not fall," said Sancho Panza, "but from the shock I got at seeing my master fall, my body aches so that I feel as if I had had a thousand thwacks."

"That may well be," said the young girl, "for it has many a time happened to me to dream that I was falling down from a tower and never coming to the ground, and when I awoke from the dream to find myself as weak and shaken as if I had really fallen."

"There is the point, señora," replied Sancho Panza, "that I without dreaming at all, but being more awake than I am now, find myself with scarcely less wheals than my master, Don Quixote."

"How is the gentleman called?" asked Maritornes the Asturian.

"Don Quixote of La Mancha," answered Sancho Panza, "and he is a knight-adventurer, and one of the best and stoutest that have been seen in the world this long time past."

"What is a knight-adventurer?" said the lass.

"Are you so new in the world as not to know?" answered Sancho Panza. "Well, then, you must know, sister, that a knight-adventurer is a thing that in two words is seen drubbed and emperor, that is today the most miserable and needy being in the world, and tomorrow will have two or three crowns of kingdoms to give his squire."

"Then how is it," said the hostess, "that, belonging to so good a master as this, you have not, to judge by appearances, even so much as a county?"

"It is too soon yet," answered Sancho, "for we have only been a month going in quest of adventures, and so far we have met with nothing that can be called one, for it will happen that when one thing is looked for another thing is found; however, if my master Don Quixote gets well of this wound, or fall, and I am left none the worse for it, I would not change my hopes for the best title in Spain."

To all this conversation Don Quixote was listening very attentively, and sitting up in bed as well as he could, and taking the hostess by the hand he said to her:

"Believe me, fair lady, you may call yourself fortunate in having in this castle of yours sheltered my person, which is such that if I do not myself praise it, it is because of what is commonly said, that self-praise debaseth; but my squire will inform you who I am. I only tell you that I shall preserve for ever inscribed on my memory the service you have rendered me in order to tender you my gratitude while life shall last me; and would to Heaven love held me not so enthralled and subject to its laws and to the eyes of that fair ingrate whom I name between my teeth, but those of this lovely damsel might be the masters of my liberty."

The hostess, her daughter, and the worthy Maritornes listened in bewilderment to the words of the knight-errant, for they understood about as much of them as if he had been talking Greek, though they could perceive they were all meant for expressions of good-will and blandishments; and not being accustomed to this kind of language, they stared at him and wondered to themselves, for he seemed to them a man of different sort from those they were used to, and thanking him in pot-house phrase for his civility they left him, while the Asturian gave her attention to Sancho, who needed it no less than his master. . . .

Early in the morning Don Quixote called, " Rise, Sancho, if thou canst, and call the *alcaide* of this fortress, and get him to give me a little oil, wine, salt, and rosemary to make the salutiferous balsam, for indeed I believe I have great need of it now.

Sancho got up with pain enough in his bones, and going after the innkeeper in the dark, said to him:

" Señor, whoever you are, do us the favor and kindness to give us a little rosemary, oil, salt, and wine, for it is wanted to cure one of the best knights-errant on earth, who lies on yonder bed sorely wounded."

The host furnished him with what he required, and Sancho brought it to Don Quixote, who took the materials, of which he made a compound, mixing them all and boiling them a good while until it seemed to him they had come to perfection. He then asked for some vial to pour it into, and as there was not one in the inn, he decided on putting it into a tin oil-bottle or flask of which the host made him a free gift; and over the flask he repeated more than eighty *paternosters* and as many more *ave-marias*, *salves*, and *credos*, accompanying each word with a cross by way of benediction.

This being accomplished, he felt anxious to make trial himself, on the spot, of the virtue of this precious balsam, as he considered it, and so he drank near a quart of what could not be put into the flask and remained in the pipkin in which it had been boiled; but scarcely had he done drinking when he began to vomit in such a way that nothing was left in his stomach, and with the pangs and spasms of vomiting he broke into a profuse sweat, on account of which he bade them cover him up and leave him alone. They did so, and he lay sleeping more than three hours, at the end of which he awoke and felt very great bodily relief and so much ease from his bruises that he thought himself cured, and verily believed he had hit upon the balsam of Fierabras; and that with this remedy he might thenceforward, without any fear, face any kind of destruction, battle, or combat, however perilous it might be.

Sancho Panza, who also regarded the amendment of his master as miraculous, begged him to give him what was left in the pipkin, which was no small quantity. Don Quixote consented, and he, taking it with both hands, in good faith and with a better will, gulped down and drained off very little less than his master. But the fact is, that the stomach of poor Sancho was of necessity not so delicate as that of his master, and so, before vomiting, he was seized with such gripings and retchings, and such sweats and faintness, that verily and truly he believed his last hour had come, and finding himself so racked and tormented he cursed the balsam and the thief that had given it to him. Don Quixote, seeing him in this state, said:

" It is my belief, Sancho, that this mischief comes of thy not being dubbed a knight, for I am persuaded this liquor cannot be good for those who are not so."

" If your worship knew that," returned Sancho,—" woe betide me and all my kindred!— Why did you let me taste it?"

Don Quixote, however, who, as has been said, felt himself relieved and well, was eager to take his departure at once in quest of adventrues, as it seemed to him that all the time he loitered there was a fraud upon the world and those in it who stood in need of his help and protection, all the more when he had the security and confidence his balsam afforded him; and so, urged by this impulse, he saddled Rocinante himself and put the pack-saddle on his squire's beast, whom likewise he helped to dress and mount the ass; after which he mounted his horse and turning to a corner of the inn he laid hold of a pike that stood there, to serve him by way of a lance. All that were in the inn, who were more than twenty persons, stood watching him; the inn-keeper's daughter was likewise observing him, and he too never took his eyes off her, and from time to time fetched a sigh that he seemed to pluck up from the depths of his bowels; but they all thought it must be from the pain he felt in his ribs; at any rate, they who had seen him plastered the night before thought so. As soon as they were both mounted, at the gate of the inn, he called to the host and said in a very grave and measured voice:

"Many and great are the favors, Señor Alcaide, that I have received in this castle of yours, and I remain under the deepest obligation to be grateful to you for them all the days of my life; if I can repay them in avenging you of any arrogant foe who may have wronged you, know that my calling is no other than to aid the weak, to avenge those who suffer wrong, and to chastise perfidy. Search your memory, and if you find anything of this kind you need only tell me of it, and I promise you by the order of knighthood which I have received to procure you satisfaction and reparation to the utmost of your desire."

The innkeeper replied to him with equal calmness: "Sir Knight, I do not want your worship to avenge me of any wrong, because when any is done me I can take what vengeance seems good to me; the only thing I want is that you pay me the score that you have run up in the inn last night, as well for the straw and barley for your two beasts, as for supper and beds."

"Then this is an inn?" said Don Quixote.

"And a very respectable one," said the innkeeper.

"I have been under a mistake all this time," answered Don Quixote, "for in truth I thought it was a castle, and not a bad one; but since it appears that it is not a castle but an inn, all that can be done now is that you should excuse the payment, for I cannot contravene the rule of knights-errant, of whom I know as a fact (and up to the present I have read nothing to the contrary) that they never paid for lodging or anything else in the inn where they might be; for any hospitality that might be offered them is their due by law and right in return for the insufferable toil they endure in seeking adventures by night and by day, summer and in winter, on foot and on horseback, in hunger and thirst, cold and heat, exposed to all the inclemencies of heaven and all the hardships of earth."

"I have little to do with that," replied the innkeeper; "pay me what you owe me, and let us have no more talk of chivalry, for all I care about is to get my money."

"You are a stupid, scurvy innkeeper," said Don Quixote, and putting spurs to Rocinante and bringing his pike to the slope he rode out of the inn before anyone could stop him, and pushed on some distance without looking to see if his squire was following him.

The innkeeper, when he saw him go without paying him, ran to get payment of Sancho, who said that as his master would not pay neither would he, because, being as he was, squire to a knight-errant, the same rule and reason held good for him as for his master with regard to not paying anything in inns and hostelries. At this the innkeeper waxed very wroth, and threatened if he did not pay to compel him in a way that he would not like. To which Sancho made answer that by the law of chivalry his master had received he would not pay a rap, though it cost him his life; for the excellent and ancient usage of knights-errant was not going to be violated by him, nor should the squires of such as were yet to come into the world ever complain of him or reproach him with breaking so just a law.

The ill-luck of the unfortunate Sancho so ordered it that among the company in the inn there were four wool-carders from Segovia, three needle-makers from the Colt of Cordova, and two lodgers from the Fair of Seville, lively fellows, tender-hearted, fond of a joke, and playful, who, almost as if instigated and moved by a common impulse, made up to Sancho and dismounted him from his ass, while one of them went in for the blanket of the host's bed; but on flinging him into it they looked up, and seeing that the ceiling was somewhat lower than what they required for their work, they decided upon going out into the yard, which was bounded by the sky, and there, putting Sancho in the middle of the blanket, they began to make sport with him as they would with a dog at Shrovetide.

The cries of the poor blanketed wretch were so loud that they reached the ears of his master, who, halting to listen attentively, was persuaded that some new adventure was coming, until he clearly perceived that it was his squire who uttered them. Wheeling about, he came up to the inn with a laborious gallop, and finding it shut went round it to see if he could find some way of getting in; but as soon as he came to the wall of the yard, which was not very high, he discovered the game that was being played with his squire. He saw him rising and falling in the air with such grace and nimbleness that, had his rage allowed him, it is my belief he would have laughed. He tried to climb from his horse on to the top of the wall, but he was so bruised and battered that he could not even dismount; and so from the back of his horse he began to utter such maledictions and objurgations against those who were blanketing Sancho as it would be impossible to write down accurately; they, however, did not stay their laughter or their work for this, nor did the flying Sancho cease his lamentations, mingled now with threats, now with entreaties, but all to little purpose, or none at all, until from pure weariness they left off. They then brought him his ass, and mounting him on top of it they put his jacket round him; and the compassionate Maritornes, seeing him so exhausted, thought fit to refresh him with a jug of water, and that it might be all the cooler she fetched it from the well. Sancho took it, and as he was raising it to his mouth he was stopped by the cries of his master exclaiming:

" Sancho, my son, drink not water; drink it not, my son, for it will kill thee; see, here I have the blessed balsam " (and he held up the flask of liquor), " and with drinking two drops of it thou wilt certainly be restored."

At these words Sancho turned his eyes asquint, and in a still louder voice said, " Can it be your worship has forgotten that I am not a knight, or do you want me to end by vomiting up what bowels I have left after last night?

Keep your liquor in the name of all the devils, and leave me to myself!" and at one and the same instant he left off talking and began drinking; but as at the first sup he perceived it was water, he did not care to go on with it, and begged Maritones to fetch him some wine, which she did with right good will, and paid for it with her own money; for indeed they say of her that, though she was in that line of life, there was some faint and distant resemblance to a Christian about her. When Sancho had done drinking he dug his heels into his ass, and the gate of the inn being thrown open, he passed out very well pleased at having paid nothing and carried his point, though it had been at the expense of his usual sureties, his shoulders. It is true that the innkeeper detained his wallets in payment of what was owing to him, but Sancho took his departure in such a flurry that he never missed them. The innkeeper, as soon as he saw him off, wanted to bar the gate close, but the blanketers would not agree to it, for they were fellows who would not have cared two farthings for Don Quixote, even had he been really one of the knights-errant of the Round Table.

CHAPTER XIII

S ANCHO reached his master so limp and faint that he could not urge on his beast. When Don Quixote saw the state he was in he said: "I have now come to the conclusion, good Sancho, that this castle or inn is beyond a doubt enchanted, because those who have so atrociously diverted themselves with thee, what can they be but phantoms or beings of another world? And I hold this confirmed by having noticed that when I was by the wall of the yard witnessing the acts of thy sad tragedy, it was out of my power to mount upon it, nor could I even dismount from Rocinante, because they no doubt had me enchanted; for I swear to thee by the faith of what I am that if I had been able to climb up or dismount, I would have avenged thee in such a way that those braggart thieves would have remembered their freak forever, even though in so doing I knew that I contravened the laws of chivalry, which, as I have often told thee, do not permit a knight to lay hands on him who is not one, save in case of urgent and great necessity in defense of his own life and person."

"I would have avenged myself, too, if I could," said Sancho, "whether I had been dubbed knight or not, but I could not; though for my part I am persuaded those who amused themselves with me were not phantoms or enchanted men, as your worship says, but men of flesh and

bone like ourselves; and they all had their names, for I
heard them name them when they were tossing me, and
one was called Pedro Martinez, and another Tenorio Hernandez, and the innkeeper, I heard, was called Juan Palo-
meque the Left-handed; so that, señor, your not being
able to leap over the wall of the yard or dismount from
your horse came of something else besides enchantments;
and what I make out clearly from all this is, that these
adventures we go seeking will in the end lead us into such
misadventures that we shall not know which is our right
foot; and that the best and wisest thing, according to my
small wits, would be for us to return home, now that it
is harvest-time, and attend to our business, and give over
wandering from Zeca to Mecca and from pail to bucket,
as the saying is."

"How little thou knowest about chivalry, Sancho," replied Don Quixote; "hold thy peace and have patience;
the day will come when thou shalt see with thine own
eyes what an honorable thing it is to wander in the pursuit of this calling; nay, tell me, what greater pleasure
can there be in the world, or what delight can equal that
of winning a battle, and triumphing over one's enemy?
None, beyond all doubt."

"Verly likely," answered Sancho, "though I do not know
it; all I know is that since we have been knights-errant,
or since your worship has been one (for I have no right
to reckon myself one of so honorable a number), we have
never won any battle except the one with the Biscayan,
and even out of that your worship came with half an ear
and half a helmet the less; and from that till now it has
been all cudgelings and more cudgelings, cuffs and more
cuffs, I getting the blanketing over and above, and falling
in with enchanted persons on whom I cannot avenge myself so as to know what the delight, as your worship calls
it, of conquering an enemy is like."

"That is what vexes me, and what ought to vex thee,
Sancho," replied Don Quixote; "but henceforward I will
endeavor to have at hand some sword made by such craft

that no kind of enchantments can take effect upon him who carries it, and it is even possible that fortune may procure for me that which belonged to Amadis when he was called 'The Knight of the Burning Sword,' which was one of the best swords that ever knight in the world possessed, for, besides having the said virtue, it cut like a razor, and there was no armor, however strong and enchanted it might be, that could resist it."

"Such is my luck," said Sancho, "that even if that happened, and your worship found some such sword, it would, like the balsam, turn out serviceable and good for dubbed knights only, and as for the squires, they might sup sorrow."

"Fear not that, Sancho," said Don Quixote; "Heaven will deal better by thee."

Thus talking, Don Quixote and his squire were going along, when, on the road they were following, Don Quixote perceived approaching them a large and thick cloud of dust, on seeing which he turned to Sancho and said: "This is the day, O Sancho, on which will be seen the boon my fortune is reserving for me; this, I say, is the day on which as much as on any other shall be displayed the might of my arm, and on which I shall do deeds that shall remain written in the book of fame for all ages to come. Seest thou that cloud of dust which rises yonder? Well, then, all that is churned up by a vast army composed of various and countless nations that comes marching there."

"According to that there must be two," said Sancho, "for on this opposite side also there rises just such another cloud of dust."

Don Quixote turned to look and found that it was true, and rejoicing exceedingly, he concluded that they were two armies about to engage and encounter in the midst of that broad plain; for at all times and seasons his fancy was full of the battles, enchantments, adventures, crazy feats, loves, and defiances that are recorded in the books of chivalry, and everything he said, thought, or did had reference to such things. Now the cloud of dust he had seen was raised by two great droves of sheep coming along the same

road in opposite directions, which, because of the dust, did
not become visible until they drew near, but Don Quixote
asserted so positively that they were armies that Sancho
was led to believe it and say, "Well, and what are we to
do, señor?"

"What?" said Don Quixote: "give aid and assistance
to the weak and those who need it; and thou must know,
Sancho, that this which comes opposite to us is conducted
and led by the mighty emperor Alifanfaron, lord of the
great isle of Trapobana; this other that marches behind me
is that of his enemy, the king of the Garamantas, Pentapolin of the Bare Arm, for he always goes into battle with
his right arm bare."

"But why are these two lords such enemies?" asked
Sancho.

"They are at enmity," replied Don Quixote, "because
this Alifanfaron is a furious pagan and is in love with
the daughter of Pentapolin, who is a very beautiful and,
moreover, gracious lady, and a Christian, and her father is
unwilling to bestow her upon the pagan king unless he
first abandons the religion of his false prophet Mahomet,
and adopts his own."

"By my beard," said Sancho, "but Pentapolin does quite
right, and I will help him as much as I can."

"In that thou wilt do what is thy duty, Sancho," said
Don Quixote; "for to engage in battles of this sort it is
not requisite to be a dubbed knight."

"That I can well understand," answered Sancho; "but
where shall we put this ass where we may be sure to find
him after the fray is over? for I believe it has not been
the custom so far to go into battle on a beast of this kind."

"That is true," said Don Quixote, "and what you had
best to do with him is to leave him to take his chance
whether he be lost or not, for the horses we shall have
when we come out victors will be so many that even Rocinante will run a risk of being changed for another. But
attend to me and observe, for I wish to give thee some
account of the chief knights who accompany these two

armies; and that thou mayest the better see and mark, let us withdraw to the hillock which rises yonder, whence both armies may be seen."

They did so, and placed themselves on a rising ground from which the two droves that Don Quixote made armies of might have been plainly seen if the clouds of dust they raised had not obscured them and blinded the sight; nevertheless, seeing in his imagination what he did not see and what did not exist, he began thus in a loud voice:

" That knight whom thou seest yonder in yellow armor, who bears upon his shield a lion crowned crouching at the feet of a damsel, is the valiant Laurcalco, lord of the Silver Bridge; that one in armor with flowers of gold, who bears on his shield three crowns argent on an azure field, is the dreaded Micocolembo, grand duke of Quirocia; that other of gigantic frame, on his right hand, is the ever dauntless Brandabarbaran de Boliche, lord of the three Arabias, who for armor wears that serpent skin, and has for shield a gate which, according to tradition, is one of those of the temple that Samson brought to the ground when by his death he revenged himself upon his enemies; but turn thine eyes to the other side, and thou shalt see in front and in the van of this other army the ever victorious and never vanquished Timonel of Carcajona, prince of New Biscay, who comes in armor with arms quartered azure, vert, argent, and or, and bears on his shield a cat or on a field tawny with a motto which says *Miau,* which is the beginning of the name of his lady, who according to report is the peerless Miaulina, daughter of the duke Alfeñiquén of the Algarve; the other, who burdens and presses the loins of that powerful charger and bears arms white as snow and a shield blank and without any device, is a novice knight, a Frenchman by birth, Pierres Papin by name, lord of the baronies of Utrique; that other, who with iron-shod heels strikes the flanks of that nimble party-colored zebra, and for arms bears azure cups, is the mighty duke of Nervia, Espartafilardo del Bosque, who bears for device on his shield an asparagus plant with a motto in Castilian

that says, '*Rastrea mi suerte.*'" And so he went on nam-
ing a number of knights of one squadron or the other out
of his imagination, and to all he assigned off-hand their
arms, colors, devices, and mottoes, carried away by the
illusions of his unheard-of craze; and without a pause he
continued: "People of divers nations compose this squadron in front; here are those that drink of the sweet waters
of the famous Xanthus, those that scour the woody Mas-
silian plains, those that sift the pure fine gold of Arabia
Felix, those that enjoy the famed cool banks of the crystal
Thermodon, those that in many and various ways divert
the streams of the golden Pactolus, the Numidians, faith-
less in their promises, the Persians renowned in archery,
the Parthians and the Medes that fight as they fly, the
Arabs that ever shift their dwellings, the Scythians as cruel
as they are fair, the Ethiopians with pierced lips, and an
infinity of other nations whose features I recognize and
descry, though I cannot recall their names. In this other
squadron there come those that drink of the crystal streams
of the olive-bearing Betis, those that make smooth their
countenances with the water of the ever rich and golden
Tagus, those that rejoice in the fertilizing flow of the divine
Genil, those that roam the Tartesian plains abounding in
pasture, those that take their pleasure in the elysian meadows of Jerez, the rich Manchegans crowned with ruddy
ears of corn, the wearers of iron, old relics of the Gothic
race, those that bathe in the Pisuerga renowned for its
gentle current, those that feed their herds along the spread-
ing pastures of the winding Guadiana famed for its hidden
course, those that tremble with the cold of the pine-clad
Pyrenees or the dazzling snows of the lofty Apennine; in
a word, as many as all Europe includes and contains."

Good God! what a number of countries and nations he
named! giving to each its proper attributes with marvelous readiness; brimful and saturated with what he had
read in his lying books! Sancho Panza hung upon his
words without speaking, and from time to time turned to
try if he could see the knights and giants his master was

describing, and as he could not make out one of them, he said to him:

"Señor, devil take it if there's a sign of any man you talk of, knight or giant, in the whole thing; maybe it's all enchantment, like the phantoms at the inn."

"How canst thou say that!" answered Don Quixote; "dost thou not hear the neighing of the steeds, the braying of the trumpets, the roll of the drums?"

"I hear nothing but a great bleating of ewes and sheep," said Sancho; which was true, for by this time the two flocks had come close.

"The fear thou art in, Sancho," said Don Quixote, "prevents thee from seeing or hearing correctly, for one of the effects of fear is to derange the senses and make things appear different from what they are; if thou art in such fear, withdraw to one side and leave me to myself, for alone I suffice to bring victory to that side to which I shall give my aid;" and so saying he gave Rocinante the spur, and putting the lance in rest, shot down the slope like a thunderbolt. Sancho shouted after him, crying:

"Come back, Señor Don Quixote; I vow to God they are sheep and ewes you are charging! Come back! Unlucky the father that begot me! what madness is this! Look, there is no giant, nor knight, nor cats, nor arms, nor shields quartered or whole, nor cups azure or bedeviled. What are you about? Sinner that I am before God!" But not for all these entreaties did Don Quixote turn back; on the contrary, he went on, shouting out:

"Ho, knights, ye who follow and fight under the banners of the valiant emperor Pentapolin of the Bare Arm, follow me all; ye shall see how easily I shall give him his revenge over his enemy Alifanfaron of Trapobana."

So saying, he dashed into the midst of the squadron of ewes, and began spearing them with as much spirit and intrepidity as if he were transfixing mortal enemies in earnest. The shepherds and drovers accompanying the flock shouted to him to desist; but seeing it was no use, they ungirt their slings and began to salute his ears with stones as big as one's fist. Don Quixote gave no heed to the stones, but, letting drive right and left, kept saying:

"Where art thou, proud Alifanfaron? Come before me; I am a single knight who would fain prove thy prowess hand to hand, and make thee yield thy life a penalty for the wrong thou dost to the valiant Pentapolin Garamanta."

Here came a sugar-plum from the brook that struck him on the side and buried a couple of ribs in his body. Feeling himself so smitten, he imagined himself slain or badly wounded for certain, and recollecting his liquor, he drew out his flask, and putting it to his mouth began to pour the contents into his stomach; but ere he had succeeded in swallowing what seemed to him enough, there came another almond which struck him on the hand and on the flask so fairly that it smashed it to pieces, knocking three or four teeth and grinders out of his mouth in its course, and sorely crushing two fingers of his hand. Such was the force of the first blow and of the second, that the poor knight in spite of himself came down backwards off his horse. The shepherds came up, and felt sure they had killed him; so in all haste they collected their flock together, took up the dead beasts, of which there were more than seven, and made off without waiting to ascertain anything further.

All this time Sancho stood on the hill watching the crazy feats his master was performing, and tearing his beard and cursing the hour and the occasion when fortune had made him acquainted with him. Seeing him, then, brought to the ground, and that the shepherds had taken themselves off, he came down the hill and ran to him and found him in very bad case, though not unconscious; and said he:

"Did I not tell you to come back, Señor Don Quixote; and that what you were going to attack were not armies but droves of sheep?"

"That's how that thief of a sage, my enemy, can alter and falsify things," answered Don Quixote; "thou must know, Sancho, that it is a very easy matter for those of his sort to make us take what form they choose; and this malignant being who persecutes me, envious of the glory he knew I was to win in this battle, has turned the squadrons of the enemy into droves of sheep. At any rate, do this much, I beg of thee, Sancho, to undeceive thyself, and see that what I say is true; mount thy ass and follow them quietly, and thou shalt see that when they have gone some little distance from this they will return to their original shape and, ceasing to be sheep, become men in all respects as I described them to thee at first. But go not just yet, for I want thy help and assistance; come hither and see how many of my teeth and grinders are missing, for I feel as if there was not one left in my mouth."

Sancho came so close that he almost put his eyes into his mouth; now just at that moment the balsam had acted on the stomach of Don Quixote, so, at the very instant when Sancho came to examine his mouth, he discharged all its contents with more force than a musket, and full into the beard of the compassionate squire.

"Holy Mary!" cried Sancho, "what is this that has happened to me? Clearly this sinner is mortally wounded, as he vomits blood from the mouth;" but considering the matter a little more closely he perceived by the color, taste, and smell, that it was not blood but the balsam from the flask which he had seen him drink; and he was taken with such a loathing that his stomach turned, and he vomited up his inside over his very master, and both were left in a precious state. Sancho ran to his ass to get something wherewith to clean himself, and relieve his master, out of his wallets; but not finding them, he well-nigh took leave of his senses, and cursed himself anew, and in his heart resolved to quit his master and return home, even though he forfeited the wages of his service and all hopes of the government of the promised island.

Don Quixote now rose, and putting his left hand to his mouth to keep his teeth from falling out altogether, with the other he laid hold of the bridle of Rocinante, who had never stirred from his master's side—so loyal and well-behaved was he—and betook himself to where the squire stood leaning over his ass with his hand to his cheek, like one in deep dejection. Seeing him in this mood, looking so sad, Don Quixote said to him:

"Bear in mind, Sancho, that one man is no more than another, unless he does more than another; all these tempests that fall upon us are signs that fair weather is coming shortly, and that things will go well with us, for it is impossible for good or evil to last forever; and hence it follows that the evil having lasted long, the good must be now nigh at hand; so thou must not distress thyself at the misfortunes which happen to me, since thou hast no share in them."

"How have I not?" replied Sancho. "Was he whom they blanketed yesterday perchance any other than my father's son? and the wallets that are missing today with all my treasures, did they belong to any other but myself?"

"What! are the wallets missing, Sancho?" said Don Quixote.

"Yes, they are missing," answered Sancho.

"In that case we have nothing to eat today," replied Don Quixote.

"It would be so," answered Sancho, "if there were none of the herbs your worship says you know in these meadows, those with which knights-errant as unlucky as your worship are wont to supply such-like shortcomings."

"For all that," answered Don Quixote, "I would rather have just now a quarter of bread, or a loaf and a couple of pilchards' heads, than all the herbs described by Dioscorides, even with Doctor Laguna's notes. Nevertheless, Sancho the Good, mount thy beast and come along with me, for God, who provides for all things, will not fail us (more especially when we are so active in his service as we are), since he fails not the midges of the air, nor the grubs of the earth, nor the tadpoles of the water, and is so merciful that he maketh his sun to rise on the evil and on the good, and sendeth rain on the just and on the unjust."

"Your worship would make a better preacher than knight-errant," said Sancho.

"Knights-errant knew and ought to know everything, Sancho," said Don Quixotè; "for there were knights-errant in former times as well qualified to deliver a sermon or discourse in the middle of a highway, as if they had graduated in the University of Paris; whereby we may see that the lance has never blunted the pen, nor the pen the lance."

"Well, be it as your worship says," replied Sancho; "let us be off now and find some place of shelter for the night, and God grant it may be somewhere where there are no blankets, nor blanketeers, nor phantoms, nor enchanted Moors; for if there are, may the devil take the whole concern."

"Ask that of God, my son," said Don Quixote; "and do thou lead on where thou wilt, for this time I leave our lodging to thy choice; but reach me here thy hand, and feel with thy finger, and find out how many of my teeth and grinders are missing from this right side of the upper jaw, for it is there I feel the pain."

Sancho put in his fingers, and feeling about asked him, "How many grinders used your worship have on this side?"

"Four," replied Don Quixote, "besides the backtooth, all whole and quite sound."

"Mind what you are saying, señor," said Sancho.

"I say four, if not five," answered Don Quixote, "for never in my life have I had tooth or grinder drawn, nor has any fallen out or been destroyed by any decay or rheum."

"Well, then," said Sancho, "in this lower side your worship has no more than two grinders and a half, and in the upper neither a half nor any at all, for it is all as smooth as the palm of my hand."

"Luckless that I am!" said Don Quixote, hearing the sad news his squire gave him; "I had rather they had despoiled me of an arm, so it were not the sword-arm; for I tell thee, Sancho, a mouth without teeth is like a mill without a millstone, and a tooth is much more to be prized than a diamond; but we who profess the austere order of chivalry are liable to all this. Mount, friend, and lead the way, and I will follow thee at whatever pace thou wilt."

Sancho did as he bade him, and proceeded in the direction in which he thought he might find refuge without quitting the high road, which was there very much frequented. As they went along, then, at a slow pace—for the pain in Don Quixote's jaws kept him uneasy and ill-disposed for speed—Sancho thought it well to amuse and divert him by talk of some kind, and among the things he said to him was that which will be told in the following chapter.

CHAPTER XIV

OF THE SHREWD DISCOURSE WHICH SANCHO HELD WITH
HIS MASTER, AND OF THE ADVENTURE THAT BEFELL
HIM WITH A DEAD BODY, TOGETHER WITH OTHER
NOTABLE OCCURRENCES

"IT seems to me, señor, that all these mishaps that have befallen us of late have been without any doubt a punishment for the offense committed by your worship against the order of chivalry in not keeping the oath you made not to eat bread off a table-cloth or embrace the queen, and all the rest of it that your worship swore to observe until you had taken that helmet of Malandrino's, or whatever the Moor is called, for I do not very well remember."

"Thou art very right, Sancho," said Don Quixote, "but to tell the truth, it had escaped my memory; and likewise thou mayest rely upon it that the affair of the blanket happened to thee because of thy fault in not reminding me of it in time; but I will make amends, for there are ways of compounding for everything in the order of chivalry."

"Why! have I taken an oath of some sort, then?" said Sancho.

"It makes no matter that thou hast not taken an oath," said Don Quixote; "suffice it that I see thou art not quite clear of complicity; and whether or not, it will not be ill done to provide ourselves with a remedy."

"In that case," said Sancho, "mind that your worship does not forget this as you did the oath; perhaps the phantoms may take it into their heads to amuse themselves once more with me; or even with your worship if they see you so obstinate."

While engaged in this and other talk, night overtook them on the road before they had reached or discovered any place of shelter; and what made it still worse was that they were dying of hunger, for with the loss of the wallets they had lost their entire larder and commissariat; and to complete the misfortune they met with an adventure which without any invention had really the appearance of one. It so happened that the night closed in somewhat darkly, but for all that they pushed on, Sancho feeling sure that as the road was the king's highway they might reasonably expect to find some inn within a league or two. Going along, then, in this way, the night dark, the squire hungry, the master sharp-set, they saw coming towards them on the road they were traveling a great number of lights which looked exactly like stars in motion. Sancho was taken aback at the sight of them, nor did Don Quixote altogether relish them: the one pulled up his ass by the halter, the other his hack by the bridle, and they stood still, watching anxiously to see what all this would turn out to be, and found that the lights were approaching them, and the nearer they came the greater they seemed, at which spectacle Sancho began to shake like a man dosed with mercury, and Don Quixote's hair stood on end; he, however, plucking up spirit a little, said:

"This, no doubt, Sancho, will be a most mighty and perilous adventure, in which it will be needful for me to put forth all my valor and resolution."

"Unlucky me!" answered Sancho; "if this adventure happens to be one of phantoms, as I am beginning to think it is, where shall I find the ribs to bear it?"

"Be they phantoms ever so much," said Don Quixote, "I will not permit them to touch a thread of thy garments; for if they played tricks with thee the time before, it was because I was unable to leap the walls of the yard; but now we are on a wide plain, where I shall be able to wield my sword as I please."

"And if they enchant and cripple you as they did the last time," said Sancho, "what difference will it make being on the open plain or not?"

"For all that," replied Don Quixote, "I entreat thee, Sancho, to keep a good heart, for experience will tell thee what mine is."

"I will, please God," answered Sancho, and the two retiring to one side of the road set themselves to observe closely what all these moving lights might be; and very soon afterwards they made out some twenty *encamisados*, all on horseback, with lighted torches in their hands, the awe-inspiring aspect of whom completely extinguished the courage of Sancho, who began to chatter with his teeth like one in the cold fit of an ague; and his heart sank and his teeth chattered still more when they perceived distinctly that behind them there came a litter covered over with black and followed by six more mounted figures in mourning down to the very feet of their mules—for they could perceive plainly they were not horses by the easy pace at which they went. And as the *encamisados* came along they muttered to themselves in a low plaintive tone. This strange spectacle at such an hour and in such a solitary place was quite enough to strike terror into Sancho's heart, and even into his master's; and (save in Don Quixote's case) did so, for all Sancho's resolution had now broken down. It was just the opposite with his master, whose imagination immediately conjured up all this to him vividly as one of the adventures of his books. He took it into his head that the litter was a bier on which was borne some sorely wounded or slain knight, to avenge whom was a task reserved for him alone; and without any further reasoning he laid his lance in rest, fixed himself firmly in his saddle, and with gallant spirit and bearing took up his position in the middle of the road where the *encamisados* must of necessity pass; and as soon as he saw them near at hand he raised his voice and said:

"Halt, knights, whosoever ye may be, and render me account of who ye are, whence ye come, what it is ye carry upon that bier, for, to judge by appearances, either ye have done some wrong or some wrong has been done to you, and it is fitting and necessary that I shoud know, either that I may chastise you for the evil ye have done, or else that I may avenge you for the injury that has been inflicted upon you."

"We are in haste," answered one of the *encamisados*, "and the inn is far off, and we cannot stop to render you such an account as you demand;" and spurring his mule he moved on.

Don Quixote was mightily provoked by this answer, and seizing the mule by the bridle he said:

"Halt, and be more mannerly, and render an account of what I have asked of you; else, take my defiance to combat, all of you."

The mule was shy, and was so frightened at her bridle being seized that rearing up she flung her rider to the ground over her haunches. An attendant who was on foot, seeing the *encamisado* fall, began to abuse Don Quixote, who now moved to anger, without any more ado, laying his lance in rest charged one of the men in mourning and brought him badly wounded to the ground, and as he wheeled round upon the others the agility with which he attacked and routed them was a sight to see, for it seemed just as if wings had that instant grown upon Rocinante, so lightly and proudly did he bear himself. The *encamisados* were all timid folk and unarmed, so they speedily made their escape from the fray and set off at a run across the plain with their lighted torches, looking exactly like maskers running on some gala or festival night. The mourners, too, enveloped and swathed in their skirts and gowns, were unable to bestir themselves, and so with entire safety to himself Don Quixote belabored them all and drove them off against their will, for they all thought it was no man but a devil from hell come to carry away the dead body they had in the litter.

Sancho beheld all this in astonishment at the intrepidity of his lord, and said to himself, "Clearly this master of mine is as bold and valiant as he says he is."

A burning torch lay on the ground near the first man

whom the mule had thrown, by the light of which Don Quixote perceived him, and coming up to him he presented the point of the lance to his face, calling on him to yield himself prisoner, or else he would kill him; to which the prostrate man replied:

"I am prisoner enough as it is; I cannot stir, for one of my legs is broken: I entreat you, if you be a Christian gentleman, not to kill me, which will be committing grave sacrilege, for I am a licentiate and I hold first orders."

"Then what the devil brought you here, being a churchman?" asked Don Quixote.

"What, señor?" said the other. "My bad luck."

"Then still worse awaits you," said Don Quixote, "if you do not satisfy me as to all I asked you at first."

"You shall be soon satisfied," said the licentiate; "you must know, then, that though just now I said I was a licentiate, I am only a bachelor, and my name is Alonzo Lopez; I am a native of Alcobendas; I come from the city of Boeza with eleven others, priests, the same who fled with the torches, and we are going to the city of Segovia accompanying a dead body which is in that litter, and is that of a gentleman who died in Baeza, where he was interred; and now, as I said, we are taking his bones to their burial-place, which is in Segovia, where he was born."

"And who killed him?" asked Don Quixote.

"God, by means of a malignant fever that took him," answered the bachelor.

"In that case," said Don Quixote, "the Lord has relieved me of the task of avenging his death had any other slain him; but, he who slew him having slain him, there is nothing for it but to be silent, and shrug one's shoulders; I should do the same were he to slay myself: and I would have your reverence know that I am a knight of La Mancha, Don Quixote by name, and it is my business and calling to roam the world righting wrongs and redressing injuries."

"I do not know how that about righting wrongs can be," said the bachelor, "for from straight you have made me crooked, leaving me with a broken leg that will never see itself straight again all the days of its life; and the injury you have redressed in my case has been to leave me injured in such a way that I shall remain injured forever; and the height of misadventure it was to fall in with you who go in search of adventures."

"Things do not all happen in the same way," answered Don Quixote; "it all came, Sir Bachelor Alonzo Lopez, of your going, as you did, by night, dressed in those surplices, with lighted torches, praying, covered with mourning, so that naturally you looked like something evil and of the other world; and so I could not avoid doing my duty in attacking you, and I should have attacked you even had I known positively that you were the very devils of hell, for such I certainly believed and took you to be."

"As my fate has so willed it," said the bachelor, "I entreat you, Sir Knight-errant, whose errand has been such an evil one for me, to help me to get from under this mule that holds one of my legs caught between the stirrup and the saddle."

"I would have talked on till tomorrow," said Don Quixote; "how long were you going to wait before telling me of your distress?"

He at once called to Sancho, who, however, had no mind to come, as he was just then engaged in unloading a sumpter mule, well laden with provender, which these worthy gentlemen had brought with them. Sancho made a bag of his coat, and, getting together as much as he could, and as the mule's sack would hold, he loaded his beast, and then hastened to obey his master's call, and helped him to remove the bachelor from under the mule; then putting him on her back he gave him the torch, and Don Quixote bade him follow the track of his companions, and beg pardon of them on his part for the wrong which he could not help doing them.

And said Sancho, "If by chance these gentlemen should want to know who was the hero that served them so, your worship may tell them that he is the famous Don Quixote of La Mancha, otherwise called the Knight of the Rueful Countenance."

The bachelor then took his departure. I forgot to mention that before he did so he said to Don Quixote, " Remember that you stand excommunicated for having laid violent hands on a holy thing, *juxta illud, si quis, suadente diabolo*."

" I do not understand that Latin," answered Don Quixote, " but I know well I did not lay hands, only this pike; besides, I did not think I was committing an assault upon priests or things of the Church, which, like a Catholic and faithful Christian as I am, I respect and revere, but upon phantoms and specters of the other world; but even so, I remember how it fared with Cid Ruy Diaz when he broke the chair of the ambassador of that king before his Holiness the Pope, who excommunicated him for the same; and yet the good Roderick of Bivar bore himself that day like a very noble and valiant knight."

On hearing this the bachelor took his departure, as has been said, without making any reply; and Don Quixote asked Sancho what had induced him to call him the " Knight of the Rueful Countenance " more then than at any other time.

" I will tell you," answered Sancho; " it was because I have been looking at you for some time by the light of the torch held by that unfortunate, and verily your worship has got of late the most ill-favored countenance I ever saw; it must be either owing to the fatigue of this combat, or else to the want of teeth and grinders."

" It is not that," replied Don Quixote, " but because the sage whose duty it will be to write the history of my achievements must have thought it proper that I should take some distinctive name as all knights of yore did; one being ' He of the Burning Sword,' another ' He of the Unicorn,' this one ' He of the Damsels,' that ' He of the Phœnix,' another ' The Knight of the Griffin,' and another ' He of the Death,' and by these names and designations they were known all the world round; and so I say that the sage aforesaid must have put it into your mouth and mind just now to call me ' The Knight of the Rueful Countenance,' as I intend to call myself from this day forward; and that the said name may fit me better, I mean, when the opportunity offers, to have a very rueful countenance painted on my shield."

" There is no occasion, señor, for wasting time or money on making that countenance," said Sancho; " for all that need be done is for your worship to show your own, face to face, to those who look at you, and without anything more, either image or shield, they will call you ' Him of the Rueful Countenance '; and believe me I am telling you the truth, for I assure you, señor (and in good part be it said), hunger and the loss of your grinders have given you such an ill-favored face that, as I say, the rueful picture may be very well spared."

Don Quixote laughed at Sancho's pleasantry; nevertheless he resolved to call himself by that name, and have his shield or buckler painted as he had devised.

Don Quixote would have looked to see whether the body in the litter were bones or not, but Sancho would not have it, saying, " Señor, you have ended this perilous adventure more safely for yourself than any of those I have seen: perhaps these people, though beaten and routed, may bethink themselves that it is a single man that has beaten them, and feeling sore and ashamed of it may take heart and come in search of us and give us trouble enough. The ass is in proper trim, the mountains are near at hand, hunger presses, we have nothing more to do but make good our retreat, and, as the saying is, let the dead go to the grave and the living to the loaf; " and driving his ass before him, he begged his master to follow, who, feeling that Sancho was right, did so without replying; and after proceeding some little distance between two hills they found themselves in a wide and retired valley, where they alighted, and Sancho unloaded his beast, and stretched upon the green grass, with hunger for sauce, they breakfasted, dined, lunched, and supped all at once, satisfying their appetites with more than one store of cold meat which the dead man's clerical gentlemen (who seldom put themselves on short allowance) had brought with them on their sumpter mule. But another piece of ill-luck befell them, which Sancho held the worst of all, and that was that they had no wine to drink, nor even water to moisten their lips; and as thirst tormented them, Sancho, observing that the meadow where they were was full of green and tender grass, said what will be told in the following chapter.

CHAPTER XV

"IT cannot be, señor, but that this grass is a proof that there must be hard by some spring or brook to give it moisture, so it would be well done to move a little farther on, that we may find some place where we may quench this terrible thirst that plagues us, which beyond a doubt is more distressing than hunger."

The advice seemed good to Don Quixote, and, he leading Rocinante by the bridle and Sancho the ass by the halter, after he had packed away upon him the remains of the supper, they advanced up the meadow, feeling their way, for the darkness of the night made it impossible to see anything; but they had not gone two hundred paces when a loud noise of water, as if falling from great high rocks, struck their ears. The sound cheered them greatly; but halting to make out by listening from what quarter it came they heard unseasonably another noise which spoiled the satisfaction the sound of the water gave them, especially for Sancho, who was by nature timid and faint-hearted; they heard, I say, strokes falling with a measured beat, and a certain rattling of iron and chains that, together with the furious din of the water, would have struck terror into any heart but Don Quixote's. The night was, as has been said, dark, and they had happened to reach a spot in among some tall trees, whose leaves stirred by a gentle breeze made a low ominous sound; so that, what with the solitude, the place, the darkness, the noise of the water, and the rustling of the leaves, everything inspired awe and dread; more especially as they perceived that the strokes did not cease, nor the wind lull, nor morning approach; to all which might be added their ignorance as to where they were. But Don Quixote, supported by his intrepid heart, leaped on Rocinante, and bracing his buckler on his arm, brought his pike to the slope, and said:

"Friend Sancho, know that I by Heaven's will have been born in this our iron age to revive in it the age of gold, or the golden as it is called; I am he for whom perils, mighty achievements, and valiant deeds are reserved; I am, I say again, he who is to revive the Knights of the Round Table, the Twelve of France and the Nine Worthies; and he who is to consign to oblivion the Platirs, the Tablantes, the Olivantes and Tirantes, the Phœbuses and Belianises, with the whole herd of famous knights-errant of days gone by, performing in these in which I live such exploits, marvels, and feats of arms as shall obscure their brightest deeds. Thou dost mark well, faithful and trusty squire, the gloom of this night, its strange silence, the dull confused murmur of those trees, the awful sound of that water in quest of which we came, that seems as though it were precipitating and dashing itself down from the lofty mountains of the moon, and that incessant hammering that wounds and pains our ears; which things all together and each of itself are enough to instil fear, dread, and dismay into the breast of Mars himself, much more into one not used to hazards and adventures of the kind. Well, then, all this that I put before thee is but an incentive and stimulant to my spirit, making my heart burst in my bosom through eagerness to engage in this adventure, arduous as it promises to be; therefore tighten Rocinante's girths a little, and God be with thee; wait for me here three days and no more, and if in that time

CERVANTES' "DON QUIXOTE"

I come not back, thou canst return to our village, and thence, to do me a favor and a service, thou wilt go to El Toboso, where thou shalt say to my incomparable lady Dulcinea that her captive knight hath died in attempting things that might make him worthy of being called hers."

When Sancho heard his master's words he began to weep in the most pathetic way, saying:

"Señor, I know not why your worship wants to attempt this so dreadful adventure; it is night now, no one sees us here, we can easily turn about and take ourselves out of danger, even if we don't drink for three days to come; and as there is no one to see us, all the less will there be any one to set us down as cowards; besides, I have many a time heard the curate of our village, whom your worship knows well, preach that he who seeks danger perishes in it; so it is not right to tempt God by trying so tremendous a feat from which there can be no escape save by a miracle, and Heaven has performed enough of them for your worship in delivering you from being blanketed as I was, and bringing you out victorious and safe and sound from among all those enemies that were with the dead man; and if all this does not move or soften that hard heart, let this thought and reflection move it, that you will have hardly quitted this spot when from pure fear I shall yield my soul up to any one that will take it. I left home and wife and children to come and serve your worship, trusting to do better and not worse; but, as covetousness bursts the bag, it has rent my hopes asunder, for just as I had them highest about getting that wretched unlucky island your worship has so often promised me, I see that instead and in lieu of it you mean to desert me now in a place so far from human reach: for God's sake, master mine, deal not so unjustly by me, and if your worship will not entirely give up attempting this feat, at least put it off till morning, for by what the lore I learned when I was a shepherd tells me it cannot want three hours of dawn now, because the mouth of the Horn is overhead and makes midnight in the line of the left arm."

"How canst thou see, Sancho," said Don Quixote, "where it makes that line, or where the mouth or head is that thou talkest of, when the night is so dark that there is not a star to be seen in the whole heaven?"

"That's true," said Sancho, "but fear has sharp eyes, and sees things underground, much more above in the heavens; besides, there is good reason to show that it now wants but little of day."

"Let it want what it may," replied Don Quixote, "it shall not be said of me now or at any time that tears or entreaties turned me aside from doing what was in accordance with knightly usage; and so I beg of thee, Sancho, to hold thy peace, for God, who has put it into my heart to undertake now this so unexampled and terrible adventure, will take care to watch over my safety and console thy sorrow; what thou hast to do is to tighten Rocinante's girth well, and wait here, for I shall come back shortly, alive or dead."

Sancho perceiving it his master's final resolve, and how little his tears, counsels, and entreaties prevailed with him, determined to have recourse to his own ingenuity and compel him if he could to wait till daylight; and so, while tightening the girths of the horse, he quietly and without being felt, tied both Rocinante's fore-legs, so that when Don Quixote strove to go he was unable as the horse could only move by jumps. Seeing the success of his trick, Sancho Panza said:

"See there, señor! Heaven, moved by my tears and prayers, has so ordered it that Rocinante cannot stir; and if you will be obstinate, and spur and strike him, you will only provoke fortune, and kick, as they say, against the pricks."

Don Quixote at this grew desperate, but the more he drove his heels into the horse, the less he stirred him; and not having any suspicion of the tying, he was fain to resign himself and wait till daybreak or until Rocinante could move, firmly persuaded that all this came of something other than Sancho's ingenuity. So he said to him:

CERVANTES' "DON QUIXOTE"

"As it is so, Sancho, and as Rocinante cannot move, I am content to wait till dawn smiles upon us, even though I weep while it delays its coming."

"There is no need to weep," answered Sancho, "for I will amuse your worship by telling stories from this till daylight, unless indeed you like to dismount and lie down to sleep a little on the green grass after the fashion of knights-errant, so as to be fresher when day comes and the moment arrives for attempting this extraordinary adventure you are looking forward to."

"What art thou talking about dismounting or sleeping for?" said Don Quixote. "Am I, thinkest thou, one of those knights that take their rest in the presence of danger? Sleep thou who art born to sleep, or do as thou wilt, for I will act as I think most consistent with my character."

"Be not angry, master mine," replied Sancho, "I did not mean to say that;" and coming close to him he laid one hand on the pommel of the saddle and the other on the cantle, so that he held his master's left thigh in his embrace, not daring to separate a finger's length from him; so much afraid was he of the strokes which still resounded with a regular beat. Don Quixote bade him tell some story to amuse him as he had proposed, to which Sancho replied that he would if his dread of what he heard would let him.

"Still," said he, "I will strive to tell a story which, if I can manage to relate it, and it escapes me not, is the best of stories, and let your worship give me your attention, for here I begin. What was, was; and may the good that is to come be for all, and the evil for him who goes to look for it—your worship must know that the beginning the old folk used to put to their tales was not just as each one pleased; it was a maxim of Cato Zonzorino the Roman that says 'the evil for him that goes to look for it,' and it comes as pat to the purpose now as ring to finger, to show that your worship should keep quiet and not go looking for evil in any quarter, and that we should go back by some other road, since nobody forces us to follow this in which so many terrors affright us."

"Go on with thy story, Sancho," said Don Quixote, "and leave the choice of our road to my care."

"I say then," continued Sancho, "that in a village of Estremadura there was a goat-shepherd—that is to say, one who tended goats—which shepherd or goat-herd, as my story goes, was called Lope Ruiz, and this Lope Ruiz was in love with a shepherdess called Torralva, which shepherdess called Torralva was the daughter of a rich grazier, and this rich grazier——"

"If that is the way thou tellest thy tale, Sancho," said Don Quixote, "repeating twice all thou hast to say, thou wilt not have done these two days; go straight on with it, and tell it like a reasonable man, or else say nothing."

"Tales are always told in my country in the very way I am telling this," answered Sancho, "and I cannot tell it in any other, nor is it right of your worship to ask me to make new customs."

"Tell it as thou wilt," replied Don Quixote; "and as fate will have it that I cannot help listening to thee, go on."

"And so, lord of my soul," continued Sancho, "as I have said, this shepherd was in love with Torralva the shepherdess, who was a wild buxom lass with something of the look of a man about her, for she had little mustaches; I fancy I see her now."

"Then you knew her?" said Don Quixote.

"I did not know her," said Sancho, "but he who told me the story said it was so true and certain that when I told it to another I might safely declare and swear I had seen it all myself. And so in course of time, the devil, who never sleeps and puts everything in confusion, contrived that the love the shepherd bore the shepherdess turned into hatred and ill-will, and the reason, according to evil tongues, was some little jealousy she caused him that crossed the line and trespassed on forbidden ground; and so much did the shepherd hate her from that time forward that, in order to escape from her, he determined to quit the country and go where he should never set eyes on her again. Torralva, when she found herself spurned by Lope, was immediately smitten with love for him, though she had never loved him before."

"That is the natural way of women," said Don Quixote, "to scorn the one that loves them, and love the one that hates them: go on, Sancho."

"It came to pass," said Sancho, "that the shepherd carried out his intention, and driving his goats before him took his way across the plains of Estremadura to pass over into the Kingdom of Portugal. Torralva, who knew of it, went after him, and on foot and barefoot followed him at a distance, with a pilgrim's staff in her hand and a scrip round her neck, in which she carried, it is said, a bit of looking-glass, and a piece of a comb and some little pot or other of paint for her face; but let her carry what she did, I am not going to trouble myself to prove it; all I say is, that the shepherd, they say, came with his flock to cross over the river Guadiana, which was at that time swollen and almost overflowing its banks, and at the spot he came to there was neither ferry nor boat nor any one to carry him or his flock to the other side, at which he was much vexed, for he perceived that Torralva was approaching and would give him great annoyance with her tears and entreaties; however, he went looking about so closely that he discovered a fisherman who had alongside of him a boat so small that it could only hold one person and one goat; but for all that he spoke to him and agreed with him to carry himself and his three hundred goats across. The fisherman got into the boat and carried one goat over; he came back and carried another over; he came back again, and again brought over another—let your worship keep count of the goats the fisherman is taking across, for if one escapes the memory there will be an end of the story, and it will be impossible to tell another word of it. To proceed, I must tell you the landing place on the other side was miry and slippery, and the fisherman lost a great deal of time in going and coming; still he returned for another goat, and another, and another."

"Take it for granted he brought them all across," said Don Quixote, "and don't keep going and coming in this way, or thou wilt not make an end of bringing them over this twelvemonth."

"How many have gone across so far?" said Sancho.

"How the devil do I know?" replied Don Quixote.

"There it is," said Sancho, "what I told you, that you must keep a good count; well then, by God, there is an end of the story, for there is no going any farther."

"How can that be?" said Don Quixote; "is it so essential to the story to know to a nicety the goats that have crossed over, that if there be a mistake of one in the reckoning, thou canst not go on with it?"

"No señor, not a bit," replied Sancho; "for when I asked your worship to tell me how many goats had crossed, and you answered you did not know, at that very instant all I had to say passed away out of my memory, and faith, there was much virtue in it, and entertainment."

"So then," said Don Quixote, "the story has come to an end?"

"As much as my mother has," said Sancho.

"In truth," said Don Quixote, "thou hast told one of the rarest stories, tales, or histories, that any one in the world could have imagined, and such a way of telling it and ending it was never seen nor will be in a lifetime; though I expected nothing else from thy excellent understanding. But I do not wonder, for perhaps those careless strokes may have confused thy wits."

"All that may be," replied Sancho, "but I know that as to my story, all that can be said is that it ends there where the mistake in the count of the passage of the goats begins."

"Let it end where it will, well and good," said Don Quixote, "and let us see if Rocinante can go; and again he spurred him, and again Rocinante made jumps and remained where he was, so well tied was he. . . .

With this and other talk of the same sort master and

man passed the night, till Sancho, perceiving that daybreak was coming on apace, very cautiously untied Rocinante. As soon as Rocinante found himself free, though by nature he was was not at all mettlesome, he seemed to feel lively and began pawing—for as to capering, begging .his pardon, he knew not what it meant. Don Quixote, then, observing that Rocinante could move, took it as a good sign and a signal that he should attempt the dread adventure. By this time day had fully broken and everything showed distinctly, and Don Quixote saw that he was among some tall trees, chestnuts, which cast a very deep shade; he perceived likewise that the sound of the strokes did not cease, but could not discover what caused it, and so without any further delay he let Rocinante feel the spur, and once more taking leave of Sancho, he told him to wait for him there three days at most, as he had said before, and if he should not have returned by that time, he might feel sure it had been God's will that he should end his days in that perilous adventure. He again repeated the message and commission with which he was to go on his behalf to his lady Dulcinea, and said he was not to be uneasy as to the payment of his services, for before leaving home he had made his will, in which he would find himself fully recompensed in the matter of wages in due proportion to the time he had served; but if God delivered him safe, sound, and unhurt out of that danger, he might look upon the promised island as much more than certain. Sancho began weeping afresh on again hearing the affecting words of his good master, and resolved to stay with him until the final issue and end of the business. From these tears and this honorable resolve of Sancho Panza's the author of this history infers that he must have been of good birth and at least an old Christian; and the feeling he displayed touched his master somewhat, but not so much as to make him show any weakness; on the contrary, hiding what he felt as well as he could, he began to move towards that quarter whence the sound of the water and of the strokes seemed to come.

Sancho followed him on foot, leading by the halter, as

his custom was, his ass, his constant comrade in prosperity or adversity; and advancing some distance through the shady chestnut trees they came upon a little meadow at the foot of some high rocks, down which a mighty rush of water flung itself. At the foot of the rocks were some rudely constructed houses looking more like ruins than houses, from among which came, they perceived, the din and clatter of blows, which still continued without intermission. Rocinante took fright at the noise of the water and of the blows, but quieting him Don Quixote advanced step by step towards the houses, commending himself with all his heart to his lady, imploring her support in that dread pass and enterprise, and on the way commending himself to God, too, not to forget him. Sancho, who never quitted his side, stretched his neck as far as he could and peered between the legs of Rocinante to see if he could now discover what it was that caused him such fear and apprehension. They went it might be a hundred paces farther, when on turning a corner the true cause, beyond the possibility of any mistake, of that dread-sounding and to them awe-inspiring noise that had kept them all the night in such fear and perplexity, appeared plain and obvious; and it was (if, reader, thou art not disgusted and disappointed) six fulling hammers which by their alternate strokes made all the din.

When Don Quixote saw what it was, he was struck dumb and rigid from head to foot. Sancho glanced at him and saw him with his head bent down upon his breast in manifest mortification; and Don Quixote glanced at Sancho and saw him with his cheeks puffed out and his mouth full of laughter, and evidently ready to explode with it, and in spite of his vexation he could not help laughing at the sight of him; and when Sancho saw his master begin he let go so heartily that he had to hold his sides with both hands to keep himself from bursting with laughter. Four times he stopped, and as many times did his laughter break out afresh with the same violence as at first, whereat Don Quixote grew furious, above all when he heard him say mockingly:

CERVANTES' "DON QUIXOTE"

"Thou must know, friend Sancho, that of Heaven's will I was born in this our iron age to revive in it the golden or age of gold; I am he for whom are reserved perils, mighty achievements, valiant deeds;" and here he went on repeating all or most of the words that Don Quixote uttered the first time they heard the awful strokes.

Don Quixote, then, seeing that Sancho was turning him into ridicule, was so mortified and vexed that he lifted up his pike and smote him two such blows that if, instead of catching him on his shoulders, he had caught them on his head, there would have been no wages to pay, unless indeed to his heirs. Sancho seeing that he was getting an awkward return in earnest for his jest, and fearing his master might carry it still further, said to him very humbly:

"Calm yourself, sir, for by God I am only joking."

"Well, then, if you are joking I am not," replied Don Quixote. "Look here, my lively gentleman, if these, instead of being fulling hammers, had been some perilous adventure, have I not, think you, shown the courage required for the attempt and achievement? Am I, perchance, being, as I am, a gentleman, bound to know and distinguish sounds and tell whether they come from fulling mills or not; and that, when perhaps, as is the case, I have never in my life seen any as you have, low boor as you are, that have been born and bred among them? But turn me these six hammers into six giants, and bring them to beard me, one by one or all together, and if I do not knock them head over heels, then make what mockery you like of me."

"No more of that, señor," returned Sancho; "I own I went a little too far with the joke. But tell me, your worship, now that peace is made between us (and may God bring you out of all the adventures that may befall you as safe and sound as he has brought you out of this one), was it not a thing to laugh at, and is it not a good story, the great fear we were in?—at least that I was in; for as to your worship I see now that you neither know nor understand what either fear or dismay is."

"I do not deny," said Don Quixote, "that what hap-·
pened to us may be worth laughing at, but it is not worth
making a story about, for it is not every one that is shrewd
enough to hit the right point of a thing."

"At any rate," said Sancho, "your worship knew how
to hit the right point with your pike, aiming at my
head and hitting me on the shoulders, thanks be to God
and my own smartness in dodging it. But let that pass;
all will come out in the scouring; for I have heard say ' he
loves thee well that makes thee weep;' and moreover that
it is the way with great lords after any hard words they
give a servant to give him a pair of breeches; though I do
not know what they give after blows, unless it be that
knights-errant after blows give islands, or kingdoms on
the mainland."

"It may be on the dice," said Don Quixote, "that all
thou ·sayest will come true; overlook the past, for thou
art shrewd enough to know that our first movements are
not in our own control; and one thing for the future bear
in mind, that thou curb and restrain thy loquacity in my
company; for in all the books of chivalry that I have read,
and they are innumerable, I never met with a squire who
talked so much to his lord as thou dost to thine; and in
fact I feel it to be a great fault of thine and of mine: of
thine, that thou hast so little respect for me; of mine, that
I do not make myself more respected. There was Ganda-
lin, the squire of Amadis of Gaul, that was Count of the
Insula Firme, and we read of him that he always addressed
his lord with his cap in his hand, his head bowed down
and his body bent double, *more turquesco*. And then,
what shall we say of Gasabal, the squire of Galaor, who
was so silent that in order to indicate to us the greatness
of his marvelous taciturnity his name is only once mentioned in the whole of that history, as long as it is truthful? From all I have said thou wilt gather, Sancho, that
there must be a difference between master and man, between lord and lackey, between knight and squire: so that
from this day forward in our intercourse we must observe

more respect and take less liberties, for in whatever way
I may be provoked with you it will be bad for the pitcher.
The favors and benefits that I have promised you will come
in due time, and if they do not your wages at least will
not be lost, as I have already told you."

"All that your worship says in very well," said Sancho,
"but I should like to know (in case the time of favors
should not come, and it might be necessary to fall back
upon wages) how much did the squire of a knight-errant
get in those days, and did they agree by the mouth, or
by the day like bricklayers?"

"I do not believe," replied Don Quixote, "that such
squires were ever on wages, but were dependent on favor;
and if I have now mentioned thine in the sealed will I have
left at home, it was with a view to what may happen; for
as yet I know not how chivalry will turn out in these
wretched times of ours, and I do not wish my soul to suffer
for trifles in the other world; for I would have thee know,
Sancho, that in this there is no condition more hazardous
than that of adventures."

"That is true," said Sancho, "since the mere noise of
the hammers of a fulling mill can disturb and disquiet the
heart of such a valiant errant adventurer as your worship;
but you may be sure I will not open my lips henceforth
to make light of anything of your worship's, but only to
honor you as my master and natural lord."

"By so doing," replied Don Quixote, "shalt thou live
long on the face of the earth; for next to parents, masters
are to be respected as though they were parents."

CHAPTER XVI

IT now began to rain a little, and Sancho was for going into the fulling mills, but Don Quixote had taken such a disgust to them on account of the late joke that he would not enter them on any account; so turning aside to the right they came upon another road, different from that which they had taken the night before. Shortly afterwards Don Quixote perceived a man on horseback who wore on his head something that shone like gold, and the moment he saw him he turned to Sancho and said:

"I think, Sancho, there is no proverb that is not true, all being maxims drawn from experience itself the mother of all the sciences, especially that one that says, 'Where one door shuts, another opens.' I say so because if last night fortune shut the door of the adventure we were looking for against us, cheating us with the fulling mills, it now opens wide another one for another better and more certain adventure, and if I do not contrive to enter it, it will be my own fault, and I cannot lay it to my ignorance of fulling mills, or the darkness of the night. I say this because, if I mistake not, there comes towards us one who wears on his head the helmet of Mambrino, concerning which I took the oath thou rememberest."

"Mind what you say, your worship, and still more what you do," said Sancho, "for I don't want any more fulling mills to finish off fulling and knocking our sense out."

"The devil take thee, man," said Don Quixote; "what has a helmet to do with fulling mills?"

"I don't know," replied Sancho, "but, faith, if I might speak as I used, perhaps I could give such reasons that your worship would see you were mistaken in what you say."

"How can I be mistaken in what I say, unbelieving traitor?" returned Don Quixote; "tell me, seest thou not yonder knight coming towards us on a dappled gray steed, who has upon his head a helmet of gold?"

"What I see and make out," answered Sancho, "is only a man on a gray ass like my own, who has something that shines on his head."

"Well, that is the helmet of Mambrino," said Don Quixote; "stand to one side and leave me alone with him; thou shalt see how, without saying a word, to save time, I shall bring this adventure to an issue and possess myself of the helmet I have so longed for."

"I will take care to stand aside," said Sancho; "but God grant, I say once more, that it may be marjoram and not fulling mills."

"I have told thee, brother, on no account to mention those fulling mills to me again," said Don Quixote, "or I vow—and I say no more—I'll full the soul out of you."

Sancho held his peace in dread lest his master should carry out the vow he had hurled like a bowl at him.

The fact of the matter as regards helmet, steed, and knight that Don Quixote saw, was this. In that neighborhood there were two villages, one of them so small that it had neither apothecary's shop, nor barber, which the other that was close to it had, so the barber of the larger served the smaller, and in it there was a sick man who required to be bled and another man who wanted to be shaved, and on this errand the barber was going, carrying with him a brass basin; but as luck would have it, as he was on the way it began to rain, and not to spoil his hat, which probably was a new one, he put the basin on his head, and being clean it glittered at half a league's distance.

He rode upon a gray ass, as Sancho said, and this was what made it seem to Don Quixote to be a dapple-gray steed and a knight and a golden helmet; for everything he saw he made to fall in with his crazy chivalry and ill-errant notions; and when he saw the poor knight draw near, without entering into any parley with him, at Rocinante's top speed he bore down upon him with the pike pointed low, fully determined to run him through and through, and as he reached him, without checking the fury of his charge, he cried to him:

"Defend thyself, miserable being, or yield me of thine own accord that which is so reasonably my due."

The barber, who without any expectation or apprehension of it saw this apparition coming down upon him, had no other way of saving himself from the stroke of the lance but to let himself fall off his ass; and no sooner had he touched the ground than he sprang up more nimbly than a deer and sped away across the plain faster than the wind.

He left the basin on the ground, with which Don Quixote contented himself, saying that the pagan had shown his discretion and imitated the beaver, which finding itself pressed by the hunters bites and cuts off with its teeth that for which, by its natural instinct, it knows it is pursued.

He told Sancho to pick up the helmet, and he taking it in his hand said, "By God the basin is a good one, and worth a *real* of eight if it is worth a *maravedi*," and handed it to his master, who immediately put it on his head, turning it round, now this way, now that, in search of the visor, and not finding it he said, 'Clearly the pagan to whose measure this famous head-piece was first forged must have had a very large head; but the worst of it is, half of it is wanting."

When Sancho heard him call the basin a head-piece he was unable to restrain his laughter, but remembering his master's wrath he checked himself in the midst of it.

"What art thou laughing at, Sancho?" said Don Quixote.

"I am laughing," said he, "to think of the great head the pagan must have had who owned this helmet, for it looks exactly like a regular barber's basin."

"Dost thou know what I suspect, Sancho?" said Don Quixote; "that this wonderful piece of this enchanted helmet must by some strange accident have come into the hands of some one who was unable to recognize or realize its value, and who, not knowing what he did, and seeing it to be of the purest gold, must have melted down one half for the sake of what it might be worth, and of the other made this which is like a barber's basin as thou sayest; but be it as it may, to me who recognize it, its transformation makes no difference, for I will set it to rights at the first village where there is a blacksmith, and in such style that that helmet the god of smithies forged for the god of battles shall not surpass it or even come up to it; and in the meantime I will wear it as well as I can, for something is better than nothing, all the more as it will be quite enough to protect me from any chance blow of a stone."

"That is," said Sancho, "if it is not shot with a sling as they were in the battle of the two armies, when they signed the cross on your worship's grinders and smashed the flask with that blessed draught that made me vomit my bowels up."

"It does not grieve me much to have lost it," said Don Quixote, "for thou knowest, Sancho, that I have the recipe in my memory."

"So have I," answered Sancho, "but if ever I make it, or try it again as long as I live, may this be my last hour; moreover, I have no intention of putting myself in the way of wanting it, for I mean, with all my five senses, to keep myself from being wounded or from wounding any one: as to being blanketed again I say nothing, for it is hard to prevent mishaps of that sort, and if they come there is nothing for it but to squeeze our shoulders together, hold our breath, shut our eyes, and let ourselves go where luck and the blanket may send us."

TALES FROM THE SPANISH

"Thou art a bad Christian, Sancho," said Don Quixote
on hearing this, "for once an injury has been done thee
thou never forgettest it: but know that it is the part of a
noble and generous heart not to attach importance to trifles.
What lame leg hast thou got by it, what broken rib, what
cracked head, that thou canst not forget that jest? For
jest and sport it was, properly regarded, and had I not
seen it in that light I would have returned and done more
mischief in revenging thee than the Greeks did for the
rape of Helen, who, if she were alive now, or if my Dulcinea had lived then, might depend upon it she would not
be so famous for her beauty as she is;" and here he heaved
a sigh and sent it aloft; and said Sancho:

"Let it pass for a jest as it cannot be revenged in
earnest, but I know what sort of jest and earnest it was,
and I know it will never be rubbed out of my memory any
more than off my shoulders. But putting that aside, will
your worship tell me what are we to do with this dapple-
gray steed that looks like a gray ass, which that Martino
that your worship overthrew has left deserted here? for,
from the way he took to his heels and bolted, he is not
likely ever to come back for it; and by my beard but the
gray is a good one,"

"I have never been in the habit," said Don Quixote,
"of taking spoil of those whom I vanquish, nor is it the
practice of chivalry to take away their horses and leave
them to go on foot, unless indeed it be that the victor have
lost his own in the combat, in which case it is lawful to
take that of the vanquished as a thing won in lawful war;
therefore, Sancho, leave this horse, or ass, or whatever
thou wilt have it to be; for when its owner sees us gone
hence he will come back for it."

"God knows I should like to take," returned Sancho,
"or at least to change it for my own, which does not seem
to me as good a one: verily the laws of chivalry are strict,
since they cannot be stretched to let one ass be changed
for another; I should like to know if I might at least
change trappings."

122

"On that head I am not quite certain," answered Don Quixote, "and the matter being doubtful, pending better information, I say thou mayest change them, if so be thou hast urgent need of them."

"So urgent is it," answered Sancho, "that if they were for my own person I could not want them more;" and forthwith, fortified by this license, he effected the *mutatio capparum,* and rigged out his beast to the ninety-nines, making quite another thing of it. This done, they broke their fast on the remains of the spoils of war plundered from the sumpter mule, and drank of the brook that flowed from the fulling mills, without casting a look in that direction, in such loathing did they hold them for the alarm they had caused them; and, all anger and gloom removed, they mounted and, without taking any fixed road (not to fix upon any being the proper thing for true knights-errant), they set out, guided by Rocinante's will, which carried along with it that of his master, not to say that of the ass, which always followed him wherever he led, lovingly and sociably; nevertheless they returned to the high road, and pursued it at a venture without any other aim.

As they went along, then, in this way Sancho said to his master:

"Señor, would your worship give me leave to speak a little to you? For since you laid that hard injunction of silence on me several things have gone to rot in my stomach, and I have now just one on the tip of my tongue that I don't want to be spoiled."

"Say on, Sancho," said Don Quixote, "and be brief in thy discourse, for there is no pleasure in one that is long."

"Well then, señor," returned Sancho, "I say that for some days past I have been considering how little is got or gained by going in search of these adventures that your worship seeks in these wilds and cross-roads, where, even if the most perilous are victoriously achieved, there is no one to see or know of them, and so they must be left untold forever, to the loss of your worship's object and the credit they deserve; therefore it seems to me it would be better (saving your worship's better judgment) if we were to go and serve some emperor or other great prince who may have some war on hand, in whose service your worship may prove the worth of your person, your great might, and greater understanding, on perceiving which the lord in whose service we may be will perforce have to reward us, each according to his merits; and there you will not be at a loss for some one to set down your achievements in writing so as to preserve their memory forever. Of my own I say nothing, as they will not go beyond squirely limits, though I make bold to say that, if it be the practice in chivalry to write the achievements of squires, I think mine must not be left out."

"Thou speakest not amiss, Sancho," answered Don Quixote, "but before that point is reached it is requisite to roam the world, as it were on probation, seeking adventures, in order that, by achieving some, name and fame may be acquired, such that when he betakes himself to the court of some great monarch the knight may be already known by his deeds, and that the boys, the instant they see him enter the gate of the city, may all follow him and surround him, crying, 'This is the Knight of the Sun'— or the Serpent, or any other title under which he may have achieved great deeds. 'This,' they will say, 'is he who vanquished in single combat the gigantic Brocabruno of mighty strength; he who delivered the great Mameluke of Persia out of the long enchantment under which he had been for almost nine hundred years.' So from one to another they will go proclaiming his achievements; and presently at the tumult of the boys and the others the king of that kingdom will appear at the windows of his royal palace, and as soon as he beholds the knight, recognizing him by his arms and the device on his shield, he will as a matter of course say, 'What ho! Forth all ye, the knights of my court, to receive the flower of chivalry who cometh hither!' At which command all will issue forth, and he himself, advancing half-way down the stairs, will embrace him closely, and salute him, kissing him on the cheek, and will then lead him to the queen's chamber, where the knight will find her with the princess her daughter, who will be one of the most beautiful and accomplished damsels that could with the utmost pains be discovered anywhere in the known world.

Straightway it will come to pass that she will fix her eyes upon the knight and he his upon her, and each will seem to the other something more divine than human, and, without knowing how or why, they will be taken and entangled in the inextricable toils of love, and sorely distressed in their hearts not to see any way of making their pains and sufferings known by speech. Thence they will lead him, no doubt, to some richly adorned chamber of the palace, where, having removed his armor, they will bring him a rich mantle of scarlet wherewith to robe himself, and if he looked noble in his armor he will look still more so in a doublet. When night comes he will sup with the king, queen, and princess; and all the time he will never take his eyes off her, stealing stealthy glances, unnoticed by those present, and she will do the same, and with equal cautiousness, being, as I have said, a damsel of great disrcetion. The tables being removed, suddenly through the door of the hall there will enter a hideous and diminutive dwarf followed by a fair dame, between two giants, who comes with a certain adventure, the work of an ancient sage; and he who shall achieve it shall be deemed the best knight in the world. The king will then command all those present to essay it, and none will bring it to an end and conclusion save the stranger knight, to the great enchantment of his fame, whereat the princess will be overjoyed and will esteem herself happy and fortunate in having fixed and placed her thoughts so high.

And the best of it is that this king, or prince, or whatever he is, is engaged in a very bitter war with another as powerful as himself, and the stranger knight, after having been some days at his court, requests leave from him to go and serve him in the said war. The king will grant it very readily, and the knight will courteously kiss his hands for the favor done to him; and that night he will take leave of his lady the princess at the grating of the chamber where she sleeps, which looks upon a garden, and at which he has already many times conversed with her, the go-between and confidante in the matter being a damsel much trusted by the princess. He will sigh, she will swoon, the damsel will fetch water, he will be distressed because morning approaches, and for the honor of his lady he would not that they were discovered; at last the princess will come to herself and will present her white hands through the grating to the knight, who will kiss them a thousand and a thousand times, bathing them with his tears. It will be arranged between them how they are to inform each other of their good or evil fortunes, and the princess will entreat him to make his absence as short as possible, which he will promise to do with many oaths; once more he kisses her hands, and takes his leave in such grief that he is well-nigh ready to die. He betakes him thence to his chamber, flings himself on his bed, cannot sleep for sorrow at parting, rises early in the morning, goes to take leave of the king, queen, and princess, and, as he takes his leave of the pair, it is told him that the princess in indisposed and cannot receive a visit; the knight thinks it is from grief at his departure, his heart is pierced, and he is hardly able to keep from showing his pain. The confidante is present, observes all, goes to tell her mistress, who listens with tears and says that one of her greatest distresses is not knowing who this knight is, and whether he is of kingly lineage or not; the damsels assures her that so much courtesy, gentleness, and gallantry of bearing as her knight possesses could not exist in any save one who was royal and illustrious; her anxiety is thus relieved, and she strives to be of good cheer lest she should excite suspicion in her parents, and at the end of two days she appears in public.

Meanwhile the knight has taken his departure; he fights in the war, conquers the king's enemy, wins many cities, triumphs in many battles, returns to the court, sees his lady where he was wont to see her, and it is agreed that he shall demand her in marriage of her parents as the reward of his services; the king is unwilling to give her, as he knows not who he is, but nevertheless, whether carried off or in whatever other way it may be, the princess comes to be his bride, and her father comes to regard it as very good fortune; for it so happens that this knight is proved to be the son of a valiant king of some kingdom, I know not what, for I fancy it is not likely to be on the map; the father dies, the princess inherits, and in two words the knight becomes king. And here comes in at once the bestowal of rewards upon his squire and all who have aided him in rising to so exalted a rank. He marries his squire to a damsel of the princess's, who will be, no doubt, the one who was confidante in their *amour,* and is daughter of a very great duke."

"That's what I want, and no mistake about it!" said Sancho. "That's what I'm waiting for; for all this, word for word, is in store for your worship under the title of The Knight of the Rueful Countenance."

"Thou needst not doubt it, Sancho," replied Don Quixote, "for in the same manner, and by the same steps I have described here, knights-errant rise and have risen to be kings and emperors; all we want now is to find out what king, Christian or pagan, is at war and has a beautiful daughter; but there will be time enough to think of that, for, as I have told thee, fame must be won in other quarters before repairing to the court. There is another thing, too, that is wanting; for supposing we find a king who is at war and has a beautiful daughter, and that I have won incredible fame throughout the universe, I know not how it can be made out that I am of royal lineage, or even second cousin to an emperor; for the king will not be willing to give me his daughter in marriage unless he is first thoroughly satisfied on this point, however much my famous deeds may deserve it; so that by this deficiency I fear I shall lose what my arm has fairly earned.

"True it is I am a gentleman of a known house, of estate and property, and entitled to the five hundred *sueldos* mulct; and it may be that the sage who shall write my history will so clear up my ancestry and pedigree that I may find myself fifth or sixth in descent from a king; for I would have thee know, Sancho, that there are two kinds of lineages in the world; some there be tracing and deriving their descent from kings and princes, whom time has reduced little by little until they end in a point like a pyramid upside down; and others who spring from the common herd and go on rising step by step until they come to be great lords; so that the difference is that the one were what they no longer are, and the others are what they formerly were not. And I may be of such that after investigation my origin may prove great and famous, with which the king, my father-in-law that is to be, ought to be satisfied; and should he not be, the princess will so love me that even though she well knew me to be the son of a water-carrier, she will take me for her lord and husband in spite of her father; if not, then it comes to seizing her and carrying her off where I please; for time or death will put an end to the wrath of her parents."

"It comes to this, too," said Sancho, "what some naughty people say, 'Never ask a favor what thou canst take by force;' though it would fit better to say, 'A clear escape is better than good men's prayers.' I say so because if my lord the king, your worship's father-in-law, will not condescend to give you my lady the princess, there is nothing for it but, as your worship says, to seize her and transport her. But the mischief is that until peace is made and you come into the peaceful enjoyment of your kingdom, the poor squire is famishing as far as rewards go, unless it be that the confidante damsel that is to be his wife comes with the princess, and that with her he tides over his bad luck until Heaven otherwise orders things; for his master, I suppose, may as well give her to him at once for a lawful wife."

"Nobody can object to that," said Don Quixote.

"Then since that may be," said Sancho, "there is nothing for it but to command ourselves to God, and let fortune take what course it will."

"God guide it according to my wishes and thy wants," said Don Quixote, "and mean be he who makes himself mean."

"In God's name let him be so," said Sancho; "I am an old Christian, and to fit me for a count that's enough."

"And more than enough for thee," said Don Quixote; "and even wert thou not, it would make no difference, because I, being the king, can easily give thee nobility without purchase or service rendered by thee, for when I make thee a count, then thou art at once a gentleman; and they may say what they will, but by my faith they will have to call thee 'your lordship,' whether they like it or not."

"Not a doubt of it; and I'll know how to support the tittle," said Sancho.

"Title thou shouldst say, not tittle," said his master.

"So be it," answered Sancho, "I say I will know how to behave, for once in my life I was beadle of a brotherhood, and the beadle's gown sat so well on me that all said I looked as if I was fit to be steward of the same brotherhood. What will it be, then, when I put a duke's robe on my back, or dress myself in gold and pearls like a foreign count? I believe they will come a hundred leagues to see me."

"Thou wilt look well," said Don Quixote, "but thou must shave thy beard often, for thou hast it so thick and rough and unkempt, that if thou dost not shave it every second day at least, they will see what thou art at the distance of a musket shot."

"What more will it be," said Sancho, "than having a barber, and keeping him at wages in the house? and even if it be necessary, I will make him go behind me like a nobleman's equerry."

"Why, how dost thou know that noblemen have equerries behind them?" asked Don Quixote.

"I will tell you," answered Sancho. "Years ago I was for a month at the capital, and there I saw taking the air a very small gentleman who they said was a very great man, and a man following him on horseback in every turn he took, just as if he was his tail. I asked why this man did not join the other man, instead of always going behind him; they answered me that he was his equerry, and that it was the custom with nobles to have such persons behind them, and ever since then I know it, for I have never forgotten it."

"Thou art right," said Don Quixote, "and in the same way thou mayest carry thy barber with thee, for customs did not come into use all together, nor were they all invented at once, and thou mayest be the first count to have a barber follow him; and, indeed, shaving one's beard is a greater trust than saddling one's horse."

"Let the barber business be my look-out," said Sancho; "and your worship's be it to strive to become a king, and make me a count."

"So it shall be," answered Don Quixote, and raising his eyes he saw what will be told in the following chapter.

CHAPTER XVII

OF THE FREEDOM DON QUIXOTE CONFERRED ON SEVERAL UN-
FORTUNATES WHO AGAINST THEIR WILL WERE BEING
CARRIED WHERE THEY HAD NO WISH TO GO

CID HAMET BENENGELI, the Arab and Manche-
gan author, relates in this most grave, high-sounding,
minute, delightful, and original history that after the discussion between the famous Don Quixote of La Mancha
and his squire Sancho Panza which is set down at the end
of chapter sixteen, Don Quixote raised his eyes and saw
coming along the road he was following some dozen men
on foot strung together by the neck, like beads, on a great
iron chain, and all with manacles on their hands. With
them there came also two men on horseback and two on
foot; those on horseback with wheel-lock muskets, those
on foot with javelins and swords, and as soon as Sancho
saw them he said:

"That is a chain of galley slaves, on the way to the
galleys by force of the king's orders."

"How by force?" asked Don Quixote; "is it possible
that the king uses force against any one?"

"I do not say that," answered Sancho, "but that these
are people condemned for their crimes to serve by force
in the king's galleys."

"In fact," replied Don Quixote, "however it may be,
these people are going where they are taking them by
force, and not of their own will."

"Just so," said Sancho.

"Then if so," said Don Quixote, "here is a case for the exercise of my office, to put down force and to succor and help the wretched."

"Recollect, your worship," said Sancho, "Justice, which is the king himself, is not using force or doing wrong to such persons, but punishing them for their crimes."

The chain of galley slaves had by this time come up, and Don Quixote in very courteous language asked those who were in custody of it to be good enough to tell him the reason or reasons for which they were conducting these people in this manner. One of the guards on horseback answered that they were galley slaves belonging to his majesty, that they were going to the galleys, and that was all that was to be said and all he had any business to know."

"Nevertheless," replied Don Quixote, "I should like to know from each of them separately the reason of his misfortune;" to this he added more to the same effect to induce them to tell him what he wanted so civilly that the other mounted guard said to him, "Though we have here the register and certificate of the sentence of every one of these wretches, this is no time to take them out or read them; come and ask themselves; they can tell if they choose, and they will, for these follows take a pleasure in doing and talking about rascalities."

With this permission, which Don Quixote would have taken even had they not granted it, he approached the chain and asked the first for what offenses he was now in such a sorry case.

He made answer that it was for being a lover.

"For that only?" replied Don Quixote. "Why, if for being lovers they send people to the galleys, I might have been rowing in them long ago."

"The love is not the sort your worship is thinking of," said the galley slave; "mine was that I loved a washerwoman's basket of clean linen so well, and held it so close in my embrace, that if the arm of the law had not forced it from me, I should never have let it go of my own will to this moment; I was caught in the act, there was no occasion for torture, the case was settled, they treated me to a hundred lashes on the back, and three years of *gurapas* besides, and that was the end of it."

"What are *gurapas?*" asked Don Quixote.

"*Gurapas* are galleys," answered the galley slave, who was a young man of about four-and-twenty, and said he was a native of Piedrahita.

Don Quixote asked the same question of the second, who made no reply, so downcast and melancholy was he; but the first answered for him, and said, "He, sir, goes as a canary, I mean as a musician and a singer."

"What!" said Don Quixote, "for being musicians and singers do people go to the galleys, too?"

"Yes, sir," answered the galley slave, "for there is nothing worse than singing under suffering."

"On the contrary, I have heard say," said Don Quixote, "that he who sings scares away his woes."

"Here it is the reverse," said the galley-slave; "for he who sings once weeps all his life."

"I do not understand it," said Don Quixote; but one of the guards said to him, "Sir, to sing under suffering means with the *non sancta* fraternity to confess under torture; they put this sinner to the torture, and he confessed his crime, which was being a *cuatrero*, that is, a cattle-stealer, and on his confession they sentenced him to six years in the galleys, besides two hundred lashes that he has already had on the back; and he is always dejected and downcast because the other thieves that were left behind and that march here ill-treat, and snub, and jeer, and despise him for confessing and not having spirit enough to say nay; for, say they, 'nay' has no more letters in it than 'yea,' and a culprit is well off when life or death with him depends on his own tongue and not on that of witnesses or evidence; and to my thinking they are not very far out."

"And I think so, too," answered Don Quixote; then passing on to the third, he asked him what he had asked the others, and the man answered very readily and un-concernedly, "I am going for five years to their ladyships the *gurapas* for the want of ten ducats."

"I will give twenty with pleasure to get you out of that trouble," said Don Quixote.

"That," said the galley-slave, "is like a man having money at sea when he is dying of hunger and has no way of buying what he wants; I say so because, if at the right time I had had those twenty ducats that your wor-ship now offers me, I would have greased the notary's pen and freshened up the attorney's wit with them, so that today I should be in the middle of the plaza of the Zocodover at Toledo, and not on this road coupled like a greyhound. But God is great; patience—there, that's enough of it."

Don Quixote passed on to the fourth, a man of vener-able aspect with a white beard falling below his breast, who on hearing himself asked the reason of his being there began to weep without answering a word, but the fifth acted as his tongue and said:

"This worthy man is going to the galleys for four years, after having gone the rounds in the robe of ceremony and on horseback."

"That means," said Sancho Panza, "as I take it, to have been exposed to shame in public."

"Just so," replied the galley-slave, "and the offense for which they gave him that punishment was having been an ear-broker, nay body-broker; I mean, in short, that this gentleman goes as a pimp, and for having be-sides a certain touch of the sorcerer about him."

"If that touch had not been thrown in," said Don Quixote, "he would not deserve, for mere pimping, to row in the galleys, but rather to command and be admiral of them; for the office of pimp is no ordinary one, being the office of persons of discretion, one very necessary in a well-ordered state, and only to be exercised by persons of good birth; nay, there ought to be an inspector and overseer of them, as in other offices, and a fixed and

recognized number, as with the brokers on change; in
this way many of the evils would be avoided which are
caused by this office and calling being in the hands of
stupid and ignorant people, such as women more or less
silly, and pages and jesters of little standing and experience, who on the most urgent occasions, and when ingenuity of contrivance is needed, let the crumbs freeze on
the way to their mouths, and know not which is their
right hand. I would go further, and give reasons to
show that it is advisable to choose those who are to hold
so necessary an office in the state, but this is not the fit
place for it; some day I will expound the matter to
someone able to see to and rectify it; all I say now is,
that the additional fact of his being a sorcerer has removed the sorrow it gave me to see these white hairs and
this venerable countenance in so painful a position on
account of his being a pimp; though I know well there
are no sorceries in the world that can move or compel
the will as some simple folk fancy, for our will is free,
nor is there herb or charm that can force it. All that
certain silly women and quacks do is to turn men mad
with potions and poisons, pretending that they have power
to cause love, for, as I say, it is an impossibility to compel the will."

"It is true," said the good old man, "and indeed, sir,
as far as the charge of sorcery goes I was not guilty;
as to that of being a pimp, I cannot deny it; but I never
thought I was doing any harm by it, for my only object
was that all the world should enjoy itself and live in
peace and quiet, without quarrels or troubles; but my
good intentions were unavailing to save me from going
where I never expect to come back from, with this weight
of years upon me and a urinary ailment that never gives
me a moment's ease;" and again he fell to weeping as
before, and such compassion did Sancho feel for him that
he took out a *real* of four from his bosom and gave it to
him in alms.

Don Quixote went on and asked another what his crime

was, and the man answered with no less but rather much more sprightliness than the last one, " I am here because I carried the joke too far with a couple of cousins of mine, and with a couple of other cousins who were none of mine; in short, I carried the joke so far with them all that it ended in such a complicated increase of kindred that no accountant could make it clear: it was all proved against me, I got no favor, I had no money, I was near having my neck stretched, they sentenced me to the galleys for six years, I accepted my fate, it is the punishment of my fault; I am a young man; let life only last, and with that all will come right. If you, sir, have anything wherewith to help the poor, God will repay it to you in heaven, and we on earth will take care in our petitions to him to pray for the life and health of your worship, that they may be as long and as good as your amiable appearance deserves." This one was in the dress of a student, and one of the guards said he was a great talker and a very elegant Latin scholar.

Behind all these there came a man of thirty, a very personable fellow, except that when he looked his eyes turned in a little, one towards the other. He was bound differently from the rest, for he had to his leg a chain so long that it was wound all round his body, and two rings on his neck, one attached to the chain, the other to what they call a " keep-friend " or " friend's foot," from which hung two irons reaching to his waist with two manacles fixed to them in which his hands were secured by a big padlock, so that he could neither raise his hands to his mouth nor lower his head to his hands. Don Quixote asked why this man carried so many more chains than the others. The guard replied that it was because he alone had committed more crimes than all the rest put together, and was so daring and such a villain that, though they marched him in that fashion, they did not feel sure of him, but were in dread of his making his escape.

" What crimes can he have committed," said Don

Quixote, "if they have not deserved a heavier punishment than being sent to the galleys?"

"He goes for ten years," replied the guard, "which is the same thing as civil death, and all that need be said is that this good fellow is the famous Gines de Pasamonte, otherwise called Ginesillo de Parapilla."

"Gently, señor commissary," said the galley-slave at this; "let us have no fixing of names or surnames; my name is Gines, not Ginesillo, and my family name is Pasamonte, not Parapilla, as you say; let each one mind his own business, and he will be doing enough."

"Speak with less impertinence, master thief of extra measure," replied the commissary, "if you don't want me to make you hold your tongue in spite of your teeth."

"It is easy to see," returned the galley-slave, "that man goes as God pleases, but someone shall know some day whether I am called Ginesillo de Parapilla or not."

"Don't they call you so, you liar?" said the guard.

"They do," returned Gines, "but I will make them give over calling me so with a vengeance; where, I won't say. If you, sir, have anything to give us, give it to us at once, and God speed you, for you are becoming tiresome with all this inquisitiveness about the lives of others; if you want to know about mine, let me tell you I am Gines de Pasamonte, whose life is written by these fingers."

"He says true," said the commissary, "for he has himself written his story as grand as you please, and has left the book in the prison in pawn for two hundred *reals.*"

"And I mean to take it out of pawn," said Gines, "though it were in for two hundred ducats."

"Is it so good?" said Don Quixote.

"So good is it," replied Gines, "that a fig for *Lazarillo de Tormes,* and all of that kind that have been written, or shall be written, compared with it; all I will say about it is that it deals with facts, and facts so neat and diverting that no lies could match them."

"And how is the book entitled?" asked Don Quixote.

" The *Life of Gines de Pasamonte,*" replied the subject of it.

" And it is finished? " asked Don Quixote.

" How can it be finished," said the other, " when my life is not yet finished? All that is written is from my birth down to the point when they sent me to the galleys this last time."

" Then you have been there before? " said Don Quixote.

" In the service of God and the king I have been there for four years before now, and I know by this time what the biscuit and courbash are like," replied Gines; " and it is no great grievance to me to go back to them, for there I shall have time to finish my book; I have still many things left to say, and in the galleys of Spain there is more than enough leisure; though I do not want much for what I have to write, for I have it by heart."

" You seem a clever fellow," said Don Quixote.

" And an unfortunate one," replied Gines, " for misfortune always persecutes wit."

" It persecutes rogues," said the commissary.

" I told you already to go gently, master commissary," said Pasamonte; " their lordships yonder never gave you that staff to ill-treat us wretches here, but to conduct and take us where his majesty orders you; if not, by the life of —never mind—; it may be that some day the stains made in the inn will come out in the scouring; let every one hold his tongue and behave well and speak better; and now let us march on, for we have had quite enough of this entertainment."

The commissary lifted his staff to strike Pasamonte in return for his threats, but Don Quixote came between them, and begged him not to ill-use him, as it was not too much to allow one who had his hands tied to have his tongue a trifle free; and turning to the whole chain of them he said:

" From all you have told me, dear brethren, I make out clearly that though they have punished you for your faults, the punishments you are about to endure do not give you much pleasure, and that you go to them very much against the grain and against your will, and that perhaps this one's want of courage under torture, that one's want of money, the other's want of advocacy, and lastly the perverted judgment of the judge may have been the cause of your ruin and of your failure to obtain the justice you had on your side. All which presents itself now to my mind, urging, persuading, and even compelling me to demonstrate in your case the purpose for which Heaven sent me into the world and caused me to make profession of the order of chivalry to which I belong, and the vow I took therein to give aid to those in need and under the oppression of the strong. But as I know that it is a mark of prudence not to do by foul means what may be done by fair, I will ask these gentlemen, the guards and commissary, to be so good as to release you and let you go in peace, as there will be no lack of others to serve the king under more favorable circumstances; for it seems to me a hard case to make slaves of those whom God and nature have made free. Moreover, sirs of the guard," added Don Quixote, " these poor fellows have done nothing to you; let each answer for his own sins yonder; there is a God in heaven who will not forget to punish the wicked or reward the good; and it is not fitting that honest men should be the instruments of punishment to others, they being therein no way concerned. This request I make thus gently and quietly, that, if you comply with it, I may have reason for thanking you; and, if you will not voluntarily, this lance and sword together with the might of my arm shall compel you to comply with it by force."

" Nice nonsense ! " said the commissary; " a fine piece of pleasantry he has come out with at last ! He wants us to let the king's prisoners go, as if we had any authority to release them, or he to order us to do so ! Go your way, sir, and good luck to you; put that basin straight that you've got on your head, and don't go looking for three feet on a cat."

" 'Tis you that are the cat, rat, and rascal," replied Don Quixote, and acting on the word he fell upon him so suddenly that without giving him time to defend himself he brought him to the ground sorely wounded with a lance-thrust; and lucky it was for him that it was the one that had the musket. The other guards stood thunderstruck and amazed at this unexpected event, but recovering presence of mind, those on horseback seized their swords, and those on foot their javelins, and attacked Don Quixote, who was waiting for them with great calmness; and no doubt it would have gone badly with him if the galley slaves seeing the chance before them of liberating themselves had not effected it by contriving to break the chain on which they were strung. Such was the confusion, that the guards, now rushing at the galley slaves who were breaking loose, now to attack Don Quixote who was waiting for them, did nothing at all that was of any use. Sancho, on his part, gave a helping hand to release Gines de Pasamonte, who was the first to leap forth upon the plain free and unfettered, and who, attacking the prostrate commissary, took from him his sword and the musket, with which, aiming at one and leveling at another, he, without ever discharging it, drove every one of the guards off the field, for they took to flight, as well to escape Pasamonte's musket, as the showers of stones the now released galley slaves were raining upon them. Sancho was greatly grieved at the affair, because he anticipated that those who had fled would report the matter to the Holy Brotherhood, who at the summons of the alarm-bell would at once sally forth in quest of the offenders; and he said so to his master, and entreated him to leave the place at once, and go into hiding in the *sierra* that was close by.

"That is all very well," said Don Quixote, "but I know what must be done now;" and calling together all the galley slaves, who were now running riot, and had stripped the commissary to the skin, he collected them round him to hear what he had to say, and addressed them as follows:

"To be grateful for benefits received is the part of persons of good birth, and one of the sins most offensive to God is ingratitude; I say so because, sirs, ye have already seen by manifest proof the benefit ye have received of me; in return for which I desire, and it is my good pleasure that, laden with that chain which I have taken off your necks, ye at once set out and proceed to the city of El Toboso, and there present yourselves before the lady Dulcinea del Toboso, and say to her that her knight, he of the Rueful Countenance, sends to commend himself to her; and that ye recount to her in full detail all the particulars of this notable adventure, up to the recovery of your longed-for liberty; and this done ye may go where ye will, and good fortune attend you."

Gines de Pasamonte made answer for all, saying, " That which you, sir, our deliverer, demand of us, is of all impossibilities the most impossible to comply with, because we cannot go together along the roads, but only singly and separate, and each one his own way, endeavoring to hide ourselves in the bowels of the earth to escape the Holy Brotherhood, which, no doubt, will come out in search of us. What your worship may do, and fairly do, is to change this service and tribute as regards the lady Dulcinea del Toboso for a certain quantity of *ave-marias* and *credos* which we will say for your worship's intention, and this is a condition that can be complied with by night as well as by day, running or resting, in peace or in war; but to imagine that we are going now to return to the flesh-pots of Egypt, I mean, to take up our chain and set out for El Toboso, is to imagine that it is now night, though it is not yet ten in the morning, and to ask this of us is like asking pears of the elm tree."

" Then by all that's good," said Don Quixote (now stirred to wrath), " Don Ginesillo de Paropillo, or whatever your name is, you will have to go yourself alone, with your tail between your legs and the whole chain on your back."

Pasamonte, who was anything but meek (being by this time thoroughly convinced that Don Quixote was not quite right in his head as he had committed such a vagary as trying to set them free), finding himself abused in this fashion, gave the wink to his companions, and falling back they began to shower stones on Don Quixote at such a rate that he was quite unable to protect himself with his buckler, and poor Rocinante no more heeded the spur than if he had been made of brass. Sancho planted himself behind his ass, and with him sheltered himself from the hailstorm that poured on both of them. Don Quixote was unable to shield himself so well but that more pebbles than I could count struck him full on the body with such force that they brought him to the ground; and the instant he fell the student pounced upon him, snatched the basin from his head, and with it struck three or four blows on his shoulders, and as many more on the ground knocking it almost to pieces. They then stripped him of a jacket that he wore over his armor, and they would have stripped off his stockings if his greaves had not prevented them. From Sancho they took his coat, leaving him in his shirt-sleeves; and dividing among themselves the remaining spoils of the battle, they went each one his own way, more solicitous about keeping clear of the Holy Brotherhood they dreaded, than about burdening themselves with the chain, or going to present themselves before the lady Dulcinea del Toboso. The ass and Rocinante, Sancho and Don Quixote, were all that were left upon the spot; the ass with drooping head, serious, shaking his ears from time to time as if he thought the storm of stones that assailed them was not yet over; Rocinante stretched beside his master, for he too had been brought to the ground with a stone; Sancho stripped, and trembling with fear of the Holy Brotherhood; and Don Quixote fuming to find himself so served by the very persons for whom he had done so much.

CHAPTER XVIII

OF WHAT BEFELL DON QUIXOTE IN THE SIERRA MORENA,
WHICH WAS ONE OF THE RAREST ADVENTURES RELATED IN
THIS VERACIOUS HISTORY.

SEEING himself served in this way, Don Quixote said
to his squire, " I have always heard it said, Sancho,
that to do good to boors is to throw water into the sea. If
I had believed thy words, I should have avoided this trouble;
but it is done now, it is only to have patience and take
warning from this for the future."

" Your worship will take warning as much as I am a
Turk," returned Sancho; " but, as you say this mischief
might have been avoided if you had believed me, believe
me now, and a still greater one will be avoided; for I tell
you chivalry is of no account with the Holy Brotherhood,
and they don't care two *maravedis* for all the knights-
errant in the world; and I can tell you I fancy I hear their
arrows whistling past my ears this minute."

" Thou art a coward by nature, Sancho," said Don Quixote, " but lest thou shouldst say I am obstinate, and that
I never do as thou dost advise, this once I will take thy advice, and withdraw out of reach of that fury thou dread-
est; but it must be on one condition, that never, in life or
in death, thou art to say to any one that I retired or withdrew from this danger out of fear, but only in compliance
with thy entreaties; for if thou sayest otherwise thou wilt
lie therein, and from this time to that, and from that to
this, I give thee the lie, and say thou liest and wilt lie every
time thou thinkest or sayest it; and answer me not again;

for at the mere thought that I am withdrawing or retiring from any danger, above all from this, which does seem to carry some little shadow of fear with it, I am ready to take my stand here and await alone, not only that Holy Brotherhood you talk of and dread, but the brothers of the twelve tribes of Israel, and the Seven Maccabees, and Castor and Pollux, and all the brothers and brotherhoods in the world."

"Señor," replied Sancho, "to retire is not to flee, and there is no wisdom in waiting when danger outweighs hope, and it is the part of wise men to preserve themselves today for tomorrow, and not risk all in one day; and let me tell you, though I am a clown and a boor, I have got some notion of what they call safe conduct: so repent not of having taken my advice, but mount Rocinante if you can, and if not I will help you; and follow me, for my mother-wit tells me we have more need of legs than hands just now."

Don Quixote mounted without replying, and, Sancho leading the way on his ass, they entered the side of the Sierra Morena, which was close by, as it was Sancho's design to cross it entirely and come out again at El Viso or Almodovar del Campo, and hide for some days among its crags so as to escape the search of the Brotherhood should they come to look for them. He was encouraged in this by perceiving that the stock of provisions carried by the ass had come safe out of the fray with the galley slaves, a circumstance that he regarded as a miracle, seeing how they pillaged and ransacked.

That night they reached the very heart of the Sierra Morena, where it seemed prudent to Sancho to pass the night and even some days, at least as many as the stores he carried might last, and so they encamped between two rocks and among some cork trees; but fatal destiny, which, according to the opinion of those who have not the light of the true faith, directs, arranges, and settles everything in its own way, so ordered it that Gines de Pasamonte, the famous knave and thief who by the virtue and madness of Don Quixote had been released from the chain, driven by fear of the Holy Brotherhood, which he had good reason to dread, resolved to take hiding in the mountains; and his fate and fear led him to the same spot to which Don Quixote and Sancho Panza had been led by theirs, just in time to recognize them and leave them to fall asleep: and as the wicked are always ungrateful, and necessity leads to wrongdoing, and immediate advantage overcomes all considerations of the future, Gines, who was neither grateful nor well-principled, made up his mind to steal Sancho Panza's ass, not troubling himself about Rocinante, as being a prize that was no good either to pledge or sell. While Sancho slept he stole his ass, and before day dawned he was far out of reach.

Aurora made her appearance bringing gladness to the earth but sadness to Sancho Panza, for he found that his Dapple was missing, and seeing himself bereft of him he began the saddest and most doleful lament in the world, so loud that Don Quixote awoke at his exclamations and heard him saying:

"O son of my bowels, born in my very house, my children's plaything, my wife's joy, the envy of my neighbors, relief of my burdens, and, lastly half supporter of myself, for with the six-and-twenty *maravedis* thou didst earn me daily I met half my charges."

Don Quixote, when he heard the lament and learned the cause, consoled Sancho with the best arguments he could, entreating him to be patient, and promising to give him a letter of exchange ordering three out of five ass-colts that he had at home to be given to him. Sancho took comfort at this, dried his tears, suppressed his sobs, and returned thanks for the kindness shown him by Don Quixote. He on his part was rejoiced to the heart on entering the mountains, as they seemed to him to be just the place for the adventures he was in quest of. They brought back to his memory the marvelous adventures that had befallen knights-errant in like solitudes and wilds, and he went along reflecting on these things, so absorbed and carried away by them that he had no thought for anything else. Nor had Sancho any other care (now that he fancied he was traveling in a safe quarter) than to satisfy his appetite with such remains as were left of the clerical spoils, and so he marched behind his master laden with what Dapple used to carry, emptying the sack and packing his paunch, and so long as he could go that way, he would not have given a farthing to meet with another adventure.

While so engaged he raised his eyes and saw that his master had halted, and was trying with the point of his pike to lift some bulky object that lay upon the ground, on which he hastened to join him and help him if it were needful, and reached him just as with the point of the pike he was raising a saddle-pad with a valise attached to it, half or rather wholly rotten and torn; but so heavy were they that Sancho had to help to take them up, and his master directed him to see what the valise contained. Sancho did so with great alacrity, and though the valise was secured by a chain and padlock, from its torn and rotten condition he was able to see its contents, which were four shirts of fine holland, and other articles of linen no less curious than clean; and in a handkerchief he found a good lot of gold crowns, and as soon as he saw them he exclaimed, "Blessed be all Heaven for sending us an adventure that is good for something!" Searching further he found a little memorandum book richly bound; this Don Quixote asked of him, telling him to take the money and keep it for himself. Sancho kissed his hands for the favor, and cleared the valise of its linen, which he stowed away in the provision sack. Considering the whole matter, Don Quixote observed:

"It seems to me, Sancho—and it is impossible it can be otherwise—that some strayed traveler must have crossed this sierra and been attacked and slain by foot-pads, who brought him to this remote spot to bury him."

"That cannot be," answered Sancho, "because if they had been robbers they would not have left this money."

"Thou art right," said Don Quixote, "and I cannot guess or explain what this may mean; but stay; let us see if in this memorandum book there is anything written by which we may be able to trace out or discover what we want to know."

He opened it, and the first thing he found in it, written roughly but in a very good hand, was a sonnet, and reading it aloud that Sancho might hear it, he found that it ran as follows:

SONNET

Or Love is lacking in intelligence,
  Or to the height of cruelty attains,
  Or else it is my doom to suffer pains
Beyond the measure due to my offense.
But if Love be a God, it follows thence
  That he knows all, and certain it remains
  No God loves cruelty; then who ordains
This penance that inthralls while it torments?
It were a falsehood, Chloe, thee to name;
  Such evil with such goodness cannot live;
And against Heaven I dare not charge the blame,
  I only know it is my fate to die.
To him who knows not whence his malady
A miracle alone a cure can give.

"There is nothing to be learned from that rhyme," said Sancho, "unless by that clew there's in it, one may draw out the ball of the whole matter."

"What clew is there?" said Don Quixote.

"I thought your worship spoke of a clew in it," said Sancho.

"I only said Chloe," replied Don Quixote; "and that, no doubt, is the name of the lady of whom the author of the sonnet complains; and, faith, he must be a tolerable poet, or I know little of the craft."

"Then your worship understands rhyming too?" said Sancho.

"And better than thou thinkest," replied Don Quixote, "as thou shalt see when thou carriest a letter written in verse from beginning to end to my lady Dulcinea del Toboso, for I would have thee know, Sancho, that all or most of the knights-errant in days of yore were great troubadours and great musicians, for both of these accomplishments, or more properly speaking gifts, are the peculiar property of lovers-errant: true it is that the verses of the knights of old have more spirit than neatness in them."

"Read more, your worship," said Sancho, "and you will find something that will enlighten us."

Don Quixote turned the page and said, "This is prose and seems to be a letter."

"A correspondence letter, señor?" asked Sancho.

"From the beginning it seems to be a love-letter," replied Don Quixote.

"Then let your worship read it aloud," said Sancho, "for I am very fond of these love matters."

"With all my heart," said Don Quixote, and reading it aloud as Sancho had requested him, he found it ran thus:

Thy false promise and my sure misfortune carry me to a place whence the news of my death will reach thy ears before the words of my complaint. Ungrateful one, thou hast rejected me for one more wealthy, but not more worthy; but if virtue were esteemed wealth I should neither envy the fortunes of others nor weep for misfortunes of my own. What thy beauty raised up thy deeds have laid low; by it I believed thee to be an angel, by them I know thou art a woman...Peace be with thee who hast sent war to me, and Heaven grant that the deceit of thy husband be ever hidden from thee, so that thou repent not of what thou hast done, and I reap not a revenge I would not have.

When he had finished the letter, Don Quixote said, "There is less to be gathered from this than from the verses, except that he who wrote it is some rejected lover;" and turning over nearly all the pages of the book he found more verses and letters, some of which he could read, while others he could not: but they were all made up of complaints, laments, misgivings, desires and aversions, favors and rejections, some rapturous, some doleful. While Don Quixote examined the book, Sancho examined the valise, not leaving a corner in the whole of it or in the pad that he did not search, peer into, and explore, or seam that he did not rip, or tuft of wool that he did not pick to pieces, lest anything should escape for want of care and pains; so keen was the covetousness excited in him by the discovery of the crowns, which amounted to near a hundred; and though he found no more booty, he held the blanket flights, balsam vomits, stake benedictions, carriers' fisticuffs, missing wallets, stolen coat, and all the hunger, thirst, and weariness he had endured in the service of his good master, cheap at the price; as he considered himself more than fully indemnified for all by the payment he received in the gift of the treasure-trove. . . .

They proceeded slowly, making their way into the most rugged part of the mountain, Sancho all the while dying to have a talk with his master, and longing for him to begin, so that there should be no breach of the injunction laid upon him; but unable to keep silence so long he said to him:

"Señor Don Quixote, give me your worship's blessing and dismissal, for I'd like to go home at once to my wife and children with whom I can at any rate talk and converse as much as I like; for to want me to go through these solitudes day and night and not speak to you when I have a mind is burying me alive. If luck would have it that animals spoke as they did in the days of Guisopete, it would not be so bad, because I could talk to Rocinante about whatever came into my head, and so put up with my ill-fortune; but it is a hard case, and not to be borne with patience, to go seeking adventures all one's life and get nothing but kicks and blanketings, brickbats and punches, and with all this to have to sew up one's mouth without daring to say what is in one's heart, just as if one were dumb."

"I understand thee, Sancho," replied Don Quixote; "thou art dying to have the interdict I placed upon thy tongue removed; consider it removed, and say what thou wilt, on condition that the removal is not to last longer than while we are wandering in these mountains. . . .

"Señor," began Sancho, "is it a good rule of chivalry

149

that we should go astray through these mountains without path or road?"

"Peace, Sancho," said Don Quixote, "for let me tell thee the desire that leads me into these regions is that of performing among them an achievement wherewith I shall win eternal name and fame throughout the known world; and it shall be such that I shall thereby set the seal on all that can make a knight-errant perfect and famous."

"And is it very perilous, this achievement?" asked Sancho.

"No," replied he of the Rueful Countenance; "though it may be in the dice that we may throw deuce-ace instead of sixes; but all will depend on thy diligence."

"On my diligence!" said Sancho.

"Yes," said Don Quixote, "for if thou dost return soon from the place where I mean to send thee, my penance will be soon over, and my glory will soon begin. . . .

"What is it in reality," said Sancho, "that your worship means to do in such an out-of-the-way place as this?"

"Have I not told thee," answered Don Quixote, "that I mean to imitate Amadis here, playing the victim of despair, the madman, the maniac. . . .

"It seems to me," said Sancho, "that the knights who behaved in this way had provocation and cause for those follies and penances; but what cause has your worship for going mad? What lady has rejected you, or what evidence have you found to prove that the lady Dulcinea del Toboso has been trifling with Moor or Christian?"

"There is the point," replied Don Quixote, "and that is the beauty for this business of mine; no thanks to a knight-errant for going mad when he has a cause; the thing is to turn crazy without any provocation, and to let my lady know, if I do this in the dry, what I would do in the moist; moreover I have abundant cause in the long separation I have endured from my lady till death, Dulcinea del Toboso. . . .

"But tell me, Sancho, hast thou got Mambrino's helmet

safe; for I saw thee take it up from the ground when that wretch tried to break it in pieces but could not, by which the fineness of its temper may be seen?"

To which Sancho made answer, " By the living God, Sir Knight of the Rueful Countenance, I cannot endure or bear with patience some of the things that your worship says; and from them I begin to suspect that all you tell me about chivalry, and winning kingdoms and empires, and giving islands, and bestowing other rewards and dignities after the custom of knights-errant, must be all made up of wind and lies, and all pigments or figments, or whatever we may call them; for what would any one think that heard your worship calling a barber's basin Mambrino's helmet without ever seeing the mistake all this time, but that one who says and maintains such things must have his brains addled? I have the basin in my sack all dinted, and I am taking it home to have it mended, to trim my beard in it, if by God's grace I am allowed to see my wife and children some day or other."

" Look here, Sancho," said Don Quixote, " by him thou didst swear by just now I swear thou hast the most limited understanding that any squire in the world has or ever had. Is it possible that all this time thou hast been going about with me thou hast never found out that all things belonging to knights-errant seem to be illusions and nonsense and ravings, and to go always by contraries? And not because it really is so, but because there is always a swarm of enchanters in attendance upon us that change and alter everything with us, and turn things as they please, and according as they are disposed to aid or destroy us; thus what seems to thee a barber's basin seems to me Mambrino's helmet, and to another it will seem something else; and rare foresight it was in the sage who is on my side to make what is really and truly Mambrino's helmet seem a basin to everybody, for, being held in such estimation as it is, all the world would pursue me to rob me of it; but when they see it is only a barber's basin they do not take the trouble to obtain it; as was plainly shown by him

who tried to break it, and left it on the ground without
taking it, for, by my faith, had he known it he would
never have have left it behind. Keep it safe, my friend,
for just now I have no need of it; indeed, I shall have to
take off all this armor and remain as naked as I was born,
if I have a mind to follow Roland rather than Amadis
in my penance."

Thus talking they reached the foot of a high mountain
which stood like an isolated peak among the others that
surrounded it. Past its base there flowed a gentle brook,
all around it spread a meadow so green and luxuriant that it
was a delight to the eyes to look upon it, and forest trees
in abundance, and shrubs and flowers, added to the charms
of the spot. Upon this place the Knight of the Rueful
Countenance fixed his choice for the performance of his
penance, and as he beheld it exclaimed in a loud voice as
though he were out of his senses:

"This is the place, oh, ye heavens, that I select and
choose for bewailing the misfortune in which ye yourselves have plunged me: this is the spot where the over-
flowings of mine eyes shall swell the waters of yon little
brook, and my deep and endless sighs shall stir unceasingly
the leaves of these mountain trees, in testimony and token
of the pain my persecuted heart is suffering " . . . and so
saying he dismounted from Rocinante, and in and instant
relieved him of saddle and bridle, and giving him a slap
on the croup, said, " He gives thee freedom who is bereft of it himself, oh steed as excellent in deed as thou
art unfortunate in thy lot; begone where thou wilt, for
thou bearest written on thy forehead that neither Astolfo's
hippogriff, nor the famed Frontino that cost Bradamante
so dear, could equal thee in speed."

Seeing this Sancho said, " Good luck to him who has
saved us the trouble of stripping the pack-saddle off Dapple! By my faith he would not have gone without a slap
on the croup and something said in his praise; though if he
were here I would not let any one strip him, for there
would be no occasion, as he had nothing of the lover or vic-

tim of despair about him, inasmuch as his master, which I was while it was God's pleasure, was nothing of the sort; and indeed, Sir Knight of the Rueful Countenance, if my departure and your worship's madness are to come off in earnest, it will be as well to saddle Rocinante again in order that he may supply the want of Dapple, because it will save me time in going and returning; for if I go on foot I don't know when I shall get there or when I shall get back, as I am, in truth, a bad walker."

"I declare, Sancho," returned Don Quixote, "it shall be as thou wilt, for thy plan does not seem to me a bad one, and three days hence thou wilt depart, for I wish thee to observe in the meantime what I do and say for her sake, that thou mayest be able to tell it."

"But what more have I to see besides what I have seen?" said Sancho.

"Much thou knowest about it!" said Don Quixote. "I have now got to tear up my garments, to scatter about my armor, knock my head against these rocks, and more of the same sort of thing, which thou must witness."

"For the love of God," said Sancho, "be careful, your worship, how you give yourself those knocks on the head, for you may come across such a rock, and in such a way, that the very first may put an end to the whole contrivance of this penance; and I should think, if indeed knocks on the head seem necessary to you, and this business cannot be done without them, you might be content—as the whole thing is feigned, and counterfeit, and in joke—you might be content, I say, with giving them to yourself in the water, or against something soft, like cotton; and leave it all to me; for I'll tell my lady that your worship knocked your head against a point of rock harder than a diamond."

"I thank thee for thy good intentions, friend Sancho," answered Don Quixote, "but I would have thee know that all these things I am doing are not in joke, but very much in earnest, for anything else would be a transgression of the ordinances of chivalry, which forbid us to tell any lie whatever under the penalties due to apostasy; and to do one thing instead of another is just the same as lying; so my knocks on the head must be real, solid, and valid, without anything sophisticated or fancied about them, and it will be needful to leave me some lint to dress my wounds, since fortune has compelled us to do without the balsam we lost."

"It was worse losing the ass," replied Sancho, "for with him lint and all were lost; but I beg of your worship not to remind me again of that accursed liquor, for my soul, not to say my stomach, turns at hearing the very name of it; and I beg of you, too, to reckon as past the three days you allowed me for seeing the mad things you do, for I take them 'as seen already and pronounced upon, and I will tell wonderful stories to my lady; so write the letter and send me off at once, for I long to return and take your worship out of this purgatory where I am leaving you."

"Purgatory dost thou call it, Sancho?" said Don Quixote, "rather call it hell, or even worse if there be anything worse."

"For one who is in hell," said Sancho, "*nulla est retentio*, as I have already said."

"I do not understand what *retentio* means," said Don Quixote.

"*Retentio*," answered Sancho, "means that whoever is in hell never comes nor can come out of it, which will be the opposite case with your worship or my legs will be idle, that is if I have spurs to enliven Rocinante: let me once get to El Toboso and into the presence of my lady Dulcinea, and I will tell her such things of the follies and madnesses (for it is all one) that your worship has done and is still doing, that I will manage to make her softer than a glove though I find her harder than a cork tree; and with her sweet and honeyed answer I will come back through the air like a witch, and take your worship out of this purgatory that seems to be hell but is not, as there is hope of getting out of it; which, as I have said, those in hell have not, and I believe your worship will not say anything to the contrary."

"That is true," said he of the Rueful Countenance, "but how shall we manage to write the letter?"

"And the ass-colt order too," added Sancho.

"All shall be included," said Don Quixote; "and as there is no paper, it would be well done to write it on the leaves of trees, as the ancients did, or on tablets of wax; though that would be as hard to find just now as paper. But it has just occurred to me how it may be conveniently and even more than conveniently written, and that is in a note-book, and thou wilt take care to have it copied on paper, in a good hand, at the first village thou comest to where there is a schoolmaster, or if not, any sacristan will copy it; but see thou give it not to any notary to copy, for they write a law hand that Satan could not make out."

"But what is to be done about the signature?" said Sancho.

"The letters of Amadis were never signed," said Don Quixote.

"That is all very well," said Sancho, "but the order must needs be signed, and if it is copied they will say the signature is false, and I shall be left without ass-colts."

"The order shall go signed in the same book," said Don Quixote, "and on seeing it my niece will make no difficulty about obeying it; as to the love-letter thou canst put by way of signature, '*Yours till death, the Knight of the Rueful Countenance.*' And it will be no great matter if it is in some other person's hand, for as well as I can recollect Dulcinea can neither read nor write, nor in the whole course of her life has she seen handwriting or letter of mine.

"For my love and hers have been always platonic, not going beyond a modest look, and even that so seldom that I can safely swear I have not seen her four times in all these twelve years I have been loving her more than the light of these eyes that the earth will one day devour; and perhaps even of those four times she has not once perceived that I was looking at her: such is the retirement and seclusion in which her father Lorenzo Corchuelo and her mother Aldonza Nogales have brought her up."

"So, so!" said Sancho; "Lorenzo Corchuelo's daughter is the lady Dulcinea del Toboso, otherwise called Aldonza Lorenzo?"

"She it is," said Don Quixote, "and she it is that is worthy to be lady of the universe."

"I know her well," said Sancho, "and let me tell you she can fling a crowbar as well as the lustiest lad in all the town. Giver of all good; but she is a brave lass, and a right and stout one, and fit to be helpmate to my knight-errant that is or is to be, who may make her his lady: the whoreson wench, what pith she has and what a voice! I can tell you one day she posted herself on the top of the belfry of the village to call some laborers of theirs that were in a ploughed field of her father's, and though they were better than half a legaue off they heard her as well as if they were at the foot of the tower; and the best of her is that she is not a bit prudish, for she has plenty of affability, and jokes with everybody, and has a grin and a jest for everything.

"So, Sir Knight of the Rueful Countenance, I say you not only may and ought to do mad freaks for her sake, but you have a good right to give way to despair and hang yourself; and no one who knows of it but will say you did well, though the devil should take you, and I wish I were on my road already, simply to see her, for it is many a day since I saw her, and she must be altered by this time, for going about the fields always, and the sun and the air spoil women's looks greatly. But I must own the truth to your worship, Señor Don Quixote; until now I have been under a great mistake, for I believed truly and honestly that the lady Dulcinea must be some princess your worship was in love with, or some person great enough to deserve the rich presents you have sent her, such as the Biscayan and the galley slaves, and many more no doubt, for your worship must have won many victories in the time when I was not yet your squire. But all things considered, what good can it do the lady Aldonza Lorenzo (I mean the lady Dulcinea del Toboso) to have the vanquished your worship sends or will send coming to her and going down on their knees before her? Because maybe when they came she'd be hackling flax or threshing on the threshing floor, and they'd be ashamed to see her, and she'd laugh, or resent the present."

" I have before now told thee many times, Sancho," said Don Quixote, " that thou art a mighty great chatterer, and that with a blunt wit thou art always striving at sharpness. . . . It is not to be supposed that all those poets who sang the praises of ladies under the fancy names they give them, had any such mistresses. Thinkest thou that the Amaryllises, the Phillises, the Sylvias, the Dianas, the Galateas, the Filidas, and all the rest of them, that the books, the ballads, the barber's shops, the theaters are full of, were really and truly ladies of flesh and blood, and mistresses of those that glorify and have glorified them? Nothing of the kind; they only invent them for the most part to furnish a subject for their verses, and that they may pass for lovers, or for men who have some pretentions to be so; and so it is enough for me to think and believe that the good Aldonza Lorenzo is fair and virtuous; and as to her pedigree it is very little matter, for no one will examine into it for the purpose of conferring any order upon her, and I, for my part, reckon her the most exalted princess in the world. For thou shouldst know, Sancho, if thou dost not know, that two things alone beyond all others are incentives to love, and these are great beauty and a good name, and these two things are to be found in Dulcinea in the highest degree, for in beauty no one equals her and in good name few approach her; and to put the whole thing in a nutshell, I persuade myself that all I say is as I say, neither more nor less, and I picture her in my imagination as I would have her to be, as well in beauty as in condition; Helen approaches her not nor

157

does Lucretia come up to her, nor any other of the famous women of times past, Greek, Barbarian, or Latin; and let each say what he will, for if in this I am taken to task by the ignorant, I shall not be censured by the critical."

" I say that your worship is entirely right," said Sancho, " and that I am an ass. But I know not how the name of ass came into my mouth, for a rope is not to be mentioned in the house of him who has been hanged; but now for the letter, and then, God be with you, I am off."

Don Quixote took out the note-book, and, retiring to one side, very deliberately began to write the letter, and when he had finished it he called to Sancho, saying he wished to read it to him, so that he might commit it to memory, in case of losing it on the road; for with evil fortune like his anything might be apprehended. To which Sancho replied:

" Write it two or three times there in the book and give it to me, and I will carry it very carefully, because to expect me to keep it in my memory is all nonsense, for I have such a bad one that I often forget my own name; but for all that repeat it to me, as I shall like to hear it, for surely it will run as if it was in print."

" Listen," said Don Quixote, " this is what it says:

" *Don Quixote's Letter to Dulcinea del Toboso.*

" Sovereign and exalted Lady,—The pierced by the point of absence, the wounded to the heart's core, sends thee, sweetest Dulcinea del Toboso, the health that he himself enjoys not. If thy beauty despises me, if thy worth is not for me, if thy scorn is my affliction, though I be sufficiently long-suffering, hardly shall I endure this anxiety, which, besides being oppressive, is protracted. My good squire Sancho will relate to thee in full, fair ingrate, dear enemy, the condition to which I am reduced on thy account: if it be thy pleasure to give me relief, I am thine; if not, do as may be pleasing to thee; for by ending my life I shall satisfy thy cruelty and my desire.

" Thine till death,
" THE KNIGHT OF THE RUEFUL COUNTENANCE."

" By the life of my father," said Sancho, when he heard the letter, " it is the loftiest thing I ever heard. Body of me! how your worship says everything as you like in it! And how well you fit in ' The Knight of the Rueful Countenance ' into the signature. I declare your worship is indeed the very devil, and there is nothing you don't know."

" Everything is needed for the calling I follow," said Don Quixote.

" Now then," said Sancho, " let your worship put the order for the three ass-colts on the other side, and sign it very plainly, that they may recognize it at first sight."

" With all my heart," said Don Quixote, and as soon as he had written it he read it to this effect:

" Mistress Niece,—By this first of ass-colts please pay to Sancho Panza, my squire, three of the five I left at home in your charge: said three ass-colts to be paid and delivered for the same number received here in hand, which upon this and upon his receipt shall be duly paid. Done in the heart of the Sierra Morena, the twenty-seventh of August of this present year."

" That will do," said Sancho; " now let your worship sign it."

" There is no need to sign it," said Don Quixote, " but merely to put my flourish, which is the same as a signature, and enough for three asses, or even three hundred."

" I can trust your worship," returned Sancho; " let me go and saddle Rocinante, and be ready to give me your blessing, for I mean to go at once without seeing the fooleries your worship is going to do; I'll say I saw you do so many that she will not want any more."

" At any rate, Sancho," said Don Quixote, " I should like—and there is reason for it—I should like thee, I say, to see me stripped to the skin and performing a dozen or two of insanities, which I can get done in less than half an hour; for having seen them with thine own eyes, thou canst then safely swear to the rest that thou wouldst add; and I promise thee thou wilt not tell of as many as I mean to perform."

"For the love of God, master mine," said Sancho, "let me not see your worship stripped, for it will sorely grieve me, and I shall not be able to keep from tears, and my head aches so with all I shed last night for Dapple, that I am not fit to begin any fresh weeping; but if it is your worship's pleasure that I should see some insanities, do them in your clothes, short ones, and such as come readiest to hand; for I myself want nothing of the sort, and, as I have said, it will be a saving of time for my return, which will be with the news your worship desires and deserves. If not, let the lady Dulcinea look at it; if she does not answer reasonably, I swear as solemnly as I can that I will fetch a fair answer out of her stomach with kicks and cuffs; for why should it be borne that a knight-errant as famous as your worship should go mad without rhyme or reason for a—? her ladyship had best not drive me to say it, for by God I will speak out and have done with it, though it stop the sale: I am pretty good at that; she little knows me; faith, if she knew me she'd be afraid of me."

"In faith, Sancho," said Don Quixote, "to all appearances thou art not sounder in thy wits than I am."

"I am not so mad," answered Sancho, "but I am more peppery; but apart from all this, what has your worship to eat until I come back? Will you sally out on the road to force it from the shepherds?"

"Let not that anxiety trouble thee," replied Don Quixote, for even if I had it I should not eat anything but the herbs and the fruits which this meadow and these trees may yield me; the beauty of this business of mine lies in not eating, and in performing other mortifications."

"Do you know what I am afraid of?" said Sancho upon this; "that I shall not be able to find my way back to this spot where I am leaving you, it is such an out-of-the-way place."

"Observe the landmarks well," said Don Quixote, "for I will try not to go far from this neighborhood, and I will ever take care to mount the highest of these rocks to see if I can discover thee returning; however, not to miss me and lose thyself, the best plan will be to cut some branches of the broom that is so abundant about here, and as thou goest to lay them at intervals until thou hast come out upon the plain; these will serve thee, after the fashion of the clew in the labyrinth of Theseus, as marks and signs for finding me on thy return."

"So I will," said Sancho Panza, and having cut some, he asked his master's blessing, and not without many tears on both sides took his leave of him, and mounting Rocinante, of whom Don Quixote charged him earnestly to have as much care as of his own person, he set out for the plain, strewing at intervals the branches of broom as his master had recommended him; and so he went his way, though Don Quixote still entreated him to see him do were it only a couple of mad acts. He had not gone a hundred paces, however, when he returned and said:

"I must say, señor, your worship said quite right, that in order to be able to swear without a weight on my conscience that I had seen you do mad things, it would be well for me to see if it were only one; though in your worship's remaining here I have seen a very great one."

"Did I not tell thee so?" said Don Quixote. "Wait, Sancho, and I will do them in the saying of a *credo*," and pulling off his breeches in all haste he stripped himself to his skin and his shirt, and then, without more ado, he cut a couple of gambados in the air, and a couple of somersaults, heels over head, making such a display that, not to see it a second time, Sancho wheeled Rocinante round, and felt easy, and satisfied in his mind that he could swear he had left his master mad; and so we will leave him to follow his road until his return, which was a quick one.

CHAPTER XIX

RETURNING to the proceedings of him of the Rueful
Countenance when he found himself alone, the history says that when Don Quixote had completed the performance of the somersaults or capers, naked from the
waist down and clothed from the waist up, and saw that
Sancho had gone off without waiting to see any more crazy
feats, he climbed up to the top of a high rock, and there
set himself to consider what he had several times before
considered without ever coming to any conclusion on the
point, namely whether it would be better and more to his
purpose to imitate the outrageous madness of Roland, or
the melancholy madness of Amadis. . . . He solaced himself with pacing up and down the little meadow, and writing and carving on the bark of the trees and on the fine
sand a multitude of verses all in harmony with his sadness,
and some in praise of Dulcinea; but, when he was found
there afterwards, the only ones completely legible that
could be discovered were those that follow here:

> Ye on the mountain side that grow,
>   Ye green things all, trees, shrubs, and bushes,
> Are ye aweary of the woe
>   That this poor aching bosom crushes?
> If it disturb you, and I owe
>   Some reparation, it may be a
> Defense for me to let you know
> Don Quixote's tears are on the flow,
>   And all for distant Dulcinea
>   Del Toboso.

CERVANTES' "DON QUIXOTE"

The lealest lover time can show,
  Doomed for a lady-love to languish,
Among these solitudes doth go,
  A prey to every kind of anguish.
Why Love should like a spiteful foe
  Thus use him, he hath no idea,
But hogsheads full—this doth he know—
Don Quixote's tears are on the flow,
  And all for distant Dulcinea
        Del Toboso.

Adventure-seeking doth he go
  Up rugged heights, down rocky valleys,
But hill or dale, or high or low,
  Mishap attendeth all his sallies:
Love still pursues him to and fro,
  And plies his cruel scourge—ah me! a
Relentless fate, an endless woe;
Don Quixote's tears are on the flow,
  And all for distant Dulcinea
        Del Toboso.

The addition of "Del Toboso" to Dulcinea's name gave rise to no little laughter among those who found the above lines, for they suspected Don Quixote must have fancied that unless he added "del Toboso" when he introduced the name of Dulcinea the verse would be unintelligible; which was indeed the fact, as he himself afterwards admitted. He wrote many more, but, as has been said, these three verses were all that could be plainly and perfectly deciphered. In this way, and in sighing and calling on the fauns and satyrs of the woods and the nymphs of the streams, and Echo, moist and mournful, to answer, console, and hear him, as well as in looking for herbs to sustain him, he passed his time until Sancho's return; and had that been delayed three weeks, as it was three days, the Knight of the Rueful Countenance would have worn such an altered countenance that the mother that bore him would not have known him: and here it will be well to leave him, wrapped up in sighs and verses, to relate how Sancho Panza fared on his mission.

As for him, coming out upon the high road, he made for El Toboso, and the next day reached the inn where the mishap of the blanket had befallen him. As soon as he

163

recognized it he felt as if he were once more flying through the air, and he could not bring himself to enter it though it was an hour when he might well have done so, for it was dinner-time, and he longed to taste something hot as it had been all cold fare with him for many days past. This craving drove him to draw near to the inn, still undecided whether to go in or not, and as he was hesitating there came out two persons who at once recognized him, and said one to the other:

"Señor licentiate, is not he on the horse there Sancho Panza who, our adventurer's housekeeper told us, went off with her master as esquire?"

"So it is," said the licentiate, "and that is our friend Don Quixote's horse;" and if they knew him so well it was because they were the curate and the barber of his own village; and as soon as they recognized Sancho Panza and Rocinante, being anxious to hear of Don Quixote, they approached, and calling him by his name the curate said:

"Friend Sancho Panza, where is your master?"

Sancho recognized them at once, and determined to keep secret the place and circumstances where and under which he had left his master, so he replied that his master was engaged in a certain quarter on a certain matter of great importance to him which he could not disclose for the eyes in his head.

"Nay, nay," said the barber, "if you don't tell us where he is, Sancho Panza, we will suspect, as we suspect already, that you have murdered and robbed him, for here you are mounted on his horse; in fact, you must produce the master of the hack, or else take the consequences."

"There is no need of threats with me," said Sancho, "for I am not a man to rob or murder anybody; let his own fate, or God who made him, kill each one; my master is engaged very much to his taste doing penance in the midst of these mountains;" and then, offhand and without stopping, he told them how he had left him, what adventures had befallen him, and how he was carrying a letter to the lady Dulcinea del Toboso, the daughter of Lorenzo Corchuelo, with whom he was over head and ears in love. They were both amazed at what Sancha Panza told them; for though they were aware of Don Quixote's madness and the nature of it, each time they heard of it they were filled with fresh wonder. Then they asked Sancho Panza to show them the letter he was carrying to the lady Dulcinea del Toboso. He said it was written in a note-book, and that his master's directions were that he should have it copied on paper at the first village he came to. On this the curate said if he showed it to him, he himself would make a fair copy of it. Sancho put his hand into his bosom in search of the note-book, but could not find it, nor, if he had been searching until now, could he have found it, for Don Quixote had kept it, and had never given it to him, nor had he himself thought of asking for it. When Sancho discovered he could not find the book his face grew deadly pale, and in great haste he again felt his body all over, and seeing plainly it was not to be found, without more ado he seized his beard with both hands and plucked away half of it, and then, as quick as he could and without stopping, gave himself half a dozen cuffs on the face and nose till they were bathed in blood.

Seeing this, the curate and the barber asked him what had happened him that he gave himself such rough treatment.

"What should happen me," replied Sancho, "but to have lost from one hand to the other, in a moment, three ass-colts, each of them like a castle?"

"How is that?" said the barber.

"I have lost the note-book," said Sancho, "that contained the letter to Dulcinea, and an order signed by my master in which he directed his niece to give me three ass-colts out of four or five he had at home;" and he then told them about the loss of Dapple.

The curate consoled him, telling him that when his master was found he would get him to renew the order, and, make a fresh draft on paper, as was usual and customary; for those made in note-books were never accepted or honored.

Sancho comforted himself with this, and said if that were so the loss of Dulcinea's letter did not trouble him much, for he had it almost by heart, and it could be taken down from him wherever and whenever they liked.

" Repeat it then, Sancho," said the barber, " and we will write it down afterwards."

Sancho Panza stopped to scratch his head to bring back the letter to his memory, and balanced himself now on one foot, now the other, one moment staring at the ground, the next at the sky, and after having half gnawed off the end of a finger and kept them in suspense waiting for him to begin, he said, after a long pause:

" By God, señor licentiate, devil a thing can I recollect of the letter; but it said at the beginning, ' Exalted and scrubbing Lady.' "

" It cannot have said ' scrubbing,' " said the barber, " but ' superhuman ' or ' sovereign.' "

" That is it," said Sancho; " then, as well as I remember, it went on, ' The wounded, and wanting of sleep, and the pierced, kisses your worship's hands, ungrateful and very unrecognized fair one;' and it said something or other about health and sickness that he was sending her; and from that it went tailing off until it ended with ' Yours till death, the Knight of the Rueful Countenance.' "

It gave them no little amusement, both of them, to see what a good memory Sancho had, and they complimented him greatly upon it, and begged him to repeat the letter a couple of times more, so that they too might get it by heart to write it out by-and-by. Sancho repeated it three times, and as he did, uttered three thousand more absurdities; then he told them more about his master; but he never said a word about the blanketing that had befallen himself in that inn, into which he refused to enter. He told them, moreover, how his lord, if he brought him a favorable answer from the lady Dulcinea del Toboso, was to put himself in the way of endeavoring to become an emperor, or at least a monarch; for it had been so settled between them, and with his personal worth and the might of his arm it was an easy matter to come to be one: and how on becoming one his lord was to make a marriage for him (for he would be a widower by that time, as a matter of course) and was to give him as a wife one of the damsels of the empress, the heiress of some rich and grand state on the mainland, having nothing to do with islands of any sort, for he did not care for them now. All this Sancho delivered with so much composure—wiping his nose from time to time—and with so little common-sense that his two hearers were again filled with wonder at the force of Don Quixote's madness that could run away with this poor man's reason. They did not care to take the trouble of disabusing him of his error, as they considered that since it did not in any way hurt his conscience it would be better to leave him in it, and they would have all the more amusement in listening to his simplicities; and so they bade him pray to God for his lord's health, as it was a very likely and a very feasible thing for him in course of time to come to be an emperor, as he said, or at least an archbishop or some other dignitary of equal rank. To which Sancho made answer:

"If fortune, sirs, should bring things about in such a way that my master should have a mind, instead of being an emperor, to be an archbishop, I should like to know what archbishops-errant commonly give their squires?"

"They commonly give them," said the curate, "some simple benefice or cure, or some place as sacristan which brings them a good fixed income, not counting the altar fees, which may be reckoned at as much more."

"But for that," said Sancho, "the squire must be unmarried, and must know, at any rate, how to help at mass, and if that be so, woe is me, for I am married already and I don't know the first letter of the A B C. What will become of me if my master takes a fancy to become an archbishop and not an emperor, as is usual and customary with knights-errant? "

" Be not uneasy, friend Sancho," said the barber, " for we will entreat your master, and advise him, even urging it upon him as a case of conscience, to become an emperor and not an archbishop, because it will be easier for him as he is more valiant than lettered."

" So I have thought," said Sancho; "though I can tell you he is fit for anything: what I mean to do for my part is to pray to our Lord to place him where it may be best for him, and where he may be able to bestow most favors upon me."

" You speak like a man of sense," said the curate, " and you will be acting like a good Christian; but what must now be done is to take steps to coax your master out of that useless penance you say he is performing; and we had best turn into this inn to consider what plan to adopt, and also to dine, for it is now time."

Sancho said they might go in, but that he would wait there outside, and that he would tell them afterwards the reason why he was unwilling, and why it did not suit him to enter it; but he begged them to bring him out something to eat, and to let it be hot, and also to bring barley for Rocinante. They left him and went in, and presently the barber brought him out something to eat. By-and-by, after they had between them carefully thought over what they should do to carry out their object, the curate hit upon an idea very well adapted to humor Don Quixote, and effect their purpose; and his notion, which he explained to the barber, was that he himself should assume the disguise of a wandering damsel, while the other should try as best he could to pass for a squire, and that they should thus proceed to where Don Quixote was, and he, pretending to be an aggrieved and distressed damsel, should ask a favor of him, which as a valiant knight-errant he could not refuse to grant; and the favor he meant to ask him was that he should accompany her whither she would conduct him, in order to redress a wrong which a wicked knight had done her, while at the same time she should entreat him not to require her to remove her mask, nor ask her any question touching her circumstances until he had righted her with the wicked knight. And he had no doubt that Don Quixote would comply with any request made in these terms, and that in this way they might remove him and take him to his own village, where they would endeavor to find out if his extraordinary madness admitted of any kind of remedy.

CHAPTER XX

THE curate's plan did not seem a bad one to the barber, but on the contrary so good that they immediately set about putting it in execution. They begged a petticoat and hood of the landlady, leaving her in pledge a new cassock of the curate's; and the barber made a beard out of a gray or red ox-tail in which the landlord used to stick his comb. The landlady asked them what they wanted these things for, and the curate told her in a few words about the madness of Don Quixote, and how this disguise was intended to get him away from the mountain where he then was. The landlord and landlady immediately came to the conclusion that the madman was their guest, the balsam man and master of the blanketed squire, and they told the curate all that had passed between him and them, not omitting what Sancho had been so silent about. Finally the landlady dressed up the curate in a style that left nothing to be desired; she put on him a cloth petticoat with black velvet stripes a palm broad, all slashed, and a bodice of green velvet set off by a binding of white satin, which as well as the petticoat must have been made in the time of king Wamba. The curate would not let them cover him with the hood, but put on his head a little quilted linen cap which he used for a night-cap, and bound his forehead with a strip of black silk, while with another he made a

mask with which he concealed his beard and face very well.
He then put on his hat, which was broad enough to serve
him for an umbrella, and enveloping himself in his cloak
seated himself woman-fashion on his mule, while the barber mounted his with a beard down to the waist of mingled
red and white, for it was, as has been said, the tail of a
red ox. They took leave of all, and of the good Maritornes, who, sinner as she was, promised to pray a rosary
of prayers that God might grant them success in such an
arduous and Christian undertaking as that they had in hand.
But hardly had he sallied forth from the inn when it struck
the curate that he was doing wrong in rigging himself
out in that fashion, as it was an indecorous thing for a
priest to dress himself that way even though much might
depend upon it; and saying so to the barber he begged him
to change dresses, as it was fitter he should be the distressed damsel, while he himself would play the squire's
part, which would be less derogatory to his dignity; otherwise he was resolved to have nothing more to do with the
matter, and let the devil take Don Quixote. Just at this
moment Sancho came up, and on seeing the pair in such
a costume he was unable to restrain his laughter; the barber, however, agreed to do as the curate wished, and, al-
tering their plan, the curate went on to instruct him how
to play his part and what to say to Don Quixote to induce
and compel him to come with them and give up his fancy
for the place he had chosen for his idle penance. The
barber told him he could manage it properly without any
instruction, and as he did not care to dress himself up
until they were near where Don Quixote was, he folded
up the garments, and the curate adjusted his beard, and
they set out under the guidance of Sancho Panza.

The next day they reached the place where Sancho had
laid the broom-branches as marks to direct him to where
he had left his master, and recognizing it he told them that
here was the entrance, and that they would do well to dress
themselves, if that was required to deliver his master; for
they had already told him that going in this guise and

dressing in this way were of the highest importance in order to rescue his master from the pernicious life he had adopted; and they charged him strictly not to tell his master who they were, or that he knew them, and should he ask, as ask he would, if he had given the letter to Dulcinea, to say he had, and that, as she did not know how to read, she had given an answer by word of mouth, saying that she commanded him, on pain of her displeasure, to come and see her at once; and it was a very important matter for himself, because in this way and with what they meant to say to him they felt sure of bringing him back to a better mode of life and inducing him to take immediate steps to become an emperor or monarch, for there was no fear of his becoming an archbishop. All this Sancho listened to and fixed it well in his memory, and thanked them heartily for intending to recommend his master to be an emperor instead of an archbishop, for he felt sure that in the way of bestowing rewards on their squires emperors could do more than archbishops-errant. He said, too, that it would be as well for him to go on before them to find him, and give him his lady's answer; for that perhaps might be enough to bring him away from the place without putting them to all this trouble. They approved of what Sancho proposed, and resolved to wait for him until he brought back word of having found his master.

Sancho pushed into the glens of the *sierra,* leaving them in one through which there flowed a little gentle rivulet, and where the rocks and trees afforded a cool and grateful shade. It was an August day with all the heat of one, and the heat in those parts is intense, and the hour was three in the afternoon, all which made the spot the more inviting and tempted them to wait there for Sancho's return, which they did.

They were reposing, then, in the shade, when a voice unaccompanied by the notes of any instrument, but sweet and pleasing in its tone, reached their ears, at which they were not a little astonished, as the place did not seem to them likely quarters for one who sang so well; for though it is often said that shepherds of rare voice are to be found in the woods and fields, this is rather a flight of the poet's fancy than the truth. . . .

The hour, the summer season, the solitary place, the voice and skill of the singer, all contributed to the wonder and delight of the two listeners, who remained still waiting to hear something more; finding, however, that the silence continued some little time, they resolved to go in search of the musician who sang with so fine a voice; but just as they were about to do so they were checked by the same voice. . . .

The song ended with a deep sigh, and again the listeners remained waiting attentively for the singer to resume; but perceiving that the music had now turned to sobs and heart-rending moans they determined to find out who the unhappy being could be whose voice was as rare as his sighs were piteous, and they had not proceeded far when on turning the corner of a rock they discovered a man of wild aspect. He, showing no astonishment when he saw them, stood still with his head bent down upon his breast like one in deep thought, without raising his eyes to look at them after the first glance when they suddenly came upon him. The curate, being a man of good address, approached him and in a few sensible words entreated and urged him to quit a life of such misery, lest he should end it there, which would be the greatest of all misfortunes. The stranger, seeing them dressed in a fashion so unusual among the frequenters of those wlids, could not help showing some surprise; so he replied to them thus:

"I see plainly, sirs, whoever you may be, that Heaven, whose care it is to succor the good, and even the wicked very often, here, in this remote spot, cut off from human intercourse, sends me, though I deserve it not, those who seek to draw me away from this to some better retreat, showing me by many and forcible arguments how unreasonably I act in leading the life I do; but as they know not what I know, that if I escape from this evil I shall fall into another still greater, perhaps they will set me down as a weak-minded man, or, what is worse, one devoid of reason; nor would it be any wonder, for I myself can perceive that the effect of the recollection of my misfortunes is so great and works so powerfully to my ruin, that in spite of myself I become at times like a stone, without feeling or consciousness; and I come to feel the truth of it when they tell me and show me proofs of the things I have done when the terrible fit overmasters me; and all I can do is bewail my lot in vain, and idly curse my destiny, and plead for my madness by telling how it was caused, to any that care to hear it; for no reasonable beings on learning the cause will wonder at the effects; and if they cannot help me at least they will not blame me, and the repugnance they feel at my wild ways will turn into pity for my woes. If it be, sirs, that you are here with the same design as others have come with, before you proceed with your wise arguments, I entreat you to hear the story of my countless misfortunes, for perhaps when you have heard it you will spare yourselves the trouble you would take in offering consolation to grief that is beyond the reach of it."

As they, both of them, desired nothing more than to hear from his own lips the cause of his suffering, they entreated him to tell it, promising not to do anything for his relief or comfort that he did not wish. . . .

[" My name is Cardenio, my family one of the noblest in Andalusia. In that same country lived Luscinda, a damsel as noble and as rich as I, whom I loved, worshiped, and adored from my earliest years. But in my youth my father sent me to serve Duke Ricardo, whose son, Don Fernando, became my closest friend. To him I extolled the beauty of Luscinda, till he, under pretense of buying horses, came with me to my own city. He too fell in love with Luscinda. Finding my presence an obstacle to his treacherous design, he sent me to his elder brother for money. Luscinda warned me by letter that Don Fernando had secured her father's consent to a marriage. Hastening back, I arrived in time to see Luscinda faint at the ceremony. Half-mad with jealousy and anger at

her falsity, I fled to the wild passes of these mountains,
resolved to end here the life I hated as if it were my
mortal enemy."]

Just as the curate was going to offer consolation to
Cardenio, he was interrupted by a voice that fell upon
his ear saying in plaintive tones:

"O God! is it possible I have found a place that may
serve as a secret grave for the weary load of this body
that I support so unwillingly? If the solitude these mountains promise deceive me not, it is so; ah! woe is me! how
much more grateful to my mind will be the society of
these rocks and brakes that permit me to complain of
my misfortune to Heaven, than that of any human being,
for there is none on earth to look to for counsel in doubt,
comfort in sorrow, or relief in distress!"

All this was heard distinctly by the curate and those
with him, and as it seemed to them to be uttered close
by, as indeed it was, they got up to look for the speaker,
and before they had gone twenty paces they discovered
behind a rock, seated at the foot of an ash tree, a youth
in the dress of a peasant, whose face they were unable
at the moment to see, as he was leaning forward, bathing
his feet in the brook that flowed past. . . . As soon
as he had wiped them with a towel, he raised his face,
and those who were watching him had an opportunity of
seeing a beauty so exquisite that Cardenio said to the
curate in a whisper:

"As this is not Luscinda, it is no human creature, but
a divine being."

The youth then took off the cap, and shaking his head
from side to side there broke loose and spread out a mass
of hair that the beams of the sun might have envied. . . .
To learn who she was, the three beholders resolved to show
themselves, and at the stir they made in getting upon their
feet the fair damsel raised her head, and parting her hair
from before her eyes with both hands, she looked to see
who had made the noise, and the instant she perceived
them she started to her feet, and without waiting to put

on her shoes or gather up her hair, hastily snatched up a bundle as though of clothes that she had beside her, and, scared and alarmed, endeavored to take flight; but before she had gone six paces she fell to the ground, her delicate feet being unable to bear the roughness of the stones; seeing which, the three hastened towards her, and the curate addressing her first said:

"Stay, señora, whoever you may be, for those whom you see here only desire to be of service to you; you have no need to attempt a flight so heedless, for neither can your feet bear it, nor we allow it."

Taken by surprise and bewildered, she made no reply to these words. They, however, came towards her, and the curate taking her hand went on to say:

"What your dress would hide, señora, is made known to us by your hair; a clear proof that it can be no trifling cause that has disguised your beauty in a garb so unworthy of it, and sent it into solitudes like these where we have had the good fortune to find you, if not to relieve your distress, at least to offer you comfort; for no distress, as long as life lasts, can be so oppressive or reach such a height as to make the sufferer refuse to listen to comfort offered with good intention. And so, señora, or señor, or whatever you prefer to be, dismiss the fears that our appearance has caused you and make us acquainted with your good or evil fortunes, for from all of us together, or from each one of us, you will receive sympathy in your trouble."

While the curate was speaking, the disguised damsel stood as if spell-bound, looking at them without opening her lips or uttering a word, just like a village rustic to whom something strange that he has never seen before has been suddenly shown; but on the curate addressing some further words to the same effect to her, sighing deeply, she broke silence and said:

"Since the solitude of these mountains has been unable to conceal me, and the escape of my dishevelled tresses will not allow my tongue to deal in falsehoods, it would be idle for me now to make any further pretense of what, if you were to believe me, you would believe more out of courtesy than for any other reason. This being so, I say I thank you, sirs, for the offer you have made me, which places me under the obligation of complying with the request you have made of me; though I fear the account I shall give you of my misfortunes will excite in you as much concern as compassion, for you will be unable to suggest anything to remedy them or any consolation to alleviate them. However, that my honor may not be left a matter of doubt in your minds, now that you have discovered me to be a woman, and see that I am young, alone, and in this dress, things that taken together or separately would be enough to destroy my good name, I feel bound to tell what I would willingly keep secret if I could."

All this she who was now seen to be a lovely woman delivered without any hesitation, with so much ease and in so sweet a voice that they were not less charmed by her intelligence than by her beauty, and as they again repeated their offers and entreaties to her to fulfill her promise, she without further pressing . . . told a piteous story of her betrayal by Don Fernando, of her following him to the city only to learn of his marriage with Luscinda, and of her wanderings in the forest.

CHAPTER XXI

WHICH TREATS OF THE DROLL DEVICE AND METHOD
ADOPTED TO EXTRICATE OUR LOVE-STRICKEN KNIGHT
FROM THE SEVERE PENANCE HE HAD IMPOSED UPON
HIMSELF

WHILE she was speaking, the color that overspread
her face showed plainly the pain and shame she
was suffering at heart. In theirs the listeners felt as much
pity as wonder at her misfortunes; but as the curate was
just about to offer her some consolation and advice, Cardenio forestalled him, saying:

"So, then, señora, you are the fair Dorothea, the only
daughter of the rich Clenardo?"

Dorothea was astonished at hearing her father's name,
and at the miserable appearance of him who mentioned it,
for it has been already said how wretchedly clad Cardenio
was; so she said to him:

"And who may you be, brother, who seem to know
my father's name so well? For so far, if I remember
rightly, I have not mentioned it in the whole story of
my misfortunes."

"I am that unhappy being, señora," replied Cardenio,
"whom, as you have said, Luscinda declared to be her
husband; I am the unfortunate Cardenio, whom the
wrong-doing of him who has brought you to your present
condition has reduced to the state you see me in, bare,
ragged, bereft of all human comfort, and, what is worse,
of reason, for I only possess it when Heaven is pleased for

178

some short space to restore it to me. . . . Fate has preserved me for the good fortune I have had in meeting you; for if that which you have just told us be true, as I believe it to be, it may be that Heaven has yet in store for both of us a happier termination to our misfortunes than we look for; because, seeing that Luscinda cannot marry Don Fernando, being mine, and that Don Fernando cannot marry her, as he is yours, we may reasonably hope that Heaven will restore to us what is ours, as it is still in existence and not yet alienated or destroyed. And as we have this consolation springing from no very visionary hope or wild fancy, I entreat you, señora, to form new resolutions in your better mind, as I mean to do in mine, preparing yourself to look forward to happier fortunes; for I swear to you by the faith of a gentleman and a Christian not to desert you until I see you in possession of Don Fernando, and if I cannot by words induce him to recognize his obligation to you, in that case to avail myself of the right which my rank as a gentleman gives me, and with just cause challenge him on account of the injury he has done you, not regarding my own wrongs, which I shall leave to Heaven to avenge, while I on earth devote myself to yours." . . .

At this moment they heard a shout, and recognized it as coming from Sancho Panza, who, not finding them where he had left them, was calling aloud to them. They went to meet him, and in answer to their inquires about Don Quixote, he told them how he had found him stripped to his shirt, lank, yellow, half dead with hunger, and sighing for his lady Dulcinea; and although he had told him that she commanded him to quit that place and come to El Toboso, where she was expecting him, he had answered that he was determined not to appear in the presence of her beauty until he had done deeds to make him worthy of her favor; and if this went on, Sancho said, he ran the risk of not becoming an emperor as in duty bound, or even an archbishop, which was the least he could be; for which reason they ought to consider what

was to be done to get him away from there. The licentiate in reply told him not to be uneasy, for they would
fetch him away in spite of himself. He then told Cardenio and Dorothea what they had proposed to do to cure
Don Quixote, or at any rate take him home; upon which
Dorothea said that she could play the distressed damsel
better than the barber; especially as she had there the
dress in which to do it to the life, and that they might
trust to her acting the part in every particular requisite
for carrying out their scheme, for she had read a great
many books of chivalry, and knew exactly the style in
which afflicted damsels begged boons of knights-errant.

"In that case," said the curate, "there is nothing more
required than to set about it at once, for beyond a doubt
fortune is declaring itself in our favor, since it has so
unexpectedly begun to open a door for your relief, and
smoothed the way for us to our object."

Dorothea then took out of her pillow-case a complete
petticoat of some rich stuff, and a green mantle of some
other fine material, and a necklace and other ornaments
out of a little box, and with these in an instant she so
arrayed herself that she looked like a great and rich lady.
All this, and more, she said, she had taken from home in
case of need, but that until then she had had no occasion
to make use of it. They were all highly delighted with
her grace, air, and beauty, and declared Don Fernando to
be a man of very little taste when he rejected such charms.
But the one who admired her most was Sancho Panza, for
it seemed to him (what indeed was true) that in all the
days of his life he had never seen such a lovely creature;
and he asked the curate with great eagerness who this
bautiful lady was, and what she wanted in these out-of-
the-way quarters.

"This fair lady, brother Sancho," replied the curate,
"is no less a personage than the heiress in the direct male
line of the great kingdom of Micomicon, who has come
in search of your master to beg a boon of him, which is
that he redress a wrong or injury that a wicked giant has

done her; and from the fame as a good knight which your master has acquired far and wide, this princess has come from Guinea to seek him."

"A lucky seeking and a lucky finding!" said Sancho Panza at this; "especially if my master has the good fortune to redress that injury, and right that wrong, and kill that son of a bitch of a giant your worship speaks of; as kill him he will if he meets him, unless, indeed, he happens to be a phantom; for my master has no power at all against phantoms. But one thing among others I would beg of you, señor licentiate, which is, that, to prevent my master taking a fancy to be an archbishop, for that is what I'm afraid of, your worship would recommend him to marry this princess at once; for in this way he will be disabled from taking archbishop's orders, and will easily come into his empire, and I to the end of my desires; I have been thinking over the matter carefully, and by what I can make out I find it will not do for me that my master should become an archbishop, because I am no good for the Church, as I am married; and for me now, having as I have a wife and children, to set about obtaining dispensations to enable me to hold a place of profit under the Church, would be endless work; so that, señor, it all turns on my master marrying this lady at once—for as yet I do not know her grace, and so I cannot call her by her name."

"She is called the Princess Micomicona," said the curate; "for as her kingdom is Micomicon, it is clear that must be her name."

"There's no doubt of that," replied Sancho, "for I have known many to take their name and title from the place where they were born and call themselves Pedro of Alcala, Juan of Úbeda, and Diego of Valladolid; and it may be that over there in Guinea queens have the same way of taking the names of their kingdoms."

"So it may," said the curate; "and as for your master's marrying, I will do all in my power towards it:" with which Sancho was as much pleased as the curate was amazed at his simplicity and at seeing what a hold the absurdities of his master had taken of his fancy, for he had evidently persuaded himself that he was going to be an emperor.

By this time Dorothea had seated herself upon the curate's mule, and the barber had fitted the ox-tail beard to his face, and they now told Sancho to conduct them to where Don Quixote was, warning him not to say that he knew either the licentiate or the barber, as his master's becoming an emperor entirely depended on his not recognizing them; neither the curate nor Cardenio, however, thought fit to go with them; Cardenio lest he should remind Don Quixote of a quarrel he had with him, and the curate as there was no necessity for his presence just yet, so they allowed the others to go on before them, while they themselves followed slowly on foot. The curate did not forget to instruct Dorothea how to act, but she said they might make their minds easy, as everything would be done exactly as the books of chivalry required and described.

They had gone about three-quarters of a league when they discovered Don Quixote in a wilderness of rocks, by this time clothed, but without his armor; and as soon as Dorothea saw him and was told by Sancho that that was Don Quixote, she whipped her palfrey, the well-bearded barber following her, and on coming up to him her squire sprang from his mule and came forward to receive her in his arms, and she dismounting with great ease of manner advanced to kneel before the feet of Don Quixote; and though he strove to raise her up, she without rising addressed him in this fashion, " From this spot I will not rise, O valiant and doughty knight, until your goodness and courtesy grant me a boon, which will redound to the honor and renown of your person and render a service to the most disconsolate and afflicted damsel the sun has seen; and if the might of your strong arm corresponds to the repute of your immortal fame, you are bound to aid the helpless being who, led by the savor of your renowned name, hath come from far distant lands to seek your aid in her misfortunes."

SHE ADVANCED TO KNEEL BEFORE THE FEET OF DON QUIXOTE
(From the tercentenary edition of "Don Quixote," published in Madrid
in 1905)

" I will not answer a word, beauteous lady," replied Don Quixote, "nor will I listen to anything further concerning you, until you rise from the earth."

" I will not rise, señor," answered the afflicted damsel, "unless of your courtesy the boon I ask is first granted me."

" I grant and accord it," said Don Quixote, "provided without detriment or prejudice to my king, my country, or her who holds the key of my heart and freedom, it may be complied with."

" It will not be to the detriment or prejudice of any of them, my worthy lord," said the afflicted damsel; and here Sancho Panza drew close to his master's ear and said to him very softly, " Your worship may very safely grant the boon she asks; it's nothing at all; only to kill a big giant; and she who asks it is the exalted princess Micomicona, queen of the great kingdom of Micomicon of Ethiopia."

" Let her be who she may," replied Don Quixote, "I will do what is my bounden duty, and what my conscience bids me, in conformity with what I have professed;" and turning to the damsel he said, " Let your great beauty rise, for I grant the boon which you would ask of me."

" Then what I ask," said the damsel, " is that your magnanimous person accompany me at once whither I will conduct you, and that you promise not to engage in any other adventure or quest until you have avenged me of a traitor who, against all human and divine law, has usurped my kingdom."

" I repeat that I grant it," replied Don Quixote; "and so, lady, you may from this day forth lay aside the melancholy that distresses you, and let your failing hopes gather new life and strength, for with the help of God and of my arm you will soon see yourself restored to your kingdom, and seated upon the throne of your ancient and mighty realm, notwithstanding and despite of the felons who would gainsay it; and now hands to the work, for, as they say, in delay there is apt to be danger."

The distressed damsel strove with much pertinacity to

kiss his hands; but Don Quixote, who was in all things a polished and courteous knight, would by no means allow it, but made her rise and embraced her with great courtesy and politeness, and ordered Sancho to look to Rocinante's girths, and to arm him without a moment's delay. Sancho took down the armor, which was hung up on a tree like a trophy, and having seen to the girths armed his master in a trice, who as soon as he found himself in his armor exclaimed:

"Let us be gone in the name of God to bring aid to this great lady."

The barber was all this time on his knees at great pains to hide his laughter and not let his beard fall, for had it fallen maybe their fine scheme would have come to nothing; but now seeing the boon granted, and the promptitude with which Don Quixote prepared to set out in compliance with it, he rose and took his lady's hand, and between them they placed her upon the mule. Don Quixote then mounted Rocinante, and the barber settled himself on his beast, Sancho being left to go on foot, which made him feel anew the loss of his Dapple, finding the want of him now. But he bore all with cheerfulness, being persuaded that his master had now fairly started and was just on the point of becoming an emperor; for he felt no doubt at all that he would marry this princess, and be king of Micomicon at least. The only thing that troubled him was the reflection that this kingdom was in the land of the blacks, and that the people they would give him for vassals would all be black; but for this he soon found a remedy in his fancy, and said he to himself:

"What is it to me if my vassals are blacks? What more have I to do than make a cargo of them and carry them to Spain, where I can sell them and get ready money for them, and with it buy some title or some office in which to live at ease all the days of my life? Not unless you go to sleep and haven't the wit or skill to turn things to account and sell three, six, or ten thousand vassals while you would be talking about it! By God I will stir them up, big and little, or as best I can, and let them be ever so black I'll turn them into white or yellow. Come, come, what a fool I am!" And so he jogged on, so occupied with his thoughts and easy in his mind that he forgot all about the hardship of traveling on foot.

Cardenio and the curate were watching all this from among some bushes, not knowing how to join company with the others; but the curate, who was very fertile in devices, soon hit upon a way of effecting their purpose, and with a pair of scissors that he had in a case he quickly cut off Cardenio's beard, and putting on him a gray jerkin of his own he gave him a black cloak, leaving himself in his breeches and doublet, while Cardenio's appearance was so different from what it had been that he would not have known himself had he seen himself in a mirror. Having effected this, although the others had gone on ahead while they were disguising themselves, they easily came out on the high road before them, for the brambles and awkward places they encountered did not allow those on horseback to go as fast as those on foot. They then posted themselves on the level ground at the outlet of the *sierra*, and as soon as Don Quixote and his companions emerged from it the curate began to examine him very deliberately, as though he were striving to recognize him, and after having stared at him for some time he hastened towards him with open arms exclaiming:

"A happy meeting with the mirror of chivalry, my worthy compatriot Don Quixote of La Mancha, the flower and cream of high breeding, the protection and relief of the distressed, the quintessence of knights-errant!"

And so saying he clasped in his arms the knee of Don Quixote's left leg. He, astonished at the stranger's words and behavior, looked at him attentively, and at length recognized him, very much surprised to see him there, and made great efforts to dismount. This, however, the curate would not allow, on which Don Quixote said:

"Permit me, señor licentiate, for it is not fitting that I

should be on horseback and so reverend a person as your worship on foot."

" On no account will I allow it," said the curate; " your mightiness must remain on horseback, for it is on horseback you achieve the greatest deeds and adventures that have been beheld in our age; as for me, an unworthy priest, it will serve me well enough to mount on the haunches of one of the mules of these gentlefolk who accompany your worship, if they have no objection, and I will fancy I am mounted on the steed Pegasus, or on the zebra or charger that bore the famous Moor, Muzaraque, who to this day lies enchanted in the great hill of Zulema, a little distance from the great Complutum."

" Nor even that will I consent to, señor licentiate," answered Don Quixote, " and I know it will be the good pleasure of my lady the princess, out of love for me, to order her squire to give up the saddle of his mule to your worship, and he can sit behind if the beast will bear it."

" It will, I am sure," said the princess, " and I am sure, too, that I need not order my squire, for he is too courteous and too good a Christian to allow a churchman to go on foot when he might be mounted."

" That he is," said the barber, and at once alighting, he offered his saddle to the curate, who accepted it without much entreaty; but unfortunately as the barber was mounting behind, the mule, being as it happened a hired one, which is the same thing as saying ill-conditioned, lifted its hind hoofs and let fly a couple of kicks in the air, which would have made Master Nicholas wish his expedition in quest of Don Quixote at the devil had they caught him on the breast or head. As it was, they so took him by surprise that he came to the ground, giving so little heed to his beard that it fell off, and all he could do when he found himself without it was to cover his face hastily with both his hands and moan that his teeth were knocked out. Don Quixote when he saw all that bundle of beard detached, without jaws or blood, from the face of the fallen squire, exclaimed:

"By the living God, but this is a great miracle! it has knocked off and plucked away the beard from his face as if it had been shaved off designedly."

The curate, seeing the danger of discovery that threatened his scheme, at once pounced upon the beard and hastened with it to where Master Nicholas lay, still uttering moans, and drawing his head to his breast had it on in an instant, muttering over him some words which he said were a certain special charm for sticking on beards, as they would see; and as soon as he had it fixed he left him, and he squire appeared well bearded and whole as before, whereat Don Quixote was beyond measure astonished, and begged the curate to teach him that charm when he had an opportunity, as he was persuaded its virtue must extend beyond the sticking on of beards, for it was clear that where the beard had been stripped off the flesh must have remained torn and lacerated, and when it could heal all that it must be good for more than beards.

"And so it is," said the curate, and he promised to teach it to him on the first opportunity. They then agreed that for the present the curate should mount, and that the three should ride by turns until they reached the inn, which might be about six leagues from where they were.

Three then being mounted, that is to say, Don Quixote, the princess, and the curate, and three on foot, Cardenio, the barber and Sancho Panza, Don Quixote said to the damsel, "Let your highness, lady, lead on whithersoever is most pleasing to you;" but before she could answer the licentiate said, "Towards what kingdom would your ladyship direct our course? Is it perchance towards that of Micomicon? It must be, or else I know little about kingdoms."

She, being ready on all points, understood that she was to answer "Yes," so she said, "Yes, señor, my way lies towards that kingdom."

"In that case," said the curate, "we must pass right through my village, and there your worship will take the road to Cartagena, where you will be able to embark, fortune favoring; and if the wind be fair and the sea smooth and tranquil, in somewhat less than nine years you may come in sight of the great lake Meona, I mean Meotides, which is little more than a hundred day's journey this side of your highness's kingdom."

"Your worship is mistaken, señor," said she; "for it is not two years since I set out from it, and though I never had good weather, nevertheless I am here to behold what I so longed for, and that is my lord Don Quixote of La Mancha, whose fame came to my ears as soon as I set foot in Spain and impelled me to go in search of him, to commend myself to his courtesy, and intrust the justice of my cause to the might of his invincible arm."

"Enough; no more praise," said Don Quixote at this, "for I hate flattery; and though this may not be so, still language of the kind is offensive to my chaste ears. I will only say, señora, that whether it has might or not, that which it may or may not have shall be devoted to your service even to death; and now, leaving this to its proper season, I would ask the señor licentiate to tell me what it is that has brought him into these parts, alone, unattended, and so lightly clad that I am filled with amazement."

"I will answer that briefly," replied the curate; "you must know then, Señor Don Quixote, that Master Nicholas, our friend and barber, and I were going to Seville to receive some money that a relative of mine who went to the Indies many years ago had sent me, and not such a small sum but that it was over sixty thousand pieces of eight, full weight, which is something; and passing by this place yesterday we were attacked by four footpads, who stripped us even to our beards, and them they stripped off so that the barber found it necessary to put on a false one, and even this young man here"—pointing to Cardenio—"they completely transformed. But the best of it is, the story goes in the neighborhood that those who attacked us belong to a number of galley slaves who, they say, were set free almost on the very same spot by a man of such valor that, in spite of the commissary and of the guards, he released the whole of them; and beyond all doubt he must have been out of his senses, or he must be as great a scoundrel as they, or some man without heart or conscience to let the wolf loose among the sheep, the fox among the hens, the fly among the honey. He has defrauded justice, and opposed his king and lawful master, for he opposed his just commands; he has, I say, robbed the galleys of their feet, stirred up the Holy Brotherhood which for many years past has been quiet, and, lastly, has done a deed by which his soul may be lost without any gain to his body."

Sancho had told the curate and the barber of the adventure of the galley slaves, which, so much to his glory, his master had achieved, and hence the curate in alluding to it made the most of it to see what would be said or done by Don Quixote; who changed color at every word, not daring to say that it was he who had been the liberator of those worthy people.

"These, then," said the curate, "were they who robbed us; and God in his mercy pardon him who would not let them go to the punishment they deserved."

CHAPTER XXII

WHICH TREATS OF THE ADDRESS DISPLAYED BY THE FAIR
DOROTHEA, WITH OTHER MATTERS PLEASANT AND AMUS-
ING

THE curate had hardly ceased speaking, when Sancho
said:

"In faith, señor licentiate, he who did that deed was my
master; and it was not for want of my telling him beforehand and warning him to mind what he was about, and
that it was a sin to set them at liberty, as they were all
on the march there because they were special scoun-
drels."

"Blockhead!" said Don Quixote at this, "it is no business or concern of knights-errant to inquire whether any
persons in affliction, in chains, or oppressed that they may
meet on the high roads go that way and suffer as they do
because of their faults or because of their misfortunes.
It only concerns them to aid them as persons in need of
help, having regard to their sufferings and not to their
rascalities. I encountered a chaplet or string of miserable
and unfortunate people, and did for them what my sense
of duty demands of me, and as for the rest be that as it
may; and whoever takes objection to it, saving the sacred
dignity of the señor licentiate and his honored person, I
say he knows little about chivalry and lies like a whoreson
villian, and this I will give him to know to the fullest extent with my sword;" and so saying he settled himself in
his stirrups and pressed down his morion; for the barber's

basin, which according to him was Mambrino's helmet, he carried hanging at the saddle-bow until he could repair the damage done to it by the galley slaves.

Dorothea, who was shrewd and sprightly, and by this time thoroughly understood Don Quixote's crazy turn, and that all except Sancho Panza were making game of him, not to be behind the rest said to him, on observing his irritation:

" Sir Knight, remember the boon you have promised me, and that in accordance with it you must not engage in any other adventure, be it ever so pressing; calm yourself, for if the licentiate had known that the galley slaves had been set free by that unconquered arm he would have stopped his mouth thrice over, or even bitten his tongue three times before he would have said a word that tended towards disrespect of your worship."

" That I swear heartily," said the curate, " and I would have even plucked off a mustache."

" I will hold my peace, señora," said Don Quixote, " and I will curb the natural anger that had arisen in my breast, and will proceed in peace and quietness until I have fulfilled my promise; but in return for this consideration I entreat you to tell me, if you have no objection to do so, what is the nature of your trouble, and how many, who, and what are the persons of whom I am to require due satisfaction, and on whom I am to take vengeance on your behalf?"

" That I will do with all my heart," replied Dorothea, " if it will not be wearisome to you to hear of miseries and misfortunes."

" It will not be wearisome, señora," said Don Quixote; to which Dorothea replied, " Well, if that be so, give me your attention." As soon as she said this, Cardenio and the barber drew close to her side, eager to hear what sort of story the quick-witted Dorothea would invent for herself; and Sancho did the same, for he was as much taken in by her as his master; and she having settled herself comfortably in the saddle, and with the help of coughing

and other preliminaries taken time to think, began with
great sprightliness of manner in this fashion.

"First of all, I would have you know, sirs, that my name
is——" and here she stopped for a moment, for she forgot
the name the curate had given her; but he came to her relief, seeing what her difficulty was, and said:

"It is no wonder, señora, that your highness should be
confused and embarrassed in telling the tale of your misfortunes; for such afflictions often have the effect of depriving the sufferers of memory, so that they do not even
remember their own names, as is the case now with your
ladyship, who has forgotten that she is called the Princess
Micomicona, lawful heiress of the great kingdom of Micomicon; and with this cue your highness may now recall
to your sorrowful recollection all you may wish to tell us."

"That is the truth," said the damsel; "but I think from
this on I shall have no need of any prompting, and I shall
bring my true story safe into port, and here it is. The
king my father, who was called Tinacrio the Sapient, was
very learned in what they call magic arts, and became
aware by his craft that my mother, who was called Queen
Jaramilla, was to die before he did, and that soon after
he too was to depart this life, and I was to be left an orphan
without father or mother. But all this, he declared, did
not so much grieve or distress him as his certain knowledge
that a prodigious giant, the lord of a great island close to
our kingdom, Pandafilando of the Scowl by name—for it
is averred that, though his eyes are properly placed and
straight, he always looks askew as if he squinted, and this
he does out of malignity, to strike fear and terror into
those he looks at—that he knew, I say, that this giant on
becoming aware of my orphan condition would overrun my
kingdom with a mighty force and strip me of all, not leaving me even a small village to shelter me; but that I could
avoid all this ruin and misfortune if I were willing to
marry him; however, as far as he could see, he never
expected that I would consent to a marriage so unequal;
and he said no more than the truth in this, for it has never

entered my mind to marry that giant, or any other, let him
be ever so great or enormous. My father said, too, that
when he was dead, and I saw Pandafilando about to in-
vade my kingdom, I was not to wait an attendant to defend myself, for that would be destructive to me, but that
I should leave the kingdom entirely open to him if I wished
to avoid the death and total destruction of my good and
loyal vassals, for there would be no possibility of defending
myself against the giant's devilish power; and that I should
at once with some of my followers set out for Spain,
where I should obtain relief in my distress on finding a
certain knight-errant whose fame by that time would extend over the whole kingdom, and who would be called,
if I remember rightly, Don Azote or Don Gigote."

" 'Don Quixote,' he must have said, señora," observed
Sancho at this, " otherwise called the Knight of the Rueful
Countenance."

" That is it," said Dorothea; " he said, moreover, that
he would be tall of stature and lank featured; and that
on his right side under the left shoulder, or thereabouts, he
would have a gray mole with hairs like bristles."

On hearing this, Don Quixote said to his squire, " Here,
Sancho my son, bear a hand and help me to strip, for I
want to see if I am the knight that sage king foretold."

" What does your worship want to strip for? " said Dorothea.

" To see if I have that mole your father spoke of,"
answered Don Quixote.

" There is no occasion to strip," said Sancho; " for I
know your worship has just such a mole on the middle
of your backbone, which is the mark of a strong man."

" That is enough," said Dorothea, " for with friends we
must not look too closely into trifles; and whether it be
on the shoulder or on the backbone matters little; it is
enough if there is a mole, be it where it may, for it is
all the same flesh; no doubt my good father hit the truth
in every particular, and I have made a lucky hit in commending myself to Don Quixote; for he is the one my

father spoke of, as the features of his countenance correspond with those assigned to this knight by that wide fame he has acquired not only in Spain but in all La Mancha; for I had scarcely landed at Osuna when I heard such accounts of his achievements, that at once my heart told me he was the very one I had come in search of."

"But how did you land at Osuna, señora," asked Don Quixote, "when it is not a seaport?"

But before Dorothea could reply the curate anticipated her, saying, "The princess meant to say that after she had landed at Malaga the first place where she heard of your worship was Osuna."

"That is what I meant to say," said Dorothea.

"And that would be only natural," said the curate. "Will your majesty please proceed?"

"There is no more to add," said Dorothea, "save that in finding Don Quixote I have had such good fortune, that I already reckon and regard myself queen and mistress of my entire dominions, since of his courtesy and magnanimity he has granted me the boon of accompanying me whithersoever I may conduct him, which will be only to bring him face to face with Pandafilando of the Scowl, that he may slay him and restore me what has been unjustly usurped by him: for all this must come to pass satisfactorily since my good father Tinacrio the Sapient foretold it, who likewise left it declared in writing in Chaldee or Greek characters (for I cannot read them), that if this predicted knight, after having cut the giant's throat, should be disposed to marry me I was to offer myself at once without demur as his lawful wife, and yield him possession of my kingdom together with my person."

"What thinkest thou now, friend Sancho?" said Don Quixote at this. "Hearest thou that? Did I not tell thee so? See how we have already got a kingdom to govern and a queen to marry!"

"On my oath it is so," said Sancho; "and foul fortune to him who won't marry after slitting Señor Pandahilado's windpipe! And then, how ill-favored the queen is! I

wish the fleas in my bed were that sort!" and so saying
he cut a couple of capers in the air with every sign of extreme satisfaction, and then ran to seize the bridle of Dorothea's mule, and checking it fell on his knees before her,
begging her to give him her hand to kiss in token of his
acknowledgment of her as his queen and mistress. Which
of the by-standers could have helped laughing to see the
madness of the master and the simplicity of the servant?
Dorothea therefore gave her hand, and promised to make
him a great lord in her kingdom, when Heaven should be so
good as to permit her to recover and enjoy it, for which
Sancho returned thanks in words that set them all laughing again.

" This, sirs," continued Dorothea, " is my story; it only
remains to tell you that of all the attendants I took with me
from my kingdom I have none left except this well-bearded
squire, for all were drowned in a great tempest we encountered when in sight of port; and he and I came to land
on a couple of planks as if by a miracle; and indeed the
whole course of my life is a miracle and a mystery as
you may have observed; and if I have been over minute
in any respect or not as precise as I ought, let it be ac-
counted for by what the licentiate said at the beginning
of my tale, that constant and excessive troubles deprive
the sufferers of their memory."

" They shall not deprive me of mine, exalted and worthy
princess," said Don Quixote, " however great and unexampled those which I shall endure in your service may be;
and here I confirm anew the boon I have promised you,
and I swear to go with you to the end of the world until
I find myself in the presence of your fierce enemy, whose
haughty head I trust by the aid of God and of my arm
to cut off with the edge of this—I will not say good sword,
thanks to Gines de Pasamonte who carried away mine "—
(this he said between his teeth, and then continued), " and
when it has been cut off and you have been put in peaceful
possession of your realm it shall be left to your own decision to dispose of your person as may be most pleasing

to you; for so long as my memory is occupied, my will enslaved, and my understanding enthralled by her—I say no more—it is impossible for me for a moment to contemplate marriage, even with a Phœnix."

The last words of his master about not wanting to marry were so disagreeable to Sancho that raising his voice he exclaimed with great irritation:

" By my oath, Señor Don Quixote, you are not in your right senses; for how can your worship possibly object to marrying such an exalted princess as this? Do you think Fortune will offer you behind every stone such a piece of luck as is offered you now? Is my lady Dulcinea fairer, perchance? Not she; nor half as fair; and I will even go so far as to say she does not come up to the shoe of this one here. A poor chance I have of getting that county I am waiting for if your worship goes looking for dainties in the bottom of the sea. In the devil's name, marry, marry, and take this kingdom that comes to hand without any trouble, and when you are king make me a marquis or governor of a province, and for the rest let the devil take it all."

Don Quixote, when he heard such blasphemies uttered against his lady Dulcinea, could not endure it, and lifting his pike, without saying anything to Sancho or uttering a word, he gave him two such thwacks that he brought him to the ground; and had it not been that Dorothea cried out to him to spare him he would have no doubt taken his life on the spot.

"Do you think," he said to him after a pause, "you scurvy clown, that you are to be always interfering with me, and that you are to be always offending and I always pardoning? Don't fancy it, impious scoundrel, for that beyond a doubt thou art, since thou hast set thy tongue going against the peerless Dulcinea. Know you not, lout, vagabond, beggar, that were it not for the might which she infuses into my arm I should not have strength enough to kill a flea? Say, O scoffer with a viper's tongue, what think you has won this kingdom and cut off this giant's head and made you a marquis (for all this I count as already accomplished and decided), but the might of Dulcinea, employing my arm as the instrument of her achievements? She fights in me and conquers in me, and I live and breathe in her, and owe my life and being to her. O whoreson scoundrel, how ungrateful you are, you see yourself raised from the dust of the earth to be a titled lord, and the return you make for so great a benefit is to speak evil of her who has conferred it upon you!"

Sancho was not so stunned but that he heard all his master said, and rising with some degree of nimbleness he ran to place himself behind Dorothea's palfrey, and from that position he said to his master:

"Tell me, señor; if your worship is resolved not to marry this queen, now that we have got her here as if showered down from heaven, and afterwards you may go back to my lady Dulcinea; for there must have been kings in the world who kept mistresses. As to beauty, I have nothing to do with it; and if the truth is to be told, I like them both; though I have never seen the lady Dulcinea."

"How! never seen her, blasphemous traitor!" exclaimed Don Quixote; "hast thou not just now brought me a message from her?"

"I mean," said Sancho, "that I did not see her so much at my leisure that I could take particular notice of her beauty, or of her charms piecemeal; but taken in the lump I like her."

"Now I forgive thee," said Don Quixote; "and do thou forgive me the injury I have done thee; for our first impulses are not in our control."

"That I see," replied Sancho, "and with me the wish to speak is always the first impulse, and I cannot help saying, once at any rate, what I have on the tip of my tongue."

"For all that, Sancho," said Don Quixote, "take heed of what thou sayest, for the pitcher goes so often to the well—I need say no more to thee."

"Well, well," said Sancho, "God is in heaven, and sees

all tricks, and will judge who does most harm, I in speaking right, or your worship in doing it."

"That is enough," said Dorothea; "run, Sancho and kiss your lord's hand and beg his pardon, and henceforward be more circumspect with your praise and abuse; and say nothing in disparagement of that lady Toboso, of whom I know nothing save that I am her servant; and put your trust in God, for you will not fail to obtain some dignity so as to live like a prince."

Sancho advanced hanging his head and begged his master's hand, which Don Quixote with dignity presented to him, giving him his blessing as soon as he had kissed it; he then bade him go on ahead a little, as he had questions to ask him and matters of great importance to discuss with him. Sancho obeyed, and when the two had gone some distance in advance Don Quixote said to him:

"Since thy return I have had no opportunity or time to ask thee many particulars touching thy mission and the answer thou hast brought back, and now that chance has granted us the time and opportunity, deny me not the happiness thou canst give me by such good news."

"Let your worship ask what you will," answered Sancho, "for I shall find a way out of all as easily as I found a way in; but I implore you, señor, not to be so revengeful in future."

"Why dost thou say that, Sancho?" said Don Quixote.

"I say it," he returned, "because those blows just now were more because of the quarrel the devil stirred up between us both the other night, than for what I said against my lady Dulcinea, whom I love and reverence as I would a relic—though there is nothing of that about her—merely as something belonging to your worship."

"Say no more on that subject for thy life, Sancho," said Don Quixote, "for it is displeasing to me; I have already pardoned thee for that, and thou knowest the common saying, 'For a fresh sin a fresh penance.'"

While this was going on they saw coming along the road they were following a man mounted on an ass, who when he came close seemed to be a gypsy; but Sancho Panza, whose eyes and heart were there wherever he saw asses, no sooner beheld the man than he knew him to be Gines de Pasamonte; and by the thread of the gypsy he got at the ball, his ass, for it was, in fact, Dapple that carried Pasamonte, who to escape recognition and to sell the ass had disguised himself as a gypsy, being able to speak the gypsy language, and many more, as well as if they wese his own. Sancho saw him and recognized him, and the instant he did so he shouted to him:

"Ginesillo, you thief, give up my treasure, release my life, embarrass thyself not with my repose, quit my ass, leave my delight, be off, rip, get thee gone, thief, and give up what is not thine."

There was no necessity for so many words or objurgations, for at the first one Gines jumped down, and at a trot like racing speed made off and got clear of them all. Sancho hastened to his Dapple, and embracing him he said, " How hast thou fared, my blessing, Dapple of my eyes, my comrade? " all the while kissing him and caressing him as if he were a human being. The ass held his peace, and let himself be kissed and caressed by Sancho without answering a single word. They all came up and congratulated him on having found Dapple, Don Quixote especially, who told him that notwithstanding this he would not cancel the order for the three ass-colts, for which Sancho thanked him.

While the two had been going along conversing in this fashion, the curate observed to Dorothea that she had shown great cleverness, as well in the story itself as in its conciseness, and the resemblance it bòre to those of the books of chivalry. She said that she had many times amused herself reading them; but that she did not know the situation of the provinces or seaports, and so she had said at hap-hazard that she had landed at Osuna.

"So I saw," said the curate, "and for that reason I made haste to say what I did, by which it was all set right. But it is not a strange thing to see how readily this unhappy gentleman believes all these figments and lies, simply because they are in the style and manner of the absurdities of his books?"

"So it is," said Cardenio; "and so uncommon and un-exampled, that were one to attempt to invent and concoct it in fiction, I doubt if there be any wit keen enough to imagine it."

"But another strange thing about it," said the curate, "is that, apart from the silly things which this worthy gentleman says in connection with his craze, when other subjects are dealt with, he can discuss them in a perfectly rational manner, showing that his mind is quite clear and composed; so that, provided his chivalry is not touched upon, no one would take him to be anything but a man of thoroughly sound understanding."

While they were holding this conversation Don Quixote continued his with Sancho.

"Friend Panza, let us forgive and forget as to our quarrels, and tell me now, dismissing anger and irritation, where, how, and when didst thou find Dulcinea? What was she doing? What didst thou say to her? What did she answer? How did she look when she was reading my letter? Who copied it out for thee? and everything in the matter that seems to thee worth knowing, asking, and learning, neither adding nor falsifying to give me pleasure, nor yet curtailing lest you should deprive me of it."

"Señor," replied Sancho, "if the truth is to be told, nobody copied out the letter for me, for I carried no letter at all."

"It is as thou sayest," said Don Quixote, "for the note-book in which I wrote it I found in my own possession two days after thy departure, which gave me very great vexation, as I knew not what thou wouldst do on finding thyself without any letter; and I made sure thou wouldst return from the place where thou didst first miss it."

"So I should have done," said Sancho, "if I had not got it by heart when your worship read it to me, so that I repeated it to a sacristan, who copied it out for me from hearing it, so exactly that he said in all the days of his life, though he had read many a letter of excommunication, he had never seen or read so pretty a letter as that."

"And hast thou got it still in thy memory, Sancho?" said Don Quixote.

"No, señor," replied Sancho, "for as soon as I had repeated it, seeing there was no further use for it, I set about forgetting it; and if I recollect any of it, it is that about 'Scrubbing,' I mean to say 'Sovereign Lady,' and the end 'Yours till death, the Knight of the Rueful Countenance;' and between these two I put into it more than three hundred 'my souls' and 'my life's' and 'my eyes.'"

CHAPTER XXIII

OF THE DELECTABLE DISCUSSION BETWEEN DON QUIXOTE AND
SANCHO PANZA, HIS SQUIRE, TOGETHER WITH OTHER
INCIDENTS

"ALL that is not satisfactory to me," said Don Quixote. "Go on; thou didst reach her; and what was that queen of beauty doing? Surely thou didst find her stringing pearls, or embroidering some device in gold thread for this her enslaved knight."

"I did not," said Sancho, "but I found her winnowing two bushels of wheat in the yard of her house."

"Then depend upon it," said Don Quixote, "the grains of that wheat were pearls when touched by her hands; and didst thou look, friend? was it white wheat or brown?"

"It was neither, but red," said Sancho.

"Then I promise thee," said Don Quixote, "that, winnowed by her hands, beyond a doubt the bread it made was of the whitest; but go on; when thou gavest her my letter, did she kiss it? Did she place it on her head? Did she perform any ceremony befitting such a letter, or what did she do?"

"When I went to give it to her," replied Sancho, "she was hard at it swaying from side to side with a lot of wheat she had in the sieve, and she said to me, 'Lay the letter, friend, on the top of that sack, for I cannot read it until I have done sifting all this.'"

"Discreet lady!" said Don Quixote; "that was in order to read it at her leisure and enjoy it; proceed, Sancho;

while she was engaged in her occupation what converse did she hold with thee? What did she ask about me, and what answer didst thou give? Make haste; tell me all, and let not an atom be left behind in the ink-bottle."

"She asked me nothing," said Sancho; "but I told her how your worship was left doing penance in her service, naked from the waist up, in among these mountains like a savage, sleeping on the ground, not eating bread off a table-cloth nor combing your beard, weeping and cursing your fortune."

"In saying I cursed my fortune thou saidst wrong," said Don Quixote; "for rather do I bless it and shall bless it all the days of my life for having made me worthy of aspiring to love so lofty a lady as Dulcinea del Toboso."

"And so lofty she is," said Sancho, "that she overtops me by more than a hand's-breadth."

"What! Sancho," said Don Quixote, "didst thou measure with her?"

"I measured in this way," said Sancho; "going to help her to put a sack of wheat on the back of an ass, we came so close together that I could see she stood more than a good palm over me."

"Well!" said Don Quixote, "and doth she not of a truth accompany and adorn this greatness with a thousand million charms of mind! But one thing thou wilt not deny, Sancho; when thou camest close to her didst thou not perceive a Sabæan odor, an aromatic fragrance, a, I know not what, delicious, that I cannot find a name for; I mean a redolence, an exhalation, as if thou wert in the shop of some dainty glover?"

"All I can say is," said Sancho, "that I did perceive a little odor, something goaty; it must have been that she was all in a sweat with hard work."

"It could not be that," said Don Quixote, "but thou must have been suffering from cold in the head, or must have smelt thyself; for I know well what would be the scent of that rose among thorns, that lily of the field, that dissolved amber."

"Maybe so," replied Sancho; "there often comes from myself that same odor which then seemed to me to come from her grace the lady Dulcinea; but that's no wonder, for one devil is like another."

"Well then," continued Don Quixote, "now she has done sifting the corn and sent it to the mill; what did she do when she read the letter?"

"As for the letter," said Sancho, "she did not read it, for she said she could neither read nor write; instead of that she tore it up into small pieces, saying that she did not want to let any one read it lest her secrets should become known in the village, and that what I had told her by word of mouth about the love your worship bore her, and the extraordinary penance you were doing for her sake, was enough; and, to make an end of it, she told me to tell your worship that she kissed your hands, and that she had a greater desire to see you than to write to you; and that therefore she entreated and commanded you, on sight of this present, to come out of these thickets, and to have done with carrying on absurdities, and to set out at once for El Toboso, unless something else of greater importance should happen, for she had a great desire to see your worship. She laughed greatly when I told her how your worship was called The Knight of the Rueful Countenance; I asked her if that Biscayan the other day had been there; and she told me he had, and that he was a very honest fellow; I asked her too about the galley slaves, but she said she had not seen any as yet."

"So far all goes well," said Don Quixote; "but tell me what jewel was it that she gave thee on taking thy leave, in return for thy tidings of me? For it is a usual and ancient custom with knights and ladies errant to give the squires, damsels, or dwarfs who bring tidings of their ladies to the knights, or of their knights to the ladies, some rich jewel as a guerdon for good news, and acknowledgment of the message."

"That is very likely," said Sancho, "and a good custom it was, to my mind; but that must have been in days gone by, for now it would seem to be the custom only to give a piece of bread and cheese; because that was what my lady Dulcinea gave me over the top of the yard-wall when I took leave of her; and more by token it was sheep's-milk cheese."

"She is generous in the extreme," said Don Quixote, "and if she did not give thee a jewel of gold, no doubt it must have been because she had not one to hand there to give thee; but sleeves are good after Easter; I shall see her and all shall be made right. But knowest thou what amazes me, Sancho? It seems to me thou must have gone and come through the air, for thou hast taken but little more than three days to go to El Toboso and return, though it is more than thirty leagues from here to there. From which I am inclined to think that the sage magician who is my friend, and watches over my interests (for of necessity there is and must be one, or else I should not be a right knight-errant), that this same, I say, must have helped thee to travel without thy knowledge; for some of these sages will catch up a knight-errant sleeping in his bed, and without his knowing how or in what way it happened, he wakes up the next day more than a thousand leagues away from the place where he went to sleep.

"And if it were not for this, knights-errant would not be able to give aid to one another in peril, as they do at every turn. For a knight, maybe, is fighting in the mountains of Armenia with some dragon, or fierce serpent, or another knight, and gets the worst of the battle, and is at the point of death; but when he least looks for it, there appears over against him on a cloud, or chariot of fire, another knight, a friend of his, who just before had been in England, and who takes his part, and delivers him from death; and at night he finds himself in his own quarters supping very much to his satisfaction; and yet from one place to the other will have been two or three thousand leagues. And all this is done by the craft and skill of the sage enchanters who take care of those valiant knights; so that, friend Sancho, I find no difficulty in believing that thou mayest have gone from this place to El Toboso and returned in such a short time, since, as I have said, some friendly sage must have carried thee through the air without thy perceiving it."

"That must have been it," said Sancho, "for indeed Rocinante went like a gypsy's ass with quicksilver in his ears."

"Quicksilver!" said Don Quixote, "ay, and what is more, a legion of devils, folk that can travel and make others travel without being weary, exactly as the whim seizes them. But putting this aside, what thinkest thou I ought to do about my lady's command to go and see her? For though I feel that I am bound to obey her mandate, I feel too that I am debarred by the boon I have accorded to the princess that accompanies us, and the law of chivalry compels me to have regard for my word in preference to my inclination; on the one hand the desire to see my lady pursues and harasses me, on the other my solemn promise and the glory I shall win in this enterprise urge and call me; but what I think I shall do is to travel with all speed and reach quickly the place where this giant is, and on my arrival I shall cut off his head, and establish the princess peacefully in her realm, and forthwith I shall return to behold the light that lightens my senses, to whom I shall make such excuses that she will be led to approve of my delay, for she will see that it entirely tends to increase her glory and fame; for all that I have won, am winning, or shall win by arms in this life, comes to me of the favor she extends to me, and because I am hers."

"Ah! what a bad state your worship's brains are in!" said Sancho. "Tell me, señor, do you mean to travel all that way for nothing, and to let slip and lose so rich and great a match as this where they give as a portion a kingdom that in sober truth I have heard say is more than twenty thousand leagues round about, and abounds with all things necessary to support human life, and is bigger than Portugal and Castile put together? Peace, for the love of God! Blush for what you have said, and take my advice, and forgive me, and marry at once in the first village where there is a curate; if not, here is our licentiate who will do the business beautifully; remember, I am old enough to give advice, and this I am giving comes pat to the purpose; for a sparrow in the hand is better than a vulture on the wing, and he who has the good to his hand and chooses the bad, that the good he complains of may not come to him."

"Look here, Sancho," said Don Quixote. "If thou art advising me to marry, in order that immediately on slaying the giant I may become king, and be able to confer favors on thee, and give thee what I have promised, let me tell thee I shall be able very easily to satisfy thy desires without marrying; for before going into battle I will make it a stipulation that, if I come out victorious, even if I do not marry, they shall give me a portion of the kingdom, that I may bestow it upon whomsoever I choose, and when they give it to me upon whom wouldst thou have me bestow it but upon thee?"

"That is plain speaking," said Sancho; "but let your worship take care to choose it on the sea-coast, so that if I don't like the life, I may be able to ship off my black vassals and deal with them as I have said; don't mind going to see my lady Dulcinea now, but go and kill this giant and let us finish off this business; for by God it strikes me it will be one of great honor and great profit."

"I hold thou art in the right of it, Sancho," said Don Quixote, "and I will take thy advice as to accompanying the princess before going to see Dulcinea; but I counsel thee not to say anything to anyone, or to those who are with us, about what we have considered and discussed, for as Dulcinea is so decorous that she does not wish her thoughts to be known it is not right that I or any one for me should disclose them."

"Well then, if that be so," said Sancho, "how is it that your worship makes all those you overcome by your arm go to present themselves before thy lady Dulcinea, this being the same thing as signing your name to it that you love her and are her lover? And as those who go must perforce kneel before her and say they come from your worship to submit themselves to her, how can the thoughts of both of you be hid?"

"O, how silly and simple thou art!" said Don Quixote; "seest thou not, Sancho, that this tends to her greater exaltation? For thou must know that according to our way of thinking in chivalry, it is a high honor to a lady to have many knights-errant in her service, whose thoughts never go beyond serving her for her own sake, and who look for no other reward for their great and true devotion than that she should be willing to accept them as her knights."

"It is with that kind of love," said Sancho, "I have heard preachers say we ought to love our Lord, for himself alone, without being moved by the hope of glory or the fear of punishment; though for my part, I would rather love and serve him for what he could do."

"The devil take thee for a clown!" said Don Quixote, "and what shrewd things thou sayest at times! One would think thou hadst studied."

"In faith, then, I cannot even read," answered Sancho. Master Nicholas here called out to them to wait a while, as they wanted to halt and drink at a little spring there was there. Don Quixote drew up, not a little to the satisfaction of Sancho, for he was by this time weary of telling so many lies, and in dread of his master catching him tripping, for though he knew that Dulcinea was a peasant girl of El Toboso, he had never seen her in all his life. Cardenio had now put on the clothes which Dorothea was wearing when they found her, and though they were not very good, they were far better than those he put off. They dismounted together by the side of the spring, and with what the curate had provided himself with at the inn they appeased, though not very well, the keen appetite they all of them brought with them.

While they were so employed there happened to come by a youth passing on his way, who, stopping to examine the party at the spring, the next moment ran to Don Quixote and clasping him round the legs, began to weep freely, saying:

"Oh, señor, do you not know me? Look at me well; I am that lad Andres that your worship released from the oak-tree where I was tied."

Don Quixote recognized him, and taking his hand he turned to those present and said:

"That your worships may see how important it is to have knights-errant to redress the wrongs and injuries done by tyrannical and wicked men in this world, I may tell you that some days ago, passing through a wood, I heard cries and piteous complaints, as of a person in pain and distress; I immediately hastened, impelled by my bounden duty, to the quarter whence the plaintive accents seemed to me to proceed, and I found tied to an oak this lad who now stands before you, which in my heart I rejoice at, for his testimony will not permit me to depart from the truth in any particular. He was, I say, tied to an oak, naked from the waist up, and a clown, whom I afterwards found to be his master, was scarifying him by lashes with the reins of his mare. As soon as I saw him I asked the reason of so cruel a flagellation. The boor replied that he was flogging him because he was his servant and because of carelessness that proceeded rather from dishonesty than stupidity; on which this boy said, 'Señor, he flogs me only because I ask for my wages.' The master made I know not what speeches and explanations, which, though I listened to them, I did not accept. In short, I compelled the clown to unbind him, and to swear he would take him with him, and pay him *real* by *real*, and perfumed into the bargain. Is not all this true, Andres, my son? Didst thou not mark what authority I commanded him, and with what humility he promised to do all I enjoined, specified, and required of him? Answer without confusion or hesitation; tell these gentlemen what took place, that they may see and observe that it is as great an advantage as I say to have knights-errant abroad."

"All that your worship has said is quite true," answered the lad; "but the end of the business turned out just the opposite of what your worship supposes."

"How! the opposite?" said Don Quixote; "did not the clown pay thee then?"

"Not only did he not pay me," replied the lad, "but as soon as your worship had passed out of the wood and we were alone, he tied me up again to the same oak and gave me a fresh flogging, that left me like a flayed Saint Bartholomew; and every stroke he gave me he followed up with some jest or gibe about having made a fool of your worship, and but for the pain I was suffering I should have laughed at the things he said. In short he left me in such a condition that I have been until now in a hospital getting cured of the injuries which that rascally clown inflicted on me then; for all which your worship is to blame; for if you had gone your own way and not come where there was no call for you, nor meddled in other people's affairs, my master would have been content with giving me one or two dozen lashes, and would have then loosed me and paid me what he owed me; but when your worship abused him so out of measure, and gave him so many hard words, his anger was kindled; and as he could not revenge himself on you, as soon as he saw you had left him the storm burst upon me in such a way that I feel as if I should never be a man again as long as I live."

"The mischief," said Don Quixote, "lay in my going away; for I should not have gone until I had seen thee paid; because I ought to have known well by long experience that there is no clown who will keep his word if he finds it will not suit him to keep it; but thou rememberest, Andres, that I swore if he did not pay thee I would go and seek him, and find him though he were to hide himself in the whale's belly."

"That is true," said Andres; "but it was of no use."

"Thou shalt see now whether it is of use or not," said Don Quixote; and so saying, he got up hastily and bade Sancho bridle Rocinante, who was browsing while they were eating. Dorothea asked him what he meant to do. He replied that he meant to go in search of this clown and chastise him for such iniquitous conduct, and see Andres paid to the last *maravedi,* despite and in the teeth of all the clowns in the world. To which she replied that he must remember that in accordance with his promise he could not engage in any enterprise until he had brought hers to a conclusion; and that as he knew this better than anyone, he should restrain his ardor until his return from her kingdom.

"That is true," said Don Quixote, "and Andres must have patience until my return, as you say, señora; but I once more swear and promise afresh not to stop until I have seen him avenged and paid."

"I have no faith in those oaths," said Andres; "I would rather have now something to help me to get to Seville than all the revenges in the world: if you have here anything to eat that I can take with me, give it to me, and God be with your worships and all knights-errant; and may their errands turn out as well for themselves as they have for me."

Sancho took out from his store a piece of bread and another of cheese, and giving them to the lad he said, "Here, take this, brother Andres, for we have all of us a share in your misfortune."

"Why, what share have you got?" asked Andres.

"This share of bread and cheese I am giving you," answered Sancho; "and God knows whether I shall feel the want of it myself or not; for I would have you know, friend, that we squires to knights-errant have to bear a great deal of hunger and hard fortune, and even other things more easily felt than told."

Andres seized his bread and cheese, and seeing that nobody gave him anything more, bent his head, and took hold of the road, as the saying is. However, before leaving he said to Don Quixote: "For the love of God, Sir Knight-errant, if you ever meet me again, though you may see them cutting me to pieces, give me no aid or succor, but leave me to my misfortune, which will not be so great but that a greater will come to me by being helped by your worship, on whom and all the knights-errant that have ever been born God send his curse."

Don Quixote was getting up to chastise him, but he took to his heels at such a pace that no one attempted to follow him; and mightily chapfallen was Don Quixote at the story of Andres, and the others had to take great care to restrain their laughter so as not to put him entirely out of countenance.

CHAPTER XXIV

WHICH TREATS OF WHAT BEFELL ALL DON QUIXOTE'S PARTY AT THE INN

THEIR dainty repast being finished, they saddled at once, and without any adventure worth mentioning they reached next day the inn, the object of Sancho Panza's fear and dread; but though he would have rather not entered it, there was no help for it. The landlady, the landlord, their daughter, and Maritornes, when they saw Don Quixote and Sancho coming, went out to welcome them with signs of hearty satisfaction, which Don Quixote received with dignity and gravity, and bade them make up a better bed for him than the last time: to which the landlady replied that if he paid better than he did the last time she would give him one fit for a prince. Don Quixote said he would, so they made up a tolerable one for him in the same garret as before; and he lay down at once, being sorely shaken and in want of sleep.

No sooner was the door shut upon him than the landlady made at the barber, and seizing him by the beard, said:

"By my faith you are not going to make a beard of my tail any longer; you must give me back my tail, for it is a shame the way that thing of my husband's goes tossing about on the floor; I mean the comb that I used to stick in my good tail."

But for all she tugged at it the barber would not give it up until the licentiate told him to let her have it, as there was now no further occasion for that stratagem, because he might declare himself and appear in his own character, and tell Don Quixote that he had fled to this inn when those thieves the galley slaves robbed him; and should he ask for the princess's squire, they could tell him that she had sent him on before her to give notice to the people of her kingdom that she was coming, and bringing with her the deliverer of them all. On this the barber cheerfully restored the tail to the landlady, and at the same time they returned all the accessories they had borrowed to effect Don Quixote's deliverance. All the people of the inn were struck with astonishment at the beauty of Dorothea, and even at the comely figure of the shepherd Cardenio. The curate made them get ready such fare as there was in the inn, and the landlord, in hope of better payment, served them up a tolerably good dinner. All this time Don Quixote was asleep, and they thought it best not to waken him, as sleeping would now do him more good than eating.

While at dinner, the company consisting of the landlord, his wife, their daughter, Maritornes, and all the travelers, they discussed the strange craze of Don Quixote and the manner in which he had been found; and then, looking round to see if Sancho was there, when she saw he was not, she gave them the whole story of his blanketing, which they received with no little amusement. But on the curate observing that it was the books of chivalry which Don Quixote had read that had turned his brain, the landlord said:

"I cannot understand how that can be, for in truth to my mind there is no better reading in the world, and I have here two or three of them, with other writings that are the very life, not only of myself but of plenty more; for when it is harvest-time, the reapers flock here on holidays, and there is always one among them who can read and who takes up one of these books, and we gather round him, thirty or more of us, and stay listening to him with a delight that makes our gray hairs grow young again.

At least I can say for myself that when I hear of what furious and terrible blows the knights deliver, I am seized with the longing to do the same, and I would like to be hearing about them night and day."

"And I just as much," said the landlady, "because I never have a quiet moment in my house except when you are listening to someone reading; for then you are so taken up that for the time being you forget to scold."

"That is true," said Maritornes; "and, faith, I relish hearing these things greatly too, for they are very pretty; especially when they describe some lady or another in the arms of her knight under the orange trees, and the duenna who is keeping watch for them half dead with envy and fright; all this, I say, is as good as honey."

"And you, what do you think, young lady?" said the curate turning to the landlord's daughter.

"I don't know indeed, señor," said she; "I listen too, and to tell the truth, though I do not understand it, I like hearing it; but it is not the blows that my father likes that I like, but the laments the knights utter when they are separated from their ladies; and indeed they sometimes make me weep with the compassion I feel for them."

"Then you would console them if it was for you they wept, young lady?" said Dorothea.

"I don't know what I should do," said the girl; "I only know that there are some of those ladies so cruel that they call their knights tigers and lions and a thousand other foul names: and, Jesus! I don't know what sort of folk they can be, so unfeeling and heartless, that rather than bestow a glance upon a worthy man they leave him to die or go mad. I don't know what is the good of such prudery; if it is for honor's sake, why not marry them? That's all they want."

"Hush, child," said the landlady; "it seems to me thou knowest a great deal about these things, and it is not fit for girls to know or talk so much."

"As the gentleman asked me, I could not help answering him," said the girl.

"Well then," said the curate, "bring me these books, señor landlord, for I would like to see them."

"With all my heart," said he, and going into his own room he brought out an old valise secured with a little chain, on opening which the curate found in it three large books and some manuscripts written in a very good hand. The first he opened he found to be *Don Cirongilio of Thrace*, and the second *Don Felixmarte of Hircania*, and the other the *History of the Great Captain Gonzalo Hernandez de Cordova, with the Life of Diego Garcia de Paredes.*

When the curate read the first two titles he looked over at the barber and said, "We want my friend's housekeeper and niece here now."

"Nay," said the barber, "I can do just as well to carry them to the yard or to the hearth, and there is a very good fire there."

"What! your worship would burn my books!" said the landlord.

"Only these two," said the curate, *"Don Cirongilio"* and *"Felixmarte."*

"Are my books, then, heretics or phlegmatics that you want to burn them?" said the landlord.

"Schismatics you mean, friend," said the barber, "not phlegmatics."

"That's it," said the landlord; "but if you want to burn any, let it be that about the Great Captain and that Diego Garcia; for I would rather have a child of mine burnt than either of the others."

"Brother," said the curate, "those two books are made up of lies, and are full of folly and nonsense; but this of the Great Captain is true history, and contains the deeds of Gonzalo Hernandez of Cordova, who by his many and great achievements earned the title all over the world of the Great Captain, a famous and illustrious name, and deserved by him alone; and this Diego Garcia de Paredes was a distinguished knight of the city of Trujillo in Estremadura, a most gallant soldier, and of such bodily strength that with one finger he stopped a mill-wheel in full motion;

and posted with a two-handed sword at the foot of a bridge he kept the whole of an immense army from passing over it, and achieved such other exploits that if, instead of his relating them himself with the modesty of a knight and of one writing his own history, some free and unbiased writer had recorded them, they would have thrown into the shade of the deeds of the Hectors, Achilleses, and Rolands."

"Tell that to my father," said the landlord. "There's a thing to be astonished at! Stopping a mill-wheel! By God your worship should read what I have read of Felixmarte of Hircania, how with one single backstroke he cleft five giants asunder through the middle as if they had been made of bean-pods like the little friars the children make; and another time he attacked a very great and powerful army, in which there were more than a million six hundred thousand soldiers, all armed from head to foot, and he routed them all as if they had been flocks of sheep. And then, what do you say to the good Cirongilio of Thrace, that was so stout and bold; as may be seen in the book, where it is related that as he was sailing along a river there came up out of the midst of the water against him a fiery serpent, and he, as soon as he saw it, flung himself upon it and got astride of its scaly shoulders, and squeezed its throat with both hands with such force that the serpent, finding he was throttling it, had nothing for it but to let itself sink to the bottom of the river, carrying with it the knight who would not let go his hold; and when they got down there he found himself among palaces and gardens so pretty that it was a wonder to see; and then the serpent changed itself into an old ancient man, who told him such things as were never heard. Hold your peace, señor; for if you were to hear this you would go mad with delight. A couple of figs for your Great Captain and your Diego Garcia!"

Hearing this Dorothea said in a whisper to Cardenio, "Our Landlord is almost fit to play a second part to Don Quixote."

"I think so," said Cardenio, "for as he shows, he accepts it as a certainty that everything those books relate took place exactly as it is written down; and the barefooted friars themselves would not persuade him to the contrary."

"But consider, brother," said the curate once more, "there never was any Felixmarte of Hircania in the world, nor any Cirongilio of Thrace, or any of the other knights of the same sort, that the books of chivalry talk of; the whole thing is the fabrication and invention of idle wits, devised by them for the purpose you describe of beguiling the time, as your reapers do when they read: for I swear to you in all seriousness there never were any such knights in the world, and no such exploits or nonsense ever happened anywhere."

"Try that bone on another dog," said the landlord; "as if I did not know how many make five, and where my shoe pinches me; don't think to feed me with pap, for by God I am no fool. It is a good joke for your worship to try and persuade me that everything these good books say is nonsense and lies, and they printed by the license of the Lords of the Royal Council, as if they were people who would allow such a lot of lies to be printed all together, and so many battles and enchantments that they take away one's senses."

"I have told you, friend," said the curate, "that this is done to divert our idle thoughts; and as in well-ordered states games of chess, fives, and billiards are allowed for the diversion of those who do not care, or are not obliged, or are unable to work, so books of this kind are allowed to be printed, on the supposition that, what indeed is the truth, there can be nobody so ignorant as to take any of of them for true stories; and if it were permitted me now, and the present company desired it, I could say something about the qualities books of chivalry should possess to be good ones, that would be to the advantage and even to the taste of some; but I hope the time will come when I can communicate my ideas to some one who may be able to mend matters; and in the meantime, señor landlord, be-

lieve what I have said, and take your books, and make up
your mind about their truth or falsehood, and much good
may they do you; and God grant you may not fall lame
of the same foot your guest Don Quixote halts on."

"No fear of that," returned the landlord; "I shall not
be so mad as to make a knight-errant of myself; for I
see well enough that things are not now as they used to
be in those days, when they say those famous knights
roamed about the world."

Sancho had made his appearance in the middle of this
conversation, and he was very much troubled and cast down
by what he heard said about knights-errant being now no
longer in vogue, and all books of chivalry being folly and
lies; and he resolved in his heart to wait and see what came
of this journey of his master's, and if it did not turn out
as happily as his master expected, he determined to leave
him and go back to his wife and children and his ordinary labor. . . .

But before long he burst forth in wild excitement from
the garret where Don Quixote was lying, shouting, "Run,
sirs! quick; and help my master, who is in the thick of
the toughest and stiffest battle I ever laid eyes on. By
the living God he has given the giant, the enemy of my lady
the Princess Micomicona, such a slash that he has sliced
his head clean off as if it were a turnip."

"What are you talking about, brother?" said the curate.
"Are you in your senses, Sancho? How the devil can it
be as you say, when the giant is two thousand leagues
away?"

Here they heard a loud noise in the chamber, and Don
Quixote shouting out, "Stand, thief, brigand, villain; now
I have got thee and thy cimeter shall not avail thee!" And
then it seemed as though he were slashing vigorously at the
wall.

"Don't stop to listen," said Sancho, "but go in and part
them or help my master: though there is no need of that
now, for no doubt the giant is dead by this time and giving
account to God of his past wicked life; for I saw the

blood flowing on the ground, and the head cut off and fallen on one side, and it is as big as a large wine-skin."

" May I die," said the landlord at this, " if Don Quixote or Don Devil has not been slashing some of the skins of red wine that stand full at his bed's head and the spilt wine must be what this good fellow takes for blood;" and so saying he went into the room and the rest after him, and there they found Don Quixote in the strangest costume in the world. He was in his shirt, which was not long enough in front to cover his thighs completely and was six fingers shorter behind; his legs were very long and lean, covered with hair, and anything but clean; on his head he had a little greasy red cap that belonged to the host, round his left arm he had rolled the blanket of the bed, to which Sancho, for reasons best known to himself, owed a grudge, and in his right hand he held his unsheathed sword, with which he was slashing about on all sides, uttering exclamations as if he were actually fighting some giant: and the best of it was his eyes were not open, for he was fast asleep, and dreaming that he was doing battle with the giant. For his imagination was so wrought upon by the adventure he was going to accomplish, that it made him dream he had already reached the kingdom of Micomicon, and was engaged in combat with his enemy; and believing he was laying on to the giant, he had given so many cuts to the skins that the whole room was full of wine. On seeing this the landlord was so enraged that he fell on Don Quixote, and with his clinched fist began to pummel him in such a way, that if Cardenio and the curate had not dragged him off, he would have brought the war of the giant to an end. But in spite of all the poor gentleman never woke until the barber brought a great pot of cold water from the well and flung it with one dash all over his body, on which Don Quixote woke up, but not so completely as to understand what was the matter. Dorothea, seeing how short and slight his attire was, would not go in to witness the battle between her champion and her opponent. As for Sancho, he went searching all over the floor for the head of the giant, and not finding it he said. "I see now that it's all enchantment in this house; for this head is not to be seen anywhere about, though I saw it cut off with my own eyes and the blood running from the body as if from a fountain."

"What blood and fountains are you talking about, enemy of God and his saints?" said the landlord. "Don't you see, you thief, that the blood and the fountain are only these skins here that have been stabbed and the red wine swimming all over the room?—and I wish I saw the soul of him that stabbed them swimming in hell."

"I know nothing about that," said Sancho; "all I know is it will be my bad luck that through not finding this head my county will melt away like salt in water;"—for Sancho awake was worse than his master asleep, so much had his master's promises addled his wits.

The landlord was beside himself at the coolness of the squire and the mischievous doings of the master, and swore it should not be like the last time when they went without paying; and that their privileges of chivalry should not hold good this time to let one or other of them off without paying, even to the cost of the plugs that would have to be put to the damaged wine-skins. The curate was holding Don Quixote's hands, who, fancying he had now ended the adventure and was in the presence of the Princess Micomicona, knelt before the curate and said:

"Exalted and beauteous lady, your highness may live from this day forth fearless of any harm this base being could do you; and I too from this day forth am released from the promise I gave you, since by the help of God on high and by the favor of her by whom I live and breathe, I have fulfilled it so successfully."

"Did not I say so?" said Sancho on hearing this. "You see I wasn't drunk; there you see my master has already salted the giant; there's no doubt about the bulls: my county is all right!"

Who could have helped laughing at the absurdities of the pair, master and man? And laugh they did, all except the landlord, who cursed himself; but at length the barber, Cardenio, and the curate contrived with no small trouble to get Don Quixote on the bed, and he fell asleep with every appearance of excessive weariness. They left him to sleep, and came out to the gate of the inn to console Sancho Panza on not having found the head of the giant; but much more work had they to appease the landlord, who was furious at the sudden death of his wine-skins; and said the landlady, half scolding, half crying:

"At an evil moment and in an unlucky hour he came into my house, this knight-errant—would that I had never set eyes on him, for dear he has cost me; the last time he went off with the overnight score against him for supper, bed, straw, and barley, for himself and his squire and a hack and an ass, saying he was a knight adventurer—God send unlucky adventures to him and all the adventurers in the world—and therefore not bound to pay anything, for it was so settled by the knight-errantry tariff: and then, all because of him, came the other gentleman and carried off my tail, and gives it back more than two *quartillos* the worse, all stripped of its hair, so that it is no use for my husband's purpose; and then, for a finishing touch to all, to burst my wine-skins and spill my wine! I wish I saw his own blood spilt! But let him not deceive himself, for, by the bones of my father and the shade of my mother, they shall pay me down every *quarto;* or my name is not what it is, and I am not my father's daughter."

All this and more to the same effect the landlady delivered with great irritation, and her good maid Maritornes backed her up, while the daughter held her peace and smiled from time to time. The curate smoothed matters by promising to make good all losses to the best of his power, not only as regarded the wine-skins, but also the wine, and above all the depreciation of the tail which they set such store by. Dorothea comforted Sancho, telling him that she pledged herself, as soon as it should appear certain that his master had decapitated the giant, and she found herself peacefully established in her kingdom, to bestow upon him the best county there was in it. With this Sancho consoled himself, and assured the princess she might rely upon it that he had seen the head of the giant, and more by token it had a beard that reached to the girdle, and that if it was not to be seen now it was because everything that happened in that house went by enchantment, as he himself had proved the last time he had lodged there. Dorothea said she fully believed it, and that he need not be uneasy, for all would go well and turn out as he wished. . . .

CHAPTER XXV

JUST at that instant the landlord, who was standing at
the gate of the inn, exclaimed, "Here comes a fine
troop of guests; if they stop here we may say *gaudeamus.*"

"What are they?" said Cardenio.

"Four men," said the landlord, "riding on high saddles,
with lances and bucklers, and all with black veils, and with
them there is a woman in white on a side-saddle, whose face
is also veiled, and two attendants on foot."

"Are they very near?" said the curate.

"So near," answered the landlord, "that here they come."

Hearing this Dorothea covered her face, and Cardenio
retreated into Don Quixote's room, and they hardly had
time to do so before the whole party the host had described
entered the inn, and the four that were on horseback,
who were of high-bred appearance and bearing, dismounted,
and came forward to take down the woman who rode on the
side-saddle, and one of them taking her in his arms placed
her in a chair that stood at the entrance of the room where
Cardenio had hidden himself. All this time neither she
nor they had removed their veils or spoken a word, only on
sitting down on the chair the woman gave a deep sigh
and let her arms fall like one that was ill and weak. The
attendants on foot then led the horses away to the stable.
Observing this the curate, curious to know who these
people in such a dress and preserving such silence were,

went to where the servants were standing and put the question to one of them, who answered him:

"Faith, sir, I cannot tell you who they are, I only know they seem to be people of distinction, particularly he who advanced to take the lady you saw in his arms; and I say so because all the rest show him respect, and nothing is done except what he directs and orders."

"And the lady, who is she?" asked the curate.

"That I cannot tell you either," said the servant, "for I have not seen her face all the way: I have indeed heard her sigh many times and utter such groans that she seems to be giving up the ghost every time; but it is no wonder if we do not know more than we have told you, as my comrade and I have only been in their company two days, for having met us on the road they begged and persuaded us to accompany them to Andalusia, promising to pay us well."

"And have you heard any of them called by his name?" asked the curate.

"No, indeed," replied the servant; "they all preserve a marvelous silence on the road, for not a sound is to be heard among them except the poor lady's sighs and sobs, which make us pity her; and we feel sure that wherever it is she is going, it is against her will, and as far as one can judge from her dress she is a nun or, what is more likely, about to become one; and perhaps it is because taking the vows is not of her own free will, that she is so unhappy as she seems to be."

"That may well be," said the curate, and leaving them he returned to where Dorothea was, who, hearing the veiled lady sigh, moved by natural compassion drew near to her and said, "What are you suffering from, señora? If it be anything that women are accustomed and know how to relieve, I for my part offer you my services with all my heart."

To this the unhappy lady made no reply; and though Dorothea repeated her offers more earnestly she still kept silence, until the gentleman with the veil, who, the servant said, was obeyed by the rest, approached and said to Dorothea:

"Do not give yourself the trouble, señora, of making any offers to that woman, for it is her way to give no thanks for anything that is done for her; and do not try to make her answer unless you want to hear some lie from her lips."

"I have never told a lie," was the immediate reply of her who had been silent until now; "on the contrary, it is because I am so truthful and so ignorant of lying devices that I am now in this miserable condition; and this I call you yourself to witness, for it is my unstained truth that has made you false and a liar."

Cardenio heard these words clearly and distinctly, being quite close to the speaker, for there was only the door of Don Quixote's room between them, and the instant he did so, uttering a loud exclamation he cried:

"Good God! what is that I hear? What voice is this that has reached my ears?"

Startled at the voice the lady had turned her head; and not seeing the speaker she stood up and attempted to enter the room; observing which the gentleman held her back, preventing her from moving a step. In her agitation and sudden movement the silk with which she had covered her face fell off and disclosed a countenance of incomparable and marvelous beauty, but pale and terrified; for she kept turning her eyes, everywhere she could direct her gaze, with an eagerness that made her look as if she had lost her senses, and so marked that it excited the pity of Dorothea and all who beheld her, though they knew not what caused it. The gentleman grasped her firmly by the shoulders, and being so fully occupied with holding her back, he was unable to put a hand to his veil which was falling off, as it did at length entirely, and Dorothea, who was holding the lady in her arms, raising her eyes saw that he who likewise held her was her husband, Don Fernando. The instant she recognized him, with a prolonged plaintive cry drawn from the depths of her heart, she fell backwards fainting, and but for the barber being close by to catch her in his arms she would have fallen completely to the ground. The curate at once hastened to uncover her face and throw water on it, and as he did so Don Fernando, for he it was who held the other in his arms, recognized her and stood as if death-stricken by the sight; not, however, relaxing his grasp of Luscinda, for it was she that was struggling to release herself from his hold, having recognized Cardenio by his voice, as he had recognized her. Cardenio also heard Dorothea's cry as she fell fainting, and imagining that it came from his Luscinda burst forth in terror from the room, and the first thing he saw was Don Fernando with Luscinda in his arms. Don Fernando, too, knew Cardenio at once; and all three, Luscinda, Cardenio, and Dorothea, stood in silent amazement scarcely knowing what had happened to them.

They gazed at one another without speaking, Dorothea at Don Fernando, Don Fernando at Cardenio, Cardenio at Luscinda, and Luscinda at Cardenio. The first to break silence was Luscinda, who thus addressed Don Fernando: "Leave me, Señor Don Fernando, for the sake of what you owe to yourself; if no other reason will induce you, leave me to cling to the wall of which I am the ivy, to the support from which neither your importunities nor your threats, nor your promises, nor your gifts have been able to detach me. See how Heaven, by ways strange and hidden from our sight, has brought me face to face with my true husband; and well you know by dear-bought experience that death alone will be able to efface him from my memory. May this plain declaration, then, lead you, as you can do nothing else, to turn your love into rage, your affection into resentment, and so to take my life; for if I yield it up in the presence of my beloved husband I count it well bestowed; it may be by my death he will be convinced that I kept my faith to him to the last moment of life."

Meanwhile Dorothea had come to herself, and had heard Luscinda's words, by means of which she divined who she was; but seeing that Don Fernando did not yet release her or reply to her, summoning up her resolution as well as she could she rose and knelt at his feet, and with a flood of bright and touching tears addressed him thus:

"If, my lord, the beams of that sun that thou holdest eclipsed in thine arms did not dazzle and rob thine eyes of sight, thou wouldst have seen by this time that she who kneels at thy feet is, so long as thou wilt have it so, the unhappy and unfortunate Dorothea. I am that lowly peasant girl whom thou in thy goodness or for thy pleasure wouldst raise high enough to call herself thine; I am she who in the seclusion of innocence led a contented life until at the voice of thy importunity, and thy true and tender passion, as it seemed, she opened the gates of her modesty and surrendered to thee the keys of her liberty; a gift received by thee but thanklessly, as is clearly shown by my forced retreat to the place where thou dost find me, and by thy appearance under the circumstances in which I see thee. Nevertheless, I would not have thee suppose that I have come here driven by my shame; it is only grief and sorrow at seeing myself forgotten by thee that have led me. It was thy will to make me thine, and thou didst so follow thy will, that now, even though thou repentest, thou canst not help being mine. Bethink thee, my lord, the unsurpassable affection I bear thee may compensate for the beauty and noble birth for which thou wouldst desert me. Thou canst not be the fair Luscinda's because thou art mine, nor can she be thine because she is Cardenio's; and it will be easier, remember, to bend thy will to love one who adores thee, than to lead one to love thee who abhors thee now. Thou didst address thyself to my simplicity, thou didst lay siege to my virtue, thou wert not ignorant of my station, well dost thou know how I yielded wholly to thy will; there is no ground or reason for thee to plead deception, and if it be so, as it is, and if thou art a Christian as thou art a gentleman, why dost thou by such subterfuges put off making me happy at last as thou didst at first? And if thou wilt not have me for what I am, thy true and lawful wife, at least take and accept me as thy slave, for so long as I am thine I will count myself happy and fortunate.

"Do not by deserting me let my shame become the talk of the gossips in the streets; make not the old age of my parents miserable; for the loyal services they as faithful vassals have ever rendered thine are not deserving of such a return; and if thou thinkest it will debase thy blood to mingle it with mine, reflect that there is little or no nobility in the world that has not traveled the same road, and that in illustrious lineages it is not the woman's blood that is of account; and, moreover, that true nobility consists in virtue, and if thou art wanting in that, refusing me what in justice thou owest me, then even I have higher claims to nobility than thine. To make an end, señor, these are my last words to thee: whether thou wilt, or wilt not, I am thy wife; witness thy words, which must not and ought not to be false, if thou dost pride thyself on that for want of which thou scornest me; witness the pledge which thou didst give me, and witness Heaven, which thou thyself didst call to witness the promise thou hadst made me; and if all this fail, thy own conscience will not fail to lift up its silent voice in the midst of all thy gayety, and vindicate the truth of what I say and mar thy highest pleasure and enjoyment."

All this and more the injured Dorothea delivered with such earnest feeling and such tears that all present, even those who came with Don Fernando, were constrained to join her in them. Don Fernando listened to her without replying, until, ceasing to speak, she gave way to such sobs and sighs that it must have been a heart of brass that was not softened by the sight of so great sorrow. Luscinda stood regarding her with no less compassion for her sufferings than admiration for her intelligence and beauty, and would have gone to her to say some words of comfort to her, but was prevented by Don Fernando's grasp which held her fast. He, overwhelmed with confusion and astonishment, after regarding Dorothea for some moments with a fixed gaze, opened his arms, and, releasing Luscinda, exclaimed:

"Thou hast conquered, fair Dorothea, thou hast conquered, for it is impossible to have the heart to deny the united force of so many truths."

Luscinda in her feebleness was on the point of falling to the ground when Don Fernando released her, but Cardenio, who stood near, having retreated behind Don Fernando to escape recognition, casting fear aside and regardless of what might happen, ran forward to support her, and said as he clasped her in his arms:

"If Heaven in its compassion is willing to let thee rest at last, mistress of my heart, true, constant, and fair, nowhere canst thou rest more safely than in these arms that receive thee, and received thee before when fortune permitted me to call thee mine."

At these words Luscinda looked up at Cardenio, at first beginning to recognize him by his voice and then satisfying herself by her eyes that it was he, and hardly knowing what she did, and heedless of all considerations of decorum, she flung her arms around his neck and pressing her face close to his, said:

"Yes, my dear lord, you are the true master of this your slave, even though adverse fate interpose again, and fresh dangers threaten this life that hangs on yours."

A strange sight was this for Don Fernando and those that stood around, filled with surprise at an incident so unlooked for. Dorothea fancied that Don Fernando changed color and looked as though he meant to take vengeance on Cardenio, for she observed him put his hand to his sword; and the instant the idea struck her, with wonderful quickness she clasped him round the knees, and kissing them and holding him so as to prevent his moving, she said, while her tears continued to flow:

"What is it thou wouldst do, my only refuge, in this unforeseen event? Thou hast thy wife at thy feet, and she whom thou wouldst have for thy wife is in the arms of her husband: reflect whether it will be right for thee, whether it will be possible for thee to undo what Heaven has done, or whether it will be becoming in thee to seek to raise her to be thy mate who in spite of every obstacle, and strong in her truth and constancy, is before thine eyes, bathing with the tears of love the face and bosom of her lawful husband. For God's sake I entreat of thee, for thine own I implore thee, let not this open manifestation rouse thy anger; but rather so calm it as to allow these two lovers to live in peace and quiet without any interference from thee so long as Heaven permits them; and in so doing thou wilt prove the generosity of thy lofty noble spirit, and the world shall see that with thee reason has more influence than passion."

All the time Dorothea was speaking Cardenio, though he held Luscinda in his arms, never took his eyes off Don Fernando, determined, if he saw him make any hostile movement, to try and defend himself and resist as best he could all who might assail him, though it should cost him his life. But now Don Fernando's friends, as well as the curate and the barber, who had been present all the while, not forgetting the worthy Sancho Panza, ran forward and gathered around Don Fernando, entreating him to have regard for the tears of Dorothea, and not suffer her reasonable hopes to be disappointed, since, as they firmly believed, what she said was but the truth; and bidding him observe that it was not, as it might seem, by accident, but by a special disposition of Providence that they had all met in a place where no one could have expected a meeting.

And the curate bade him remember that only death could part Luscinda from Cardenio; that even if some sword were to separate them they would think their death most happy; and that in a case that admitted of no remedy his wisest course was, by conquering and putting a constraint upon himself, to show a generous mind, and of his own accord suffer these two 'o enjoy the happiness Heaven had granted them. He bade him, too, turn his eyes upon the beauty of Dorothea and he would see that few if any could equal much less excel her; while to that beauty should be added her modesty and the surpassing love she bore him. But besides all this, he reminded him that if he prided himself on being a gentleman and a Christian, he could not do otherwise than keep his plighted word; and that in doing so he would obey God and meet the approval of all sensible poeple, who know and recognize it to be the privilege of beauty, even in one of humble birth, provided virtue accompany it, to be able to raise itself to the level of any rank, without any slur upon him who places it upon an equality with himself; and furthermore that when the potent sway of passion asserts itself, so long as there be no mixture of sin in it, he is not to be blamed who gives way to it.

To be brief, they added to these such other forcible arguments that Don Fernando's manly heart, being after all nourished by noble blood, was touched, and yielded to the truth which, even had he wished it, he could not gainsay; and he showed submission, and acceptance of the good advice that had been offered to him, by stooping down and embracing Dorothea, saying to her:

"Rise, dear lady, it is not right that what I hold in my heart should be kneeling at my feet; and if until now I have shown no sign of what I own, it may have been by Heaven's decree in order that, seeing the constancy with which you love me, I may learn to value you as you deserve. What I entreat of you is that you reproach me not with my transgression and grievous wrong-doing; for the same cause and force that drove me to make you mine impelled me to struggle against being yours; and to prove this, turn and look at the eyes of the now happy Luscinda, and you will see in them an excuse for all my errors; and as she has found and gained the object of her desires, and I have found in you what satisfies all my wishes, may she live in peace and contentment as many happy years with her Cardenio, as on my knees I pray Heaven to allow me to live with my Dorothea;" and with these words he once more embraced her and pressed his face to hers with so much tenderness that he had to take great heed to keep his tears from completing the proof of his love and repentance in the sight of all.

Not so Luscinda, and Cardenio, and almost all the others, for they shed so many tears, some in their own happiness, some at that of the others, that one would have supposed a heavy calamity had fallen upon them all. Even Sancho Panza was weeping; though afterwards he said he only wept because he saw that Dorothea was not as he fancied, the queen Micomicona, of whom he expected such great favors. Their wonder as well as their weeping lasted some time, and then Cardenio and Luscinda went and fell on their knees before Don Fernando, returning him thanks for the favor he had rendered them in language so grateful that he knew not how to answer them, and raising them up embraced them with every mark of affection and courtesy.

He then asked Dorothea how she had managed to reach a place so far removed from her own home, and she in a few fitting words told all that she had previously related to Cardenio. Don Fernando then recounted what had befallen him in the city after Luscinda's fainting when he found in her bosom a paper in which she declared that she was Cardenio's wife, and never could be his, he said he meant to kill her, and would have done so had he not been prevented by her parents, and that he quitted the house full of rage and shame, and resolved to avenge himself when a more convenient opportunity should offer. The next day he learned that Luscinda had disappeared from her father's house, and that no one could tell whither she had gone.

Finally, at the end of some months he ascertained that she was in a convent and meant to remain there all the rest of her life, if she were not to share it with Cardenio; and as soon as he had learned this, taking these three gentlemen as his companions, he arrived at the place where she was, but avoided speaking to her, fearing that if it were known he was there stricter precautions would be taken in the convent; and watching a time when the porter's lodge was open he left two to guard the gate, and he and the other entered the convent in quest of Luscinda, whom they found in the cloisters in conversation with one of the nuns, and carrying her off without giving her time to resist, they reached a place with her where they provided themselves with what they required for taking her away; all which they were able to do in complete safety, as the convent was in the country at a considerable distance from the city. He added that when Luscinda found herself in his power she lost all consciousness, and after returning to herself did nothing but weep and sigh without speaking a word; and thus in silence and tears they reached that inn, which for him was reaching heaven where all the mischances of earth are over and at an end.

CHAPTER XXVI

TO all this Sancho listened with no little sorrow at heart
to see how his hopes of dignity were fading away and
vanishing in smoke, and how the fair princess Micomicona had turned into Dorothea, and the giant into Don Fernando, while his master was sleeping tranquilly, totally unconscious of all that had come to pass. Dorothea was unable to persuade herself that her present happiness was not
all a dream; Cardenio was in a similar state of mind, and
Luscinda's thoughts ran in the same direction. Don Fernando gave thanks to Heaven for the favor shown to him
and for having been rescued from the intricate labyrinth
in which he had been brought so near the destruction of his
good name and of his soul; and in short everybody in the
inn was full of contentment and satisfaction at the happy
issue of such a complicated and hopeless business. The
curate as a sensible man made sound reflections upon the
whole affair, and congratulated each upon his good fortune; but the one that was in the highest spirits and good
humor was the landlady, because of the promise Cardenio
and the curate had given her to pay for all the losses and
damage she had sustained through Don Quixote's means.
Sancho, as has been already said, was the only one who
was distressed, unhappy, and dejected; and so with a long
face he went in to his master, who had just awoke, and said
to him:

235

"Sir Rueful Countenance, your worship may as well sleep on as much as you like, without troubling yourself about killing any giant or restoring her kingdom to the princess; for that is all over and settled now."

"I should think it was," replied Don Quixote, "for I have had the most prodigious and stupendous battle with the giant that I ever remember having had all the days of my life; and with one back-stroke—swish!—I brought his head tumbling to the ground, and so much blood gushed forth from him that it ran in rivulets over the earth like water."

"Like red wine, your worship had better say," replied Sancho; "for I would have you know, if you don't know it, that the dead giant is a hacked wine-skin, and the blood four-and-twenty gallons of red wine that it had in its belly, and the devil take it all."

"What art thou talking about, fool?" said Don Quixote; "art thou in thy senses?"

"Let your worship get up," said Sancho, "and you will see the nice business you have made of it, and what we have to pay; and you will see the queen turned into a private lady called Dorothea, and other things that will astonish you, if you understand them."

"I shall not be surprised at anything of the kind," returned Don Quixote; "for if thou dost remember the last time we were here I told thee that everything that happened here was a matter of enchantment, and it would be no wonder if it were the same now."

"I could believe all that," replied Sancho, "if my blanketing was the same sort of thing also; only it wasn't, but real and genuine; for I saw the landlord, who is here today, holding one end of the blanket and jerking me up to the skies very neatly and smartly, and with as much laughter as strength; and when it comes to be a case of knowing people, I hold for my part, simple and sinner as I am, that there is no enchantment about it at all, but a great deal of bruising and plenty of bad luck."

"Well, well, God will give me a remedy," said Don Quixote; "hand me my clothes and let me go out, for I want to see these transformations and things thou speakest of."

Sancho fetched him his clothes; and while he was dress-- ing, the curate gave Don Fernando and the others present an account of Don Quixote's madness and of the stratagem they had made use of to withdraw him from that Peña Pobre where he fancied himself stationed because of his lady's scorn. He described to them also nearly all the adventures that Sancho had mentioned, at which they mar- veled and laughed not a little, thinking it, as all did, the strangest form of madness a crazy intellect could be capable of. But now, the curate said, that the lady Dorothea's good fortune prevented her from proceeding with their purpose, it would be necessary to devise or discover some other way of getting him home.

Cardenio proposed to carry out the scheme they had be- gun, and suggested that Luscinda would act and support Dorothea's part sufficiently well.

" No," said Don Fernando, " that must not be, for I want Dorothea to follow out this idea of hers; and if the worthy gentleman's village is not very far off, I shall be happy if I can do anything for his relief."

" It is not more than two day's journey from this," said the curate.

" Even if it were more," said Don Fernando, " I would gladly travel so far for the sake of doing so good a work."

At this moment Don Quixote came out in full panoply, with Mambrino's helmet, all dinted as it was, on his head, his buckler on his arm, and leaning on his staff or pike. The strange figure he presented filled Don Fernando and the rest with amazement as they contemplated his lean yel- low face half a league long, his armor of all sorts, and the solemnity of his deportment. They stood silent, waiting to see what he would say, and he, fixing his eyes on the fair Dorothea, addressed her with great gravity and composure:

" I am informed, fair lady, by my squire here that your greatness has been annihilated and your being abolished, since, from a queen and lady of high degree as you used to be, you have been turned into a private maiden. If this has been done by the command of the magician king your father, through fear that I should not afford you the aid you need and are entitled to, I may tell you he did not know and does not know half the mass, and was little versed in the annals of chivalry; for, if he had read and gone through them as attentively and deliberately as I have, he would have found at every turn that knights of less renown than mine, have accomplished things more difficult: it is no great matter to kill a whelp of a giant, however arrogant he may be; for it is not many hours since I myself was engaged with one, and—I will not speak of it, that they may not say I am lying; time, however, that reveals all, will tell the tale when we least expect it."

"You were engaged with a couple of wine-skins, and not a giant," said the landlord at this; but Don Fernando told him to hold his tongue and on no account interrupt Don Quixote, who continued:

"I say in conclusion, high and disinherited lady, that if your father has brought about this metamorphosis in your person for the reason I have mentioned, you ought not to attach any importance to it; for there is no peril on earth through which my sword will not force a way, and with it, before many days are over, I will bring your enemy's head to the ground and place on yours the crown of your kingdom."

Don Quixote said no more, and waited for the reply of the princess, who, aware of Don Fernando's determination to carry on the deception until Don Quixote had been conveyed to his home, with great ease of manner and gravity made answer:

"Whoever told you, valiant Knight of the Rueful Countenance, that I had undergone any change or transformation did not tell you the truth, for I am the same as I was yesterday. It is true that certain strokes of good fortune, that have given me more than I could have hoped for, have made some alteration in me; but I have not therefore ceased to be what I was before, or to entertain the same desire I have had all through of availing myself of the might of your valiant and invincible arm. And so, señor, let your goodness reinstate the father that begot me in your good opinion, and be assured that he was a wise and prudent man, since by his craft he found out such a sure and easy way of remedying my misfortune; for I believe, señor, that had it not been for you I should never have lit upon the good fortune I now possess; and in this I am saying what is perfectly true; as most of these gentlemen who are present can fully testify. All that remains is to set out on our journey tomorrow, for today we could not make much way; and for the rest of the happy result I am looking forward to, I trust to God and the valor of your heart."

So said the sprightly Dorothea, and on hearing her Don Quixote turned to Sancho, and said to him, with an angry air:

"I declare now, little Sancho, thou art the greatest little villain in Spain. Say, thief and vagabond, hast thou not just now told me that this princess had been turned into a maiden called Dorothea, and that the head which I am persuaded I cut off from a giant was the wretch that bore thee, and other nonsense that put me in the greatest perplexity I have ever been in in all my life? I vow" (and here he looked to heaven and ground his teeth) "I have a mind to play the mischief with thee, in a way that will teach sense for the future to all lying squires of knights-errant in the world."

"Let your worship be calm, señor," returned Sancho, "for it may well be that I have been mistaken as to the change of the lady princess Micomicona; but as to the giant's head, or at least as to the piercing of the wine-skins, and the blood being red wine, I make no mistake, as sure as there is a God; because the wounded skins are there at the head of your worship's bed, and the red wine has made a lake of the room; if not you will see when the eggs come to be fried; I mean when his worship the landlord here calls for all the damages: for the rest, I am heartily glad that her ladyship the queen is as she was, for it concerns me as much as any one."

"I tell thee again, Sancho, thou art a fool," said Don Quixote; "forgive me, and that will do."

"That will do," said Don Fernando; "let us say no more about it; and as her ladyship the princess proposes to set out tomorrow because it is too late today, so be it, and we will pass the night in pleasant conversation, and tomorrow we will all accompany Señor Don Quixote; for we wish to witness the valiant and unparalleled achievements he is about to perform in the course of this mighty enterprise which he has undertaken."

"It is I who shall wait upon and accompany you," said Don Quixote; "and I am much gratified by the favor that is bestowed upon me, and the good opinion entertained of me, which I shall strive to justify or it shall cost me my life, or even more, if it can possibly cost me more."

Many were the compliments and expressions of politeness that passed between Don Quixote and Don Fernando; but they were brought to an end by a traveler who at this moment entered the inn, and who seemed from his attire to be a Christian lately come from the country of the Moors, for he was dressed in a short-skirted coat of blue cloth with half-sleeves and without a collar; his breeches were also of blue cloth, and his cap of the same color, and he wore yellow buskins and had a Moorish cutlass slung from a baldric across his breast. Behind him, mounted upon an ass, there came a woman dressed in Moorish fashion, with her face veiled and a scarf on her head, and wearing a little brocaded cap, and a mantle that covered her from her shoulders to her feet. The man was of a robust and well-proportioned frame, in age a little over forty, rather swarthy in complexion, with long moustaches and a full beard, and, in short, his appearance was such that if he had been well dressed he would have been taken for a person of quality and good birth. On entering he asked for a room, and when they told him there was none in the inn he seemed distressed, and approaching her who by her dress seemed to be a Moor, he took her down from the saddle in his arms. Luscinda, Dorothea, the landlady, her daughter and Maritornes, attracted by the strange, and to them entirely new costume, gathered round her; and Dorothea, who was always kindly, courteous, and quick-witted, perceiving that both she and the man who had brought her were annoyed at not finding a room, said to her:

"Do not be put out, señora, by the discomfort and want of luxuries here, for it is the way of road-side inns to be without them; still, if you will be pleased to share our lodging with us (pointing to Luscinda) perhaps you will have found worse accommodations in the course of your journey."

To this the veiled lady made no reply; all she did was to rise from her seat, crossing her hands upon her bosom, bowing her head and bending her body as a sign that she returned thanks. From her silence they concluded that she must be a Moor and unable to speak a Christian tongue.

At this moment the captive came up, having been until now otherwise engaged, and seeing that they all stood round his companion and that she made no reply to what they addressed to her, he said, "Ladies, this damsel hardly understands my language and can speak none but that of her own country, for which reason she does not and can not answer what has been asked of her."

"Nothing has been asked of her," returned Luscinda; "she has only been offered our company for this evening and a share of the quarters we occupy, where she shall be made as comfortable as the circumstances allow, with the good will we are bound to show all strangers that stand in need of it, especially if it be a woman to whom the service is rendered."

"On her part and my own, señora," replied the captive, 'I kiss your hands, and I esteem highly, as I ought, the favor you have offered, which, on such an occasion and coming from persons of your appearance, is, it is plain to see, a very great one."

"Tell me, señor," said Dorothea, "is this lady a Christian or a Moor? for her dress and her silence lead us to imagine that she is what we could wish she was not."

"In dress and outwardly," said he, "she is a Moor, but at heart she is a thoroughly good Christian, for she has the greatest desire to become one."

"Then she has not been baptized?" returned Luscinda.

"There has been no opportunity for that," replied the captive, "since she left Algiers, her native country and home; and up to the present she has not found herself in any such imminent danger of death as to make it necessary to baptize her before she has been instructed in all the ceremonies our holy mother Church ordains; but, please God, ere long she shall be baptized with the solemnity befitting her quality, which is higher than her dress or mine indi-cates."

By these words he excited a desire in all who heard him, to know who the Moorish lady and the captive were, but no one liked to ask just then, seeing that it was a fitter moment for helping them to rest themselves than for questioning them about their lives. Dorothea took the Moorish lady by the hand and leading her to a seat beside herself, requested her to remove her veil. She looked at the captive as if to ask him what they meant and what she was to do. He said to her in Arabic that they asked her to take off her veil, and thereupon she removed it and disclosed a countenance so lovely, that to Dorothea she seemed more beautiful than Luscinda, and to Luscinda more beautiful than Dorothea, and all the bystanders felt that if any beauty could compare with theirs it was the Moorish lady's, and there were even those who were inclined to give it somewhat the preference. And as it is the privilege and charm of beauty to win the heart and secure good-will, all forthwith became eager to show kindness and attention to the lovely Moor.

Don Fernando asked the captive what her name was, and he replied that it was Lela Zoraida; but the instant she heard him, she guessed what the Christian had asked, and said hastily, with some displeasure and energy, "No, not Zoraida; Maria, Maria!" giving them to understand that she was called "Maria" and not "Zoraida." These words, and the touching earnestness with which she uttered them, drew more than one tear from some of the listeners, particularly the women, who are by nature tender-hearted and compassionate. Luscinda embraced her affectionately, saying, "Yes, yes, Maria, Maria," to which the Moor replied, "Yes, yes, Maria; Zoraida *mecange,*" which means "not Zoraida."

Night was now approaching, and by the orders of those who accompanied Don Fernando the landlord had taken care and pains to prepare for them the best supper that was in his power. The hour therefore having arrived they all took their seats at a long table like a refectory one, for round or square table there was none in the inn, and the seat of honor at the head of it, though he was for refusing it, they assigned to Don Quixote, who desired the lady Micomicona to place herself by his side, as he was her protector. Luscinda and Zoraida took their places next her, opposite to them were Don Fernando and Cardenio, and next the captive and the other gentlemen, and by the side of the ladies, the curate and the barber. And so they supped in high enjoyment, which was increased when they observed Don Quixote leave off eating, and, moved by an impulse like that which made him deliver himself at such length when he supped with the goatherds, begin to address them:

"Verily, gentlemen, if we reflect upon it, great and marvelous are the things they see, who make profession of the order of knight-errantry. Say, what being is there in this world, who entering the gate of this castle at this moment, and seeing us as we are here, would suppose or imagine us to be what we are? Who would say that this lady who is beside me was the great queen that we all know her to be, or that I am that Knight of the Rueful Countenance, trumpeted far and wide by the mouth of Fame? Now, there can be no doubt that this art and calling surpasses all those that mankind has invented, and is the more deserving of being held in honor in proportion as it is the more exposed to peril.

" Away with those who assert that letters have the pre-eminence over arms; I will tell them, whosoever they may be, that they know not what they say. For the reason which such persons commonly assign, and upon which they chiefly rest, is, that the labors of the mind are greater than those of the body, and that arms give employment to the body alone; as if the calling were a porter's trade, for which nothing more is required than sturdy strength; or as if, in what we who profess them call arms, there were not included acts of vigor for the execution of which high intelligence is requisite; or as if the soul of the warrior, when he has an army, or the defense of a city under his care, did not exert itself as much by mind as by body. Nay; see whether by bodily strength it be possible to learn or divine the intentions of the enemy, his plans, strata-gems, or obstacles, or to ward off impending mischief; for all these are the work of the mind, and in them the body has no share whatever.

" Since, therefore, arms have need of the mind, as much as letters, let us see now which of the two minds, that of the man of letters or that of the warrior, has most to do; and this will be seen by the end and goal that each seeks to attain; for that purpose is the more estimable which has for its aim the nobler object. The end and goal of letters —I am not speaking now of divine letters, the aim of which is to raise and direct the soul to Heaven; for with an end so infinite no other can be compared—I speak of human letters, the end of which is to establish distributive justice, give to every man that which is his, and see and take care that good laws are observed: an end undoubt-edly noble, lofty, and deserving of high praise, but not such as should be given to that sought by arms, which have for their end and object peace, the greatest boon that man can desire in this life. The first good news the world and mankind received was that which the angels announced on the night that was our day, when they sang in the air,

CERVANTES' "DON QUIXOTE"

'Glory to God in the highest, and peace on earth to men of good will;' and the salutation which the great Master of heaven and earth taught his disciples and chosen followers when they entered any house, was to say, 'Peace be on this house;' and many other times he said to them, 'My peace I give unto you, my peace I leave you, peace be with you;' a jewel and a precious gift given and left by such a hand: a jewel without which there can be no happiness either on earth or in heaven. This peace is the true end of war; and war is only another name for arms. This, then, being admitted, that the end of war is peace, and that so far it has the advantage of the end of letters, let us turn to the bodily labors of the man of letters, and those of him who follows the profession of arms, and see which are the greater."

Don Quixote delivered his discourse in such a manner and in such correct language, that for the time being he made it impossible for any of his hearers to consider him a madman; on the contrary, as they were mostly gentlemen, to whom arms are an appurtenance by birth, they listened to him with great pleasure as he continued:

"Here, then, I say is what the student has to undergo; first of all poverty; not that all are poor, but to put the case as strongly as possible: and when I have said that he endures poverty, I think nothing more need be said about his hard fortune, for he who is poor has no share of the good things of life. This poverty he suffers from in various ways, hunger, or cold, or nakedness, or all together; but for all that it is not so extreme but that he gets something to eat, though it may be at somewhat unseasonable hours and from the leavings of the rich; for the greatest misery of the student is what they call 'going out for soup,' and there is always some neighbor's brazier or hearth for them, which, if it does not warm, at least tempers the cold to them, and lastly, they sleep comfortably at night under a roof. I will not go into other particulars, as for example want of shirts, and no superabundance of shoes, thin and threadbare garments, and gorging themselves to surfeit in their voracity when good luck has treated them to a banquet of some sort. By this road that I have described, rough and hard, stumbling here, falling there, getting up again to fall again, they reach the rank they desire, and that once attained, we have seen many who have passed these Syrtes and Scyllas and Charybdises, as if borne flying on the wings of favoring fortune; we have seen them, I say, ruling and governing the world from a chair, their hunger turned into satiety, their cold into comfort, their nakedness into fine raiment, their sleep on a mat into repose in holland and damask, the justly earned reward of their virtue; but, contrasted and compared with what the warrior undergoes, all they have undergone falls far short of it." . . .

They finished their supper, the cloth was removed, and while the hostess, her daughter, and Maritornes were getting Don Quixote of La Mancha's garret ready, in which it was arranged that the women were to be quartered by themselves for the night, Don Fernando begged the captive to tell them the story of his life, for it could not fail to be strange and interesting, to judge by the hints he had let fall on his arrival in company with Zoraida. To this the captive replied that he would very willingly yield to his request, only he feared his tale would not give them as much pleasure as he wished; nevertheless, not to be wanting in compliance, he would tell it. The curate and the others thanked him and added their entreaties, and he finding himself so pressed said there was no occasion to ask, where a command had such weight, and added, "If your worships will give me your attention you will hear a true story which, perhaps, fictitious ones constructed with ingenious and studied art cannot come up to." These words made them settle themselves in their places and preserve a deep silence, and he seeing them waiting on his words in mute expectation, began thus in a pleasant quiet voice.

CHAPTER XXVII

MY family had its origin in a village in the mountains of Leon, and nature had been kinder and more generous to it than fortune; though in the general poverty of those communities my father passed for being even a rich man; and he would have been so in reality had he been as clever in preserving his property as he was in spending it. This tendency of his to be liberal and profuse he had acquired from having been a soldier in his youth, for the soldier's life is a school in which the niggard becomes freehanded and the free-handed prodigal; and if any soldiers are to be found who are misers, they are monsters of rare occurrence. My father went beyond liberality and bordered on prodigality, a disposition by no means advantageous to a married man who has children to succeed to his name and position. My father had three, all sons, and all of sufficient age to make choice of a profession. Finding, then, that he was unable to resist his propensity, he resolved to divest himself of the instrument and cause of his prodigality and lavishness, to divest himself of wealth, without which Alexander himself would have seemed parsimonious; and so calling us all three aside one day into a room, he addressed us in words somewhat to the following effect:

" My sons, to assure you that I love you, no more need be known or said than that you are my sons; and to encourage a suspicion that I do not love you, no more is

247

needed than the knowledge that I have no self-control as far as preservation of your patrimony is concerned; therefore, that you may for the future feel sure that I love you like a father, and have no wish to ruin you like a stepfather, I propose to do with you what I have done for some time back meditated, and after mature deliberation decided upon. You are now of an age to choose your line of life or at least make choice of a calling that will bring you honor and profit when you are older; and what I have resolved to do is to divide my property into four parts; three I will give to you, to each his portion without making any difference, and the other I will retain to live upon and support myself for whatever remainder of life Heaven may be pleased to grant me.

"But I wish each of you on taking possession of the share that falls to him to follow one of the paths I shall indicate. In this Spain of ours there is a proverb, to my mind very true—as they all are, being short aphorisms drawn from long practical experience—and the one I refer to says, 'The church, or the sea, or the king's house;' as much as to say, in plainer language, whoever wants to flourish and become rich, let him follow the church, or go to sea, adopting commerce as his calling, or go into the king's service in his household, for they say, 'Better a king's crumb than a lord's favor.' I say so because it is my will and pleasure that one of you should follow letters, another trade, and the third serve the king in the wars, for it is a difficult matter to gain admission to his service in his household, and if war does not bring much wealth it confers great distinction and fame. Eight days hence I will give you your full shares in money, without defrauding you of a farthing, as you will see in the end. Now tell me if you are willing to follow out my idea and advice as I have laid it before you."

Having called upon me as the eldest to answer, I, after urging him not to strip himself of his property but to spend it all as he pleased, for we were young men able to gain our living, consented to comply with his wishes, and said that

mine were to follow the profession of arms and thereby
serve God and my king. My second brother having made
the same proposal, decided upon going to the Indies, em-
barking the portion that fell to him in trade. The young-
est, and in my opinion the wisest, said he would rather
follow the church, or go to complete his studies at Salamanca. As soon as we had come to an understanding, and
made choice of our porfessions, my father embraced us all,
and in the short time he mentioned carried into effect all he
had promised; and when he had given to each his share,
which as well as I remember was three thousand ducats
apiece in cash (for an uncle of ours bought the estate
and paid for it down, not to let it go out of the family),
we all three on the same day took leave of our good father;
and at the same time, as it seemed to me inhuman to leave
my father with such scanty means in his old age, I induced
him to take two of my three thousand ducats, as the
remainder would be enough to provide me with all a soldier
needed. My two brothers, moved by my example, gave
him each a thousand ducats, so that there was left for my
father four thousand ducats in money, besides three thousand, the value of the portion that fell to him which he
preferred to retain in land instead of selling it. Finally,
as I said, we took leave of him, and of our uncle whom
I have mentioned, not without sorrow and tears on both
sides, they charging us to let them know whenever an opportunity offered how we fared well or ill. We promised
to do so, and when he had embraced us and given us his
blessing, one set out for Salamanca, the other for Seville,
and I for Alicante, where I had heard there was a Genoese
vessel taking in a cargo of wool for Genoa.

It is now some twenty-two years since I left my father's
house, and all that time, though I have written several letters, I have had no news whatever of him or of my
brothers; my own adventures during that period I will now
relate briefly. I embarked at Alicante, reached Genoa after a prosperous voyage, and proceeded thence to Milan,
where I provided myself with arms and a few soldier's

accoutrements; then it was my intention to go and take
service in Piedmont, but as I was already on the road to
Alessandria della Paglia, I learned that the great Duke
of Alva was on his way to Flanders. I changed my plans,
joined him, served under him in the campaigns he made,
was present at the deaths of the Counts Egmont and Horn,
and was promoted to be ensign under a famous captain of
Guadalajara, Diego de Urbina by name. Some time after
my arrival in Flanders news came of the league that his
Holiness Pope Pius V. of happy memory had made with
Venice and Spain against the common enemy, the Turk,
who had just then with his fleet taken the famous island
of Cyprus, which belonged to the Venetians, a loss de-
plorable and disastrous. It was known as a fact that the
Most Serene Don John of Austria, natural brother of our
good king Don Philip, was coming as commander-in-chief
of the allied forces, and rumors were abroad of the vast
warlike preparations which were being made, all which
stirred my heart and filled me with a longing to take part
in the campaign which was expected; and though I had
reason to believe, and most certain promises, that on the
first opportunity that presented itself I should be promoted
to be captain, I preferred to leave all and betake myself, as
I did, to Italy; and it was my good fortune that Don John
had just arrived at Genoa, and was going on to Naples to
join the Venetian fleet, as he afterwards did at Messina.

I may say, in short, that I took part in that glorious
expedition, promoted by this time to be a captain of infantry, to which honorable charge my good luck rather
than my merits raised me; and that day— so fortunate for
Christendom, because then all the nations of the earth
were disabused of the error under which they lay in imagining the Turks to be invincible on sea—on that day, I say,
on which the Ottoman pride and arrogance were broken,
among all that were there made happy (for the Christians
who died that day were happier than those who remained
alive and victorious) I alone was miserable; for, instead
of some naval crown that I might have expected had it

been in Roman times, on the night that followed that famous day I found myself with fetters on my feet and manacles on my hands.

It happened in this way: El Uchali, the King of Algiers, a daring and successful corsair, having attacked and taken the leading Maltese galley (only three knights being left alive in it, and they badly wounded), the chief galley of John Andrea, on board of which I and my company were placed, came to its relief, and doing as I was bound to do in such a case, I leaped on board the enemy's galley, which, sheering off from that which had attacked it, prevented my men from following me, and so I found myself alone in the mdist of my enemies, who were in such numbers that I was unable to resist; in short I was taken, covered with wounds; El Uchali, as you know, sirs, made his escape with his entire squadron, and I was left a prisoner in his power, the only sad being among so many filled with joy, and the only captive among so many free; for there were fifteen Christians, all at the oar in the Turkish fleet, that regained their longed for liberty that day.

They carried me to Constantinople, where the Grand Turk, Selim, made my master general at sea for having done his duty in the battle and carried off as evidence of his bravery the standard of the Order of Malta. The following year, which was the year seventy-two, I found myself at Navarino rowing in the leading galley with the three lanterns. There I saw and observed how the opportunity of capturing the whole Turkish fleet in harbor was lost; for all the marines and janizzaries that belonged to it made sure that they were about to be attacked inside the very harbor, and had their kits and *pasamaques*, or shoes, ready to flee at once on shore without waiting to be assailed, in so great fear did they stand of our fleet. But Heaven ordered it otherwise, not for any fault or neglect of the general who commanded on our side, but for the sins of Christendom, and because it was God's will and pleasure that we should always have instruments of punishment to chastise us. As it was, El Uchali took refuge at Modon,

251

which is an island near Navarino, and landing his forces
fortified the mouth of the harbor and waited quietly until
Don John retired. On this expedition was taken the galley
called the Prize, whose captain was a son of the famous
corsair Barbarossa. It was taken by the chief Neapolitan
galley called the *She-wolf,* commanded by that thunderbolt of war, that father of his men, that successful and unconquered captain Don Alvaro de Bazan, Marquis of Santa
Cruz; and I cannot help telling you what took place at the
capture of the Prize.

The son of Barbarossa was so cruel, and treated his
slaves so badly, that, when those who were at the oars saw
that the She-wolf galley was bearing down upon them and
gaining upon them, they all at once dropped their oars
and seized their captain who stood on the stage at the end
of the gangway shouting to them to row lustily; and passing him on from bench to bench, from the poop to the
prow, they so bit him that before he had got much past the
mast his soul had already got to hell; so great, as I said,
was the cruelty with which he treated them, and the hatred
with which they hated him.

We returned to Constantinople, and the following year,
seventy-three, it became know that Don John had seized
Tunis and taken the kingdom from the Turks, and placed
Muley Hamet in possession, putting an end to the hopes
which Muley Hamida, the cruelest and bravest Moor in
the world, entertained of returning to reign there. The
Grand Turk took the loss greatly to heart, and with the
cunning which all his race possess, he made peace with the
Venetians (who were much more eager for it than he was),
and the following year, seventy-four, he attacked the Goletta and the fort which Don John had left half built near
Tunis. While all these events were occurring, I was labor-
ing at the oar without any hope of freedom; at least I had
no hope of obtaining it by ransom, for I was firmly resolved not to write to my father telling him of my misfortunes. At length the Goletta fell, and the fort fell, before which places there were seventy-five thousand regular

Turkish soldiers, and more than four hundred thousand Moors and Arabs from all parts of Africa, and in the train of all this great host such munitions and engines of war, and so many pioneers that with their hands they might have covered the Goletta and the fort with handfuls of earth. The first to fall was the Goletta, until then reckoned impregnable, and it fell, not by any fault of its defenders, who did all that they could and should have done, but because experiment proved how easily intrenchments could be made in the desert sand there; for water used to be found at two palms depth, while the Turks found none at two yards; and so by means of a quantity of sandbags they raised their works so high that they commanded the walls of the fort, sweeping them as if from a cavalier, so that no one was able to make a stand or maintain the defense.

It was a common opinion that our men should not have shut themselves up in the Goletta, but should have waited in the open at the landing-place; but those who say so talk at random and with little knowledge of such matters; for if in the Goletta and in the fort there were barely seven thousand soldiers, how could such a small number, however resolute, sally out and hold their own against numbers like those of the enemy? And now is it possible to help losing a stronghold that is not relieved, above all when surrounded by a host of determined enemies in their own country? But many thought, and I thought so too, that it was a special favor and mercy which Heaven showed to Spain in permitting the destruction of that source and hiding-place of mischief, that devourer, sponge, and moth of countless money, fruitlessly wasted there to no other purpose save preserving the memory of its capture by the invincible Charles V.; as if to make that eternal, as it is and will be, these stones were needed to support it.

The fort also fell; but the Turks had to win it inch by inch, for the soldiers who defended it fought so gallantly and stoutly that the number of the enemy killed in twenty-two general assaults exceeded twenty-five thousand. Of three hundred that remained alive not one was taken unwounded, a clear and manifest proof of their gallantry and resolution, and how sturdily they had defended themselves and held their post. A small fort or tower which was in the middle of the lagoon under the command of Don Juan Zanoguera, a Valencian gentleman and a famous soldier, capitulated upon terms. They took prisoner Don Pedro Puertacarrero, commandant of the Goletta, who had done all in his power to defend his fortress, and took the loss of it so much to heart that he died of grief on the way to Constantinople, where they were carrying him a prisoner. They also took the commandant of the fort, Gabrio Cerbellon by name, a Milanese gentleman, a great engineer and a very brave soldier. . . .

CHAPTER XXVIII

THE Goletta and the fort being thus in their hands, the Turks gave orders to dismantle the Goletta—for the fort was reduced to such a state that there was nothing left to level—and to do the work more quickly and easily they mined it in three places; but nowhere were they able to blow up the part which seemed to be the least strong, that is to say, the old walls, while all that remained standing of the new fortification that the Fratin had made came to the ground with the greatest ease. Finally the fleet returned victorious and triumphant to Constantinople, and a few months later died my master, El Uchali, otherwise Uchali Fartax, which seems in Turkish "the scabby renegade;" for that he was; it is the practice with the Turks to name people from some defect or virtue they may possess; the reason being that there are among them only four surnames belonging to families tracing their descent from the Ottoman house, and the others, as I have said, take their names and surnames either from bodily blemishes or moral qualities.

This "scabby one" rowed at the oar as a slave of the Grand Signor's for fourteen years, and when over thirty-four years of age, in resentment at having been struck by a Turk while at the oar, turned renegade and renounced his faith in order to be able to revenge himself; and such was his valor that, without owing his advancement to the base ways and means by which most favorites of the Grand Signor rise to power, he came to be king of Algiers, and

afterwards general-at-sea, which is the third place of trust
in the realm. He was a Calabrian by birth, and a worthy
man morally, and he treated his slaves with great humanity.
He had three thousand of them, and after his death they
were divided, as he directed by his will, between the Grand
Signor (who is heir of all who die and shares with the children of the deceased) and his renegades.

I fell to the lot of a Venetian renegade who, when a
cabin-boy on board a ship, had been taken by Uchali and
was so much beloved by him that he became one of his
most favored youths. He came to be the most cruel renegade I ever saw: his name was Hassan Aga, and he grew
very rich and became king of Algiers. With him I went
there from Constantinople, rather glad to be so near Spain,
not that I intended to write to any one about my unhappy
lot, but to try if fortune would be kinder to me in Algiers
than in Constantinople, where I had attempted in a thousand ways to escape without ever finding a favorable time
or chance; but in Algiers I resolved to seek for other
means of effecting the purpose I cherished so dearly; for
the hope of obtaining my liberty never deserted me; and
when in my plots and schemes and attempts the result did
not answer my expectations, without giving way to despair
I immediately began to look out for or conjure up some
new hope to support me, however faint or feeble it might
be.

In this way I lived on immured in a building or prison
called by the Turks a *baño*, in which they confine the
Christian captives, as well those that are the king's as
those belonging to private individuals, and also what they
call those of the Almacen, which is as much as to say the
slaves of the municipality, who serve the city in the public
works and other employments; but captives of this kind
recover their liberty with great difficulty, for, as they are
public property and have no particular master, there is no
one with whom to treat for their ransom, even though
they may have the means. To these *baños*, as I have said,
some private individuals of the town are in the habit of

bringing their captives, especially when they are to be ransomed; because there they can keep them in safety and comfort until their ransom arrives. The king's captives also, that are on ransom, do not go out to work with the rest of the crew, unless when their ransom is delayed; for then, to make them write for it more pressingly, they compel them to work and go for wood, which is no light labor.

I, however, was of those on ransom, for when it was discovered that I was a captain, although I declared my scanty means and want of fortune, nothing could dissuade them from including me among the gentlemen and those waiting to be ransomed. They put a chain on me, more as a mark of this than to keep me safe, and so I passed my life in that *baño* with several other gentlemen and persons of equality marked out as held to ransom; but though at times, or rather almost always, we suffered from hunger and scanty clothing, nothing distressed us so much as hearing and seeing at every turn the unexampled and unheard-of cruelties my master inflicted upon the Christians. Every day he hanged a man, impaled one, cut off the ears of another; and all with so little provocation, or so entirely without any, that the Turks acknowledged he did it merely for the sake of doing it, and because he was by nature murderously disposed towards the whole human race.

The only one that fared at all well with him was a Spanish soldier, something de Saavedra by name, to whom he never gave a blow himself, or ordered a blow to be given, or addressed a hard word, although he had done things that will dwell in the memory of the people there for many a year, and all to recover his liberty; and for the least of the many things he did we all dreaded that he would be impaled, and he himself was in fear of it more than once; and only that time does not allow, I could tell you now something of what that soldier did, that would interest and astonish you much more than the narration of my own tale.

To go on with my story; the courtyard of our prison was overlooked by the windows of the house belonging to a wealthy Moor of high position; and these, as is usual in Moorish houses, were rather loopholes than windows, and besides were covered with thick and close blinds. It so happened, then, that as I was one day on the terrace of our prison with three other comrades, trying, to pass away the time, how far we could leap with our chains, we being alone, for all the other Christians had gone out to work, I chanced to raise my eyes, and from one of these little closed windows I saw a reed appear with a cloth attached to the end of it, and it kept waving to and fro, and moving as if making signs to us to come and take it. We watched it, and one of those who were with me went and stood under the reed to see whether they would let it drop, or what they would do, but as he did so the reed was raised and moved from side to side, as if they meant to say " no " by a shake of the head. The Christians came back, and it was again lowered, making the same movements as before. Another of my comrades went, and with him the same happened as with the first, and then the third went forward, but with the same result as the first and second. Seeing this I did not like not to try my luck, and as soon as I came under the reed it was dropped and fell inside the *baño* at my feet. I hastened to untie the cloth, in which I perceived a knot, and in this were ten *cianis,* which are coins of base gold, current among the Moors, and each worth ten *reals* of our money.

It is needless to say that I rejoiced over this godsend, and my joy was not less than my wonder as I strove to imagine how this good fortune could have come to us, but to me specially; for the evident unwillingness to drop the reed for any but me showed that it was for me the favor was intended. I took my welcome money, broke the reed, and returned to the terrace, and looking up at the window, I saw a very white hand put out that opened and shut very quickly. From this we gathered or fancied that it must be some woman living in that house that had done us this kindness, and to show that we were grateful for it, we made salaams after the fashion of the Moors, bowing the head, bending the body, and crossing the arms on the breast. Shortly afterwards at the same window a small cross made of reeds was put out and immediately withdrawn. This sign led us to believe that some Christian woman was a captive in the house, and that it was she who had been so good to us; but the whiteness of the hand and the bracelet we had perceived made us dismiss that idea, though we thought it might be one of the Christian renegades whom their masters very often take as lawful wives, and gladly, for they prefer them to the women of their own nation.

In all our conjectures we were wide of the truth; so from that time forward our sole occupation was watching and gazing at the window where the cross had appeared to us, as if it were our pole-star; but at least fifteen days passed without our seeing either it or the hand, or any other sign whatever; and though meanwhile we endeavored with the utmost pains to ascertain who it was that lived in the house, and whether there were any Christian renegade in it, nobody could ever tell us anything more than that he who lived there was a rich Moor of high position, Hadji Morato by name, formerly *alcaide* of La Pata, an office of high dignity among them. But when we least thought it was going to rain any more *cianis* from that quarter, we saw the reed suddenly appear with another cloth, tied in a larger knot, attached to it, and this at a time when, as on the former occasion, the *baño* was deserted and unoccupied.

We made trial as before, each of the same three going forward before I did; but the reed was delivered to none but me, and on my approach it was let drop. I untied the knot and I found forty Spanish gold crowns with a paper written in Arabic, and at the end of the writing there was a large cross drawn. I kissed the cross, took the crowns and returned to the terrace, and we all made our salaams; again the hand appeared, I made signs that I would read the paper, and then the window was closed. We were all puzzled, though filled with joy at what had taken place;

and as none of us understood Arabic, great was our curiosity to know what the paper contained, and still greater the difficulty of finding some one to read it.

At last I resolved to confide in a renegade, a native of Murcia, who professed a very great friendship for me, and had given pledges that bound him to keep any secret I might intrust to him; for it is the custom with some renegades, when they intend to return to Christian territory, to carry about them certificates from captives of mark testifying, in whatever form they can, that such and such a renegade is a worthy man who has always shown kindness to Christians, and is anxious to escape on the first opportunity that may present itself. Some obtain these testimonials with good intentions, others put them to a cunning use; for when they go to pillage on Christian territory, if they chance to be cast away, or taken prisoners, they produce their certificates and say that from these papers may be seen the object they came for, which was to remain on Christian ground, and that it was to this end they joined the Turks in their foray. In this way they escape the consequences of the first outburst and make their peace with the Church before it does them any harm, and then when they have the chance they return to Barbary to become what they were before. Others, however, there are who procure these papers and make use of them honestly, and remain on Christian soil. This friend of mine, then, was one of these renegades that I have described; he had certificates from all our comrades, in which we testified in his favor as strongly as we could; and if the Moors had found the papers they would have burned him alive.

I knew that he understood Arabic very well, and could not only speak but also write it; but before I disclosed the whole matter to him, I asked him to read for me this paper which I had found by accident in a hole in my cell. He opened it and remained some time examining it and muttering to himself as he translated it. I asked him if he understood it, and he told me he did perfectly, and that if I wished him to tell me its meaning word for word, I must

give him pen and ink that he might do it more satisfactorily. We at once gave him what he required, and he set
about translating it bit by bit, and when he had done he
said:

"All that is here in Spanish is what the Moorish paper
contains, and you must bear in mind that when it says,
'Lela Marien' it means Our Lady the Virgin Mary.'"
We read the paper and it ran thus:

"When I was a child my father had a slave who taught
me to pray the Christian prayer in my own language, and
told me many things about Lela Marien. The Christian
died, and I know that she did not go to the fire, but to
Allah, because since then I have seen her twice, and she
told me to go to the land of the Christians to see Lela
Marien, who had great love for me. I know not how to
go. I have seen many Christians, but except thyself none
has seemed to me to be a gentleman. I am young and
beautiful, and have plenty of money to take with me. See
if thou canst contrive how we may go, and if thou wilt
thou shalt be my husband there, and if thou wilt not it will
not distress me, for Lela Marien will find me some one
to marry me. I myself have written this: have a care to
whom thou givest it to read; trust no Moor, for they are
all perfidious. I am greatly troubled on this account, for I
would not have thee confide in any one, because if my
father knew it he would at once fling me down a well and
cover me with stones. I will put a thread to the reed; tie
the answer to it, and if thou hast no one to write for thee
in Arabic, tell it to me by signs, for Lela Marien will make
me understand thee. She and Allah and this cross, which
I often kiss as the captive bade me, protect thee."

Judge, sirs, whether we had reason for surprise and joy
at the words of this paper; and both one and the other were
so great, that the renegade perceived that the paper had
not been found by chance, but had been in reality addressed
to some one of us, and he begged us, if what he suspected
were the truth, to trust him and tell him all, for he would
risk his life for our freedom; and so saying he took out

from his breast a metal crucifix, and with many tears swore by the God the image represented, in whom, sinful and wicked as he was, he truly and faithfully believed, to be loyal to us and keep secret whatever we chose to reveal to him; for he thought and almost foresaw that by means of her who had written that paper, he and all of us would obtain our liberty, and he himself obtain the object he so much desired, his restoration to the bosom of the Holy Mother Church, from which by his own sin and ignorance he was now severed like a corrupt limb.

The renegade said this with so many tears and such signs of repentance, that with one consent we all agreed to tell him the whole truth of the matter and so we gave him a full account of all, without hiding anything from him. We pointed out to him the window at which the reed appeared, and he by that means took note of the house, and resolved to ascertain with particular care who lived in it. We agreed also that it would be advisable to answer the Moorish lady's letter, and the renegade without a moment's delay took down the words I dictated to him, which were exactly what I shall tell you, for nothing of importance that took place in this affair has escaped my memory, or ever will while life lasts. This, then, was the answer returned to the Moorish lady:

"The true Allah protect thee, lady, and that blessed Marien who is the true mother of God, and who has put it into thy heart to go to the land of the Christians, because she loves thee. Entreat her that she be pleased to show thee how thou canst execute the command she gives thee, for she will, such is her goodness. On my own part, and on that of these Christians who are with me, I promise to do all that we can for thee, even to death. Fail not to write to me and inform me what thou dost mean to do, and I will always answer thee; for the great Allah has given us a Christian captive who can speak and write thy language well, as thou mayest see by this paper; without fear, therefore, thou canst inform us of all thou wouldst. As to what thou sayest, that if thou dost reach the land of the

Christians thou wilt be my wife, I give thee my promise upon it as a good Christian; and know that the Christians keep their promises better than the Moors. Allah and Marien his mother watch over thee, my lady."

The paper being written and folded I waited two days until the *baño* was empty as before, and immediately repaired to the usual walk on the terrace to see if there were any sign of the reed, which was not long in making its appearance. As soon as I saw it, although I could not distinguish who put it out, I showed the paper as a sign to attach the thread, but it was already fixed to the reed, and to it I tied the paper; and shortly afterwards our star once more made its appearance with the white flag of peace, the little bundle. It was dropped, and I picked it up, and found in the cloth, in gold and silver coins of all sorts, more than fifty crowns, which fifty times more doubled our joy and strengthened our hope of gaining our liberty.

That very night our renegade returned and said he had learned that the Moor we had been told of lived in that house, that his name was Hadji Morato, that he was enormously rich, that he had one only daughter, the heiress of all his wealth, and that it was the general opinion throughout the city that she was the most beautiful woman in Barbary, and that several of the viceroys who came there had sought her for a wife, but that she had been always unwilling to marry; and he had learned, moreover, that she had a Christian slave who was now dead; all which agreed with the contents of the paper. We immediately took counsel with the renegade as to what means would have to be adopted in order to carry off the Moorish lady and bring us all to Christian territory; and in the end it was agreed that for the present we should wait for a second communication from Zoraida (for that was the name of her who now desires to be called Maria), because we saw clearly that she and no one else could find a way out of these difficulties.

When we had decided upon this the renegade told us not to be uneasy, for he would lose his life or restore us to liberty. For four days the *baño* was filled with people, for which reason the reed delayed its appearance for four days, but at the end of that time, when the *baño* was, as it generally was, empty, it appeared with the cloth so bulky that it promised a happy birth. Reed and cloth came down to me, and I found another paper and a hundred crowns in gold, without any other coin. The renegade was present, and in our cell we gave him the paper to read, which he said was to this effect:

" I cannot think of a plan, señor, for our going to Spain, nor has Lela Marien shown me one, though I have asked her. All that can be done is for me to give you plenty of money in gold from this window. With it ransom yourself and your friends, and let one of you go to the land of the Christians, and there buy a vessel and come back for the others; and he will find me in my father's garden, which is at the Babazon gate near the sea-shore, where I shall be all this summer with my father and my servants. You can carry me away from there by night without any danger, and bring me to the vessel. And remember thou art to be my husband, else I will pray to Marien to punish thee. If thou canst not trust any one to go for the vessel, ransom thyself and do thou go, for I know thou wilt return more surely than any other, as thou art a gentleman and a Christian. Endeavor to make thyself acquainted with the garden; and when I see thee walking yonder I shall know that the *baño* is empty and I will give thee abundance of money. Allah protect thee, señor."

These were the words and contents of the second paper, and on hearing them, each declared himself willing to be the ransomed one, and promised to go and return with scrupulous good faith; and I too made the same offer; but to all this the renegade objected, saying that he would not on any account consent to one being set free before all went together, as experience had taught him how ill those who have been set free keep promises which they made in captivity; for captives of distinction frequently had recourse to this plan, paying the ransom of one who

was to go to Valencia or Majorca with money to enable
him to arm a bark and return for the others who had
ransomed him; but who never came back; for recovered
liberty and the dread of losing it again efface from the
memory all the obligations in the world.

And to prove the truth of what he said, he told us briefly
what had happened to a certain Christian gentleman almost
at that very time, the strangest case that had ever occurred
even there, where astonishing and marvelous things are
happening every instant. In short, he ended by saying that
what could and ought to be done was to give the money
intended for the ransom of one of us Christians to him,
so that he might with it buy a vessel there in Algiers under
the pretence of becoming a merchant and trading to Tetuan
and along the coast; and when master of the vessel, it
would be easy for him to hit on some way of getting us
all out of the *baño* and putting us on board; especially if
the Moorish lady gave, as she said, money enough to ransom all, because once free it would be the easiest thing in
the world for us to embark even in open day; but the
greatest difficulty was that the Moors do not allow any
renegade to buy or own any craft, unless it be a large
vessel for going on roving expeditions, because they are
afraid that anyone who buys a small vessel, especially if
he be a Spaniard, only wants it for the purpose of escaping to Christian territory. This, however, he could get over
by arranging with a Tagarin Moor to go shares with him in
the purchase of the vessel and in the profit on the cargo;
and under cover of this he could become master of the
vessel, in which case he looked upon all the rest as accomplished.

But though to me and my comrades it had seemed a
better plan to send to Majorca for the vessel, as the
Moorish lady suggested, we did not dare to oppose him,
fearing that if we did not do as he said he would de-
nounce us, and place us in danger of losing all our lives
if he were to disclose our dealings with Zoraida, for
whose life we would have all given our own. We there-

fore resolved to put ourselves in the hands of God and in the renegade's; and at the same time an answer was given to Zoraida, telling her that we would do all she recommended, for she had given as good advice as if Lela Marien had delivered it, and that it depended on her alone whether we were to defer the business or put it in execution at once.

I renewed my promise to be her husband; and thus the next day that the *baño* chanced to be empty she at different times gave us by means of the reed and cloth two thousand gold crowns and a paper in which she said that the next Jumá, that is to say Friday, she was going to her father's garden, but that before she went she would give us more money; and if it were not enough we were to let her know, as she would give us as much as we asked, for her father had so much he would not miss it, and besides she kept all the keys.

We at once gave the renegade five hundred crowns to buy the vessel, and with eight hundred I ransomed myself, giving the money to a Valencian merchant who happened to be in Algiers at the time, and who had me released on his word, pledging it that on the arrival of the first ship from Valencia he would pay my ransom; for if he had given the money at once it would have made the king suspect that my ransom money had been for a long time in Algiers, and that the merchant had for his own advantage kept it secret. In fact, my master was so difficult to deal with that I dared not on any account pay down the money at once. The Thursday before the Friday on which the fair Zoraida was to go to the garden she gave us a thousand crowns more, and warned us of her departure, begging me, if I were ransomed, to find out her father's garden at once, and by all means to seek an opportunity of going there to see her. I answered in a few words that I would do so, and that she must remember to commend us to Lela Marien with all the prayers the captive had taught her.

This having been done, steps were taken to ransom our

three comrades, so as to enable them to quit the *baño,* and lest, seeing me ransomed and themselves not, though the money was forthcoming, they should make a disturbance about it and the devil should prompt them to do something that might injure Zoraida; for though their position might be sufficient to relieve me from this apprehension, nevertheless I was unwilling to run any risk in the matter; and so I had them ransomed in the same way as I was, handing over all the money to the merchant so that he might with safety and confidence give security; without, however, confiding our arrangement and secret to him, which might have been dangerous.

CHAPTER XXIX

BEFORE fifteen days were over our renegade had already purchased an excellent vessel with room for more than thirty persons; and to make the transaction safe and lend a color to it, he thought it well to make, as he did, a voyage to a place called Shershel, twenty leagues from Algiers on the Oran side, where there is an extensive trade in dried figs. Two or three times he made this voyage in company with the Tagarin already mentioned. The Moors of Aragon are called Tagarins in Barbary, and those of Granada Mudéjars; but in the Kingdom of Fez they call the Mudéjars Elches, and they are the people the king chiefly employs in war. To proceed: Every time he passed with his vessel he anchored in a cove that was not two cross-bow shots from the garden where Zoraida was waiting; and there the renegade, together with the two Moorish lads that rowed, used purposely to station himself, either going through his prayers, or else practicing as a part what he meant to perform in earnest. And thus he would go to Zoraida's garden and ask for fruit, which her father gave him, not knowing him; but though, as he afterwards told me, he sought to speak to Zoraida, and tell her who he was, and that by my orders he was to take her to the land of the Christians, so that she might feel satisfied and easy, he had never been able to do so; for the Moorish women do not allow themselves to be seen by any Moor or Turk, unless their husband or father bid them: with Christian captives they permit freedom of intercourse and communication, even more than might be considered proper. But for my part I should have been sorry if he had spoken to her, for perhaps it might have alarmed her to find her affairs talked of by renegades.

But God, who ordered it otherwise, afforded no opportunity for our renegade's well-meant purpose; and he, seeing how safely he could go to Shershel and return, and anchor when and how and where he liked, and that the Tagarin his partner had no will but his, and that, now I was ransomed, all we wanted was to find some Christians to row, told me to look out for any I should be willing to take with me, over and above those who had been ransomed, and to engage them for the next Friday, which he fixed upon for our departure. On this I spoke to twelve Spaniards, all stout rowers, and such as could most easily leave the city; but it was no easy matter to find so many just then, because there were twenty ships out on a cruise and they had taken all the rowers with them; and these would not have been found were it not that their master remained at home that summer without going to sea in order to finish a *galliot* that he had upon the stocks. To these men I said nothing more than that the next Friday in the evening they were to come out stealthily one by one and hang about Hadji Morato's garden, waiting for me there until I came. These directions I gave each one separately, with orders that if they saw any other Christians there they were not to say anything to them except that I had directed them to wait at that spot.

This preliminary having been settled, another still more necessary step had to be taken, which was to let Zoraida know how matters stood that she might be prepared and forewarned, so as not to be taken by surprise if we were suddenly to seize upon her before she thought the Christians' vessel could have returned. I determined, therefore, to go to the garden and try if I could speak to her; and the day before my departure I went there under the pretence of gathering herbs. The first person I met was her

father, who addressed me in the language that all over
Barbary and even in Constantinople is the medium between
captives and Moors, and is neither Morisco nor Castilian,
nor of any other nation, but a mixture of all languages,
by means of which we can all understand one another. In
this sort of language, I say, he asked me what I wanted in
his garden, and to whom I belonged. I replied that I was
a slave of the Arnaut Mami (for I knew as a certainty
that he was a very great friend of his), and that I wanted
some herbs to make a salad. He asked me then whether
I were on ransom or not, and what my master demanded
for me.

While these questions and answers were proceeding, the
fair Zoraida, who had already perceived me some time
before, came out of the house in the garden, and as Moorish women are by no means particular about letting themselves be seen by Christians, or, as I have said before, at
all coy, she had no hesitation in coming to where her
father stood with me; moreover, her father, seeing her
approaching slowly, called to her to come. It would be
beyond my power now to describe to you the great beauty,
the high-bred air, the rich, brilliant attire of my beloved
Zoraida as she presented herself before my eyes. I will
content myself with saying that more pearls hung from
her fair neck, her ears, and her hair than she had hairs on
her head. On her ankles, which, as is customary, were
bare, she had *carcajes* (for so bracelets or anklets are
called in Morisco) of the purest gold, set with so many
diamonds that she told me afterwards her father valued
them at ten thousand doubloons, and those she had on
her wrists were worth as much more. The pearls were in
profusion and very fine, for the highest display and adorn-
ment of the Moorish women is decking themselves with
rich pearls and seed-pearls; and of these there are, therefore, more among the Moors than among any other people.
Zoraida's father had the reputation of possessing a great
number, and the purest in all Algiers, and of possessing
also more than two hundred thousand Spanish crowns;

and she, who is now mistress of me only, was mistress of all this.

Whether thus adorned she would have been beautiful or not, and what she must have been in her prosperity, may be imagined from the beauty remaining to her after so many hardships; for, as everyone knews, the beauty of some women has its times and its seasons, and is increased or diminished by chance causes; and naturally the emotions of the mind will heighten or impair it, though indeed more frequently they totally destroy it. In a word, she presented herself before me that day attired with the utmost splendor, and supremely beautiful; at any rate, she seemed to me the most beautiful object I had ever seen; and when, besides, I thought of all I owed to her I felt as though I had before me some heavenly being come to earth to bring me relief and happiness.

As she approached, her father told her in his own language that I was a cáptive belonging to his friend the Arnaut Mami, and that I had come for salad.

She took up the conversation, and in that mixture of tongues I have spoken of she asked me if I was a gentleman, and why I was not ransomed.

I answered that I was already ransomed, and that by the price it might be seen what value my master set on me, as they had given one thousand five hundred *zoltanis* for me; to which she replied:

" Hadst thou been my father's, I can tell thee, I would not have let him part with thee for twice as much, for you Christians always tell lies about yourselves and make yourselves out poor to cheat the Moors."

" That may be, lady," said I; " but indeed I dealt truthfully with my master, as I do and mean to do with everybody in the world."

" And when dost thou go ? " said Zoraida.

" Tomorrow, I think," said I, " for there is a vessel here from France which sails tomorrow, and I think I shall go in her."

" Would it not be better," said Zoraida, " to wait for the

arrival of ships from Spain and go with them and not with the French, who are not your friends?"

"No," said I; "though if there were intelligence that a vessel were now coming from Spain it is true I might, perhaps, wait for it; however, it is more likely I shall depart tomorrow, for the longing I feel to return to my country and to those I love is so great that it will not allow me to wait for another opportunity, however more convenient, if it be delayed."

"No doubt thou art married in thine own country," said Zoraida, "and for that reason thou art anxious to go and see thy wife."

"I am not married," I replied, "but I have given my promise to marry on my arrival there."

"And is the lady beautiful to whom thou hast given it?" said Zoraida.

"So beautiful," said I, "that, to describe her worthily and tell thee the truth, she is very like thee."

At this her father laughed very heartily and said, "By Allah, Christian, she must be very beautiful if she is like my daughter, who is the most beautiful woman in all this kingdom: only look at her well and thou wilt see I am telling the truth."

Zoraida's father as the better linguist helped to interpret most of these words and phrases, for though she spoke the bastard language that, as I have said, is employed there, she expressed her meaning more by signs than by words.

While we were still engaged in this conversation, a Moor came running up, exclaiming that four Turks had leaped over the fence or wall of the garden, and were gathering the fruit, though it was not yet ripe. The old man was alarmed and Zoraida, too, for the Moors commonly, and, so to speak, instinctively have a dread of the Turks, but particularly of the soldiers, who are so insolent and domineering to the Moors who are under their power that they treat them worse than if they were their slaves. So her father said to Zoraida:

"Daughter, retire into the house and shut thyself in

while I go and speak to these dogs; and thou, Christian, pick they herbs, and go in peace, and Allah bring thee safe to thy own country."

I bowed, and he went away to look for the Turks, leaving me alone with Zoraida, who made as if she were about to retire as her father bade her; but the moment he was concealed by the trees of the garden, turning to me with her eyes full of tears, she said, "*Tameji, cristiano, tameji?*" that is to say, "Art thou going, Christian, art thou going?"

I made answer, "Yes, lady, but not without thee, come what may: be on the watch for me on the next Jumá, and be not alarmed when thou seest us; for most surely we shall go to the land of the Christians."

This I said in such a way that she understood perfectly all that passed between us, and throwing her arm round my neck she began with feeble steps to move towards the house; but as fate would have it (and it might have been very unfortunate if Heaven had not otherwise ordered it), just as we were moving on in the manner and position I have described, with her arm round my neck, her father, as he returned after having sent away the Turks, saw how we were walking and we perceived that he saw us; but Zoraida, ready and quick-witted, took care not to remove her arm from my neck, but on the contrary drew closer to me and laid her head on my breast, bending her knees a little and showing all the signs and tokens of fainting, while I at the same time made it seem as though I were supporting her against my will. Her father came running up to where we were, and seeing his daughter in this state asked what was the matter with her; she, however, giving no answer, he said, "No doubt she has fainted in alarm at the entrance of those dogs," and taking her from mine he drew her to his own breast, while she, sighing, her eyes still wet with tears, said again, "*Ameji, cristiano, ameji*"—"Go, Christian, go." To this her father replied, "There is no need, daughter, for the Christian to go, for he has done thee no harm, and the Turks have now gone; feel no alarm, there is nothing to hurt thee, for as I say, the Turks at my request have gone back the way they came."

"It was they who terrified her, as thou hast said, señor," said I to her father; "but since she tells me to go, I have no wish to displease her: peace be with thee, and with thy leave I will come back to this garden for herbs if need be, for my master says there are nowhere better herbs than here."

"Come back for any thou hast need of," replied Hadji Morato; "for my daughter does not speak thus because she is displeased with thee or any Christian: she only meant that the Turks should go, not thou; or that it was time for thee to look for thy herbs."

With this I at once took my leave of both; and she, looking as though her heart were breaking, retired with her father. While pretending to look for herbs I made the round of the garden at my ease, and studied carefully all the approaches and outlets, and the fastenings of the house and everything that could be taken advantage of to make our task easy. Having done so, I went and gave an account of all that had taken place to the renegade and my comrades, and looked forward with impatience to the hour when, all fear at an end, I should find myself in possession of the prize which fortune held out to me in the fair and lovely Zoraida.

The time passed at length, and the appointed day we so longed for arrived; and, following out the arrangement and plan which, after careful consideration and many a long discussion, we had decided upon, we succeeded as fully as we could have wished; for on the Friday following the day upon which I spoke to Zoraida in the garden, the renegade anchored his vessel at nightfall almost opposite the spot where she was. The Christians who were to row were ready and in hiding in different places round about, all waiting for me, anxious and elated, and eager to attack the vessel they had before their eyes; for they did not know the renegade's plan, but expected that they were to gain their liberty by force of arms and by killing the Moors who were on board the vessel. As soon, then, as I and my comrades made our appearance, all those that were in hiding seeing us came and joined us. It was now the time when the city gates are shut, and there was no one to be seen in all the space outside.

When we were collected together we debated whether it would be better first to go for Zoraida, or to make prisoners of the Moorish rowers who rowed in the vessel; but while we were still uncertain, our renegade came up asking us what kept us, as it was now the time, and all the Moors were off their guard and most of them asleep. We told him why we hesitated, but he said it was of more importance first to secure the vessel, which could be done with the greatest ease and without any danger, and then we could go for Zoraida. We all approved of what he said, and so, without further delay, guided by him we made for the vessel, and he, leaping on board first, drew his cutlass and said in Morisco, "Let no one stir from this if he does not want it to cost him his life." By this time almost all of the Christians were on board, and the Moors, who were faint-hearted, hearing their captain speak in this way, were cowed, and without any one of them taking to his arms (and indeed they had few or hardly any) they submitted without saying a word to be bound by the Christians, who quickly secured them, threatening them that if they raised any kind of outcry they would be all put to the sword.

This having been accomplished, and half of our party being left to keep guard over them, the rest of us, again taking the renegade as our guide, hastened towards Hadji Morato's garden, and as good luck would have it, on trying the gate it opened as easily as if it had not been locked; and so, quite quietly and in silence, we reached the house without being perceived by anybody. The lovely Zoraida was watching for us at a window, and as soon as she perceived that there were people there, she asked in a low voice if we were *Nizarani,* as much as to say or ask if we were Christians. I answered that we were, and begged her to come down. As soon as she recognized me she did not delay an instant, but without answering a word came down immediately, opened the door and presented herself before us all, so beautiful and so richly attired that I cannot attempt to describe her. The moment I saw her I took her hand and kissed it, and the renegade and my two comrades did the same; and the rest, who knew nothing of the circumstances, did as they saw us do, for it only seemed as if we were returning thanks to her, and recognizing her as the giver of our liberty. The renegade asked her in the Morisco language if her father was in the house. She replied that he was and that he was asleep.

"Then it will be necessary to waken him and take him with us," said the renegade, "and everything of value in this fair mansion."

"Nay," said she, "my father must not on any account be touched, and there is nothing in the house except what I shall take, and that will be quite enough to enrich and satisfy all of you; wait a little and you shall see," and so saying, she went in again, telling us she would return immediately, and bidding us keep quiet without making any noise.

I asked the renegade what had passed between them, and when he told me I declared that nothing should be done except in accordance with the wishes of Zoraida, who now came back with a little trunk so full of gold crowns that she could scarcely carry it. Unfortunately her father awoke while this was going on, and hearing a noise in the garden, came to the window, and at once perceiving that all those who were there were Christians, raising a prodigiously loud outcry, he began to call out in Arabic, "Christians, Christians! thieves, thieves!" by which cries we were all thrown into the greatest fear and embarrassment; but the renegade seeing the danger we were in and how important it was for him to effect his purpose before we were heard, mounted with the utmost quickness to where Hadji Morato was, and with him went

some of our party; I, however, did not dare to leave
Zoraida, who had fallen almost fainting in my arms.

To be brief, those who had gone upstairs acted so
promptly that in an instant they came down, carrying
Hadji Morato with his hands bound and a napkin tied
over his mouth, which prevented him from uttering a
word, warning him at the same time that to attempt to
speak would cost him his life. When his daughter caught
sight of him she covered her eyes so as not to see him,
and her father was horror-stricken, not knowing how willingly she had placed herself in our hands. But it was now
most essential for us to be on the move, and carefully
and quickly we regained the vessel, where those who had
remained on board were waiting for us in apprehension
of some mishap having befallen us. It was barely two
hours after night set in when we were all on board the
vessel, where the cords were removed from the hands of
Zoraida's father, and the napkin from his mouth; but the
renegade once more told him not to utter a word, or they
would take his life. He, when he saw his daughter there,
began to sigh piteously, and still more when he perceived
that I held her closely embraced and that she lay quiet
without resisting or complaining, or showing any reluct-
ance; nevertheless he remained silent lest they should carry
into effect the repeated threats the renegade had addressed
to him.

Finding herself now on board, and that we were about
to give way with the oars, Zoraida, seeing her father there,
and the other Moors bound, bade the renegade ask me to
do her the favor of releasing the Moors and setting her
father at liberty, for she would rather drown herself in
the sea than suffer a father that had loved her so dearly
to be carried away captive before her eyes and on her
account. The renegade repeatd this to me, and I replied
that I was very willing to do so; but he replied that it was
not advisable, because if they were left there they would
at once raise the country and stir up the city, and lead
to the dispatch of swift cruisers in pursuit, and our being

taken, by sea or land, without any possibility of escape;
and that all that could be done was to set them free on
the first Christian ground we reached.

On this point we all agreed; and Zoraida, to whom it
was explained, together with the reasons that prevented us
from doing at once what she desired, was satisfied likewise; and then in glad silence and with cheerful alacrity
each of our stout rowers took his oar, and commending
ourselves to God with all our hearts, we began to shape
our course for the island of Majorca, the nearest Christian land. Owing, however, to the Tramontana rising a
little, and the sea growing somewhat rough, it was impossible for us to keep a straight course for Majorca, and we
were compelled to coast in the direction of Oran, not without great uneasiness on our part lest we should be observed
from the town of Shershel, which lies on that coast, not
more than sixty miles from Algiers. Moreover, we were
afraid of meeting on that course one of the *galliots* that
usually come with goods from Tetuan; although each of
us for himself and all of us together felt confident that,
if we were to meet a merchant *galliot*, so that it were not
a cruiser, not only should we not be lost, but that we
should take a vessel in which we could more safely accomplish our voyage. As we pursued our course Zoraida kept
her head between my hands so as not to see her father,
and I felt sure that she was praying to Lela Marien to
help us.

We might have made about thirty miles when daybreak
found us some three musket-shots off the land, which
seemed to us deserted, and without anyone to see us. For
all that, however, by hard rowing we put out a little to
sea, for it was now somewhat calmer, and having gained
about two leagues the word was given to row by batches,
while we ate something, for the vessel was well provided;
but the rowers said it was not a time to take any rest; let
food be served out to those who were not rowing, but
they would not leave their oars on any account. This was
done, but now a stiff breeze began to blow, which obliged

us to leave off rowing and make sail at once and steer for Oran, as it was impossible to make any other course. All this was done very promptly, and under sail we ran more than eight miles an hour without any fear, except that of coming across some vessel out on a roving expedition. We gave the Moorish rowers some food, and the renegade comforted them by telling them that they were not held as captives, as we should set them free on the first opportunity.

The same was said to Zoraida's father, who replied, "Anything else, O Christian, I might hope for or think likely from your generosity and good behavior, but do not think me so simple as to imagine you will give me my liberty; for you would have never exposed yourselves to the danger of depriving me of it only to restore it to me so generously, especially as you know who I am and the sum you may expect to receive on restoring it; and if you will only name that, I here offer all you require for myself and for my unhappy daughter there; or else for her alone, for she is the greatest and most precious part of my soul."

As he said this he began to weep so bitterly that he filled us all with compassion and forced Zoraida to look at him, and when she saw him weeping she was so moved that she rose from my feet and ran to throw her arms round him, and pressing her face to his, they both gave way to such an outburst of tears that several of us were constrained to keep them company.

But when her father saw her in full dress and with all her jewels about her, he said to her in his own language, "What means this, my daughter? Last night, before this terrible misfortune in which we are plunged befell us, I saw thee in thy every-day and indoor garments; and now, without having had time to attire thyself, and without my bringing thee any joyful tidings to furnish an occasion for adorning and bedecking thyself, I see thee arrayed in the finest attire it would be in my power to give thee when fortune was most kind to us. Answer me this; for it causes me greater anxiety and surprise than even this misfortune itself."

The renegade interpreted to us what the Moor said to his daughter; she, however, returned him no answer. But when he observed in one corner of the vessel the little trunk in which she used to keep her jewels, which he well knew he had left in Algiers and had not brought to the garden, he was still more amazed, and asked her how that trunk had come into our hands, and what there was in it. To which the renegade, without waiting for Zoraida to reply, made answer: "Do not trouble thyself by asking thy daughter Zoraida so many questions, señor, for the one answer I will give thee will serve for all; I would have thee know that she is a Christian, and that it is she who has been the file for our chains and our deliverer from captivity. She is here of her own free will, as glad, I imagine, to find herself in this position as he who escapes from darkness into the light, from death to life, and from suffering to glory."

"Daughter, is this true, what he says?" cried the Moor.

"It is," replied Zoraida.

"That thou art in truth a Christian," said the old man, "and that thou hast given thy father into the power of his enemies?"

To which Zoraida made answer, "A Christian I am, but it is not I who have placed thee in this position, for it never was my wish to leave thee or do thee harm, but only to do good to myself."

"And what good hast thou done thyself, daughter?" said he.

"Ask thou that," said she, "of Lela Marien, for she can tell thee better than I."

The Moor had hardly heard these words when with marvelous quickness he flung himself head foremost into the sea, where no doubt he would have been drowned had not the long and full dress he wore held him up for a little on the surface of the water. Zoraida cried aloud to us to save him, and we all hastened to help, and seizing him by his robe we drew him in, half drowned and insensible, at which Zoraida was in such distress that she wept over him as piteously and bitterly as though he were already dead. We turned him upon his face and he voided a great quantity of water, and at the end of two hours came to himself. Meanwhile, the wind having changed, we were compelled to head for the land, and ply our oars to avoid being driven on shore; but it was our good fortune to make a cove that lies on one side of a small promontory or cape, called by the Moors that of the *cava rumia,* which in our language means "the wicked Christian woman"; for it is a tradition among them that La Cava, through whom Spain was lost, lies buried at that spot; *cava* in their language meaning "wicked woman," and *rumia* "Christian"; moreover, they count it unlucky to anchor there when necessity compels them, and they never do so otherwise.

For us, however, it was not the resting-place of the wicked woman but a haven of safety for our relief, so much had the sea now got up. We posted a look-out on shore, and never let the oars out of our hands, and ate of the stores the renegade had laid in, imploring God and Our Lady with all our hearts to help and protect us, that we might give a happy ending to a beginning so prosperous. At the entreaty of Zoraida orders were given to set on shore her father and the other Moors who were still bound, for she could not endure, nor could her tender heart bear to see her father in bonds and her fellow-countrymen prisoners before her eyes. We promised her to do this at the moment of departure, for as it was uninhabited we ran no risk in releasing them at that place.

Our prayers were not so far in vain as to be unheard by Heaven, for the wind immediately changed in our favor, and the sea grew calm, inviting us once more to resume our voyage with a good heart. Seeing this, we unbound the Moors and one by one put them on shore at which they were filled with amazement; but when we came to land Zoraida's father, who had now completely recovered his senses, he said:

"Why is it, think ye, Christians, that this wicked woman is rejoicing at your giving me my liberty? Think ye it is because of the affection she bears me? Nay, verily, it is only because of the, hindrance my presence offers to the execution of her base designs. And think not that it is her belief that yours is better than ours that has led her to change her religion; it is only because she knows that immodesty is more freely practiced in your country than in ours."

Then turning to Zoraida, while I and another of the Christians held him fast by both arms, lest he should do some mad act, he said to her:

"Infamous girl, misguided maiden, whither in thy blindness and madness art thou going in the hands of these dogs, our natural enemies? Cursed be the hour when I begot thee! Cursed the luxury and indulgence in which I reared thee!"

But seeing that he was not likely soon to cease I made haste to put him on shore, and thence he continued his maledictions and lamentations aloud; calling on Mohammed to pray to Allah to destroy us, to confound us, to make an end of us; and when, in consequence of having made sail, we could no longer hear what he said we could see what he did; how he plucked out his beard and tore his hair and lay writhing on the ground. But once he raised his voice to such a pitch that we were able to hear what he said:

"Come back, dear daughter, come back to shore; I forgive thee all; let those men have the money, for it is theirs now, and come back to thy sorrowing father, who will yield up his life on this barren strand if thou dost leave him."

All this Zoraida heard, and heard with sorrow and tears, and all she could say in answer was:

"Allah grant that Lela Marien, who has made me become a Christian, give thee comfort in thy sorrow, O my father. Allah knows that I could not do otherwise than I have done, and that these Christians owe nothing to my will; for even had I wished not to accompany them, but remain at home, it would have been impossible for me, so eagerly did my soul urge me on to the accomplishment of this purpose, which I feel to be as righteous as to thee, dear father, it seems wicked."

But neither could her father hear her nor we see him when she said this; and so, while I consoled Zoraida, we turned our attention to our voyage, in which a breeze from the right point so favored us that we made sure of finding ourselves off the coast of Spain on the morrow by daybreak. But, as good seldom or never comes pure and unmixed, without being attended or followed by some disturbing evil that gives a shock to it, our fortune, or perhaps the curses which the Moor had hurled at his daughter (for whatever kind of father they may come from these are always to be dreaded), brought it about that when we were now in mid-sea, and the night about three hours spent, as we were running with all sail set and oars lashed, for the favoring breeze saved us the trouble or using them, we saw by the light of the moon, which shone brilliantly, a square-rigged vessel in full sail close to us, luffing up and standing across our course, and so close that we had to strike sail to avoid running foul of her, while they, too, put the helm hard up to let us pass. They came to the side of the ship to ask who we were, whither we were bound, and whence we came, but as they asked this in French our renegade said:

"Let no one answer, for no doubt these are French corsairs who plunder all comers."

Acting on this warning no one answered a word, but after we had gone a little ahead, and the vessel was now lying to leeward, suddenly they fired two guns, and apparently both loaded with chain-shot, for with one they cut our mast in half and brought down both it and the sail into the sea, and the other, discharged at the same moment, sent a ball into our vessel amidships, staving her in completely, but without doing any further damage. We, however, finding ourselves sinking, began to shout for help and call upon those in the ship to pick us up, as we were beginning to fill. They then lay to, and lowering a skiff or boat, as many as a dozen Frenchmen, well armed with matchlocks, and their matches burning, got into it and came alongside; and seeing how few we were, and that our vessel was going own, they took us in, telling us that this had come to us through our incivility in not giving them an answer. Our renegade took the trunk containing Zoraida's wealth and dropped it into the sea without anyone perceiving what he did.

In short, we went on board with the Frenchmen, who, after having ascertained all they wanted to know about us, rifled us of everything we had, as if they had been our bitterest enemies, and from Zoraida they took even the anklets she wore on her feet; but the distress they caused her did not distress me so much as the fear I was in that from robbing her of her rich and precious jewels they would proceed to rob her of the most precious jewel that she valued more than all. The desires, however, of those people do not go beyond money, but of that their covetousness is insatiable, and on this occasion it was carried to such a pitch that they would have taken even the clothes we wore as captives if they had been worth anything to them.

It was the advice of some of them to throw us all into the sea wrapped up in a sail; for their purpose was to trade at some of the ports of Spain, giving themselves out as Bretons, and if they brought us alive they would be punished as soon as the robbery was discovered; but the captain (who was the one who had plundered my beloved Zoraida) said he was satisfied with the prize he had got, and that he would not touch at any Spanish port, but pass the Straits of Gibraltar by night, or as best he could, and make for Rochelle, from which he had sailed. So they agreed by common consent to give us the skiff belonging to their ship and all we required for the short voyage that

remained to us, and this they did the next day on coming
in sight of the Spanish coast, with which, and the joy we
felt, all our sufferings and miseries were as completely forgotten as if they had never been endured by us, such is
the delight of recovering lost liberty.

It may have been about mid-day when they placed us
in the boat, giving us two kegs of water and some biscuit;
and the captain, moved by I know not what compassion,
as the lovely Zoraida was about to embark gave her some
forty gold crowns, and would not permit his men to take
from her those same garments which she has on now.
We got into the boat, returning them thanks for their
kindness to us, and showing ourselves grateful rather than
indignant. They stood out to sea, steering for the straits;
we, without looking to any compass save the land we had
before us, set ourselves to row with such energy that by
sunset we were so near that he might easily, we thought,
land before the night was far advanced.

But as the moon did not show that night, and the sky
was clouded, and as we knew not whereabouts we were,
it did not seem to us a prudent thing to make for the
shore, as several of us advised, saying we ought to run
ourselves ashore even if it were on rocks and far from
any habitation, for in this way we should be relieved from
the apprehensions we naturally felt of the prowling ves-
sels of the Tetuan corsairs, who leave Barbary at nightfall
and are on the Spanish coast by daybreak, where they
commonly take some prize, and then go home to sleep in
their own houses. But of the conflicting counsels the one
which was adopted was that we should approach grad-
ually, and land where we could if the sea were calm enough
to permit us. This was done, and a little before midnight
we drew near to the foot of a huge and lofty mountain,
not so close to the sea but that it left a narrow space on
which to land conveniently. We ran our boat up on the
sand, and all sprang out and kissed the ground, and with
tears of joyful satisfaction returned thanks to God our
Lord for all His incomparable goodness to us on our voy-

age. We took out of the boat the provisions it contained, and drew it up on the shore, and then climbed a long way up the mountain, for even there we could not feel easy in our hearts, or thoroughly persuade ourselves that it was Christian soil that was now under our feet.

The dawn came, more slowly, I think, than we could have wished; we completed the ascent in order to see if from the summit any habitation or any shepherds' huts could be discovered, but strain our eyes as we might, neither dwelling, nor human being, nor path nor road could we perceive. However, we determined to push on farther, as it could not but be that ere long we must see someone who could tell us where we were. But what distressed me most was to see Zoraida going on foot over that rough ground; for though I once carried her on my shoulders, she was more wearied by my weariness than rested by the rest; and so she would never again allow me to undergo the exertion, and went on very patiently and cheerfully, while I led her by the hand.

We had gone rather less than a quarter of a league when the sound of a little bell fell on our ears, a clear proof that there were flocks hard by, and looking about carefully to see if any were within view, we observed a young shepherd tranquilly and unsuspiciously trimming a stick with his knife at the foot of a cork tree. We called to him, and he, raising his head, sprang nimbly to his feet, for, as we afterwards learned, the first who presented themselves to his sight were the renegade and Zoraida, and seeing them in Moorish dress he imagined that all the Moors of Barbary were upon him; and plunging with marvelous swiftness into the thicket in front of him, he began to raise a prodigious outcry, exclaiming:

"The Moors—the Moors have landed! To arms, to arms!"

We were all thrown into perplexity by these cries, not knowing what to do; but reflecting that the shouts of the shepherd would raise the country and that the mounted coast-guard would come at once to see what was the matter, we agreed that the renegade must strip off his Turkish

garments and put on a captive's jacket or coat, which one
of our party gave him at once, though he himself was
reduced to his shirt; and so commending ourselves to God,
we followed the same road which we saw the shepherd
take, expecting every moment that the coast-guard would
be down upon us. Nor did our expectation deceive us,
for two hours had not passed when, coming out of the
brushwood into the open ground, we perceived some fifty
mounted men swiftly approaching us at a hand-gallop. As
soon as we saw them we stood still, waiting for them; but
as they came close and, instead of the Moors they were in
quest of, saw a set of poor Christians, they were taken
aback, and one of them asked if it could be we who were
the cause of the shepherd having raised the call to arms.
I said yes, and as I was about to explain to him what had
occurred, and whence we came and who we were, one of
the Christians of our party recognized the horseman who
had put the question to us, and before I could say anything more he exclaimed:

"Thanks be to God, sirs, for bringing us to such good
quarters; for, if I do not deceive myself, the ground we
stand on is that of Velez Malaga; unless, indeed, all my
years of captivity have made me unable to recollect that
you, señor, who ask who we are, are Pedro de Busta-
mente, my uncle."

The Christian captive had hardly uttered these words,
when the horseman threw himself off his horse, and ran
to embrace the young man, crying:

"Nephew of my soul and life! I recognize thee now;
and long have I mourned thee as dead, I, and my sister,
thy mother, and all thy kin that are still alive, and whom
God has been pleased to preserve that they may enjoy the
happiness of seeing thee. We knew long since that thou
wert in Algiers, and from the appearance of thy garments
and those of all this company, I conclude that ye have had
a miraculous restoration to liberty."

"It is true," replied the young man, "and by-and-by
we will tell you all."

As soon as the horsemen understood that we were Christian captives, they dismounted from their horses, and each offered his to carry us to the city of Velez Malaga, which was a league and a half distant. Some of them went to bring the boat to the city, we having told them where we had left it; others took us up behind them, and Zoraida was placed on the horse of the young man's uncle. The whole town came out to meet us, for they had by this time heard of our arrival from one who had gone on in advance. They were not astonished to see liberated captives or Moorish captives, for people on that coast are well used to see both one and the other; but they were astonished at the beauty of Zoraida, which was just then heightened, as well by the exertion of traveling as by joy at finding herself on Christian soil, and relieved of all fear of being lost; for this had brought such a glow upon her face that, unless my affection for her were deceiving me, I would venture to say that there was not a more beautiful creature in the world—at least, that I had ever seen.

We went straight to the church to return thanks to God for the mercies we had received, and when Zoraida entered it she said there were faces there like Lela Marien's. We told her they were her images; and as well as he could the renegade explained to her what they meant, that she might adore them as if each of them were the very same Lela Marien that had spoken to her; and she, having great intelligence and a quick and clear instinct, understood at once all he said to her about them. Thence they took us away and distributed us all in different houses in the town; but as for the renegade, Zoraida, and myself, the Christian who came with us brought us to the house of his parents, who had a fair share of the gifts of fortune, and treated us with as much kindness as they did their own son.

We remained six days in the Velez, at the end of which the renegade, having informed himself of all that was requisite for him to do, set out for the city of Granada to restore himself to the sacred bosom of the Church through the medium of the Holy Inquisition. The other released captives took their departure, each the way that seemed best to him, and Zoraida and I were left alone, with nothing more than the crowns which the courtesy of the Frenchman had bestowed upon Zoraida, out of which I bought the beast on which she rides; and, I for the present attending her as her father and squire and not as her husband, we are now going to ascertain if my father is living, or if any of my brothers has had better fortune than mine has been; though, as Heaven has made me the companion of Zoraida, I think no other lot could be assigned to me, however happy, that I would rather have. The patience with which she endures the hardships that poverty brings with it, and the eagerness she shows to become a Christian, are such that they fill me with admiration, and bind me to serve her all my life; though the happiness I feel in seeing myself hers, and her mine, is disturbed and marred by not knowing whether I shall find any corner to shelter her in my own country, or whether time and death may not have made such changes in the fortunes and lives of my father and brothers, that I shall hardly find anyone who knows me, if they are not to be found.

I have no more of my story to tell you, gentlemen; whether it be an interesting or a curious one let your better judgments decide; all I can say is I would gladly have told it to you more briefly; although my fear of wearying you has made me leave out more than one circumstance.

CHAPTER XXX

WITH these words the captive held his peace, and Don Fernando said to him:
"In truth, captain, the manner in which you have related this remarkable adventure has been such as befitted the novelty and strangeness of the matter. The whole story is curious and uncommon, and abounds with incidents that fill the hearers with wonder and astonishment; and so great is the pleasure we have found in listening to it that we should be glad if it were to begin again, even though tomorrow were to find us still occupied with the same tale."

And while he said this Cardenio and the rest of them offered to be of service to him in any way that lay in their power, and in words and language so kindly and sincere that the captain was much gratified by their goodwill. In particular Don Fernando offered, if he would go back with him, to get his brother the marquis to become godfather at the baptism of Zoraida, and on his own part to provide him with the means of making his appearance in his own country with the credit and comfort he was entitled to. For all this the captive returned thanks very courteously, but would not accept any of their generous offers.

By this time night closed in, and as it did there came up to the inn a coach attended by some men on horseback, who demanded accommodations; to which the landlady replied that there was not a hand's breadth in the whole inn unoccupied.

"Still, for all that," said one of those who had entered on horseback, "room must be found for his lordship the judge here."

At this name the landlady was taken aback, and said, "Señor, the fact is I have no beds; but if his lordship the judge carries one with him, as no doubt he does, let him come in and welcome; for my husband and I will give up our room to accommodate his worship."

"Very good, so be it," said the squire; but in the meantime a man had got out of the coach whose dress indicated at a glance the office and post he held, for the long robe with ruffled sleeves that he wore showed that he was, as his servant said, a judge of appeal. He led by the hand a young girl in a traveling dress, apparently about sixteen years of age, and of such a high-bred air, so beautiful and so graceful, that all were filled with admiration when she made her appearance, and but for having seen Dorothea, Luscinda, and Zoraida, who were there in the inn, they would have fancied that a beauty like that of this maiden's would have been hard to find. Don Quixote was present at the entrance of the judge with the young lady, and as soon as he saw him he said:

"Your worship may with confidence enter and take your ease in this castle; for though the accommodation be scanty and poor, there are no quarters so cramped or inconvenient that they cannot make room for arms and letters; above all if arms and letters have beauty for a guide and leader, as letters represented by your worship have in this fair maiden, to whom not only ought castles to throw themselves open and yield themselves up, but rocks should rend themselves asunder and mountains divide and bow themselves down to give her a reception. Enter, your worship, I say, into this paradise, for here you will find stars and suns to accompany the heaven your worship brings with you; here you will find arms in their supreme excellence and beauty in its highest perfection."

TALES FROM THE SPANISH

The judge was struck with amazement at the language of Don Quixote, whom he scrutinized very carefully, no less astonished by his figure than by his talk; and before he could find words to answer him he had a fresh surprise, when he saw opposite to him Luscinda, Dorothea, and Zoraida, who, having heard of the new guests and of the beauty of the young lady, had come to see her and welcome her; Don Fernando, Cardenio, and the curate, however, greeted him in a more intelligible and polished style. In short, the judge made his entrance in a state of bewilderment, as well with what he saw as what he heard, and the fair ladies of the inn gave the fair damsel a cordial welcome. On the whole he could perceive that all who were there were people of quality; and with the figure, countenance, and bearing of Don Quixote he was at his wits' end; and all civilities having been exchanged, and the accommodation of the inn inquired into, it was settled, as it had been before settled, that all the women should retire to the garret that has been already mentioned, and that the men should remain outside as if to guard them; the judge, therefore, was very well pleased to allow his daughter, for such the damsel was, to go with the ladies, which she did very willingly; and with part of the host's narrow bed and half of what the judge had brought with him they made a more comfortable arrangement for the night than they had expected.

The captive, whose heart had leaped within him the instant he saw the judge, telling him somehow that this was his brother, asked one of the servants who accompanied him what his name was, and whether he knew from what part of the country he came. The servant replied that he was called the Licentiate Juan Perez de Viedma, and that he heard it said he came from a village in the mountains of Leon. From this statement, and what he himself had seen, he felt convinced that this was his brother who had adopted letters by his father's advice; and excited and rejoiced, he called Don Fernando and Cardenio and the curate aside, and told them how the matter stood, assuring

them that the judge was his brother. The servant had
further informed him that he was now going to the Indies
with the appointment of judge of the Supreme Court of
Mexico; and he had learned, likewise, that the young lady
was his daughter, whose mother had died in giving birth
to her, and that he was very rich in consequence of the
dowry left to him with the daughter. He asked their advice as to what means he should adopt to make himself
known, or to ascertain beforehand whether, when he had
made himself known, his brother, seeing him so poor,
would be ashamed of him, or would receive him with a
warm heart.

"Leave it to me to find out that," said the curate;
"though there is no reason for supposing, captain, that
you will not be kindly received, because the worth and
wisdom that your brother's bearing shows him to possess
do not make it likely that he will prove haughty or insensible, or that he will not know how to estimate the acci-
dents of fortune at their proper value."

"Still," said the captain, "I would not make myself
known abruptly, but in some indirect way."

"I have told you already," said the curate, "that I will
manage it in a way to satisfy us all."

By this time supper was ready, and they all took their
seats at the table, except the captive, and the ladies, who
supped by themselves in their own room. In the middle
of supper the curate said:

"I had a comrade of your worship's name, Señor Judge,
in Constantinople, where I was a captive for several years,
and that same comrade was one of the stoutest soldiers
and captains in the whole Spanish infantry; but he had as
large a share of misfortune as he had of gallantry and
courage."

"And how was the captain called, señor?" asked the
judge.

"He was called Ruy Perez de Viedma," replied the curate, "and he was born in a village in the mountains of
Leon; and he mentioned a circumstance connected with

his father and his brothers which, had it not been told me by so truthful a man as he was, I should have set down as one of the fables the old women tell over the fire in winter; for he said his father had divided his property among his three sons and had addressed words of advice to them sounder than any of Cato's. But I can say this much, that the choice he made of going to the wars was attended with such success, that by his gallant conduct and courage, and without any help save his own merit, he rose in a few years to captain of infantry, and to see himself on the high-road and in position to be given the command of a corps before long; but Fortune was against him, for where he might have expected her favor he lost it, and with it his liberty, on that glorious day when so many recovered theirs, at the battle of Lepanto. I lost mine at the Goletta, and after a variety of adventures we found ourselves comrades at Constantinople. Thence he went to Algiers, where he met with one of the most extraordinary adventures that ever befell anyone in the world."

Here the curate went on to relate briefly his brother's adventure with Zoraida; to all of which the judge gave such an attentive hearing as he had never yet given to any cause he heard. The curate, however, only went so far as to describe how the Frenchmen plundered those who were in the boat, and the poverty and distress in which his comrade and the fair Moor were left; of whom he said he had not been able to learn what became of them, or whether they had reached Spain, or been carried to France by the Frenchmen.

The captain, standing a little to one side, was listening to all the curate said, and watching every movement of his brother, who, as soon as he perceived the curate had made an end of his story, gave a deep sigh and said with his eyes full of tears:

"Oh, señor, if you only knew what news you have given me and how it comes home to me, making me show how I feel it with these tears that spring from my eyes in spite of all my worldly wisdom and self-restraint! That brave captain that you speak of is my eldest brother, who, being of a bolder and loftier mind than my other brother and myself, chose the honorable and worthy calling of arms, which was one of the three careers our father proposed to us, as your comrade mentioned in that fable you thought he was telling you. I followed that of letters, in which God and my own exertions have raised me to the position in which you see me. My second brother is in Peru, so wealthy that with what he has sent to my father and to me he has fully repaid the portion he took with him, and has even furnished my father's hands with the means of gratifying his natural generosity, while I too have been enabled to pursue my studies in a more becoming and creditable fashion, and so to attain my present standing. My father is still alive, though dying with anxiety to hear of his eldest son, and he prays God unceasingly that death may not close his eyes until he has looked upon those of his son; but with regard to him what surprises me is, that having so much common sense as he had, he should have neglected to give any intelligence about himself, either in his troubles and sufferings, or in his prosperity, for if his father or any of us had known of his condition he need not have waited for that miracle of the reed to obtain his ransom; but what now disquiets me is the uncertainty whether those Frenchmen may have restored him to liberty, or murdered him to hide the robbery.

"All this will make me continue my journey, not with the satisfaction in which I began it, but in the deepest melancholy and sadness. Oh dear brother! that I only knew where thou art now, and I would hasten to seek thee out and deliver thee from thy sufferings, though it were to cost me suffering myself! Oh, that I could bring news to our old father that thou art alive, even wert thou in the deepest dungeon of Barbary; for his wealth and my brother's and mine would rescue thee thence! Oh, beautiful and generous Zoraida, that I could repay thy goodness to a brother! That I could be present at the new birth of thy soul, and at thy bridal that would give us all such happiness!"

All this and more the judge uttered with such deep emotion at the news he had received of his brother that all who heard him shared in it, showing their sympathy with his sorrow. The curate, seeing, then, how well he had succeeded in carrying out his purpose and the captain's wishes, had no desire to keep them unhappy any longer, so he rose from the table and going to the room where Zoraida was he took her by the hand, Luscinda, Dorothea, and the judge's daughter following her. The captain was waiting to see what the curate would do, when the latter, taking him with the other hand, advanced with both of them to where the judge and the other gentlemen were, and said:

"Let your tears cease to flow, señor judge, and the wish of your heart be gratified as fully as you could desire, for you have before you your worthy brother and your good sister-in-law. He whom you see here is the Captain Viedma, and this is the fair Moor who has been so good to him. The Frenchmen I told you of have reduced them to the state of poverty you see that you may show the generosity of your kind heart."

The captain ran to embrace his brother, who placed both hands on his breast so as to have a good look at him, holding him a little way off; but as soon as he had fully recognized him he clasped him in his arms so closely, shedding such tears of heartfelt joy, that most of those present could not but join in them. The words the brothers exchanged, the emotion they showed can scarcely be imagined, I fancy, much less put down in writing. They told each other in a few words the events of their lives; they showed the true affection of brothers in all its strength; then the judge embraced Zoraida, putting all he possessed at her disposal; then he made his daughter embrace her, and the fair Christian and the lovely Moor drew fresh tears from every eye. And there was Don Quixote observing all these strange proceedings attentively without uttering a word, and attributing the whole to chimeras of knight-errantry. Then they agreed that the captain and Zoraida should return with his brother to Seville, and send news to his father of his having been delivered and found, so as to enable him to come and be present at the marriage and baptism of Zoraida, for it was impossible for the judge to put off his journey, as he was informed that in a month from that time the fleet was to sail from Seville for New Spain, and to miss the passage would have been a great inconvenience to him.

In short, everybody was well pleased and glad at the captive's good fortune; and as now almost two-thirds of the night were past they resolved to retire to rest for the remainder of it. Don Quixote offered to mount guard over the castle lest they should be attacked by some giant or other malevolent scoundrel, covetous of the great treasure of beauty the castle contained. Those who understood him returned him thanks for this service, and they gave the judge an account of his extraordinary humor, with which he was not a little amused. Sancho Panza alone was fuming at the lateness of the hour for retiring to rest; and he of all was the one that made himself most comfortable, as he stretched himself on the trappings of his ass, which, as will be told farther on, cost him so dear.

The ladies, then, having retired to their chamber, and the others having disposed themselves with as little discomfort as they could, Don Quixote sallied out of the inn to act as sentinel of the castle as he had promised. It happened, however, that a little before the approach of dawn a voice so musical and sweet reached the ears of the ladies that it forced them all to listen attentively, but especially Dorothea, who had been awake, and by whose side Doña Clara de Viedma, for so the judge's daughter was called, lay sleeping. No one could imagine who it was that sang so sweetly, and the voice was unaccompanied by any instrument. At one moment it seemed to them as if the singer were in the court-yard, at another in the stable; and as they were all attention, wondering, Cardenio came to the door and said, " Listen, whoever is not asleep, and you will hear a muleteer's voice that enchants as it chants."

" We are listening to it already, señor," said Dorothea; on which Cardenio went away; and Dorothea, giving all her attention to it, made out the words of the song to be these:

CHAPTER XXXI

Ah me, Love's mariner am I
On Love's deep ocean sailing;
I know not where the haven lies,
I dare not hope to gain it.

One solitary distant star
Is all I have to guide me,
A brighter orb than those of old
That Palinurus lighted.

And vaguely drifting am I borne,
I know not where it leads me;
I fix my gaze on it alone,
Of all beside it heedless.

But over-cautious prudery,
And coyness cold and cruel,
When most I need it, these, like clouds,
Its longed-for light refuse me.

Bright star, goal of my yearning eyes
As thou above me beamest,
When thou shalt hide thee from my sight
I'll know that death is near me.

The singer had got so far when it struck Dorothea that
it was not fair to let Clara miss hearing such a sweet
voice, so, shaking her from side to side, she woke her,
saying:

"Forgive me, child, for waking thee, but I do so that
thou mayest have the pleasure of hearing the best voice
thou hast ever heard, perhaps, in all thy life."

299

Clara awoke quite drowsy, and not understanding at the moment what Dorothea said, asked her what it was; she repeated what she had said, and Clara became attentive at once; but she had hardly heard two lines, as the singer continued, when a strange trembling seized her, as if she were suffering from a severe attack of quartan ague, and throwing her arms round Dorothea she said:

"Ah, dear lady of my soul and life! why did you wake me? The greatest kindness fortune could do me now would be to close my eyes and ears so as neither to see or hear that unhappy musician."

"What art thou talking about, child?" said Dorothea.

"Why, they say this singer is a muleteer!"

"Nay, he is the lord of many places," replied Clara, "and that one in my heart which he holds so firmly shall never be taken from him, unless he be willing to surrender it."

Dorothea was amazed at the ardent language of the girl, for it seemed to be far beyond such experience of life as her tender years gave any promise of, so she said to her:

"You speak in such a way that I cannot understand you, Señora Clara; explain yourself more clearly, and tell me what is this you are saying about hearts and places and this musician whose voice has so moved you? But do not tell me anything now; I do not want to lose the pleasure I get from listening to the singer by giving my attention to your transports, for I perceive he is beginning to sing a new strain and a new air."

"Let him, in Heaven's name," returned Clara; and not to hear him she stopped both ears with her hands, at which Dorothea was again surprised; but turning her attention to the song she found that it ran in this fashion:

> Sweet Hope, my stay,
> That onward to the goal of thy intent
> Dost make thy way,
> Heedless of hindrance or impediment,
> Have thou no fear
> If at each step thou findest death is near.

CERVANTES' "DON QUIXOTE"

No victory,
No joy of triumph doth the faint heart know;
    Unblest is he
That a bold front to Fortune dares not show,
    But soul and sense
In bondage yieldeth up to indolence.

    If Love his wares
Do dearly sell, his right must be confest;
    What gold compares
With that whereon his stamp he hath imprest?
    And all men know
What costeth little that we rate but low.

    Love resolute
Knows not the word "impossibility";
    And though my suit
Beset by endless obstacles I see,
    Yet no despair
Shall hold me bound to earth while heaven is there.

Here the voice ceased and Clara's sobs began afresh, all which excited Dorothea's curiosity to know what could be the cause of singing so sweet and weeping so bitter, so she again asked her what it was she was going to say before. On this Clara, afraid that Luscinda might overhear her, winding her arms tightly round Dorothea put her mouth so close to her ear that she could speak safely without fear of being heard by any one else, and said:

"This singer, dear señora, is the son of a gentleman of Aragon, lord of two villages, who lives opposite my father's house at Madrid; and though my father had curtains to the windows of his house in winter, and blinds in summer, in some way—I know not how—this gentleman, who was pursuing his studies, saw me—whether in church or elsewhere, I cannot tell—and, in fact, fell in love with me, and gave me to know it from the windows of his house, with so many signs and tears that I was forced to believe him, and even to love him, without knowing what it was he wanted of me. One of the signs he used to make me was to link one hand in the other, to show me he wished to marry me; and though I should have been glad if that could be, being alone and motherless I knew not whom to open my mind to, and so I left it as it was, showing him no favor, except when my father, and his too, were from home, to raise the curtain or the blind a little and let him see me plainly, at which he would show such delight that he seemed as if he were going mad. Meanwhile the time for my father's departure arrived, which he became aware of, but not from me, for I had never been able to tell him of it. He fell sick, of grief I believe, and so the day we were going away I could not see him to take farewell of him, were it only with the eyes.

"But after we had been two days on the road, on entering the *posada* of a village a day's journey from this, I saw him at the inn door in the dress of a muleteer, and so well disguised, that if I did not carry his image graven on my heart it would have been impossible for me to recognize him. But I knew him, and I was surprised, and glad; he watched me, unsuspected by my father, from whom he always hides himself when he crosses my path on the road, or in the *posadas* where we halt; and, as I know what he is, and reflect that for love of me he makes this journey on foot in all this hardship, I am ready to die of sorrow; and where he set foot there I set my eyes. I know not with what object he has come; or how he could have got away from his father, who loves him beyond measure, having no other heir, and because he deserves it, as you will perceive when you see him. And moreover, I can tell you, all that he sings is out of his own head; for I have heard them say he is a great scholar and poet; and what is more, every time I see him or hear him sing I tremble all over, and am terrified lest my father should recognize him and come to know of our loves. I have never spoken a word to him in my life; and for all that I love him so that I could not live without him. This, dear señora, is all I have to tell you about the musician whose voice has delighted you so much; and from it alone you might easily perceive he is no muleteer, but a lord of hearts and towns, as I told you already."

"Say no more, Doña Clara," said Dorothea at this, at the same time kissing her a thousand times over, "say no more, I tell you, but wait till day comes; when I trust in God to arrange this affair of yours so that it may have the happy ending such an innocent beginning deserves."

"Ah, señora," said Doña Clara, "what end can be hoped for when his father is of such lofty position, and so wealthy, that he would think I was not fit to be even a servant to his son, much less his wife? And as to marrying without the knowledge of my father, I would not do it for all the world. I would not ask anything more than that this youth should go back and leave me; perhaps with not seeing him, and the long distance we shall have to travel, the pain I suffer now may become easier; though I dare say the remedy I propose will do me very little good. I don't know how the devil this has come about, or how this love I have for him got in; I such a young girl, and he such a mere boy; for I verily believe we are both of an age, and I am not sixteen yet; for I will be sixteen Michaelmas Day next, my father says."

Dorothea could not help laughing to hear how like a child Doña Clara spoke. "Let us go to sleep now, señora," said she, "for the little of the night that I fancy is left to us: God will soon send us daylight, and we will set all to rights, or it will go hard with me."

With this they fell asleep, and deep silence reigned all through the inn. The only person not asleep were the landlady's daughter and her servant Maritornes, who, knowing the weak point of Don Quixote's humor, and that he was outside the inn mounting guard in armor and on horseback, resolved, the pair of them, to play some trick upon him, or at any rate to amuse themselves for a while by listening to his nonsense. As it so happened there was not a window in the whole inn that looked outwards except a hole in the wall of a straw-loft through which they used to throw out the straw. At this hole the two damsels posted themselves, and observed Don Quixote on his horse, leaning on his pike and from time to time sending forth such deep and doleful sighs, that he seemed to pluck up his soul by the roots with each of them; and they could hear him, too, saying in a soft, tender, loving tone:

"Oh my lady Dulcinea del Toboso, perfection of all beauty, summit and crown of discretion, treasure house of grace, depositary of virtue, and, finally, ideal of all that is good, honorable, and delectable in this world! What is thy grace doing now? Art thou, perchance, mindful of thy enslaved knight who of his own free will hath exposed himself to so great perils, and all to serve thee? Give me tidings of her, oh luminary of the three faces! Perhaps at this moment, envious of hers, thou art regarding her, either as she paces to and fro in some gallery of her sumptuous palaces, or leans over some balcony, meditating how, whilst preserving her purity and greatness, she may mitigate the tortures this wretched heart of mine endures for her sake, what glory should recompense my sufferings, what repose my toil, and lastly what death my life, and what reward my services? And thou, oh sun, that art now doubtless harnessing thy steeds in haste to rise betimes and come forth to see my lady; when thou seest her I entreat of thee to salute her on my behalf: but have a care, when thou shalt see her and salute her, that thou kiss not her face; for I shall be more jealous of thee than thou wert of that light-footed ingrate that made thee sweat and run so on the plains of Thessaly, or on the banks of the Peneus (for I do not exactly recollect where it was thou didst run on that occasion) in thy jealousy and love."

Don Quixote had got so far in his pathetic speech when the landlady's daughter began to signal to him, saying, "Señor, come over here, please."

At these signals and voice Don Quixote turned his head and saw by the light of the moon, which then was in its full splendor, that some one was calling to him from the hole in the wall, which seemed to him to be a window, and what is more, with a gilt grating, as rich castles, such as he believed the inn to be, ought to have; and it immediately suggested itself to his imagination that, as on the former occasion, the fair damsel, the daughter of the lady of the castle, overcome by love for him, was once more endeavoring to win his affections; and with this idea, not to show himself discourteous, or ungrateful, he turned Rocinante's head and approached the hole, and as he perceived the two wenches he said:

"I pity you, beauteous lady, that you should have directed your thoughts of love to a quarter from whence it is impossible that such a return can be made to you as is due to your great merit and gentle birth, for which you must not blame this unhappy knight-errant whom love renders incapable of submission to any other than her whom, the first moment his eyes beheld her, he made absolute mistress of his soul. Forgive me, noble lady, and retire to your apartment, and do not, by any further declaration of your passion, compel me to show myself more ungrateful; and if, of the love you bear me, you should find that there is anything else in my power wherein I can gratify you, provided it be not love itself, demand it of me; for I swear to you by that sweet absent enemy of mine to grant it this instant, though it be that you require of me a lock of Medusa's hair, which was all snakes, or even the very beams of the sun shut up in a vial."

"My mistress wants nothing of that sort, Sir Knight," said Maritornes at this.

"What then, discreet dame, is it that your mistress wants?" replied Don Quixote.

"Only one of your fair hands," said Maritornes, "to enable her to vent over it the great passion which has brought her to this loophole, so much to the risk of her honor; for if the lord her father had heard her, the least slice he would cut off her would be her ear."

"I should like to see that tried," said Don Quixote; "but he had better beware of that, if he does not want to meet the most disastrous end that ever father in the world met for having laid hands on the tender limbs of a love-stricken daughter."

Maritornes felt sure that Don Quixote would present

the hand she had asked, and making up her mind what to do, she got down from the hole and went into the stable, where she took the halter of Sancho Panza's ass, and in all haste returned to the hole, just as Don Quixote had planted himself standing on Rocinante's saddle in order to reach the grated window where he supposed the love-lorn damsel to be; and giving her his hand, he said:

"Lady, take this hand, or rather this scourge of the evil-doers of the earth; take, I say, this hand which no other hand of woman has ever touched, not even hers who has complete possession of my entire body. I present it to you, not that you may kiss it, but that you may observe the contexture of the sinews, the close net-work of the muscles, the breadth and capacity of the veins, whence you may infer what must be the strength of the arm that has such a hand."

"That we shall see presently," said Maritornes, and making a running knot on the halter, she passed it over his wrist and coming down from the hole tied the other end very firmly to the bolt of the door of the straw-loft. Don Quixote, feeling the roughness of the rope on his wrist, exclaimed:

"Your grace seems to be grating rather than caressing my hand; treat it not so harshly, for it is not to blame for the offense my resolution has given you, nor is it just to wreak all your vengeance on so small a part; remember that one who loves so well should not revenge herself so cruelly."

But there was nobody now to listen to these words of Don Quixote's, for as soon as Maritornes had tied him she and the other made off, ready to die with laughing, leaving him fastened in such a way that it was impossible for him to release himself.

He was, as has been said, standing on Rocinante, with his arm passed through the hole and his wrist tied to the bolt of the door, and in mighty fear and dread of being left hanging by the arm if Rocinante were to stir one side or the other; so he did not dare to make the least movement, although from the patience and imperturbable disposition of Rocinante, he had good reason to expect that he would stand without budging for a whole century. Finding himself fast, then, and that the ladies had retired, he began to fancy that all this was done by enchantment, as on the former occasion in that same castle; and he cursed in his heart his own want of sense and judgment in venturing to enter the castle again, after having come off so badly the first time; it being a settled point with knights-errant that when they have tried an adventure, and have not succeeded in it, it is a sign that it is not reserved for them but for others, and that therefore they need not try it again. Nevertheless he pulled his arm to see if he could release himself, but it had been made so fast that all his efforts were in vain. It is true he pulled it gently lest Rocinante should move, but try as he might to seat himself in the saddle, he had nothing for it but to stand upright or pull his hand off.

Then it was he wished for the sword of Amadis, against which no enchantment whatever had any power; then he cursed his ill fortune; then he magnified the loss the world would sustain by his absence while he remained there enchanted, for what he believed was beyond all doubt; then he once more took to thinking of his beloved Dulcinea del Toboso; then he called to his worthy sqiure Sancho Panza, who, buried in sleep and stretched upon the pack-saddle of his ass, was oblivious, at that moment, of the mother that bore him; then he called upon the sages Lirgandeo and Alquife to come to his aid; then he invoked his good friend Urganda to succor him; and then, at last, morning found him in such a state of desperation and perplexity that he was bellowing like a bull, for he had no hope that day would bring any relief to his suffering, which he believed would last forever, inasmuch as he was enchanted; and of this he was convinced by seeing that Rocinante never stirred, much or little, and he felt persuaded that he and his horse were to remain in this state, without eating or drinking or sleeping, until the malign influence of the stars was overpast, or until some other more sage enchanter should disenchant him.

But he was very much deceived in this conclusion, for daylight had hardly begun to appear when there came up to the inn four men on horseback, well equipped and ac- coutred, with firelocks across their saddle-bows. They called out and knocked loudly at the gate of the inn, which was still shut; on seeing which, Don Quixote, even there where he was, did not forget to act as sentinel, and said in a loud and imperious tone:

"Knights, or squires, or whatever ye be, ye have no right to knock at the gates of this castle; for it is plain enough that they who are within are either asleep, or else are not in the habit of throwing open the fortress until the sun's rays are spread over the whole surface of the earth. With- draw to a distance, and wait till it is broad daylight, and then we shall see whether it will be proper or not to open to you."

"What the devil fortress or castle is this?" said one, "to make us stand on such ceremony? If you are the inn- keeper bid them open to us; we are travelers who only want to feed our horses and go on, for we are in haste."

"Do you think, gentlemen, that I look like an inn- keeper?" said Don Quixote.

"I don't care what you look like," replied the other; "but I know that you are talking nonsense when you call this inn a castle."

"A castle is it," returned Don Quixote, "nay, more, one of the best in this whole province, and it has within it people who have had the sceptre in the hand and the crown on the head."

"It would be better if it were the other way," said the traveler, "the sceptre on the head and the crown in the hand; but if so, maybe there is within some company of players, with whom it is a common thing to have those crowns and sceptres you speak of; for in such a small inn as this, and where such silence is kept, I do not believe any people entitled to crowns and sceptres can have taken up their quarters."

"You know but little of the world," returned Don Quixote, "since you are ignorant of what commonly occurs in knight-errantry."

But the comrades of the spokesman growing weary of the dialogue with Don Quixote, renewed their knocks with great vehemence, so much so that the host, and not only he but everybody in the inn, awoke, and he got up to ask who knocked. It happened at this moment that one of the horses of the four who were seeking admittance went to smell Rocinante, who melancholy, dejected, and with drooping ears, stood motionless, supporting his sorely stretched master; and as he was, after all, flesh, though he looked as if he were made of wood, he could not help giving way and in return smelling the one who had come to offer him attentions. But he had hardly moved at all when Don Quixote lost his footing; and slipping off the saddle, he would have come to the ground, but for being suspended by the arm, which casued him such agony that he believed either his wrist would be cut through or his arm torn off; and he hung so near the ground that he could just touch it with his feet, which was all the worse for him; for, finding how little was wanted to enable him to plant his feet firmly, he struggled and stretched himself as much as he could to gain a footing; just like those undergoing the torture of the *strappado,* when they are fixed at "touch and no touch," who aggravate their own sufferings by their violent efforts to stretch themselves, deceived by the hope which makes them fancy that with a very little more they will reach the ground.

CHAPTER XXXII

S O loud, in fact, were the shouts of Don Quixote, that
the landlord opening the gate of the inn in all haste,
came out in dismay, and ran to see who was uttering such
cries, and those who were inside joined him. Maritornes,
who had been by this time roused up by the same outcry, suspecting what it was, ran to the loft and, without any one
seeing her, untied the halter by which Don Quixote was
suspended, and down he came to the ground in the sight of
the landlord and the travelers, who approaching asked him
what was the matter with him that he shouted so. He
without replying a word took the rope off his wrist, and
rising to his feet leaped upon Rocinante, braced his buckler on his arm, put his lance in rest, and making a considerable circuit of the plain came back at a half-gallop
exclaiming:

" Whoever shall say that I have been enchanted with
just cause, provided my lady the Princess Micomicona
grants me permission to do so, I give him the lie, challenge
him and defy him to single combat."

The newly arrived travelers were amazed at the words
of Don Quixote; but the landlord removed their surprise
by telling them who he was, and not to mind him as he
was out of his senses. They then asked the landlord if
by any chance a youth of about fifteen years of age had
come to that inn, one dressed like a muleteer, and of such

and such an appearance, describing that of Doña Clara's lover. The landlord replied that there were so many people in the inn he had not noticed the person they were inquiring for; but one of them observing the coach in which the judge had come, said:

"He is here no doubt, for this is the coach he is following: let one of us stay at the gate, and the rest go in to look for him; or indeed it would be as well if one of us went round the inn, lest he should escape over the wall of the yard."

"So be it," said another; and while two of them went in, one remained at the gate and the other made the circuit of the inn; observing all which, the landlord was unable to conjecture for what reason they were taking all these precautions, though he understood they were looking for the youth whose description they had given him.

It was by this time broad daylight; and for that reason, as well as in consequence of the noise Don Quixote had made, everybody was awake and up, but particularly Doña Clara and Dorothea; for they had been able to sleep but badly that night, the one from agitation at having her lover so near her, the other from curiosity to see him. Don Quixote, when he saw that not one of the four travelers took any notice of him or replied to his challenge, was furious and ready to die with indignation and wrath; and if he could have found in the ordinances of chivalry that it was lawful for a knight-errant to undertake or engage in another enterprise, when he had plighted his word and faith not to involve himself in any until he had made an end of one to which he was pledged, he would have attacked the whole of them, and would have made them return an answer in spite of themselves. But considering that it would not become him, nor be right, to begin any new enterprise until he had established Micomicona in her kingdom, he was constrained to hold his peace and wait quietly to see what would be the upshot of the proceedings of those same travelers; one of whom found the youth they were seeking lying asleep by the side of a muleteer, without a thought of any one coming in search of him, much less finding him.

The man laid hold of him by the arm, saying, " It becomes you well indeed, Señor Don Luis, to be in the dress you wear, and well the bed in which I find you agrees with the luxury in which your mother reared you."

The youth rubbed his sleepy eyes and stared for a while at him who held him, but presently recognized him as one of his father's servants, at which he was so taken aback that for some time he could not find or utter a word; while the servant went on to say:

" There is nothing for it now, Señor Don Luis, but to submit quietly and return home, unless it is your wish that my lord, your father, should take his departure for the other world, for nothing else can be the consequence of the grief he is in at your absence."

" But how did my father know that I had gone this road and in this dress? " said Don Luis.

" It was a student to whom you confided your intentions," answered the servant, " that disclosed them, touched with pity at the distress he saw your father suffer on missing you; he therefore despatched four of his servants in quest of you, and here we all are at your service, better pleased than you can imagine that we shall return so soon and restore you to those eyes that so yearn for you."

" That shall be as I please, or as heaven orders," returned Don Luis.

" What can you please or heaven order? " said the other, " except to agree to go back? Anything else is impossible."

All this conversation between the two was overheard by the muleteer at whose side Don Luis lay, and rising, he went to report what had taken place to Don Fernando, Cardenio, and the others, who had by this time dressed themselves; and told them how the man had addressed the youth as " Don," and what words had passed, and how he wanted him to return to his father, which the youth was unwilling to do. With this, and what they already knew of the rare voice that heaven had bestowed upon him, they all felt very anxious to know more particularly who he was, and even to help him if it was attempted to employ force against him; so they hastened to where he was still talking and arguing with his servant. Dorothea at this instant came out of her room, followed by Doña Clara all in a tremor; and calling Cardenio aside, she told him in a few words the story of the musician and Doña Clara, and he at the same time told her what had happened, how his father's servants had come in search of him; but in telling her so, he did not speak low enough but that Doña Clara heard what he said, at which she was so much agitated that had not Dorothea hastened to support her she would have fallen to the ground. Cardenio then bade Dorothea return to her room, as he would endeavor to make the whole matter right, and they did as he desired. All the four who had come in quest of Don Luis had now come into the inn and surrounded him, urging him to return and console his father at once and without a moment's delay. He replied that he could not do so on any account until he had concluded some business in which his life, honor, and heart were at stake. The servants pressed him, saying that most certainly they would not return without him, and that they would take him away whether he liked it or not.

"You shall not do that," replied Don Luis, "unless you take me dead; though however you take me, it will be without life."

By this time most of those in the inn had been attracted by the dispute, but particularly Cardenio, Don Fernando, his companions, the judge, the curate, the barber, and Don Quixote; for he now considered there was no necessity for mounting guard over the castle any longer. Cardenio being already acquainted with the young man's story, asked the men who wanted to take him away, what object they had in seeking to carry off this youth against his will.

"Our object," said one of the four, "is to save the life

of his father, who is in danger of losing it through this gentleman's disappearance."

Upon this Don Luis exclaimed, "There is no need to make my affairs public here; I am free, and I will return if I please; and if not, none of you shall compel me."

"Reason will compel your worship," said the man, "and if it has no power over you, it has power over us, to make us do what we came for, and what it is our duty to do."

"Let us hear what the whole affair is about," said the judge at this; but the man, who knew him as a neighbor of theirs, replied, "Do you not know this gentleman, Señor Judge? He is the son of your neighbor, who has run away from his father's house in a dress so unbecoming his rank, as your worship may perceive."

The judge on this looked at him more carefully and recognized him, and embracing him said:

"What folly is this, Señor Don Luis, or what can have been the cause that could have induced you to come here in this way, and in this dress, which so ill becomes your condition?"

Tears came into the eyes of the young man, and he was unable to utter a word in reply to the judge, who told the four servants not to be uneasy, for all would be satisfactorily settled; and then taking Don Luis by the hand, he drew him aside and asked the reason of his having come there.

But while he was questioning him they heard a loud outcry at the gate of the inn, the cause of which was that two of the guests who had passed the night there, seeing everybody busy about finding out what it was the four men wanted, had conceived the idea of going off without paying what they owed; but the landlord, who minded his own affairs more than other people's, caught them going out of the gate and demanded his reckoning, abusing them for their dishonesty with such language that he drove them to reply with their fists, and so they began to lay on him in such a style that the poor man was forced to cry out, and call for help. The landlady and her daughter could see no one more free to give aid than Don Quixote, and to him the daughter said:

"Sir Knight, by the virtue of God has given you, help my poor father, for there are two wicked men beating him to a mummy."

To which Don Quixote very deliberately and phlegmatically replied:

"Fair damsel, at the present moment your request is inopportune, for I am debarred from involving myself in any adventure until I have brought to a happy conclusion one to which my word has pledged me; but that which I can do for you is what I will now mention: run and tell your father to stand his ground as well as he can in this battle, and on no account allow himself to be vanquished, while I go and request permission of the Princess Micomicona to enable me to succor him in his distress; and if she grants it, rest assured I will relieve him from it."

"Sinner that I am," exclaimed Maritornes, who stood by; "before you have got your permission by master will be in the other world."

"Give me leave, señora, to obtain the permission I speak of," returned Don Quixote; "and if I get it, it will matter very little if he is in the other world; for I will rescue him thence in spite of all the same world can do; or at any rate I will give you such a revenge over those who have sent him there that you will be more than moderately satisfied;" and without saying anything more he went and knelt before Dorothea, requesting her highness in knightly and errant phrase to be pleased to grant him permission to aid and succor the *castellan* of that castle, who now stood in grievous jeopardy. The princess granted it graciously, and he at once, bracing his buckler on his arm and drawing his sword, hastened to the inn-gate, where the two guests were still handling the landlord roughly; but as soon as he reached the spot he stopped short and stood still, though Maritornes and the landlady asked him why he hesitated to help their master and husband.

"I hesitate," said Don Quixote, "because it is not lawful for me to draw sword against persons of squirely condition; but call my squire Sancho to me; for this defense and vengeance are his affair and business."

Thus matters stood at the inn-gate, where there was a very lively exchange of fisticuffs and punches, to the sore damage of the landlord and to the wrath of Maritornes, the landlady, and her daughter, who were furious when they saw the pusillanimity of Don Quixote, and the hard treatment their master, husband, and father was undergoing. But let us leave him there; for he will surely find some one to help him, and if not, let him suffer and hold his tongue who attempts more than his strength allows him to do; and let us go back fifty paces to see what Don Luis said in reply to the judge whom we left questioning him privately as to his reasons for coming on foot and so meanly dressed.

To which the youth, pressing his hand in a way that showed his heart was troubled by some great sorrow, and shedding a flood of tears, made answer:

"Señor, I have no more to tell you than that from the moment when, through heaven's will and our being neighbors, I first saw Doña Clara, your daughter and my lady, from that instant I made her the mistress of my will, and if yours, my true lord and father, offers no impediment this very day she shall become my wife. For her I left my father's house, and for her I assumed this disguise, to follow her whithersoever she may go, as the arrow seeks its mark or the sailor the pole-star. She knows nothing more of my passion than what she may have learned from having sometimes seen from a distance that my eyes were filled with tears. You know already, señor, the wealth and noble birth of my parents, and that I am their sole heir; if this be a sufficient inducement for you to venture to make me completely happy, accept me at once as your son; for if my father, influenced by other objects of his own, should disapprove of this happiness I have sought for myself, time has more power to alter and change things, than human will."

CERVANTES' "DON QUIXOTE"

With this the love-smitten youth was silent, while the judge, after hearing him, was astonished, perplexed, and surprised, as well at the manner and intelligence with which Don Luis had confessed the secret of his heart, as at the position in which he found himself, not knowing what course to take in a matter so sudden and unexpected. All the answer, therefore, he gave him was to bid him to make his mind easy for the present, and arrange with his servants not to take him back that day, so that there might be time to consider what was best for all parties. Don Luis kissed his hands by force, nay, bathed them with his tears, in a way that would have touched a heart of marble, not to say that of the judge, who as a shrewd man, had already perceived how advantageous the marriage would be to his daughter; though, were it possible, he would have preferred that it should be brought about with the consent of the father of Don Luis, who he knew looked for a title for his son.

The guests had by this time made peace with the landlord, for, by persuasion and Don Quixote's fair words more than by threats, they had paid him what he demanded, and the servants of Don Luis were waiting for the end of the conversation with the judge and their master's decision, when the devil, who never sleeps, contrived that the barber, from whom Don Quixote had taken Mambrino's helmet, and Sancho Panza the trappings of his ass in exchange for those of his own, should at this instant enter the inn; which said barber, as he led his ass to the stable, observed Sancho Panza engaged in repairing something or other belonging to the pack-saddle; and the moment he saw it he knew it, and made bold to attack Sancho, exclaiming:

"Ho, Sir Thief, I have caught you! hand over that basin and my pack-saddle, and all my trappings that you robbed me of."

Sancho, finding himself so unexpectedly assailed, and hearing the abuse poured upon him, seized the pack-saddle with one hand, and with the other gave the barber a

317

cuff that bathed his teeth in blood. The barber, however, was not so ready to relinquish the prize he had made in the pack-saddle; on the contrary, he raised such an outcry that every one in the inn came running to know what the noise and quarrel meant.

"Here, in the name of the king and justice!" he cried, "this thief and highwayman wants to kill me for trying to recover my property."

"You lie," said Sancho, "I am no highwayman; it was in fair war my master Don Quixote won these spoils."

Don Quixote was standing by at the time, highly pleased to see his squire's stoutness, both offensive and defensive, and from that time forth he reckoned him a man of mettle, and in his heart resolved to dub him a knight on the first opportunity that presented itself, feeling sure that the order of chivalry would be fittingly bestowed upon him. In the course of the altercation, among other things the barber said:

"Gentlemen, this pack-saddle is mine as surely as I owe God a death, and I know it as well as if I had given birth to it, and here is my ass in the stable who will not let me lie; only try it, and if it does not fit him like a glove, call me a rascal; and what is more, the same day I was robbed of this, they robbed me likewise of a new brass basin, never yet handselled, that would fetch a crown any day."

At this Don Quixote could not keep himself from answering; and interposing between the two, and separating them, he placed the pack-saddle on the gronud, to lie there in sight until the truth was established, and said:

"Your worships may perceive clearly and plainly the error under which this worthy squire lies when he calls that a basin which was, is, and shall be the helmet of Mambrino, which I won from him in fair war, and made myself master of by legitimate and lawful possession. With the pack-saddle I do not concern myself; but I may tell you on that head that my squire Sancho asked my permission to strip off the caparison of this vanquished poltroon's steed, and with it adorn his own; I allowed him, and he took it; and as to its having been changed from a caparison into a pack-saddle, I can give no explanation except the usual one, that such transformations will take place in adventures of chivalry. To confirm all which, run, Sancho my son, and fetch hither the helmet which this good fellow calls a basin."

"Egad, master," said Sancho, "if we have no other proof of our case than what your worship puts forward, Mambrino's helmet is just as much a basin as this good fellow's caparison is a pack-saddle."

"Do as I bid thee," said Don Quixote; "it cannot be that everything in this castle goes by enchantment."

Sancho hastened to where the basin was, and brought it back with him, and when Don Quixote saw it, he took hold of it and said:

"Your worships may see with what a face this squire can assert that this is a basin and not the helmet I told you of; and I swear by the order of chivalry I profess, that this helmet is the identical one I took from him, without anything added to or taken from it."

"There is no doubt of that," said Sancho, "for from the time my master won it until now he has only fought one battle in it, when he let loose those unlucky men in chains; and if it had not been for this basin-helmet he would not have come off over well that time, for there was plenty of stone-throwing in that affair."

CHAPTER XXXIII

IN WHICH THE DOUBTFUL QUESTION OF MAMBRINO'S HEL-
MET AND THE PACK-SADDLE IS FINALLY SETTLED, WITH
OTHER ADVENTURES THAT OCCURRED IN TRUTH AND EARN-
EST

"WHAT do you think now, gentlemen," said the barber, "of what these gentles say, when they even
want to make out that this is not a basin but a helmet?"

"And whosoever says the contrary," said Don Quixote,
"I will let him know he lies if he is a knight, and if he is
a squire that he lies again a thousand times."

Our own barber, who was present at all this, and understood Don Quixote's humor so thoroughly, took it into
his head to back up his delusion and carry on the joke for
the general amusement; so addressing the other barber he
said:

"Señor barber, or whatever you are, you must know
that I belong to your profession too, and have had a license
to practice for more than twenty years, and I know the
implements of the barber craft, every one of them, perfectly well; and I was likewise a soldier for some time in
the days of my youth, and I know also what a helmet is,
and a morion, and a headpiece with a visor, and other
things pertaining to soldiering, I meant to say to soldiers'
arms; and I say—saving better opinions and always with
submission to sounder judgments—that this piece we have
now before us, which this worthy gentleman has in his
hands, not only is no barber's basin, but is as far from

being one as white is from black, and truth from falsehood; I say, moreover, that this, although it is a helmet, is
not a complete helmet."

"Certainly not," said Don Quixote, "for half of it is
wanting, that is to say the beaver."

"It is quite true," said the curate, who saw the object
of his friend the barber; and Cardenio, Don Fernando
and his companions agreed with him, and even the judge,
if his thoughts had not been so full of Don Luis's affair,
would have helped to carry on the joke; but he was so
taken up with the serious matters he had on his mind that
he paid little or no attention to these facetious proceed--
ings.

"God bless me!" exclaimed their butt the barber at
this; "is it possible that such an honorable company can
say that this is not a basin but a helmet? Why, this is a
thing that would astonish a whole university, however wise
it might be! That will do; if this basin is a helmet, why,
then the pack-saddle must be a horse's caparison, as this
gentleman has said."

"To me it looks like a pack-saddle," said Don Quixote;
"but I have already said that with that question I do not
concern myself."

"As to whether it be a pack-saddle or caparison," said
the curate, "it is only for Señor Don Quixote to say; for
in these matters of chivalry all these gentlemen and I bow
to his authority."

"By God, gentlemen," said Don Quixote, "so many
strange things have happened to me in this castle on the
two occasions on which I have sojourned in it, that I will
not venture to assert anything it contains; for it is my belief that everything that goes on within it goes by enchantment. The first time Sancho did not fare well among
certain followers of his; and last night I was kept hanging by this arm for nearly two hours, without knowing
how or why I came by such a mishap. So that now, for
me to come forward to give an opinion in such a puzzling
matter, would be to risk a rash decision. As regards the

assertion that this is a basin and not a helmet I have already given an answer; but as to the question whether this is a pack-saddle or a caparison I will not venture to give a positive opinion, but will leave it to your worships' better judgment. Perhaps as you are not dubbed knights like myself, the enchantments of this place have nothing to do with you, and your faculties are unfettered, and you can see things in this castle as they really and truly are, and not as they appear to me."

"There can be no question," said Don Fernando on this, "but that Señor Don Quixote has spoken very wisely, and that with us rests the decision of this matter; and that we may have surer ground to go on, I will take the votes of the gentlemen in secret, and declare the result clearly and fully."

To those who were in the secret of Don Quixote's humor all this afforded great amusement; but to those who knew nothing about it, it seemed the greatest nonsense in the world, in particular to the four servants of Don Luis, as well as to Don Luis himself, and to three other travelers who had by chance come to the inn, and had the appearance of officers of the Holy Brotherhood, as indeed they were; but the one who above all was at his wits' end, was the barber whose basin, there before his very eyes, had been turned into Mambrino's helmet, and whose pack-saddle he had no doubt whatever was about to become a rich caparison for a horse. All laughed to see Don Fernando going from one to another collecting the votes, and whispering to them to give him their private opinion whether the treasure over which there had been so much fighting was a pack-saddle or a caparison; but after he had taken the votes of those who knew Don Quixote, he said aloud: "The fact is, my good fellow, that I am tired of collecting such a number of opinions, for I find that there is not one of whom I ask what I desire to know, who does not tell me that it is absurd to say that this is the pack-saddle of an ass, and not the caparison of a horse, nay, of a thoroughbred horse; so you must submit, for, in spite of you and your ass, this is a caparison and no pack-saddle, and you have stated and proved your case very badly."

"May I never share heaven," said the poor barber, "if your worships are not all mistaken; and may my soul appear before God as that appears to me a pack-saddle and not a caparison; but, 'laws go,'—I say no more; and indeed I am not drunk, for I am fasting, except it be from sin."

The simple talk of the barber did not afford less amusement than the absurdities of Don Quixote, who now observed, "There is no more to be done now than for each to take what belongs to him, and to whom God has given it, may St. Peter add his blessing."

But said one of the four servants, "Unless, indeed, this is a deliberate joke, I cannot bring myself to believe that men so intelligent as those present are, or seem to be, can venture to declare and assert that this is not a basin, and that not a pack-saddle; but as I perceive that they do assert and declare it, I can only come to the conclusion that there is some mystery in this persistence in what is so opposed to the evidence of experience and truth itself; for I swear by "—and here he rapped out a round oath—" all the people in the world will not make me believe that this is not a barber's basin and that a jackass's pack-saddle."

"It might easily be a she-ass's," observed the curate.

"It is all the same,' said the servant; "that is not the point; but whether it is or is not a pack-saddle, as your worships say."

On hearing this one of the newly arrived officers of the Brotherhood, who had been listening to the dispute and controversy, unable to restrain his anger and impatience, exclaimed:

"It is a pack-saddle as sure as my father is my father, and whoever has said or will say anything else must be drunk."

"You lie like a rascally clown," returned Don Quixote; and lifting his pike, which he had never let out of his hand, he delivered such a blow at his head that, had not the officer dodged it, it would have stretched him at full length. The pike was shivered in pieces against the ground, and the rest of the officers, seeing their comrade assaulted, raised a shout, calling for help for the Holy Brotherhood. The landlord, who was of the fraternity, ran at once to fetch his staff of office and his sword, and ranged himself on the side of his comrades; the servants of Don Luis clustered round him, lest he should escape from them in the confusion; the barber, seeing the house turned upside down, once more laid hold of his pack-saddle and Sancho did the same; Don Quixote drew his sword, and charged the officers; Don Luis cried out to his servants to leave him alone and go and help Don Quixote, and Cardenio and Don Fernando, who were supporting him; the curate was shouting at the top of his voice, the landlady was screaming, her daughter was wailing, Maritornes was weeping, Dorothea was aghast, Luscinda terror-stricken, and Doña Clara in a faint. The barber cudgelled Sancho, and Sancho pommelled the barber; Don Luis gave one of his servants, who ventured to catch him by the arm to keep him from escaping, a cuff that bathed his teeth in blood; the judge took his part; Don Fernando had got one of the officers down and was belaboring him heartily; the landlord raised his voice, again calling for help for the Holy Brotherhood; so that the whole inn was nothing but cries, shouts, shrieks, confusion, terror, dismay, mishaps, sword-cuts, fisticuffs, cudgellings, kicks, and bloodshed; and in the midst of all this chaos, complication, and general entanglement, Don Quixote took it into his head that he had been plunged into the thick of the discord of Agramante's camp; and, in a voice that shook the inn like thunder, he cried out:

"Hold all, let all sheathe their swords, let all be calm and attend to me as they value their lives!"

All paused at his mighty voice, and he went on to say, "Did I not tell you, sirs, that this castle was enchanted, and that a legion or so of devils dwelt in it? In proof whereof I call upon you to behold with your own eyes how the discord of Agramante's camp has come hither, and been transferred into the midst of us. See how they fight, there for the sword, here for the horse, on that side for the eagle, on this for the helmet; we are all fighting, and all at cross purposes. Come then, you, Señor Judge, and you, Señor Curate; let the one represent King Agramante and the other King Sobrino, and make peace among us; for by God Almighty it is a sorry business that so many persons of quality as we are should slay one another for such trifling cause."

The officers, who did not understand Don Quixote's mode of speaking, and found themselves roughly handled by Don Fernando, Cardenio, and their companions, were not to be appeased; the barber was, however, for both his beard and his pack-saddle were the worse for the struggle; Sancho like a good servant obeyed the slightest word of his master; while the four servants of Don Luis kept quiet when they saw how little they gained by not doing so. The landlord alone insisted upon it that they must punish the insolence of this madman, who at every turn raised a disturbance in the inn; but at length the uproar was stilled for the present; the pack-saddle remained a caparison till the day of judgment, and the basin a helmet and the inn a castle in Don Quixote's imagination.

All having been now pacified and made friends by the persuasion of the judge and the curate, the servants of Don Luis began again to urge him to return with them at once; and while he was discussing the matter with them, the judge took counsel with Don Fernando, Cardenio, and the curate as to what he ought to do in the case, telling them how it stood, and what Don Luis had said to him. It was agreed at length that Don Fernando should tell the servants of Don Luis who he was, and that it was his desire that Don Luis should accompany him to Andalusia, where he would receive from the marquis his brother the welcome his quality entitled him to; for, otherwise, it was easy to see from the determination of Don Luis that he would not return to his father at present, though they tore him to pieces. On learning the rank of Don Fernando and the resolution of Don Luis the four then settled it between themselves that three of them should return to tell his father how matters stood, and that the other should remain to wait upon Don Luis, and not leave him until they came back for him, or his father's orders were known. Thus by the authority of Agramante and the wisdom of King Sobrino all this complication of disputes was arranged; but the enemy of concord and hater of peace, feeling himself slighted and made a fool of, and seeing how little he had gained after having involved them all in such an elaborate entanglement, resolved to try his hand once more by stirring up fresh quarrels and disturbances.

It came about in this wise: The officers were pacified on learning the rank of those with whom they had been engaged, and withdrew from the contest, considering that whatever the result might be they were likely to get the worst of the battle; but one of them, the one who had been thrashed and kicked by Don Fernando, recollected that among some warrants he carried for the arrest of certain delinquents, he had one against Don Quixote, whom the Holy Brotherhood had ordered to be arrested for setting the galley slaves free, as Sancho had, with very good reason, apprehended. Suspecting how it was, then, he wished to satisfy himself as to whether Don Quixote's features corresponded; and taking a parchment out of his bosom he lit upon what he was in search of, and setting himself to read it deliberately, for he was not a quick reader, as he made out each word he fixed his eyes on Don Quixote, and went on comparing the description in the warrant with his face, and discovered that beyond all doubt he was the person described in it. As soon as he had satisfied himself, folding up the parchment, he took the warrant in his left hand and with his right seized Don Quixote by the collar so tightly that he did not allow him to breathe, and shouted aloud:

"Help for the Holy Brotherhood! and that you may see

I demand it in earnest, read this warrant which says this highwayman is to be arrested."

The curate took the warrant and saw that what the officer said was true, and that it agreed with Don Quixote's appearance, who, on his part, when he found himself roughly handled by this rascally clown, worked up to the highest pitch of wrath, and all his joints cracking with rage, with both hands seized the officer by the throat with all his might, so that had he not been helped by his comrades he would have yielded up his life ere Don Quixote released his hold. The landlord, who had perforce to support his brother officers, ran at once to aid them. The landlady, when she saw her husband engaged in a fresh quarrel, lifted up her voice afresh, and its note was immediately caught up by Maritornes and her daughter, calling upon heaven and all present for help; and Sancho, seeing what was going on, exclaimed:

" By the Lord, it is quite true what my master says about the enchantments of this castle, for it is impossible to live an hour in peace in it!"

Don Fernando parted the officer and Don Quixote, and to their mutual contentment made them relax the grip by which they held, the one the coat collar, the other the throat of his adversary; for all this, however, the officers did not cease to demand their prisoner and call on them to help, and deliver him over bound into their power, as was required for the service of the King and of the Holy Brotherhood, on whose behalf they again demanded aid and assistance to effect the capture of this robber and footpad of the highways and byways.

Don Quixote smiled when he heard these words, and said very calmly:

" Come now, base, ill-born brood; call ye it highway robbery to give freedom to those in bondage, to release the captives, to succor the miserable, to raise up the fallen, to relieve the needy? Infamous beings, who by your vile groveling intellects deserve that heaven should not make known to you the virtue that lies in knight-errantry, or

show you the sin and ignorance in which ye lie when ye
refuse to respect the shadow, not to say the presence, of
any knight-errant! Come now; band, not of officers, but
of thieves; footpads with the license of the Holy Brotherhood; tell me who was the ignoramus who signed a warrant of arrest against such a knight as I am? Who was
he that did not know that knights-errant are independent
of all jurisdictions, that their law is their sword, their
charter their prowess, and their edicts their will? Who,
I say again, was the fool that knows not that there are no
letters patent of nobility that confer such privileges or
exemptions as a knight-errant acquires the day he is
dubbed a knight, and devotes himself to the arduous calling of chivalry? What knight-errant ever paid poll-tax,
duty, queen's pin-money, king's dues, toll or ferry? What
tailor ever took payment of him for making his clothes?
What *castellan* that received him in his castle ever made
him pay his shot? What king did not seat him at his
table? What damsel was not enamoured of him and did
not yield herself up wholly to his will and pleasure? And,
lastly, what knight-errant has there been, is there, or will
there ever be in the world, not bold enough to give, single-
handed, four hundred cudgelings to four hundred officers
of the Holy Brotherhood if they come in his way?"

CHAPTER XXXIV

OF THE END OF THE NOTABLE ADVENTURE OF THE OFFICERS OF THE HOLY BROTHERHOOD; AND OF THE GREAT FEROCITY OF OUR WORTHY KNIGHT, DON QUIXOTE.

WHILE Don Quixote was talking in this strain, the curate was endeavoring to persuade the officers that he was out of his senses, as they might perceive by his deeds and his words, and that they need not press the matter any further, for even if they arrested him and carried him off, they would have to release him by-and-by as a madman; to which the holder of the warrant replied that he had nothing to do with inquiring into Don Quixote's madness, but only to execute his superior's orders, and that once taken they might let him go three hundred times if they liked.

"For all that," said the curate, "you must not take him away this time, nor will he, it is my opinion, let himself be taken away."

In short, the curate used such arguments, and Don Quixote did such mad things, that the officers would have been more mad than he was if they had not perceived his want of wits, and so they thought it best to allow themselves to be pacified, and even to act as peacemakers between the barber and Sancho Panza, who still continued their altercation with much bitterness. In the end they, as officers of justice, settled the question by arbitration in such a manner that both sides were, if not perfectly contented, at least to some extent satisfied; for they changed the pack-saddles, but not the girths or head-stalls; and as to Mambrino's helmet, the curate, under the rose and without Don Quixote's knowing it, paid eight *reals* for the basin, and the barber executed a full receipt and engagement to make no further demand then or thenceforth for evermore, amen.

These two disputes, which were the most important and gravest, being settled, it only remained for the servants of Don Luis to consent that three of them should return while one was left to accompany him whither Don Fernando desired to take him; and good luck and better fortune, having already begun to solve difficulties and remove obstructions in favor of the lovers and warriors of the inn, were pleased to persevere and bring everything to a happy issue; for the servants agreed to do as Don Luis wished; which gave Doña Clara such happiness that no one could have looked into her face just then without seeing the joy of her heart. Zoraida, though she did not fully comprehend all she saw, was grave or gay without knowing why, as she watched and studied the various countenances, but particularly her Spaniard's, whom she followed with her eyes and clung to with her soul. The gift and compensation which the curate gave the barber had not escaped the landlord's notice, and he demanded Don Quixote's reckoning, together with the amount of the damage to his wine-skins, and the loss of his wine, swearing that neither Rocinante nor Sancho's ass should leave the inn until he had been paid to the very last farthing. The curate settled all amicably, and Don Fernando paid; though the judge had also very readily offered to pay the score; and all became so peaceful and quiet that the inn no longer reminded one of the discord of Agramante's camp, as Don Quixote said, but of the peace and tranquillity of the days of Octavianus: for all which it was the universal opinion that their thanks were due to the great zeal and eloquence of the curate, and to the unexampled generosity of Don Fernando.

Finding himself now clear and quit of all quarrels, his squire's as well as his own, Don Quixote considered that it would be advisable to continue the journey he had begun, and bring to a close that great adventure for which he had been called and chosen; and with this high resolve he went and knelt before Dorothea, who, however, would not allow him to utter a word until he had risen; so to obey her he rose, and said:

"It is a common proverb, fair lady, that 'diligence is the mother of good fortune,' and experience has often shown in important affairs that the earnestness of the negotiator brings the doubtful case to a successful termination; but in nothing does this truth show itself more plainly than in war, where quickness and activity forestall the devices of the enemy, and win the victory before the foe has time to defend himself. All this I say, exalted and esteemed lady, because it seems to me that for us to remain any longer in this castle now is useless, and may be injurious to us in a way that we shall find out some day; for who knows but that your enemy the giant may have learned by means of secret and diligent spies that I am going to destroy him, and if the opportunity be given him he may seize it to fortify himself in some impregnable castle or stronghold, against which all my efforts and the might of my indefatigable arm may avail but little? Therefore, lady, let us, as I say, forestall his schemes by our activity, and let us depart at once in quest of fair fortune; for your highness is only kept from enjoying it as fully as you could desire by my delay in encountering your adversary."

Don Quixote held his peace and said no more, calmly awaiting the reply of the beauteous princess, who, with commanding dignity and in a style adapted to Don Quixote's own, replied to him in these words:

"I give you thanks, Sir Knight, for the eagerness you, like a good knight to whom it is a natural obligation to succor the orphan and the needy, display to afford me aid in my sore trouble; and heaven grant that your wishes and mine may be realized, so that you may see that there are women in this world capable of gratitude; as to my departure, let it be forthwith, for I have no will but yours; dispose of me entirely in accordance with your good pleasure; for she who has once intrusted to you the defense of her person, and placed in your hands the recovery of her dominions, must not think of offering opposition to that which your wisdom may ordain."

"On, then, in God's name," said Don Quixote; "for, when a lady humbles herself to me, I will not lose the opportunity of raising her up and placing her on the throne of her ancestors. Let us depart at once, for the common saying that in delay there is danger lends spurs to my eagerness to take the road; and as neither heaven has created nor hell seen any that can daunt or intimidate me, saddle Rocinante, Sancho, and get ready thy ass and the queen's palfrey, and let us take leave of the *castellan* and these gentlemen, and go hence this very instant."

Sancho, who was standing by all the time, said, shaking his head, "Ah! master, master, there is more mischief in the village than one hears of, begging all good bodies' pardon."

"What mischief can there be in any village, or in all the cities of the world, you booby, that can hurt my reputation?" said Don Quixote.

"If your worship is angry," replied Sancho, "I will hold my tongue and leave unsaid what as a good squire I am bound to say, and what a good servant should tell his master."

"Say what thou wilt," returned Don Quixote, "provided thy words be not meant to work upon my fears; for thou, when thou fearest, art behaving like thyself; but I like myself, when I fear not."

"It is nothing of the sort, as I am a sinner before God," said Sancho, "but that I take it to be sure and certain that this lady, who calls herself queen of the great kingdom of Micomicon, is no more so than my mother; for, if she was what she says, she would not go rubbing noses with one that is here every instant and behind every door."

CERVANTES' "DON QUIXOTE"

Dorothea turned red at Sancho's words, for the truth was that her husband Don Fernando had now and then, when the others were not looking, gathered from her lips some of the reward his love had earned, and Sancho seeing this had considered that such freedom was more like a courtesan than a queen of a great kingdom; she, however, being unable or not caring to answer him, allowed him to proceed, and he continued:

" This, I say, señor, because, if after we have traveled roads and highways, and passed bad nights and worse days, one who is now enjoying himself in this inn is to reap the fruit of our labors, there is no need for me to be in a hurry to saddle Rocinante, put the pad on the ass,. or get ready the palfrey; for it will be better for us to stay quiet, and let every jade mind her spinning, and let us go to dinner."

Good God, what was the indignation of Don Quixote when he heard the audacious words of his squire! So great was it, that in a voice inarticualte with rage, with a stammering tongue, and eyes that flashed living fire, he exclaimed:

" Rascally clown, boorish, insolent, and ignorant, illspoken, foul-mouthed, impudent backbiter and slanderer! Hast thou dared to utter such words in my presence and in that of these illustrious ladies? Hast thou dared to harbor such gross and shameless thoughts in thy muddled imagination? Begone from my presence, thou born monster, storehouse of lies, hoard of untruths, garner of knaveries, inventor of scandals, publisher of absurdities, enemy of the respect due to royal personages! Begone, show thyself no more before me under pain of my wrath!"

So saying, he knitted his brows, puffed out his cheeks, gazed around him, and stamped on the ground violently with his right foot, showing in every way the rage that was pent up in his heart; and at his words and furious gestures Sancho was so scared and terrified that he would have been glad if the earth had opened that instant and swallowed him, and his only thought was to turn round and make his escape from the angry presence of his master. But the ready-witted Dorothea, who by this time so well understood Don Quixote's humor, said, to mollify his wrath:

" Be not irritated at the absurdities your good squire has uttered, Sir Knight of the Rueful Countenance, for perhaps he did not utter them without cause, and from his good sense and Christian conscience it is not likely that he would bear false witness against anyone. We may therefore believe, without any hesitation, that since, as you say, Sir Knight, everything in this castle goes and is brought about by means of enchantment, Sancho, I say, may possibly have seen, through this diabolical medium, what he says he saw so much to the detriment of my modesty."

" I swear by God Omnipotent," excalimed Don Quixote at this, " your highness has hit the point; and that some vile illusion must have come before this sinner of a Sancho, that made him see what it would have been impossible to see by any other means than enchantments; for I know well enough, from the poor fellow's goodness and harmlessness, that he is incapable of bearing false witness against anybody."

" True, no doubt," said Don Fernando, " for which reason, Señor Don Quixote, you ought to forgive him and restore him to the bosom of your favor, *sicut erat in principio*, before illusions of this sort had taken away his senses."

Don Quixote said he was ready to pardon him, and the curate went for Sancho, who came in very humbly, and falling on his knees begged for the hand of his master, who having presented it to him and allowed him to kiss it, gave him his blessing and said, " Now, Sancho, my son, thou wilt be convinced of the truth of what I have many a time told thee, that everything in this castle is done by means of enchantment."

" So it is, I believe," said Sancho, " except the affair of the blanket, which came to pass in reality by ordinary means."

CERVANTES' "DON QUIXOTE"

"Believe it not," said Don Quixote, "for had it been so, I would have avenged thee that instant, or even now; but neither then nor now could I, nor have I seen anyone upon whom to avenge thy wrong."

They were all eager to know what the affair of the blanket was, and the landlord gave them a minute account of Sancho's flights, at which they laughed not a little, and at which Sancho would have been no less out of countenance had not his master once more assured him it was all enchantment. For all that his simplicity never reached so high a pitch that he could persuade himself it was not the plain and simple truth, without any deception whatever about it, that he had been blanketed by beings of flesh and blood, and not by visionary and imaginary phantoms, as his master believed and protested.

The illustrious company had now been two days in the inn; and as it seemed to them time to depart, they devised a plan so that, without giving Dorothea and Don Fernando the trouble of going back with Don Quixote to his village under pretense of restoring Queen Micomicona, the curate and the barber might carry him away with them as they proposed, and the curate be able to take his madness in hand at home; and in pursuance of their plan they arranged with the owner of an ox-cart who happened to be passing that way to carry him after this fashion. They constructed a kind of cage with wooden bars, large enough to hold Don Quixote comfortably; and then Don Fernando and his companions, the servants of Don Luis, and the officers of the Brotherhood, together with the landlord, by the directions and advice of the curate, covered their faces and disguised themselves, some in one way, some in another, so as to appear to Don Quixote quite different from the persons he had seen in the castle. This done, in profound silence they entered the room where he was asleep, taking his rest after the past frays, and advancing to where he was sleeping tranquilly, not dreaming of anything of the kind happening, they seized him firmly and bound him fast hand and foot, so

335

that, when he awoke startled, he was unable to move, and could only marvel and wonder at the strange figures he saw before him; upon which he at once gave way to the idea which his crazed fancy invariably conjured up before him, and took it into his head that all these shapes were phantoms of the enchanted castle, and that he himself was unquestionably enchanted, as he could neither move nor help himself; precisely what the curate, the concocter of the scheme, expected would happen.

Of all that were there Sancho was the only one who was at once in his senses and in his own proper character, and he, though he was within very little of sharing his master's infirmity, did not fail to perceive who all these disguised figures were; but he did not dare to open his lips until he saw what came of this assault and capture of his master; nor did the latter utter a word, waiting to see the upshot of his mishap; which was that, bringing in the cage, they shut him up in it and nailed the bars so firmly that they could not be easily burst open. They then took him on their shoulders, and as they passed out of the room an awful voice—as much so as the barber, not he of the pack-saddle, but the other, was able to make it— was heard to say:

"O Knight of the Rueful Countenance, let not this captivity in which thou art placed afflict thee, for this must needs be, for the more speedy accomplishment of the adventure in which thy great heart has engaged thee; the which shall be accomplished when the raging Manchegan lion and the white Tobosan dove shall be linked together, having first humbled their haughty necks to the gentle yoke of matrimony. And from this marvelous union shall come forth to the light of the world brave whelps, that shall rival the ravening claws of their valiant father; and this shall come to pass ere the pursuer of the flying nymph shall in his swift natural course have twice visited the starry signs. And thou, O most noble and obedient squire that ever bore sword at side, beard on face, or nose to smell with, be not dismayed or grieved to see the flower of knight-errantry carried away thus before thy very eyes; for soon, if it so please the Framer of the universe, thou shalt see thyself exalted to such a height that thou shalt not know thyself, and the promises which thy good master has made thee shall not prove false; and I assure thee, on the authority of the sage Mentironiana, that thy wages shall be paid thee, as thou shalt see in due season. Follow then the footsteps of the valiant enchanted knight, for it is expedient that thou shouldst go to the destination assigned to both of you; and as it is not permitted to me to say more, God be with thee; for I return to that place I wot of."

As he brought the prophecy to a close he raised his voice to a high pitch, and then lowered it to such a soft tone, that even those who knew it was all a joke were almost inclined to take what they heard seriously.

Don Quixote was comforted by the prophecy he heard, for he at once comprehended its meaning perfectly, and perceived it was promised to him that he should see himself united in holy and lawful matrimony with his beloved Dulcinea del Toboso, from whose blessed womb should proceed the whelps, his sons, to the eternal glory of La Mancha; and being thoroughly and firmly persuaded of this, he lifted up his voice, and with a deep sigh exclaimed:

"O thou, whoever thou art, who hast foretold me so much good, I implore of thee that on my part thou entreat that sage enchanter who takes charge of my interests, that he leave me not to perish in this captivity in which they are now carrying me away, ere I see fulfilled promises so joyful and incomparable as those which have been now made me; for, let this but come to pass, and I shall glory in the pains of my prison, find comfort in these chains wherewith they bind me, and regard this bed whereon they stretch me, not as a hard battlefield, but as a soft and happy nuptial couch; and touching the consolation of Sancho Panza, my squire, I rely upon his goodness and rectitude that he will not desert me in good or evil fortune; for if, by his ill luck or mine, it may not happen to be in my power to give him the island I have promised, or any equivalent for it, at least his wages shall not be lost; for in my will, which is already made, I have declared the sum that shall be paid to him, measured, not by his many faithful services, but by the means at my disposal."

Sancho bowed his head very respectfully and kissed both his hands, for, being tied together, he could not kiss one; and then the apparitions lifted the cage upon their shoulders and fixed it upon the ox-cart.

CHAPTER XXXV

OF THE STRANGE MANNER IN WHICH DON QUIXOTE OF
LA MANCHA WAS CARRIED AWAY ENCHANTED, TOGETHER
WITH OTHER REMARKABLE INCIDENTS

WHEN Don Quixote saw himself caged and hoisted on the cart in this way, he said:
"Many grave histories of knights-errant have I read; but never yet have I read, seen, or heard of their carrying off enchanted knights-errant in this fashion, or at the slow pace that these lazy, sluggish animals promise; for they always take them away through the air with marvelous swiftness, enveloped in a dark thick cloud, or on a chariot of fire, or it may be on some hippogriff or other beast of the kind; but to carry me off like this on an ox-cart! By God, it puzzles me! But perhaps the chivalry and enchantments of our day take a different course from that of those in days gone by; and it may be, too, that, as I am a new knight in the world, and the first to revive the already forgotten calling of knight-adventurers, they may have newly invented other kinds of enchantments and other modes of carrying off the enchanted. What thinkest thou of the matter, Sancho, my son?"

"I don't know what to think," answered Sancho, "not being as well read as your worship in errant writings; but for all that I venture to say and swear that these apparitions that are about us are not quite Catholic."

"Catholic!" said Don Quixote. "Father of me! how can they be Catholic when they are all devils that have

339

taken fantastic shapes to come and do this, and bring me to this condition? And if thou wouldst prove it, touch them, and feel them, and thou wilt find they have only bodies of air, and no consistency except in appearance."

"By God, master," returned Sancho, "I have touched them already; and that devil, that goes about there so busily, has firm flesh, and another property very different from what I have heard say devils have, for by all accounts they all smell of brimstone and other bad smells; but this one smells of amber half a league off." Sancho was here speaking of Don Fernando, who, like a gentleman of his rank, was very likely perfumed as Sancho said.

"Marvel not at that, Sancho, my friend," said Don Quixote; "for let me tell thee, devils are crafty; and even if they do carry odors about with them, they themselves have no smell, because they are spirits; or, if they have any smell, they canont smell of anything sweet, but of something foul and fetid; and the reason is that as they carry hell with them wherever they go, and can get no ease whatever from their torments, and as a sweet smell is a thing that gives pleasure and enjoyment, it is impossible that they can smell sweet; if, then, this devil thou speakest of seems to thee to smell of amber, either thou art deceiving thyself, or he wants to deceive thee by making thee fancy he is not a devil."

Such was the conversation that passed between master and man; and Don Fernando and Cardenio, apprehensive of Sancho's making a complete discovery of their scheme, towards which he had already gone some way, resolved to hasten their departure, and calling the landlord aside, they directed him to saddle Rocinante and put the pack-saddle on Sancho's ass, which he did with great alacrity. In the meantime the curate had made an arrangement with the officers that they should bear them company as far as his village, he paying them so much a day. Cardenio hung the buckler on one side of the bow of Rocinante's saddle and the basin on the other, and by signs commanded Sancho to mount his ass and take Rocinate's bridle, and at each side of the cart he placed two officers with their muskets; but before the cart was put in motion, out came the landlady and her daughter and Maritornes to bid Don Quixote farewell, pretending to weep with grief at his misfortune; and to them Don Quixote said:

"Weep not, good ladies, for all these mishaps are the lot of those who follow the profession I profess; and if these reverses did not befall me I should not esteem myself a famous knight-errant; for such things never happen to knights of little renown and fame, because nobody in the world thinks about them; to valiant knights they do, for these are envied for their virtue and valor by many princes and other knights who compass the destruction of the worthy by base means. Nevertheless, virtue is of herself so mighty, that, in spite of all the magic that Zoroastes, its first inventor, knew, she will come victorious out of every trial, and shed her light upon the earth as the sun does upon the heavens. Forgive me, fair ladies, if, through inadvertence, I have in aught offended you; for intentionally and wittingly I have never done so to any; and pray to God that he deliver me from this captivity to which some malevolent enchanter has consigned me; and should I find myself released therefrom, the favors that ye have bestowed upon me in this castle shall be held in memory by me, that I may acknowledge, recognize, and requite them as they deserve."

While this was passing between the ladies of the castle and Don Quixote, the curate and the barber bade farewell to Don Fernando and his companions, to the captain, his brother, and the ladies, now all made happy, and in particular to Dorothea and Luscinda. They all embraced one another, and promised to let each other know how things went with them, and Don Fernando directed the curate where to write to him, to tell him what became of Don Quixote, assuring him that there was nothing that could give him more pleasure than to hear, and that he, too, on his part, would send him word of everything he thought he would like to know, about his marriage, Zo-

raida's baptism, Don Luis's affair, and Luscinda's return
to her home. The curate promised to comply with his
request carefully, and they embraced once more, and
renewed their promises. . . .

The order of march was this: First went the cart with
the owner leading it; at each side of it marched the officers
of the Brotherhood, as has been said, with their muskets;
then followed Sancho Panza on his ass, leading Rocinante
by the bridle; and behind all came the curate and the barber on their mighty mules, with faces covered, as aforesaid, and a grave and serious air, measuring their pace to
suit the slow steps of the oxen. Don Quixote was seated
in the cage, with his hands tied and his feet stretched
out, leaning against the bars as silent and as patient as
if he were a stone statue and not a man of flesh. Thus
slowly and silently they made, it might be, two leagues,
until they reached a valley which the carter thought a convenient place for resting and feeding his oxen, and he said
so to the curate, but the barber was of opinion that they
ought to push on a little farther, as at the other side of
a hill which appeared close by he knew there was a valley
that had more grass and much better than the one where
they proposed to halt; and his advice was taken and they
continued their journey.

Just at that moment the curate, looking back, saw coming on behind them six or seven mounted men, well found
and equipped, who soon overtook them, for they were traveling, not at the sluggish, deliberate pace of oxen, but like
men who rode canons' mules, and in haste to take their
noontide rest as soon as possible at the inn which was in
sight not a league off. The quick travelers came up with
the slow, and courteous salutations were exchanged; and
one of the newcomers, who was, in fact, a canon of Toledo and master of the others who accompanied him, observing the regular order of the procession, the cart, the
officers, Sancho, Rocinante, the curate and the barber, and
above all Don Quixote caged and confined, could not help
asking what was the meaning of carrying the man in that

fashion; though, from the badges of the officers, he already concluded that he must be some desperate highwayman or other malefactor whose punishment fell within the jurisdiction of the Holy Brotherhood. One of the officers to whom he had put the question, replied:

"Let the gentleman himself tell you the meaning of his going this way, señor, for we do not know."

Don Quixote overheard the conversation and said:

"Haply, gentlemen, you are versed and learned in matters of chivalry? Because if you are I will tell you my misfortunes; if not, there is no good in my giving myself the trouble of relating them."

But here the curate and the barber, seeing that the travelers were engaged in conversation with Don Quixote, came forward, in order to answer in such a way as to save their stratagem from being discovered. The canon, replying to Don Quixote, said:

"In truth, brother, I know more about books of chivalry than I do about Villalpando's elements of logic; so if that be all, you may safely tell me what you please."

"In God's name, then, señor," replied Don Quixote, "if that be so, I would have you know that I am held enchanted in this cage by the envy and fraud of wicked enchanters; for virtue is more persecuted by the wicked than loved by the good. I am a knight-errant, and not one of those whose names Fame has never thought of immortalizing in her record, but of those who, in defiance and in spite of envy itself, and all the magicians that Persia, or Brahmans that India, or Gymnosophists that Ethiopia ever produced, will place their names in the temple of immortality, to serve as examples and patterns for ages to come, whereby knights-errant may see the footsteps in which they must tread if they would attain the summit and crowning point of honor in arms."

"What Señor Don Quixote of La Mancha says," observed the curate, "is the truth; for he goes enchanted in this cart, not from any fault or sins of his, but because of the malevolence of those to whom virtue is odious and valor hateful. This, señor, is the Knight of the Rueful Countenance, if you have ever heard him named, whose valiant achievements and mighty deeds shall be written on lasting brass and imperishable marble, notwithstanding all the efforts of envy to obscure them and malice to hide them."

When the canon heard both the prisoner and the man who was at liberty talk in such a strain he was ready to cross himself in his astonishment, and could not make out what had befallen him; and all his attendants were in the same state of amazement.

At this point Sancho Panza, who had drawn near to hear the conversation, said, in order to make everything plain:

"Well, sirs, you may like or dislike what I am going to say, but the fact of the matter is, my master, Don Quixote, is just as much enchanted as my mother. He is in his full senses, he eats and he drinks, and he has his calls like other men and as he had yesterday, before they caged him. And if that's the case, what do they mean by wanting me to believe that he is enchanted? For I have heard many a one say that enchanted people neither eat, nor sleep, nor talk; and my master, if you don't stop him, will talk more than thirty lawyers."

Then turning to the curate he exclaimed:

"Ah, Señor Curate, Señor Curate! do you think I don't know you? Do you think I don't guess and see the drift of these new enchantments? Well, then, I can tell you I know you, for all your face is covered, and I can tell you I am up to you, however you may hide your tricks. After all, where envy reigns virtue cannot live, and where there is niggardliness there can be no liberality. Ill betide the devil! if it had not been for your worship my master would be married to the Princess Micomicona this minute, and I should be a count at least; for no less was to be expected, as well from the goodness of my master, him of the Rueful Countenance, as from the greatness of my services. But I see now how true it is what they say in these

344

parts, that the wheel of fortune turns faster than a mill-wheel, and that those who were up yesterday are down today. I am sorry for my wife and children, for when they might fairly and reasonably expect to see their father return to them a governor or viceroy of some island or kingdom, they will see him come back a horse-boy. I have said all this, Señor Curate, only to urge your paternity to lay to your conscience your ill-treatment of my master; and have a care that God does not call you to account in another life for making a prisoner of him in this way, and charge against you all the succors and good deeds that my lord Don Quixote leaves undone while he is shut up."

" Trim those lamps there! " exclaimed the barber at this; " so you are of the same fraternity as your master, too, Sancho? By God, I begin to see that you will have to keep him company in the cage, and be enchanted like him for having caught some of his humor and chivalry. It was an evil hour when you let yourself be got with child by his promises, and that island you long so much for found its way into your head."

" I am not with child by anyone," returned Sancho, "nor am I a man to let myself be got with child, if it was by the king himself. Though I am poor, I am an old Christian, and I owe nothing to nobody, and if I long for an island, other people long for worse. Each of us is the son of his own works; and being a man, I may come to be pope, not to say governor of an island, especially as my master may win so many that he will not know whom to give them to. Mind how you talk, master barber; for shaving is not everything, and there is some difference between Peter and Peter. I say this because we all know one another, and it will not do to throw false dice with me; and as to the enchantment of my master, God knows the truth; leave it as it is; it will only make it worse to stir it."

The barber did not care to answer Sancho lest by his plain speaking he should disclose what the curate and he himself were trying so hard to conceal; and under the same apprehension the curate had asked the canon to ride on a little in advance, so that he might tell him the mystery of this man in the cage, and other things that would amuse him. The canon agreed, and going on ahead with his servants, listened with attention to the account of the character, life, madness, and ways of Don Quixote, given him by the curate, who described to him briefly the beginning and origin of his craze, and told him the whole story of his adventures up to his being confined in the cage, together with the plan they had of taking him home to try if by any means they could discover a cure for his madness. The canon and his servants were surprised anew when they heard Don Quixote's strange story. . . .

While this was going on, Sancho, perceiving that he could speak to his master without having the curate and the barber, of whom he had his suspicions, present all the time, approached the cage in which Don Quixote was placed, and said:

"Señor, to ease my conscience I want to tell you the state of the case as to your enchantment, and that is that these two here, with their faces covered, are the curate of our village and the barber; and I suspect they have hit upon this plan of carrying you off in this fashion, out of pure envy because your worship surpasses them in doing famous deeds; and if this be the truth, it follows that you are not enchanted, but hoodwinked and made a fool of. And to prove this I want to ask you one thing; and if you answer me as I believe you will answer, you will be able to lay your finger on the trick, and you will see that you are not enchanted, but gone wrong in your wits."

"Ask what thou wilt, Sancho, my son," returned Don Quixote, "for I will satisfy thee and answer all thou requirest. As to what thou sayest, that these who accompany us yonder are the curate and the barber, our neighbors and acquaintances, it is very possible that they may seem to be those same persons; but that they are so in reality and in fact, believe it not on any account; what

346

thou art to believe and think is that, if they look like them, as thou sayest, it must be that those who have enchanted me have taken this shape and likeness; for it is easy for enchanters to take any form they please, and they may have taken those of our friends in order to make thee think as thou dost, and lead thee into a labyrinth of fancies from which thou wilt find no escape, though thou hadst the cord of Theseus; and they may also have done it to make me uncertain in my mind, and unable to conjecture whence this evil comes to me; for if on the one hand thou dost tell me that the barber and curate of our village are here in company with us, and on the other I find myself shut up in a cage, and know in my heart that no power on earth that was not supernatural would have been able to shut me in, what wouldst thou have me say or think, but that my enchantment is of a sort that transcends all I have ever read of in all the histories that deal with knights-errant that have been enchanted? So thou mayest set thy mind at rest as to the idea that they are what thou sayest, for they are as much so as I am a Turk. But touching thy desire to ask me something, say on, and I will answer thee, though thou shouldst ask questions from this till tomorrow morning."

"May Our Lady be good to me!" said Sancho, lifting up his voice; "and is it possible that your worship is so thick of skull and so short of brains that you cannot see that what I say is the simple truth, and that malice has more to do with your imprisonment and misfortune than enchantment? But as it is so, I will prove plainly to you that you are not enchanted. Now tell me, so may God deliver you from this affliction, and so may you find yourself when you least expect it in the arms of my lady Dulcinea——"

"Leave off conjuring me," said Don Quixote, "and ask what thou wouldst know; I have already told thee I will answer with all possible precision."

"That is what I want," said Sancho; "and what I would know, and have you tell me, without adding or leaving

347

out anything, but telling the whole truth as one expects it to be told, and as it is told, by all who profess arms, as your worship professes them, under the title of knights-errant——"

"I tell thee I will not lie in any particular," said Don Quixote; "finish thy question; for in truth thou weariest me with all these asseverations, requirements, and precautions, Sancho."

"Well, I rely on the goodness and truth of my master," said Sancho; "and so, because it bears upon what we are talking about, I would ask, speaking with all reverence, whether since your worship has been shut up and, as you think, enchanted in this cage, you have felt any desire or inclination to go anywhere, as the saying is?"

"I do not understand 'going anywhere,'" said Don Quixote; "explain thyself more clearly, Sancho, if thou wouldst have me give an answer to the point."

"Is it possible," said Sancho, "that your worship does not understand 'going anywhere'? Why, the schoolboys know that from the time they were babes. Well, then, you must know I mean have you had any desire to do what cannot be avoided?"

"Ah! now I understand thee, Sancho," said Don Quixote; "yes, often, and even this minute; get me out of this strait, or all will not go right."

CHAPTER XXXVI

WHICH TREATS OF THE SHREWD CONVERSATION WHICH SANCHO PANZA HELD WITH HIS MASTER DON QUIXOTE

"AHA, I have caught you," said Sancho; "this is what in my heart and soul I was longing to know. Come now, señor, can you deny what is commonly said around us, when a person is out of humor, 'I don't know what ails so-and-so, that he neither eats, nor drinks, nor sleeps, nor gives a proper answer to any question; one would think he was enchanted'? From which it is to be gathered that those who do not eat, or drink, or sleep, or do any of the natural acts I am speaking of—that such persons are enchanted; but not those that have the desire your worship has, and drink when drink is given them, and eat when there is anything to eat, and answer every question that is asked them."

"What thou sayest is true, Sancho," replied Don Quixote; "but I have already told thee there are many sorts of enchantments, and it may be that in the course of time they have been changed one for another, and that now it may be the way with enchanted people to do all that I do, though they did not do so before; so it is vain to argue or draw inferences against the usage of the time. I know and feel that I am enchanted, and that is enough to ease my conscience; for it would weigh heavily on it if I thought that I was not enchanted, and that in a faint-hearted and cowardly way I allowed myself to lie in this cage, defrauding multitudes of the succor I might

349

afford to those in need and distress, who at this very moment may be in sore want of my aid and protection."

" Still for all that," replied Sancho, " I say that, for your greater and fuller satisfaction, it would be well if your worship were to try to get out of this prison and I prom- ise to do all in my power to help, and even to take you out of it), and see if you could once more mount your good Rocinante, who seems to be enchanted, too, he is so melancholy and dejected; and then we might try our chance in looking for adventures again; and if we have no luck there will be time enough to go back to the cage; in which, on the faith of a good and loyal squire, I promise to shut myself up along with your worship, if so be you are so unfortunate, or I so stupid, as not to be able to carry out my plan."

" I am content to do as thou sayest, brother Sancho," said Don Quixote, " and when thou seest an opportunity for effecting my release I will obey thee absolutely; but thou wilt see, Sancho, how mistaken thou art in thy con- ception of my misfortune."

The knight-errant and the ill-errant squire kept up their conversation till they reached the place where the curate, the canon, and the barber, who had already dismounted, were waiting for them. The carter at once unyoked the oxen and left them to roam at large about the pleasant green spot, the freshness of which seemed to invite, not enchanted people like Don Quixote, but wide-awake, sen- sible folk like his squire, who begged the curate to allow his master to leave the cage for a little; for if they did not let him out, the prison might not be as clean as the propriety of such a gentleman as his master required. The curate understood him, and said he would very gladly comply with his request, only that he feared his master, finding himself at liberty, would take to his old courses and make off where nobody could ever find him again.

" I will answer for his not running away," said Sancho.

" And I for everything," said the canon, " especially if

he gives me his word as a knight not to leave us without our consent."

Don Quixote, who was listening to all this, said he would give it; and that moreover one who was enchanted as he was could not do as he liked with himself; for he who had enchanted him could prevent his moving from one place for three ages, and if he attempted to escape would bring him back flying; and that being so, they might as well release him, particularly as it would be to the advantage of all.

The canon took his hand, tied together as they both were, and on his word and promise they unbound him, and rejoiced beyond measure he was to find himself out of the cage. The first thing he did was to stretch himself all over, and then he went to where Rocinante was standing and giving him a couple of slaps on the haunches said:

" I still trust in God and in his blessed mother, O flower and mirror of steeds, that we shall soon see ourselves, both of us, as we wish to be, thou with thy master on thy back, and I mounted upon thee, following the calling for which God sent me into the world."

And so saying, accompanied by Sancho, he withdrew to a retired spot, from which he came back more eager than ever to put his squire's scheme into execution. . . .

By this time the canon's servants, who had gone to the inn to fetch the sumpter mule, had returned, and making a carpet and the green grass of the meadow serve as a table, they seated themselves in the shade of some trees and made their repast there, that the carter might not be deprived of the advantage of the spot, as has been already said. As they were eating they suddenly heard a loud noise and the sound of a bell that seemed to come from among some brambles and thick bushes that were close by, and the same instant they observed a beautiful goat, spotted all over black, white, and brown, spring out of the thicket with a goatherd after it, calling to it and uttering the usual cries to make it stop or turn back to the fold. The fugi-

tive goat, scared and frightened, ran towards the company
as if seeking protection and then stood still, and the goatherd coming up seized it by the horns and began to talk
to it as if it were possessed of reason and understanding:

"Ah, wanderer, wanderer, Spotty, Spotty; how have
you gone limping all this time? What wolves have frightened you, my daughter? Won't you tell me what is the
matter, my beauty? But what else can it be except that
you are a she, and cannot keep quiet? A plague on your
humors and the humors of those you take after! Come
back, come back, my darling; and if you will not be so
happy, at any rate you will be safe in the fold or with
your companions; for if you who ought to keep and lead
them go wandering astray in this fashion, what will become of them?"

The goatherd's talk amused all who heard it, but especially the canon, who said to him:

"As you live, brother, take it easy, and be not in such
a hurry to drive this goat back to the fold; for, being a
female, as you say, she will follow her natural instinct in
spite of all you can do to prevent it. Take this morsel
and drink a sup, and that will soothe your irritation, and
in the meantime the goat will rest herself," and so saying,
he handed him the loins of a cold rabbit on a fork. The
goatherd took it with thanks, and drank and calmed himself, and then said:

"I should be sorry if your worships were to take me
for a simpleton for having spoken so seriously as I did to
this animal; but the truth is, there is a certain mystery in
the words I used. I am a clown, but not so much of one
but that I know how to behave to men and to beasts."

"That I can well believe," said the curate, "for I know
already by experience that the woods breed men of learning, and shepherds' huts harbor philosophers."

"At all events, señor," returned the goatherd, "they
shelter men of experience; and that you may see the truth
of this and grasp it, though I may seem to put myself forward without being asked, I will, if it will not tire you,

gentlemen, and you will give me your attention for a little, tell you a true story which will confirm this gentleman's word" (and he pointed to the curate) "as well as my own."

To this Don Quixote replied: "Seeing that this affair has a certain color of chivalry about it, I for my part, brother, will hear you most gladly, and so will all these gentlemen, from the high intelligence they possess and their love of curious novelties that interest, charm, and entertain the mind, as I feel quite sure your story will do. So begin, friend, for we are all prepared to listen."

"I draw my stakes," said Sancho, "and will retreat with this pasty to the brook there, where I mean to victual myself for three days; for I have heard my lord, Don Quixote, say that a knight-errant's squire should eat until he can hold no more, whenever he has the chance, because it often happens them to get by accident into a wood so thick that they cannot find a way out of it for six days; and if the man is not well filled or his wallets well stored, there he may stay, as very often he does, turned into a dried mummy."

"Thou art in the right of it, Sancho," said Don Quixote; "go where thou wilt and eat all thou canst, for I have had enough, and only want to give my mind its refreshment, as I shall by listening to this good fellow's story."

"It is what we shall all do," said the canon; and then begged the goatherd to begin the promised tale.

The goatherd gave the goat which he held by the horns a couple of slaps on the back, saying, "Lie down here beside me, Spotty, for we have time enough to return to our fold." The goat seemed to understand him, for as her master seated himself, she stretched herself quietly beside him and looked up in his face to show him she was all attention to what he was going to say, and then in these words he began his story:

CHAPTER XXXVII

THREE leagues from this valley there is a village
which, though small, is one of the richest in all this
neighborhood, and in it there lived a farmer, a very worthy
man, and so much respected that, although to be so is the
natural consequence of being rich, he was even more respected for his virtue than for the wealth he had acquired.
But what made him still more fortunate, as he said himself, was having a daughter of such exceeding beauty, rare
intelligence, gracefulness, and virtue that everyone who
knew her and beheld her marveled at the extraordinary
gifts with which heaven and nature had endowed her. As
a child she was beautiful, she continued to grow in beauty,
and at the age of sixteen she was most lovely. The fame
of her beauty began to spread abroad through all the villages around—but why do I say the villages around,
merely, when it spread to distant cities, and even made
its way into the halls of royalty and reached the ears of
people of every class, who came from all sides to see her
as if to see something rare and curious, or some wonder-
working image?

Her father watched over her and she watched over herself; for there are no locks, or guards, or bolts that can
protect a young girl better than her own modesty. The
wealth of the father and the beauty of the daughter led
many neighbors as well as strangers to seek her for a

354

wife; but he, as one might well be who had the disposal of so rich a jewel, was perplexed and unable to make up his mind to which of her countless suitors he should intrust her. I was one among the many who felt a desire so natural, and, as her father knew who I was, and I was of the same town, of pure blood, in the bloom of life, and very rich in possessions, I had great hopes of success. There was another of the same place and qualifications who also sought her, and this made her father's choice hang in the balance, for he felt that on either of us his daughter would be well bestowed; so to escape from this state of perplexity he resolved to refer the matter to Leandra (for that is the name of the rich damsel who has reduced me to misery), reflecting that as we were both equal it would be best to leave it to his dear daughter to choose according to her inclination—a course that is worthy of imitation by all fathers who wish to settle their children in life. I do not mean that they ought to leave them to make a choice of what is contemptible and bad, but that they should place before them what is good and then allow them to make a good choice as they please. I do not know which Leandra chose; I only know her father put us both off with the tender age of his daughter and vague words that neither bound him nor dismissed us. My rival is called Anselmo and I myself Eugenio—that you may know the names of the personages that figure in this tragedy, the end of which is still in suspense, though it is plain to see it must be disastrous.

About this time there arrived in our town one Vicente de la Roca, the son of a poor peasant of the same town, the said Vicente having returned from service as a soldier in Italy and divers other parts. A captain who chanced to pass that way with his company had carried him off from our village when he was a boy of about twelve years, and now, twelve years later, the young man came back in a soldier's uniform, arrayed in a thousand colors, and all over glass trinkets and fine steel chains. Today he would appear in one gay dress, tomorrow in another; but all flimsy and gaudy, of little substance and less worth. The peasant folk, who are naturally malicious, and when they have nothing to do can be malice itself, remarked all this, and took note of his finery and jewelry, piece by piece, and discovered that he had three suits of different colors, with garters and stockings to match; but he made so many arrangements and combinations out of them, that if they had not counted them, anyone would have sworn that he had made a display of more than ten suits of clothes and twenty plumes. Do not look upon all this that I am telling you about the clothes as uncalled for or spun out, for they have a great deal to do with the story. He used to seat himself on a bench under the great poplar in our plaza, and there he would keep us all hanging open-mouthed on the stories he told us of his exploits. There was no country on the face of the globe he had not seen, nor battle he had not been engaged in; he had killed more Moors than there are in Morocco and Tunis, and fought more single combats, according to his own account, than Garcilaso, Diego Garcia de Paredes and a thousand others he named, and out of all he had come victorious without losing a drop of blood. On the other hand he showed marks of wounds, which, though they could not be made out, he said were gunshot wounds received in divers encounters and actions. Lastly, with monstrous impudence he used to say "you" to his equals and even those who knew what he was, and declare that his arm was his father and his deeds his pedigree, and that being a soldier he was as good as the king himself. And to add to these swaggering ways he was a trifle of a musician, and played the guitar with such a flourish that some said he made it speak; nor did his accomplishments end here, for he was something of a poet, too, and on every trifle that happened in the town he made a ballad a league and a half long.

This soldier, then, that I have described, this Vicente de la Roca, this bravo, gallant, musician, poet, was often seen and watched by Leandra from a window of her house which looked out on the plaza. The glitter of his showy attire took her fancy, his ballads bewitched her (for he gave away twenty copies of every one he made), the tales of his exploits which he told about himself came to her ears; and, in short, as the devil no doubt had arranged it, she fell in love with him before the presumption of making love to her had suggested itself to him; and as in love-affairs none are more easily brought to an issue than those which have the inclination of the lady for an ally, Leandra and Vicente came to an understanding without any difficulty; and before any of her numerous suitors had any suspicion of her design, she had already carried it into effect, having left the house of her dearly beloved father (for mother she had none), and disappeared from the village with the soldier, who came more triumphantly out of this enterprise than out of any of the large number he laid claim to. All the village and all who heard of it were amazed at the affair; I was aghast, Anselmo thunder-struck, her father full of grief, her relations indignant, the authorities all in a ferment, the officers of the Brotherhood in arms.

They scoured the roads, they searched the woods and all quarters, and at the end of three days they found the flighty Leandra in a mountain cave, stript to her shift, and robbed of all the money and precious jewels she had carried away from home with her. They brought her back to her unhappy father, and questioned her as to her misfortune, and she confessed without pressure that Vicente de la Roca had deceived her, and under promise of marrying her had induced her to leave her father's house, as he meant to take her to the richest and most delightful city in the whole world, which was Naples; and that she, ill-advised and deluded, had believed him, and robbed her father, and handed over all to him the night she disappeared; and that he had carried her away to a rugged mountain and shut her up in the cave where they had found her.

She said, moreover, that the soldier, without robbing her of her honor, had taken from her everything she had, and made off, leaving her in the cave, a thing that still further surprised everybody. It was not easy for us to credit the young man's continence, but she asserted it with such earnestness that it helped to console her distressed father, who thought nothing of what had been taken since the jewel that once lost can never be recovered had been left to his daughter. The same day that Leandra made her appearance her father removed her from our sight and took her away to shut her up in a convent in a town near this, in the hope that time may wear away some of the disgrace she has incurred. Leandra's youth furnished an excuse for her fault, at least with those to whom it was of no consequence whether she was good or bad; but those who knew her shrewdness and intelligence did not attribute her misdemeanor to ignorance but to wantonness and the natural disposition of women, which is for the most part flighty and ill-regulated.

Leandra withdrawn from sight, Anselmo's eyes grew blind, or at any rate found nothing to look at that gave them any pleasure, and mine were in darkness without a ray of light to direct them to anything enjoyable while Leandra was away. Our melancholy grew greater, our patience grew less; we cursed the soldier's finery and railed at the carelessness of Leandra's father. At last Anselmo and I agreed to leave the village and come to this valley; and, he feeding a great flock of sheep of his own, and I a large herd of goats of mine, we pass our life among the trees, giving vent to our sorrows, together singing the fair Leandra's praises, or upbraiding her, or else sighing alone, and to heaven pouring forth our complaints in solitude.

Following our example, many more of Leandra's lovers have come to these rude mountains and adopted our mode of life, and they are so numerous that one would fancy the place had been turned into the pastoral Arcadia, so full is it of shepherds and sheepfolds; nor is there a spot in it where the name of the fair Leandra is not heard. Here one curses her and calls her capricious, fickle, and immodest, there another condemns her as frail and frivolous; this pardons and absolves her, that spurns and reviles her; one extols her beauty, another assails her character, and, in short, all abuse her, and all adore her, and to such a pitch has this general infatuation gone that there are some who complain of her scorn without ever having exchanged a word with her, and even some that bewail and mourn the raging fever of jealousy, for which she never gave anyone cause, for, as I have already said, her misconduct was known before her passion. There is no nook among the rocks, no brookside, no shade beneath the trees that is not haunted by some shepherd telling his woes to the breezes; wherever there is an echo it repeats the name of Leandra; the mountains ring with "Leandra," "Leandra" murmur the brooks, and Leandra keeps us all bewildered and bewitched, hoping without hope and fearing without knowing what we fear. Of all this silly set the one that shows the least and also the most sense is my rival Anselmo, for having so many other things to complain of, he only complains of separation, and to the accompaniment of a rebeck, which he plays admirably, he sings his complaints in verses that show his ingenuity. I follow another easier, and to my mind worse course, and that is to rail at the frivolity of women, at their inconstancy, their double dealing, their broken promises, their unkept pledges, and in short the want of reflection they show in fixing their affections and inclinations. This, sirs, was the reason of words and expressions I made use of to this goat when I came up just now; for as she is a female I have a contempt for her, though she is the best in all my fold. This is the story I promised to tell you, and if I have been tedious in telling it, I will not be slow to serve you; my hut is close by, and I have fresh milk and dainty cheese there, as well as a variety of toothsome fruit, no less pleasing to the eye than to the palate."

CHAPTER XXXVIII

OF THE QUARREL THAT DON QUIXOTE HAD WITH THE GOAT-
HERD, TOGETHER WITH THE RARE ADVENTURE OF THE
PENITENTS, WHICH WITH AN EXPENDITURE OF SWEAT
HE BROUGHT TO A HAPPY CONCLUSION

THE goatherd's tale gave great satisfaction to all the
hearers, and the canon especially enjoyed it, for he
had remarked with particular attention the manner in
which it had been told, which was as unlike the manner
of a clownish goatherd as it was like that of a polished
city wit; and he observed that the curate had been quite
right in saying that the woods bred men of learning. They
all offered their services to Eugenio, but he who showed
himself most liberal in this way was Don Quixote, who
said to him:

"Most assuredly, brother goatherd, if I found myself
in a position to attempt any adventure, I would, this very
instant, set out on your behalf, and would rescue Leandra
from that convent (where no doubt she is kept against her
will), in spite of the abbess and all who might try to prevent me, and would place her in your hands to deal with
her according to your will and pleasure, observing, however, the laws of chivalry which lay down no violence of
any kind is to be offered to any damsel. But I trust in
God our Lord that the might of one malignant enchanter
may not prove so great but that the power of another better disposed may prove superior to it, and then I promise
you my support and assistance, as I am bound to do by

my profession, which is none other than to give aid to the weak and needy."

The goatherd eyed him, and noticing Don Quixote's sorry appearance and looks, he was filled with wonder and asked the barber, who was next him, 'Señor, who is this man who makes such a figure and talks in such a strain?"

"Who should it be," said the barber, "but the famous Don Quixote of La Mancha, the undoer of injustice, the righter of wrongs, the protector of damsels, the terror of giants, and the winner of battles?"

"That," said the goatherd, "sounds like what one reads in the books of the knights-errant, who did all that you say this man does; though it is my belief that either you are joking, or else this gentleman has empty lodgings in his head."

"You are a great scoundrel," said Don Quixote, "and it is you who are empty and a fool. I am fuller than ever was the whoreson bitch that bore you;" and passing from words to deeds, he caught up a loaf that was near him and sent it full in the goatherd's face, with such force that he flattened his nose; but the goatherd, who did not understand jokes, and found himself roughly handled in such good earnest, paying no respect to carpet, table-cloth, or diners, sprang upon Don Quixote, and seizing him by the throat with both hands would no doubt have throttled him, had not Sancho Panza that instant come to the rescue, and grasping him by the shoulders flung him down on the table, smashing plates, breaking glasses, and upsetting and scattering everything on it.

Don Quixote, finding himself free, strove to get on top of the goatherd, who, with his face covered with blood, and soundly kicked by Sancho, was on all fours feeling about for one of the table-knives to take a bloody revenge with. The canon and the curate, however, prevented him, but the barber so contrived it that he got Don Quixote under him, and rained down upon him such a shower of fisticuffs that the poor knight's face streamed with blood as freely as his own. The canon and the curate were bursting with laughter, the officers were capering with de-light, and both the one and the other hissed them on as they do dogs that are worrying one another in a fight. Sancho alone was frantic, for he could not free himself from the grasp of one of the canon's servants, who kept him from going to his master's assistance.

At last, while they were all, with the exception of the two bruisers who were mauling each other, in high glee and enjoyment, they heard a trumpet sound a note so dole-ful that it made them all look in the direction whence the sound seemed to come. But the one that was most excited by hearing it was Don Quixote, who, though sorely against his will he was under the goatherd, and something more than pretty well pummelled, said to him:

" Brother devil (for it is impossible but that thou must be one since thou hast had might and strength enough to overcome mine), I ask thee to agree to a truce for but one hour, for the solemn note of yonder trumpet that falls on our ears seems to me to summon me to some new adven-ture."

The goatherd, who was by this time tired of pum-melling and being pummelled, released him at once, and Don Quixote rising to his feet and turning his eyes to the quarter where the sound had been heard, suddenly saw coming down the slope of a hill several men clad in white like penitents.

The fact was that the clouds had that year withheld their moisture from the earth, and in all the villages of the district they were organizing processions, rogations, and penances, imploring God to open the hands of his mercy and send them rain; and to this end the people of a village that was hard by were going in procession to a holy her-mitage there was on one side of that valley. Don Quixote, when he saw the strange garb of the penitents, without re-flecting how often he had seen it before, took it into his head that this was a case of adventure, and that it fell to him alone as a knight-errant to engage in it; and he was all the more confirmed in this notion, by the idea that an image draped in black they had with them was some illustrious lady that these villains and discourteous thieves were carrying off by force. As soon as this occurred to him he ran with all speed to Rocinante who was grazing at large, and taking the bridle and the buckler from the saddle-bow, he had him bridled in an instant, and calling to Sancho for his sword he mounted Rocinante, braced his buckler on his arm, and in a loud voice exclaimed to those who stood by:

"Now, noble company, ye shall see how important it is that there should be knights in the world professing the order of knight-errantry; now, I say, ye shall see, by the deliverance of that worthy lady who is borne captive there, whether knights-errant deserve to be held in estimation."

So saying he brought his legs to bear on Rocinante— for he had no spurs—and at a full canter (for in all this veracious history we never read of Rocinante fairly galloping) set off to encounter the penitents, though the curate, the canon, and the barber ran to prevent him. But it was out of their power, nor did he even stop for the shouts of Sancho calling after him:

"Where are you going, Señor Don Quixote? What devils have possessed you to set you on against our Catholic faith? Plague take me! mind, that is a procession of penitents, and the lady they are carrying on that stand there is the blessed image of the Immaculate Virgin. Take care what you are doing, señor, for this time it may be safely said you don't know what you are about."

Sancho labored in vain, for his master was so bent on coming to quarters with these sheeted figures and releasing the lady in black that he did not hear a word; and even had he heard, he would not have turned back if the king had ordered him. He came up with the procession and reined in Rocinante, who was already anxious to slacken speed a little, and in a hoarse, excited voice he exclaimed:

"You who hide your faces, perhaps because you are not good subjects, pay attention and listen to what I am about to say to you."

The first to halt were those who were carrying the image, and one of the four ecclesiastics who were chanting the Litany, struck by the strange figure of Don Quixote, the leanness of Rocinante, and the other ludicrous peculiarities he observed, said in reply to him:

"Brother, if you have anything to say to us say it quickly, for these brethren are whipping themselves, and we cannot stop, nor is it reasonable we should stop to hear anything, unless indeed it is short enough to be said in two words."

"I will say it in one," replied Don Quixote, "and it is this; that at once, this very instant, ye release that fair lady whose tears and sad aspect show plainly that ye are carrying her off against her will, and that ye have committed some scandalous outrage against her; and I, who was born into the world to redress all such like wrongs, will not permit you to advance another step until you have restored to her the liberty she pines for and deserves."

From these words all the hearers concluded that he must be a madman, and began to laugh heartily, and their laughter acted like gunpowder on Don Quixote's fury, for drawing his word without another word he made a rush at the stand. One of those who supported it, leaving the burden to his comrades, advanced to meet him, flourishing a forked stick that he had for propping up the stand when resting, and with this he caught a mighty cut Don Quixote made at him that severed it in two; but with the portion that remained in his hand he dealt such a thwack on the shoulder of Don Quixote's sword arm (which the buckler could not protect against the clownish assault) that poor Don Quixote came to the ground in a sad plight.

Sancho Panza, who was coming on close behind puffing and blowing, seeing him fall, cried out to his assailant not to strike him again, for he was a poor enchanted knight, who had never harmed any one all the days of his life; but what checked the clown was, not Sancho's shouting, but seeing that Don Quixote did not stir hand or foot; and so, fancying he had killed him, he hastily hitched up his tunic under his girdle and took to his heels across the country like a deer.

By this time all Don Quixote's companions had come up to where he lay; but the processionists seeing them come running, and with them the officers of the Brotherhood with their crossbars, apprehended mischief, and clustering round the image, raised their hoods, and grasped their scourges, as the priests did their tapers, and awaited the attack, resolved to defend themselves and even to take the offensive against their assailants if they could. Fortune, however, arranged the matter better than they had expected, for all Sancho did was to fling himself on his master's body, raising over him the most doleful and laughable lamentation that ever was heard, for he believed he was dead. The curate was known to another curate who walked in the procession, and their recognition of one another set at rest the apprehensions of both parties; the first then told the other in two words who Don Quixote was, and he and the whole troop of penitents went to see if the poor gentleman was dead, and heard Sancho Panza saying, with tears in his eyes:

"Oh flower of chivalry, that with one blow of a stick hast ended the course of thy well-spent life! Oh pride of thy race, honor and glory of all La Mancha, nay, of all the world, that for want of thee will be full of evil-doers, no longer in fear of punishment for their misdeeds! Oh thou, generous above all the Alexanders, since for only eight months of service thou hast given me the best island the sea girds or surrounds! Humble with the proud, haughty with the humble, encounterer of dangers, endurer of outrages, enamoured without reason, imitator of the good, scourge of the wicked, enemy of the mean, in short, knight-errant, which is all that can be said!"

At the cries and moans of Sancho, Don Quixote came to himself, and the first word he said was:

"He who lives separated from you, sweetest Dulcinea, has greater miseries to endure than these. Aid me, friend Sancho, to mount the enchanted cart, for I am not in a condition to press the saddle of Rocinante, as this shoulder is all knocked to pieces."

"That I will do with all my heart, señor," said Sancho; "and let us return to our village with these gentlemen, who seek your good, and there we will prepare for making another sally, which may turn out more profitable and creditable to us."

"Thou art right, Sancho," returned Don Quixote; "it will be wise to let the malign influence of the stars which now prevails pass off."

The canon, the curate, and the barber told him he would act very wisely in doing as he said; and so, highly amused at Sancho Panza's simplicities, they placed Don Quixote in the cart as before. The procession once more formed itself in order and proceeded on its road; the goatherd took his leave of the party; the officers of the Brotherhood declined to go any farther, and the curate paid them what was due to them; the canon begged the curate to let him know how Don Quixote did, whether he was cured of his madness or still suffered from it, and then begged leave to continue his journey; in short, they all separated and went their ways, leaving to themselves the curate and the barber, Don Quixote, Sancho Panza, and the good Rocinante, who regarded everything with as great resignation as his master. The carter yoked his oxen and made Don Quixote comfortable on a truss of hay, and at his usual deliberate pace took the road the curate directed, and at the end of six days they reached Don Quixote's village, and entered it about the middle of the day, which it so happened was a Sunday, and the people were all in the plaza, through which Don Quixote's cart passed. They all flocked to see what was in the cart, and when they recognized their townsman they were filled with amazement, and a boy ran off to bring the news to his housekeeper and his niece that their master and uncle had come back all lean and yellow and stretched on a truss of hay on an ox-cart. It was piteous to hear the cries the two good ladies raised, how they beat their breasts and poured out fresh maledictions on those accursed books of chivalry; all which was renewed when they saw Don Quixote coming in at the gate.

At the news of Don Quixote's arrival Sancho Panza's wife came running, for she by this time knew that her husband had gone away with him as his squire, and on seeing Sancho, the first thing she asked him was if the ass was well. Sancho replied that he was, better than his master was.

"Thanks be to God," said she, "for being so good to me; but now tell me, my friend, what have you made by your squirings? What gown have you brought me back? What shoes for your children?"

"I will show them to you at home, wife," said Sancho; "though I bring other things of more consequence and value."

"I am very glad of that," returned his wife; "show me these things of more value and consequence, my friend; for I want to see them to cheer my heart that has been so sad and heavy all these ages that you have been away."

"I will show them to you at home, wife," said Sancho; "be content for the present; for if it please God that we should again go on our travels in search of adventures, you will soon see me a count, or governor of an island, and that not one of those every-day ones, but the best that is to be had."

"Heaven grant it, husband," said she, "for indeed we have need of it. But tell me, what's this about islands, for I don't understand it?"

"Honey is not for the mouth of the ass," returned Sancho; "all in good time thou shalt see, wife—nay, thou wilt be surprised to hear thyself called 'your ladyship,' by all thy vassals."

"What are you talking about, Sancho, with your ladyships, islands, and vassals?" returned Teresa Panza—for so Sancho's wife was called, though they were not relations, for in La Mancha it is customary for wives to take their husband's surnames.

"Don't be in such a hurry to know all this, Teresa," said Sancho; "it is enough that I am telling you the truth, so shut your mouth. But I may tell you this much by the way, that there is nothing in the world more delightful than to be a person of consideration, squire to a knight-errant, and a seeker of adventures. To be sure, most of those one finds do not end as pleasantly as one could wish, for out of a hundred that one meets with, ninety-nine will turn out cross and contrary. I know it by experience, for out of some I came blanketed, and out of others be-labored. Still, for all that, it is a fine thing to be on the lookout for what may happen, crossing mountains, search-ing woods, climbing rocks, visiting castles, putting up at inns, all at free quarters, and devil take the *maravedi* to pay."

While this conversation passed between Sancho Panza and his wife, Don Quixote's housekeeper and niece took him in and undressed him and laid him in his old bed. He eyed them askance, and could not make out where he was. The curate charged his niece to be very careful to make her uncle comfortable and to keep a watch over him lest he should make his escape from them again, telling her what they had been obliged to do to bring him home. On this the pair once more lifted up their voices and re-newed their maledictions upon the books of chivalry, and implored heaven to plunge the authors of such lies and nonsense into the midst of the bottomless pit. They were, in short, kept in anxiety and dread lest their uncle and master should give them the slip the moment he found himself somewhat better, and as they feared so it fell out.

But the author of this history, though he has devoted research and industry to the discovery of the deeds achieved by Don Quixote in his third sally, has been unable to obtain any information respecting them, at any rate derived from authentic documents; tradition has merely preserved in the memory of La Mancha the fact that Don Quixote, the third time he sallied forth from his home, betook himself to Saragossa, where he was present at some

famous jousts which came off in that city, and that he had
adventures there worthy of his valor and high intelligence.
Of his end and death he could learn no particulars, nor
would he have ascertained it or known of it, if good fortune had not produced an old physician for him who had
in his possession a leaden box, which, according to his account, had been discovered among the crumbling founda-
tions of an ancient hermitage that was being rebuilt; in
which box were found certain parchment manuscripts in
Gothic character, but in Castilian verse, containing many
of his achievements, and setting forth the beauty of Dulcinea, the form of Rocinante, the fidelity of Sancho Panza,
and the burial of Don Quixote himself, together with sun-
dry epitaphs and eulogies on his life and character. The
author of this new and unparalleled history asks of those
that shall read it nothing in return for the vast toil which
it has cost him in examining and searching the Manchegan archives in order to bring it to light, save that they
give him the same credit that people of sense give to the
books of chivalry that pervade the world and are so popu-
lar; for with this he will consider himself amply paid and
fully satisfied, and will be encouraged to seek out and
produce other histories, if not as truthful, at least equal in
invention and not less entertaining.